Acknow

To **Virginia** for her s

To all of you, **readers**—beta readers, ARC readers, bloggers, and the entire book community—you're all fabulous!

To my very **best of friends**... you know who you are!

To my **family**, I love you!

This is a work of fiction. Similarities to real people, places, or events are entirely coincidental.

JINGLE BELL ROCK

First edition. October 23, 2023.

Copyright © 2023 Lily Kate.

Written by Lily Kate.

To Christmas lovers everywhere :)

Jingle Bell Rock

Fresh out of high school, I—Tara Kendrick—was madly in love with Gavin Donovan. Until one day he disappeared in a web of secrets, and I never heard from him again. Fast forward thirteen years: I'm stranded at a rundown bed & breakfast during a snowstorm, and guess who's the new owner?

Merry Christmas to me.

While I'm locked up with my ex-flame and the current thorn-in-my-side, I'm reminded of the laundry list of items that are hard on Gavin Donovan—his biceps, his abs, his thighs...and now the massive diamond rock he slips onto my finger when I agree to be his fake fiancée for reasons I'm not comfortable repeating aloud. But I have as much incentive to make this arrangement work as he does, so falling into bed with the enemy is not on my to-do list.

As the jingle bells start to chime, however, the huge rock on my finger isn't the hardest thing between us. It's hard to keep my hands off Gavin. It's hard to pretend this relationship isn't real. It's hard to remember how I ever fell out of love with him in the first place.

You can read between the lines when I say Merry Christmas and Jingle Bell... well, *rock.*

Chapter 1

Tara

"*C'mon.*" I pounded my phone against the steering wheel with gusto. "Give me one teeny tiny bar."

I glanced at the service markers on my cell, saw the elusive bars flicker, and my chest filled with hope that I might get a call through in this disastrous area of low coverage. The barrage of snowflakes had already started, and my visibility was rapidly declining on the open stretch of highway.

"Stupid forecast," I muttered. "No snow my ass."

With two days to go before Thanksgiving, my seasonal workload was beginning to reach its peak. As an event planner with a side specialization in holiday decorating, I'd started to get the phone calls from my clients asking me to deck out hotel lobbies with massive Christmas trees, spruce up business fronts with tinsel, and my personal favorite—dress up individual homes with flair to round out the end of the year festivities.

I'd just completed my first big job of the season an hour north of my hometown. Fantasie, the place I call home, is a small town in a pretty little section of Maine that draws leaf-peepers in the fall and carolers around Christmas.

It sucks in folks for our quaint coffee shops in the spring and the cute cottages brimming with window boxes of flowers in the summer. People come to Fantasie wanting Hallmark photos and dusty used bookstores and friendly locals. I didn't *exactly* fit in with the Hallmark vibe, but it was still home nonetheless.

JINGLE BELL ROCK

Though my gig was only an hour away from Fantasie, I might as well have been in a different state with how long it would take me to travel the strip of highway back to my house. The same hotel booked me every year, two days before Thanksgiving, to layer the festive decor in the lobby and ballroom just before the holiday travel ramped up. Most years, I zipped up, did the job, and zipped home by nightfall.

Obviously, that was not the case this time around. As I'd climbed into my car after successfully lighting an eleven-foot-tall Christmas tree in the lobby at the Sweetheart Inn, my phone had pinged with a winter snowstorm warning. I'd made it all of ten minutes into my commute before the flurries had started, and by the time fifteen minutes had gone by, visibility was out the window.

My phone rang, startling me out of my focused trance.

"Thank you, sweet baby Jesus." I answered the phone with a relieved gasp. "Mom? How's Liv? I was trying to call you guys, but the service up here is horrendous."

"Olive is just fine, honey." My mother clucked at me. "I know I shouldn't say I told you so, but—"

"Then don't say it."

"Tara..." My mother continued, undeterred. "Clarice told you not to travel today. You should've listened to her."

"Yes, well, the forecast was clear up until two hours ago. Who am I supposed to believe, the self-appointed town psychic or the actual people on the news?"

My mother let the silence stretch on. Her point was very clear.

"Clarice has a very good track record." My mother's tone was quite reasonable. "You have to admit she had a point about your commute today."

It was hard to argue when I couldn't see two inches from my windshield in a very real snowstorm that Fantasie's very own Clarice (said self-appointed local psychic) had predicted but the guys down at the news station hadn't.

I blew out a breath. "I'm sorry. It's going to take me forever to get home in this mess."

"Don't be ridiculous. I booked you a stay at a nearby bed & breakfast. It's a brand spanking new place. Not even open for business to the public yet. Who knows? Maybe the owner will hire you to throw a holiday party if you play your cards right."

"I live in Maine. I know how to drive in the snow." I scoffed audibly for my mother's sake. "I'm coming home. I told Liv I'd be there to pick her up tonight."

"Honey, she's fine. We're making cookies now, and we've got *The Grinch* lined up for our seasonal viewing party. You wouldn't dare deprive your daughter and her grandmother from a snowstorm sleepover."

"I know, it's just that I promised her I'd pick her up today."

"Liv's *fine*. I figured your internet would be sketchy when I couldn't get a hold of you twenty minutes ago, so I booked you a place off that freeway entrance with that really *yum* diner. I'll put Liv on now so you can hear exactly how fine she is for yourself."

"I don't know, Mom," I said. "I don't think I need to stay overnight."

JINGLE BELL ROCK

"I paid upfront, no refunds, so you're staying. End of story. I'd feel terrible if something happened to you because you were rushing home for no reason at all."

"In that case," I said on a sigh, "I'm going to need some directions. And thanks, Mom. It's very thoughtful of you. I'll pay you back."

"Well, the directions are simple. Get off at the exit with the *yum* diner, take a right, and follow that road a mile or two. You'll hit a little bridge—drive over that—and then you'll see his sign. The nice man who owns the place says you can't miss it."

"Okay," I mumbled. "If you say so."

"Call me when you get there," my mother insisted. "Don't rush back. In fact, you should really consider viewing this as a blessing in disguise. A surprise overnight getaway. Draw a bath. Read a book. Stop working for five minutes. We'll see you once the roads are cleared."

"I'm not a workaholic."

"You're not...*not* a workaholic, Tara," my mother said kindly. "Get some rest. Do some shopping tomorrow on the way back. Have a coffee. We'll be fine."

"Let me talk to Liv, please."

In reply, I could hear my mother handing the phone over to my whole heart. Just hearing Liv's sweet greeting was enough to make me melt as she chirped *hello.*

"Hey, honey," I said. "I'm so sorry that I can't make it home tonight. The snowstorm is too dangerous to drive in, so I've got to camp out overnight at some new B&B. I'll see you in the morning, okay?"

"Mom, that's totally fine. Look, I've got to go. Grandma said we can make s'mores in the microwave and watch *The Grinch*."

"I love you, honey. Miss you."

"Love you too."

Liv clicked off the line before I could speak to my mother again. As I stared at the blank screen of the phone for a moment before returning my eyes to the road, it felt like my hands were itching to hit redial. It pained me not to ask what time my mother planned to get Liv to bed, or if Liv had eaten anything but licorice and crackers for dinner.

But I knew Liv was my independent little girl. I was raising her like I'd been raised—to take care of myself. Us Kendrick girls had bad luck with men. My father had never been in the picture. Liv's father had decided parenthood wasn't for him before his daughter was even born. If I was raising my baby girl with one thing in mind, it was to be able to fend for herself.

Guiding my car down the road, I cursed my twenty-year-old Civic as it slipped and slid with the fresh snowfall. The *yum* diner my mother had so scientifically referenced was fast approaching, and I was having my doubts that I'd be able to coax my car up the offramp without sliding right back down it.

I flicked my blinker on and crawled at a colossal pace off the highway, somewhat grateful that this drive required my whole focus. Otherwise, I'd still be feeling the sting of pain that'd zapped my chest at the way Liv had rushed me off the phone as if she didn't mind in the slightest that I'd be gone overnight.

I knew it was healthy that she had a great relationship with my mother. I loved that she'd won *Most Responsible Kid* in her class last year. I appreciated that she didn't need me the way she had when she'd been younger now that she's six going on sixteen. But that didn't mean it didn't hurt to see her growing up and stretching her wings all the same, needing me less and less with each passing day.

When I reached the stoplight at the top of the offramp, my car didn't even pretend to stop when I tapped the brakes. It just kept right on cruising through the red light. Seeing as I was the only idiot out on the road in these conditions, I just went with it. Any cop who wanted to pull me over for running a red would have to catch me first because this Civic wasn't stopping for anyone—myself included.

There was one car, already buried in snow, parked outside of the *yum* diner. The windows of the restaurant looked fuzzy-warm and welcoming, little pinpricks of light set to a backdrop of glittering snow and darkness beyond. I could see a figure through the window, sweeping up, probably preparing to head home as soon as possible.

My stomach growled, encouraging me to pull into the diner's parking lot and grab a short stack with a mountain of syrup and a pat of butter on top, but I knew if I stopped this vehicle for even a second, I wouldn't be starting it again. The only thing worse than staying at a random B&B in the middle of a blizzard was having to walk my ass there in two feet of snow.

I sincerely prayed I'd made the correct turn as I coasted down a seemingly abandoned road. I thought I could make out a few driveways tucked into the thick evergreens that lined the street, but they were already piled high with snow. I was pretty sure I could see the little bridge up ahead that was a landmark for my directions, but for all I knew, it could be nothing more than a mirage.

My fingers started to get a little sweaty, and I bit my lip as I skidded onto the shoulder and then quickly corrected to right my path. Then, I broke one of my cardinal rules out of desperation. I jabbed my finger at my downloaded Spotify Christmas playlist and let her rip. I knew it was practically sacrilege to listen to Mariah Carey before Thanksgiving, but times were desperate, and I needed a little boost of energy to distract me from the hazardous snowstorm outside.

I was starting to get a little freaked out on a road darker than sin, with no real cell service and no real directions for where I was supposed to stay. I probably should have stayed home today as Clarice had suggested. But as a single mom who counted on this time of year to make ends meet at other times of the year, I couldn't let down my clients. Lord knew I needed the money.

Then my wheels hit the bumpiness of the little bridge, and I purred sweet nothings into my dashboard as I caught sight of a teeny tiny sign dangling from a post next to a cute little mailbox. There was no way on earth I could read the sign, seeing as the letters appeared to be handwritten and illegible. The snow that had already battered against it and stuck made it worse. But it couldn't be a coincidence; this had to be the place my mother had booked.

I flicked my blinker on, which felt very unnecessary considering visibility was about the length of my pinky finger, and I coasted into the inn's driveway. My sweet nothings encouraged my car to make it halfway up the hill. That was when things started to go wrong.

For starters, my car started sliding backwards. I slammed on my brakes, which did absolutely nothing. I careened the wheel, and that did something. Something like fishtailing me off the side of the driveway and smack into a tall tree, its naked branches stretching above me as my car came circling to a stop.

The impact wasn't traumatic, but it was enough to jolt my head into the steering wheel at just the right angle so my teeth bit down on my lip, and I tasted blood. I sat still while my Christmas playlist transitioned to a very ironic chorus of "Silent Night."

I gave myself a few minutes to let my racing heart calm. Then, clearing my throat, I did my best to peek in the mirror in an attempt to make myself appear dignified which was a complete and utter failure. My lip was bleeding, my hair was drooping from a long day of work, and my eyes had bags under them. Maybe I did need a good bath and a full night's sleep.

I gathered the possessions I'd need for the night, which was quite easy seeing as I hadn't planned to stay out. I scooped up my purse, grabbed my leftover cold latte, and fished out the pepper spray I kept in my glove compartment. Not that the latter would help me all that much if the person who owned this inn was an ax murderer. Where the hell would I run in this snowstorm after I sprayed the bejeezus out of his eyeballs?

Still, I tucked the pepper spray into my purse and slid the bag onto my shoulder. As I got out of the car, I realized a very important truth about high heels: they did not double as ice picks. This morning, I'd dressed in high heels with my standard uniform of fitted jeans and a nice blouse. I'd worn the peacoat I'd splurged on five years ago that was now missing a button.

Stomping and hissing my way up the hill, I felt like a ball of yarn being batted about by a kitten. The snowstorm being the kitten, me being the yarn. I hadn't even brought a hat. I practically giggled as the thought occurred to me that whoever owned the inn might greet *me* with pepper spray. Wouldn't that be the icing on the cake.

Then, my beloved mirage bloomed in the distance. An adorable white cottage built into this hellscape of a winter tundra. Sitting atop a hill, its windows flickered with a coziness I practically craved. I could feel it in my stomach, a yearning that someone would open the door and let me tumble into its warmth. A cup of tea, a steaming bath, a leftover paperback someone else had left behind. I was seeing stars with how desperate I was for this to be my reality.

When I finally reached the front steps, I was like Elsa from *Frozen* but distinctly less princess-y and powerful and beautiful. In reality, the only thing I had in common with Elsa was that ice was dripping from every inch of my body. Unlike her, I had no control over it.

I raised a frozen hand and pounded on the door. Then, on second thought, I knocked again—this time softer. I didn't want to startle whoever was waiting for me on the other side of the door, especially since I was already bleeding and looking *quite* a fright.

JINGLE BELL ROCK

When there was no answer, I glanced around, feeling a panic rising in my chest. If this was the wrong place, and it wasn't a B&B, I was well and truly screwed. My car was a disaster. I was going to have to scoot on my butt down the hill and hitchhike back to the diner while praying the waitress hadn't left yet.

I raised a hand once more and pounded on the door, veering toward the hysterical-ax-murderer side of the spectrum. I was desperate, pounding, praying someone would let me in when, finally, the door opened, and I fell through the opening as if stumbling into Narnia. Except instead of Turkish delights and evil queens waiting for me, there was only a ghost.

"What the hell are *you* doing here?"

My ghost spoke. He had a low, gravelly voice. He had no shirt on. That was about where I stopped noticing stuff because holy guacamole, did I say he had no shirt on? My eyes stared at his—one, two, three, four, five, six, seven, was that eight?—definitely eight pack abs. Across that washboard stomach was a scar. A jagged one that hadn't been there the last time I'd laid my hands on him. There was also a tattoo on one bicep that was new.

"You must be frozen." The ghost spoke again.

"Gavin?" I croaked. "Is that you?"

Finally, the stunning male specimen laid eyes on me. Actually on *me*. Not on the sticks of ice dangling from my eyelashes or the blood dripping from my lip. Onto my face—a face he'd damn well better not have forgotten.

"Tara Kendrick."

"Who else would it be?" I stilled, and that was when I realized he was touching me.

Gavin Donovan's hands were on my arms, his palms spread wide over the ailing fabric of my peacoat. My stomach flipped as I remembered the current that had passed between us the last time we'd touched. I'd never been able to forget it, though Lord knows I'd tried.

Gavin Donovan's touch haunted my dreams. Enchanted my subconscious thoughts. Served as a comparison to every man I'd dated since. I hated it. I was pretty sure I hated him.

I took a step back and shook his hands off me. I pulled the pepper spray out of my purse and fondled it in plain sight, as if it were a warning for him to behave.

Unfortunately, my threat wasn't very ominous to Gavin because he threw his head back and barked a laugh at my bravado. A deep, infectious laugh that had my insides squirming with all sorts of conflicting feelings.

Then again, Gavin always had the ability to make girls feel special, and I wasn't immune to his charms. When we'd been together for that one, miraculous summer, he'd made me feel like the only woman in the world, the only woman for him. Which was why it'd hurt so much when he'd up and left without a word. I thought I'd meant more to him.

"*Now* you take the pepper spray out?" Gavin ran a hand down the stubble on his chin. "Now that you know who's behind the door you were trying to break down? You didn't think about having it ready before some stranger opened the door?"

Gavin Donovan looked downright edible, and I was royally pissed about it.

JINGLE BELL ROCK

"You run a horrible business," I said. "You should have a sign out front. And you should answer the door on the first knock. Have you heard of doorbells? How about directions? Maybe a nightlight left out for your guests?"

Gavin looked more and more amused with every word that flew out of my mouth. I was hurling them around like insults. It looked like he was taking it in as entertainment.

"Uh huh," he said finally, as if that made any sense.

"So are you going to let me in or what?"

I stomped right past him, pushing by that sorta-sexy tattoo on his arm, and not completely trying to avoid his bare feet with my now iced-over heels. The least I owed him was a broken toe after all he'd put me through. Toes healed. Hearts didn't.

Fortunately or unfortunately, Gavin had retained the same lithe physique he'd acquired in high school, and then he'd improved upon it as he'd aged. He danced out of the way of my stomping heels and gently rested a hand on my pepper spray canister. He pried it away easily, like he might a butter knife from a petulant toddler.

"So what the hell?" I turned to face what I'd expected to be a cozy inn and found it mostly in need of repair. "Now you own a cheap-ass inn?"

"Nice to see you too, sweetheart."

"Don't sweetheart me."

Gavin blinked. Coughed. "Technically, this inn isn't even open for business just yet."

"Then why'd you let me in?" I gaped at him. "You're telling me I stumbled upon your house randomly?"

Gavin shook his head slowly. "Some lady—who I'm now presuming is your mother—found my number online and sweet talked me into letting her daughter stay here tonight. According to her, you were in grave danger of freezing to death, and I'd be Lucifer himself if I turned you away. Her words, not mine."

"So you knew it was me this whole time?"

Gavin shook that irritatingly gorgeous head. "Your mother spoke fast, said she had to call you back so she didn't have time to talk. She just said her name was Cathy and that her daughter was looking for an inn, and could she stay here? I guess your mom found an old listing from the last couple who owned this place and figured it was worth a shot."

"You bought an inn?"

"Do you want to..." Gavin gave another throat clear before studying me. "Sit down? Come inside? Explain why you're bleeding on my floor?"

I glanced down at what was clearly still a construction site with tools scattered on various surfaces. "Like these terrible floorboards are going to stay."

Gavin gave a little grunt that I took to be humor. "Can I ask why you're bleeding or is that also too offensive?"

"Do you have tea?"

"Coffee."

"Fine," I said. "Decaf?"

"I think I can find something," he said mildly. "My Aunt Lily left some things up here last time she stopped by. You're welcome to whatever I have."

Finally, since the first time I'd fallen into my own personal Narnia, I stopped to take a breath and look at something

JINGLE BELL ROCK 15

that wasn't Gavin or his pecs. I glanced up and quickly realized my primary analysis of the place was wrong. It wasn't a dump, or a "cheap-ass" inn as I'd surmised. The place was old and quaint and had the bones to be something truly memorable.

A fresh coat of paint glistened on the entryway walls. It seemed like I might have interrupted Gavin as he'd been working on refinishing the wood on the spiral staircase. My judgment had been harsh, clouded by the fact that my nemesis was the one doing the rehabbing.

Reluctantly, I admitted that the actual structure of this place was gorgeous. It was the perfect layout for a little bed and breakfast tucked into rural Maine. It was close to the highway, close to the diner, yet perfectly secluded.

I could see a somewhat cluttered but homey kitchen to one side. A sitting room to the other side with a roaring fire in the hearth. Maybe I'd been a little harsh in thinking this place needed a complete overhaul. It wasn't as far from *cute* as I'd wanted to believe.

One of my favorite aspects of my job as a decorator was transforming a place from *blah* to *wow*. It was the way my brain worked and always had, a gift I'd been born with. And that niggling part of my brain applauded Gavin on having the smarts and vision to choose this place. The practical part of my brain zipped my lips shut and thought I'd rather die before telling him that.

"Can I take your things?" Gavin extended his arms, looking a little helpless as he scanned my body and realized I didn't have much in the way of *things*.

I smacked my lips and nodded at the pepper spray he'd plucked from my grasp. "You already did, you big bully."

Gavin winked. "You can have your little toy back after you cool down."

"Cool down," I muttered under my breath, finally reaching down to relieve my feet of the heels strapped to them. "Cool down my ass."

"You 'my ass' a lot of things." Gavin noted this with another pinch of humor dancing in his eyes. "I'm taking it to mean you have a problem with me."

"Let's just say chip on the shoulder doesn't do it justice," I said. "It's more like a boulder. But anyway, it doesn't matter. I'll leave first thing in the morning, soon as the road is cleared. The sooner I get home the better. The sooner I get away from you, also the better. My mom said she paid you already?"

"You don't need to pay me for tonight."

"That's not an answer."

"No, she didn't pay."

"Then I'll pay you."

"You don't need to pay me."

"Yes I do," I shot back. "This is not a social call. It's a business transaction."

"I told your mother that technically, the inn isn't open yet. I don't have the right licenses to run a business, so I can't accept cash from you. In fact, I don't even have a real bed for you. I told your mother all I had was a pull-out couch, and she said you've slept on worse."

I blinked at him. "I thought you talked to my mother for two seconds."

JINGLE BELL ROCK

"She talks at a very rapid pace."

I made a mental note to have a very frank discussion with my mother about the information she shared with random strangers. And also about her setting me up to couch surf on some random dude's sofa in the middle of a blizzard, not to mention the fact she'd lied about her non-refundable payment. Thank God for pepper spray after all. My mother had more courage setting me up for an overnight than a teenager bunking in a foreign hostel. At least hostels were real freaking businesses.

"Look, I'm aware we have a lot to discuss." Gavin raised his arms, arms that looked like Roman columns they were so large and in-charge, and he spread his palms in surrender. "What if I show you to the working bathroom and give you a few minutes to..."

He trailed off, studying my expression. In his defense, I did probably look murderous. I was very angry. No amount of Christmas jams were going to calm me down tonight.

"No, buster." I stepped toward him and poked that godlike chest with my finger and just about chipped my peeling manicure right off. My finger glinted off him as if I were poking a cement block.

I cleared my own throat and tried again with another prod, this time with my middle finger pointed up.

"We don't have anything to discuss." I had gotten too close to Gavin. I was looking up at him without the help of my booster heels. He was looking down at me, dwarfing me with his big shoulders and super nice hips and pretty stomach and dumb five o'clock shadow. "So if you'll just point me to my janky-ass pull out couch—"

I was on a roll with my stomping and was thinking there was no reason to stop now. I marched toward the kitchen, thinking maybe I should just climb in bed and fall asleep. Get out of Gavin's hair for the night until we'd both had some time to process our situation. I came to an abrupt halt, however, when his hand reached out and encircled my wrist.

Demanding, gentle, coaxing. But firm. Gavin spun me around in the kitchen, and I was so worked up with my stomping that I just whirled right into his chest thanks to centrifugal motion or momentum or one of those outlandish physics concepts that had never properly soaked into my brain. I wanted to step back, to stop the glorious scent of a nearly-naked Gavin from going up my nostrils and doing funny things to my lady parts, but I was in a trance.

His eyes were on mine. Gray gemstones that were the same as the last time I'd looked into them as a desperate teen, a girl who'd fallen hard and fast for the one boy she couldn't have.

First love, summer love, high school crush—all the damn cute things. Except there was no coming back from this broken heart, no matter the amount of groveling. Not that Gavin would grovel. He's forgotten about me, tossed me aside like an old handkerchief.

But for a moment, here in this magical kitchen, some of the iciness in my chest began to melt. The longer I stared into those granite eyes, the more I remembered what had enticed me to him in the first place. Those eyes weren't all that different, even a decade or so later. A little harder, crisper, sharper. A few more secrets. My breath hitched in my throat as he kept his grip on my hand.

JINGLE BELL ROCK

Then he reached over my shoulder, caging me against him as he leaned toward the sink. I hadn't realized he'd been gently guiding me backward in some odd slow dance that made my stomach hit high notes like Mariah freaking Carey.

Then he pulled something from behind me, and I jolted back to reality. He held a clean washcloth in his hand, dampened slightly by a flick of water from the faucet. He held it to my lip, pressed it gently.

My hand came up and rested on his, acting of its own accord. He looked down at me, his lips parting as our eyes caught in a standoff. Then I swallowed, and the little gulp sparked the end of the fairytale.

I swatted him away. He turned tail and headed for the freezer. He pulled out a bag of frozen peas and handed it over, taking care not to meet my gaze.

"I'll show you to your room now," he said.

"I thought I didn't have a room."

"You can have mine."

"But—"

"Just take my damn room." Gavin stared at me, daring me to challenge him.

I gulped again. Ran my tongue over my teeth. His gaze followed the movement. Despite the cold veggies on my face, I felt heated through, inside and out.

"As long as you let me pay for it," I said finally. "Where will you sleep?"

Gavin merely grunted. "Follow me."

Chapter 2

Gavin

I sat at the kitchen table. Impatient. I tapped my fingers against my cup of coffee, caffeine being the very last thing I needed considering the woman upstairs had me so wired I was concerned about insomnia for the next decade.

After a half-assed argument about sleeping arrangements and promises of payment, I'd unloaded my surprise guest into the master bedroom upstairs. It was the only finished room in the house. In fact, it was newly finished.

I'd put in the big soaking tub just a week ago, and even I had to admit that it had a pretty sweet view. The massive window I'd insisted on installing would let guests peep out onto the sloping hills that gradually rolled down to a winding river, which snaked prettily through this area. In the fall, the trees would be aflame with reds and yellows and oranges. In the winter, it'd be a sparkling tundra dotted with peeks of evergreens. In the spring, sprinkled with wildflowers. And in the summer, a lush green canvas to view while lounging in a hot bath.

Unfortunately, the thought of Tara Kendrick lounging in the soaking tub, naked—one long, lean leg hanging off the side while she sipped the glass of wine I'd set outside her door, had me rising to attention in ways I didn't need. I cussed a blue streak at my stupidity. I stood, banging my hands against the table with enough force to rattle my mug.

What the hell was she doing here? I shuffled over to the stove and yanked open the fridge. I started cracking eggs. My mind was so distracted with the daydream of Tara naked in my damn bathtub that I'd cracked a dozen damn eggs before I realized I didn't need to feed an army. I just needed to feed one pint-sized woman with a fierce temper and a happy trigger finger.

Not to mention the gorgeous face that would be burned into my mind until infinity. Tara's split lip that had my testosterone on overdrive, wishing I could protect her from the pain, the hurt, physical or otherwise. But that was impossible. I'd already hurt her, and it was a step beyond obvious that she hadn't forgotten it.

When I heard footsteps on the stairs, I just about cracked my neck whipping my head around to get a good look at her, freshly showered, her skin dewy and probably still warm from the steam. I wondered if she could tell I was downright overwhelmed at the fact that she was here, the woman who had haunted my dreams for the last thirteen years.

The sight of Tara's legs on the staircase didn't help to cool my jets in the slightest. If anything, seeing her revved me up. My brain felt like it was a slinky tumbling down a staircase, out of my control, unable to keep up. Bouncing around every which way while trying to form coherent thoughts around her.

"Hey," I grunted in a totally reasonable fashion.

I tried to say something else, but my mouth dried up when I got my first good glimpse of the first woman I'd loved. So I was stuck with "hey" as my grand prize opening line.

Tara was more wonderful than I remembered in every single way. She'd stopped wearing the high school shield of makeup she used to put on and had gone natural. Freckles popped on her cheeks; freckles I'd been too dumb to notice the first time around.

But it was her eyes that stole my breath. Warm brown stones glistening back at me, burning with a lick of fire, hiding the softness and vulnerability I remembered. The longing that had tugged on my heartstrings as I'd kissed her forehead for what I'd known then would be the last fucking time.

I looked down, frying the shit out of my eggs. The cheese was getting downright scorched. It was a good thing I wasn't wearing a shirt, because I would've lit the damn fabric on fire with how I was leaning against the stove for balance.

I reached gruffly for my mug and swigged back a jolt of coffee, mumbling something to her about there being eggs for dinner. By the time I'd gathered my thoughts enough to chance another straight look at her, she'd tentatively made her way fully into the kitchen, and I was in for another jolt straight to the gut.

Tara Kendrick was in my T-shirt. My goddamn shirt. Next to naked underneath, and I was pretty sure she'd left the bra upstairs in the bathroom judging by the faint outline of her nipples pressing against the white V-neck.

"Gavin, I hope you'll accept upfront payment—"

"Take a seat and eat something."

I thwacked the spatula against the pan, not intending to sound so pissy, but seeing her like this had caught me off-guard. It wasn't just any woman in my shirt. It was *her* in my shirt that had me feeling all sorts of things I hadn't felt in years.

Turning the heat off on the stove, I took a few deep breaths and willed myself to play things cool as I turned around, forcing a weird-ass smile onto my face while I raised the still-steaming pan. "Would you like some eggs?"

The emotions flickering across Tara's face startled me. She flicked through her expressions, one after another, like one of those old-school stereoscopes. Her frustration at seeing me. *Click.* Her surprise at my food offering. *Click.* A hint of vulnerability behind all of it. *Click, click, click.*

Finally, Tara sat. She seemed to be struggling with the idea of accepting food, but I refused to give in this easily. I'd already forced my bed on her, my bathroom, my T-shirt. If she wanted my damn eggs, she'd have to ask for them herself.

Tara tried to speak, cleared her throat, headed for a second attempt at the English language. "Sure, I guess eggs sound nice."

I gave a brief nod, grabbed two place settings from the cabinet, and divvied up the food. I'd just eaten dinner twenty minutes before she'd arrived on my doorstep. I was stuffed to the gills, but I wasn't a monster. I wasn't going to let her eat alone seeing how loathe she was to accept any sort of help.

I handed her the plate, ignoring the bolt of Zeus-sized lightning that sparked between us when our fingers brushed. Judging by the way she recoiled as if she'd been bitten by a snake, she'd felt it too.

I went to sit down, then popped right back up and grabbed the ketchup. I slid it across the table. "So fucking weird," I muttered under my breath. "Do you still use this crap?"

"It's not weird," Tara huffed. "Ketchup on eggs is a staple."

"It's disgusting," I argued. "I season my eggs just right without adding a boatload of salt and sugar."

"I can't believe you remembered." Tara wasn't looking at me as she reached for the ketchup and squirted an obscene amount of goop onto her plate. The yolks were good and buried.

Something shifted in my gut at the softness in her voice, that almost-forgotten sweetness that had been there before. Before I'd ruined everything.

"How could I forget?" I chewed a bite that felt like cardboard in my mouth. I wasn't tasting anything. How could I when all my senses were focused on the woman in front of me? "It's a little weird."

"So normal," Tara argued. "I should've known things would never work out the second you couldn't accept my affinity for ketchup."

"Affinity? You must mean obsession. Affinity would be, like, preferring to dunk your fries in ketchup rather than eat them plain." I waved with my fork at her ketchup with a side of eggs. "You have an addiction. Ketchup on your eggs, your steak, your salad. That's a serious offense."

A slight pink tinged her cheeks. "You saw me eat a salad once, and there was chicken on it. How's someone supposed to eat a chicken salad without ketchup?"

"Like this." I took a bite of my eggs and chewed, swallowed. I overexaggerated the smack of my lips. "Tastes just fine."

Tara cut a tiny bite of egg and piled an ice cream scoop's worth of condiments on top. She popped it in her mouth, barely chewed, and swallowed the whole mess in one gulp. She smacked her lips right back at me.

That little lip smack had me forgetting what we'd been arguing about in the first place. I couldn't stop staring at her lips, at the pout that was somehow even more perfect than the last time I'd had the privilege of kissing it.

The moment hung heavy between us, as if we'd both been transported back thirteen years. As if I was just finishing my degree and she was just starting college with her whole life ahead of her. Memories of us sitting side by side in a diner's peeling booth, scrounging up change to pay for dinner. The way she'd shyly glanced over her omelet at me, brushing a hand over her lips to hide her giggle as I'd teased her about her ketchup obsession back then, not all that differently than I'd done just now.

Tara had wondered aloud how I'd remembered about her taste for ketchup. The bigger question was how could I have forgotten? I had so few memories of her, of the time we'd really spent together, that I held onto every one of them like a tattered photograph. Like a precious slip of paper that had originated before digital photos had existed, and if I let those go, the memories of those days would fade away, lost forever.

I'd held fast to the thought of Tara Kendrick for over a decade. The memories had only grown in intensity, not faded. I hadn't even consciously thought about it. My past with her was simply a part of me. A large part.

Then, as if someone had snapped their fingers, I jolted back to modern day. Gone were the warm memories of two young kids tucked in a diner together, adding up dollar bills to make ends meet. Here we were, two much bigger kids still just as lost in the world. At least, that was the way I felt. I was bigger, older, richer. Not so sure about wiser.

"Why are you here?" Tara blurted the question as if she had no control of the words coming out of her mouth.

Good. I didn't want to be the only one losing control here.

"Why am *I* here?" I leaned lazily back in my chair, grateful for an opportunity to stop shoveling food into my mouth. "What do you mean?"

"How long have you been back in Maine?"

"Not long. Just a couple weeks."

"Huh." Tara sized up my answer as if she couldn't figure out whether it was the right or wrong one.

"I shouldn't have left like I did." I leaned forward, my chest tightening. "It's not that I didn't want to commit to you. I said I wouldn't marry you until you'd had the time to finish college and decide what you wanted for your life. I wasn't going to tie you up during some of the best years of your life."

"Pretty sad if the best years of my life were going to be college," Tara said. "What does that mean for the rest of my life if I peaked in college? It's just all downhill?"

"That's not what I mean. Those years, eighteen to twenty-something, are important for kids to figure themselves out. It's an opportunity to dabble, experiment, travel, date."

Tara sat back and crossed her arms across her nipples.

I tried not to stare. I failed a little bit. But it was not the time to get distracted, and I dragged my gaze back to her face.

"I was an adult when we got together, Gavin. Eighteen years old. Yes, that's young. But young doesn't equate to stupid, and I deserved to make those decisions for myself."

"I just wanted to give you the freedom to experiment."

Tara stabbed at her bites of eggs like she had a vendetta against them. "You just don't understand." *Stab, stab, stab.* "That's the whole problem. I thought you'd get it now that you're older, but maybe I was wrong."

"No argument from me." I held my hands up in surrender.

I took small solace in the fact that she liked my cooking enough to keep eating despite her obvious frustration. I reached out and rested a hand on her wrist before she started using that fork for stabbing in a different direction. Like at my eyeballs.

Tara stilled, and eventually, after a moment of touch, she rested the fork against the plate. She looked up at me, her lower lip giving a little tremble. Her eyes looked close to tears.

"Sweetheart, you don't owe me anything," I said. "What I meant to say is, I'm sorry. I know you don't owe me a damn thing. I would never presume to say I did the right thing back then, and I owe you an apology. A big, fat one. Give me a minute to process that you're here. Give me a minute to understand. Please, give me a chance."

"A chance of what?"

"Not a chance like *that*," I corrected quickly, though every fiber of my body was roaring in protest. "I meant a chance to apologize properly. I *am* sorry. But I'm still not thinking straight. I'm not going to tell you what you want to hear just to make nice. Give me a chance to have a real conversation with you. That's all I'm asking." When the look on her face seemed inconclusive, I gave one last attempt with humor. "You know, a conversation without you killing innocent eggs or pepper spraying my face."

That jolted her out of her pensive state and dragged a little smile onto her lips. "One calm conversation?"

"Just one," I said. "That's it."

"Uh huh." Tara didn't seem convinced. But she was thinking about it. "Fine. One conversation. We'll see about the calm, but I'll do my best, cowboy."

"Thank you." I took a breath. "I know you don't owe it to me. So I really do appreciate it."

Tara shifted in her seat, pushing her chair back and dragging her knees up to her chest. She seemed to have lost her rather ravenous appetite. I'd lost my non-existent appetite.

"Maybe we can sit somewhere more comfortable?" I asked. "Would you like some wine?"

"How about that decaf?"

I nodded, rose, and found the decaf beans my aunt had stashed in one of the cupboards. I ground the beans, dumped them in the pot, then took a seat as the hissing of the liquid and the smell of fresh coffee permeated the kitchen.

The brief interlude for coffee had seemed to recharge both of us. Tara cleared the plates from the table. I washed the dishes. When the coffee was done, I poured us each a mug. She returned to the table, but I gave her a nudge with my hip as I passed by behind her.

"Come on out this way," I encouraged. "It's more comfortable."

"I'm fine here." Tara remained at the table.

"Babe, when you pull your legs up on the chair like that, I can see your panties, and I'm going to find it hard to focus on a serious conversation with red lace staring me in the face."

"Oh, fuck-off, Gavin." But as she rose, her cheeks were as red as those scandalous panties she was wearing. Pretty fancy undies for a woman who had planned to go home alone.

Alone. Was she single these days? I hadn't asked.

At the thought that Tara might have someone waiting for her, for those sexy red undies, my stomach clenched in a tight knot. As she followed me into the sitting room, I figured myself to be a fool.

When I'd seen her at my door, led her up to my bedroom, cooked eggs for her, I'd simply presumed that she was still single. Which was idiotic. The woman was smart. Sweet. Downright gorgeous. There wasn't a chance in hell that she wasn't spoken for, and I wasn't sure if that made me mad or disappointed or worse.

I guided her toward the four-season porch which had storm windows and an old wood burning stove in one corner. A paisley patterned couch that was too comfortable to throw away had been left by the previous owners. Piles of blankets were situated in a wicker trunk behind it.

Tara took a seat on the cozy couch, and I unearthed a boatload of blankets and spread them over her before snagging a single threadbare one for myself. I took a seat across from her in an ancient rocking chair with what could only be a homemade cushion on it—another souvenir from the previous owners.

"Put this on." Tara threw something at me.

I glanced down, saw the white T-shirt that she must've grabbed off the railing on the way out to the porch. I vaguely remembered leaving it there on my way up to shower before I'd made dinner.

Tossing the shirt on over my bare chest, I shot her a curious glance.

"If you don't want to stare at my underwear, then I don't want to stare at..." Tara hiccupped. Then she waved her hand like a magician gesturing to my general torso area. "Get yourself decent."

I bit down on my bottom lip, feeling like finally I'd gained a little bit of even footing. If my naked chest didn't bother her, she wouldn't have said anything. A glimmer of hope? I damn well hoped so.

"So what brings you to the middle of nowhere tonight?" I asked once I'd righted my shirt and reclaimed my coffee cup from the side table.

"Work." Tara cupped her hands daintily around her mug, as if she'd wanted it more for the warmth than for the actual liquid inside of it. The movement felt familiar, reminiscent of our diner dinners from years past.

"What do you do?"

"I'm an event planner slash decorator." Tara glanced down, twitched a white knitted blanket over her legs. "It started out organically. A friend of mine asked me to help her plan her wedding. I liked it, so I offered to help out another friend. Word began to spread."

"I'm not surprised. You've always been good at whatever you put your mind to."

Tara glanced at me like I was nuts. "Don't pretend you know me anymore, Donovan."

"Just making conversation. So did you have a wedding tonight—is that where you're coming from?"

"No. Over time, as my event planning business started gaining traction, I would get requests asking for me to do decorations for other things. Businesses would hire me to come in and deck things out for a holiday party. I volunteered to dress up the Fantasie Inn for Christmas one year. Well, you know your aunt." I blinked at him. "Once I'd done that for Lily Donovan, she spread the word to other hotels and inns and whatnot. Eventually, I started getting booked up between Thanksgiving and Christmas almost a year in advance."

"That's great. You run a whole company now?"

"I mean, I guess you could say that. But it's a pretty small operation. Mostly me and some part-time help."

"You book a year out, and you haven't hired full-time help?"

"People hire me because they like *my* style." She bit down on her lip. "I have a hard time letting go of control. People like what I bring to the table, and I guess I have a hard time trusting that other people will care about the work as much as I do."

"That's very noble of you. Must keep you on your toes."

"I like to be busy." Tara leaned back against the couch and gave a small smile as she sipped her decaf. It was the first time she looked content, lost in a world I couldn't access. "I love working with my clients. Tonight, I was decorating a hotel about fifteen minutes north of here. A mom-and-pop shop. But they were one of my first clients, so I just can't bear to drop them, even though it's barely worth the hourly rate technically."

"Sweetheart Inn?"

"That's the one."

"I know Cheryl and Bob." I gave a short nod. "Good people."

"They are. I look forward to the job every year. Though it didn't quite work out as planned this year, what with the snowstorm. Usually I'm in and out in a day, and, well, that didn't happen."

"Maybe it worked out better than planned."

Tara shot me a look that told me she wasn't convinced.

We lapsed into silence. I wasn't sure how much of this conversation Tara wanted to have right now. I wasn't sure if she wanted to have it ever.

"Why are you back?" Tara asked finally. She looked at me as if she didn't want to completely care about my answer. "Literally here, of all places. In the middle of nowhere, rehabbing an old farmhouse by yourself?"

"Contrary to what it looks like, I'm not here all by my lonesome."

Tara's cheeks pinkened further, and I quickly realized how that had come out. I shook my head to correct her before she got any ideas.

"I don't mean that in a romantic context. I'm single," I added as an afterthought, as if that mattered. "I'm here because of my Aunt Lily."

"Oh." Understanding dawned in Tara's eyes. "I'd heard through the grapevine that Lily Donovan was looking at a property for a second bed and breakfast, but I wasn't sure if she'd ever gone ahead and purchased one. The Fantasie Inn is doing incredible."

"Aunt Lily bought this place a few months ago, but she's kept it quiet," I said. "I keep in contact with my aunt. I told her I was in between gigs for a bit and offered to help get this place up and running in my downtime."

"Obviously. I mean, it's your Aunt Lily, and you'd do anything for her." Tara gave a one shoulder shrug. My T-shirt slipped off her shoulder, revealing pale skin, just a light smattering of freckles. I'd never found a shoulder an erotic body part before. There was a first time for everything.

"What happens when you finish up here?"

"I've got one last job with The Company that will keep me around town for a bit." I forced my gaze back to her eyes, not ready to be completely transparent with her—mostly for her safety. "I'm not sure after that. Taking things one day at a time."

"Well, I'm sure this place will be a hit," Tara acknowledged. "You've got quite a view from here. Even though it was a blizzard when I arrived, the moon was out, and the snowfall..." Tara let her hand drop to her lap in a half-gesture beyond the windows of the porch.

Sure enough, what was visible sure was beautiful. A tundra of white spread before us down to where I knew the river was still churning beneath a layer of ice. Snow dripped from the moonlit sky like a child shaking a snow globe. There was no place I'd rather be right now. And quite frankly, no better company to be snuggled up with than Tara.

"Have you been in California this whole time?" Tara quickly looked away, into the fire, as she asked the question.

"Most of the time," I said. "My work took me traveling. But since I started in security, I've been based out there."

"I heard you enlisted in the military," Tara said. "That's what everyone assumed when you left."

"I didn't technically enlist." I picked at the blanket, feeling uneasy. "I got an offer I couldn't refuse."

"I see."

"I maybe let some people assume I'd joined the army. But that's not what happened."

Tara studied me calmly, interested. "I must admit, I thought you'd put up more of a fight admitting you were wrong to leave like you did."

"Of course not. I was an idiot," I said. "I was twenty-one and fending for myself. I made a lot of fucking mistakes."

Tara licked her lips, and I could practically see the question hovering on her tongue. Wondering if I thought that letting her go had been one of those mistakes. I prayed she asked it; I wanted her to open the door for me to grovel and make amends. But the look passed, a hardened expression came over her face, and I could see that door had already closed.

"I also realize my apology is coming thirteen years too late," I said. "I probably gave you a bit of a complex leaving like I did. I should've righted that a long time ago."

"Don't flatter yourself into thinking I've been hung up on you this whole time."

"I hope that's true." I picked at a thread on the couch. "I never, ever wanted to hurt you."

"I do believe that."

It was a whisper. A breadcrumb. Music to my fucking heart.

"And I meant it when I told you I loved you," I said. "My leaving... I never stopped loving you."

Tara nodded, jerked a hand over her face, almost as if her eyes had smarted, but that couldn't have been true because she was cool and collected when she spoke one second later.

"I forgive you," Tara said finally. "If that helps."

"I was really stupid."

Tara considered for another moment. "Well then, Gavin Donovan, if you didn't up and join the army, where the hell have you been all these years?"

Chapter 3

Tara

My brain felt like it was waterlogged. I was still processing everything that had happened, from the sudden snowstorm to the fact that I was sitting in my ex-boyfriend's bed & breakfast listening to him apologize.

Frankly, I was shocked. I wasn't sure what I'd expected from Gavin. That he'd be an asshole? That he'd try to shirk responsibility for what had happened between us? That he'd pretend nothing had happened at all?

I shifted several blankets more firmly onto my lap until I felt like I'd been anchored into place on the chilly porch. As if I let even one of those quilts slide to the floor, I'd float away like a hot air balloon from this surreal conversation in this surreal space with this surreal company.

And yet, I'd been wildly surprised. Gavin Donovan had handled the situation like a reasonably mature adult. He'd apologized and accepted responsibility for our fallout, and now the ball was in my court with how I wanted to respond. I was at a loss.

So I leaned into the change of subject and watched Gavin as his face changed while he considered what to tell me about the time we'd spent apart.

"I never went into the army," Gavin said again. "But that was the easiest way to explain my sudden desire to leave Fantasie without giving people a reason to ask a lot of questions. People never expected me to amount to much."

My mug was empty of coffee, and I was depressed about it. It had warmed me from the inside and also kept my hands busy. "I could think of a lot of different ways you could've told people, or at least *me*, about your decision. Like a phone call, email, carrier pigeon to name a few."

A slow smile appeared on Gavin's face, and he gave a slow nod. "I respectfully would argue that the method of keeping in touch wasn't so much an issue as the NDA I had to sign."

"NDA?"

"Non-disclosure—"

"I know what a non-disclosure agreement is," I said. "Why'd you have to sign one?"

"I was recruited to work for a private security firm."

"Carter's place?"

"Back then, it wasn't Carter's place," Gavin said. "Carter wasn't even working there yet. He took it over more recently."

"Uh huh." I stared at him. "So you're James Bond?"

"Not nearly as glamorous."

"What sort of things did you do for this company?"

Gavin ran his tongue over his teeth. "Remember that NDA I told you about?"

I rolled my eyes. "I'm not looking for a dossier."

"I protected people," Gavin hedged. "All different sorts of people. Celebrities, politicians, visiting foreign dignitaries—you name it."

"Okay," I trailed off. "How'd you find this place?"

"Like I said, they recruited me." Gavin bit down on his lip. "I *had* been looking into joining the army at the time—that part wasn't a lie. I'd filled out a few online applications. They must've found me that way."

"You're saying they tracked you down?"

"They look for a specific type of kid, this place."

"Do tell."

"There's all sorts of things." Gavin looked uncomfortable. "When I met with the security company's recruiter, the guy knew everything about me. My GPA. My mile time for gym class. My family situation."

My throat went dry. "Your family situation?"

"Look, I didn't have much of a family growing up, and you know that. Dad died young, sob story, blah, blah, blah." Gavin leaned forward, the rocking chair creaking as he rested his arms on his knees. "My mom was around some of the time, at least physically. But she was never..." A shadow crossed his face. "She didn't have the tools to be a great mom, let's put it that way."

Things started to click into place in my head. We'd dated just a few short months, and in that time, I'd never met his family. At the time, I hadn't thought much about it because we'd both been young and obsessed with one another, and it hadn't been long enough for me to question the oddness of it.

"I'm sorry I hid that from you back then," Gavin said, giving me a sideways gaze. "It wasn't anything you did. I just didn't want you to meet my mom when she was... that way."

"I'm sorry. I didn't know."

Memories flurried into my brain, clamoring for space. Our late-night hangouts at the diner. The look on his face as we'd leave, as if he wanted to invite me back to his place.

Now I understood he hadn't had a home that he'd felt comfortable inviting me into.

We'd spent time talking in his car, late into the night. Chowing down on short stacks in the only restaurant open until 2 a.m. He'd never had enough money. He'd never mentioned family. The wire wrapped around my heart started to soften for him just a little.

"I'm sorry."

"It's fine. My Aunt Lily knew my situation, even though she never said anything about it." Gavin gave a self-conscious throat clear. "She helped me out a lot over the years. In little ways at first, like she'd send her kids to school with an extra lunch for me. Sometimes the electricity would turn back on when I knew my mom hadn't paid the bill. New bedsheets would sometimes show up neatly folded in the closet, along with a fresh pair of pajamas and underwear."

"That's so sweet."

"Lily always wanted to help more, but every time she mentioned anything to my mom, my mom reacted terribly. Eventually, Lily gave up mentioning things to her, and anything she did for me was on the sly."

"I see."

"Then one day, my mom just left. Disappeared one day leaving behind only a note on the counter. Yes, I realize the irony now."

"I'm so sorry."

"She said she'd met a guy online and he was paying for her ticket to Florida. I never heard from her again."

"Never?"

Gavin shook his head. "I tried to look her up. Nothing. It's like she dropped off the face of the earth."

I could read the pained look in his eyes. Even I was wondering if his mother was dead—how could he *not*? A troubled woman, another Jane Doe who would never be ID'd.

"I can't imagine what that was like for you."

"I mean, I hadn't depended on her in years, so her disappearance didn't change much for me." Gavin looked like he was trying to appear neutral about it, but I could tell the way it'd gone down still stung.

"That's when the security company found me, offered me a well-paying job. I figured it would get me out of Dodge and pay me enough so that I could repay Aunt Lily back for everything she'd done for me in just a few years."

"Why didn't you tell me any of this?"

"It's a lot." Gavin rubbed his forehead. "I didn't think you needed to be saddled with that much garbage when you were just getting your start in life, when you could be anything you wanted to be, go anywhere you wanted to go. It felt selfish of me to try and rope you in when my life still felt like a fucking mess. I didn't deserve you back then, Tara."

A wave of silence washed over us. I contemplated. I'd never once considered that Gavin might've had intentions that weren't entirely selfish in the way he'd left me in the dust. I'd always assumed he'd left the way he had because he'd simply wanted to.

"Not to mention, when I joined the security company," Gavin continued, "I got a signing bonus if I stayed for seven years. If I left early, I'd have to pay it back. It was a shitload of money. Enough to almost pay my aunt back in the first few months for all the help she'd ever given me."

I nodded slowly. "So you were locked in out in California."

"There's a lot of training that goes into my type of work. The company doesn't want to invest in someone who's going to be gone in a year or two."

Questions bounced around the room, echoing off the walls. I became acutely aware that a tinge of danger seemed to hover around the conversation. Gavin hadn't joined the army, but he'd obviously been involved in something dangerous.

My mind went to the scar on his abdomen. I was desperate to ask about it, but that sort of interest would show my hand. He'd know I'd been looking, studying his body, tracing his scar with my eyes from a distance.

"Is what you were doing..." I searched for a polite way to put it. "Legal?"

A grin broadened Gavin's face. "I'm not an assassin, if that's what you're wondering."

"Are you hiding out in the middle of nowhere because the police are after you?"

"The police are not after me."

"That's not an exact confirmation on whether your job was legal or not."

Gavin gave a little snort. "You listen carefully."

I raised my eyebrows in a prompt. He grumbled something about an NDA. I decided to leave it at that.

"I just finished up a big gig." Gavin gave a one-shoulder shrug. "I'm mostly set for retirement. The thrill was getting old. I've got one job left, and then I'm out for good."

I gave a low whistle. "Nearly retired in your thirties? Not too shabby. Will you stick around here long-term?"

"I'm not sure."

I wanted to ask what the determining factors were, but that would be dipping my toe into dangerous waters, so I refrained.

"Well, this has been a great chat." I rose. "I'm exhausted. I'm going to bed."

A flash of something that looked like disappointment appeared on Gavin's face. It wiped away like an Etch-a-Sketch mere seconds later.

"Of course," he said. "I'll get you some extra blankets."

I looked down at my lap. "I'll just take a few of these. Thanks for giving me your room tonight, even though I swear I'd be fine on the couch."

"Oh, it's no problem. Thank your mom for strong-arming me into letting in guests before we were officially open. I hope you're not going to report us anywhere."

"Thanks for your apology," I said.

"Thanks for hearing me out."

We stood, then stared at one another. The snow swirled outside of the porch. For a split second, I let my brain wander. I considered if the situation were different. If I hadn't learned to hate Gavin Donovan so much over the last thirteen years, what might tonight look like?

A particularly gruesome howl of winter wind sliced through the silence, rattling the windows and shaking us from our daydreams. Gavin winced.

"Gonna be some trees down tomorrow," he mumbled. "It's a good thing you didn't drive home."

"Good night, Gavin."

"Good night, Tara Kendrick."

Chapter 4

Gavin

I shuffled into the kitchen as the sun began to rise. I'd barely slept. My lack of sleep had nothing to do with the lumpy couch or the whistling wind. Nothing to do with the flickering power outages or the stress of keeping on track with my renovations.

It had everything to do with the fact that Tara Kendrick was sleeping one floor above me. Wearing my T-shirt with her lacy underwear. The damn underwear that I couldn't stop thinking about.

Last night, something had broken loose inside me. The way the warmth in her eyes had slowly returned, lit ever so slightly, like the first glimmer of kindling on a fire as I'd apologized and explained. It hadn't been a conscious thought, to share everything with her; it had poured out of me, fueled by her gentle reaction.

I wanted more of it. More of Tara, more closeness, more familiarity. I'd wanted—needed—her to understand that she hadn't been the reason I'd left. That there had been so much I hadn't been able to say in my emotionally stunted youth. And yes, a very-binding NDA.

I hadn't been trying to do the noble thing by taking a job with The Company—a somewhat sketchy but still legal security firm. They'd sought me out, and for a good reason. They liked kids like me. Kids who had no family, no attachments. Burly, broken guys who had nothing to lose. Kids who needed money. They'd had me in their sights before I'd known they'd ever existed.

I shuffled the coffee pot into place and started it brewing. If I spent another night on the couch like the last one, I'd need to start giving myself shots of caffeine to stay awake. But I didn't see how I'd be able to get any sleep so long as Tara Kendrick was in my house. And looking at the snow still accumulating, she wasn't going anywhere just yet.

Speaking of the devil, I cursed as I spun around and caught sight of Tara standing behind me like a ghost. I hadn't heard her come down, and I stubbed my toe on the table trying to rein in my surprise.

"Sorry." Tara raised her hands. "I didn't mean to startle you. I thought you'd hear the stairs."

"Not your fault. I was thinking," I said, as if that were a very novel concept. "Did you sleep well?"

"Just fine." Silence fell, and she gave a bit of a shy smile. "Very comfortable bed. Thanks for offering it up."

"Anytime. You can keep it for tonight if you like."

"Thanks, but no." Tara nodded to where her purse sat waiting, as if she'd packed it like a suitcase. "I just came down to grab a cup of coffee, then I'm going to shower and take off."

"In a toboggan?"

"Huh?"

The woman looked fucking adorable. I had to stand still for a moment just to take it in. Her hair, which had been tied back after her shower last night, was free-flowing and wavy, with cute frizzy wisps sticking up around her forehead. Tara was makeup free and sexy as all hell.

And her nipples. Damn lighthouses beaming the way home. For the right sailor, of course. Unfortunately, that guy wasn't me. I jerked my gaze back to her face.

"Did you look out the window?" I grabbed two mugs and filled them with coffee feeling déjà vu from last night. "It's still snowing."

"Surely the plows have cleared the way."

I raised my eyebrow. "Do you know where you are? In the middle of nowhere. We're not going anywhere today."

"I'm sorry, but I'm not taking no for an answer."

Tara's angry face was just as cute as her sleepy face. She stomped around me, yanked the extra mug from the counter and spun to face me. Tara was steamed, and up close, she wasn't adorable anymore. She was fucking gorgeous.

"Don't tell me what I can and can't do." Tara poked at my chest. Then she looked up at me through thick lashes. "I am getting out of here today, okay?"

I raised my hands, and she was standing so close that as I did, my hand accidentally grazed her boob. It was wholly unintentional, but damn if it didn't have an effect on me.

Tara scowled.

"I'm sorry about the boob graze," I said. "That was not on purpose. You're the one who stomped into my space bubble."

"I'm not stomping." Tara stomped a few feet back, threw her arms across her chest. "Stop staring at my tits."

"It's hard when they're..." I gestured to her. "You know, lighthouses."

"What are you talking about?"

"Forget it." My half-explained analogy was lost on her. And it'd be worse if I explained, because then she'd know I'd been thinking about her chest. "Look, you're not in prison. You can leave if you want, but your car's all dented in and there's snow piled a foot high out there."

"I'm leaving."

"Great," I said, throwing my hands up in exasperation. "There is a shovel outside the door to dig yourself out. Alternatively, I think I saw a pair of janky old skis in the basement you can help yourself to because realistically, that's your best option."

"You are useless."

Tara stormed out of the room. She wasn't mad enough to leave her coffee cup behind, and she slurped it loudly, shooting daggers at me through the banister slats as she headed upstairs. I heard the shower flick on. Finally, I grinned. I wasn't sure what I was smiling about, but she was something all right. Something extraordinary.

While Tara showered off and presumably found herself a bra, I finished my routine in the kitchen. I was out of eggs after I'd accidentally cracked all of them last night while distracted by my new houseguest.

The fridge was looking pretty empty actually. The snowstorm had come out of the blue, and I hadn't had a chance to stock up. But there was a frozen loaf of bread Aunt Lily had stuck in the freezer, a jar of peanut butter, and some cans in the cupboards. For a single guy, it'd be plenty until Gary could clear the roads. But it wasn't much to entertain a lady with.

I settled on a breakfast of delicacies—toasted bread with peanut butter and honey—and a piping hot cup of coffee. I left two pieces of toast sitting out on a plate for Tara. I tapped my foot in the kitchen. Had a second cup of coffee. Changed into a new pair of gym shorts and a clean T-shirt. She was still nowhere to be found.

Forcing myself to stop worrying about Tara and her escape plan, I found myself drawn upstairs to one of the four bedrooms there. The room had been a nursery once upon a time, but at the time we'd purchased the house, it'd been long abandoned.

My agenda for today was to scrape down the yellow wallpaper that'd bubbled and peeled over time. Since it seemed that Tara had virtually disappeared, I figured there was no time like the present to get started.

Half an hour later, I made my way downstairs. I hadn't heard Tara get out of the shower, but at some point, it had sounded like she was talking to someone. A voice niggled in the back of my mind. A husband? A boyfriend? Then, with a flurry of hope—her mother? She had always been close with her mom.

Stopping by the kitchen, I saw with a glimmer of pride that the toast had disappeared. The plate was washed and drying on the rack. It hit me funny, the sight of a dish there—a dish I hadn't washed myself.

I stood there for far too long, literally watching a dish dry, as I contemplated why such a mundane image had triggered me. I'd lived alone for my entire adult life. I'd dated women here and there, but due to the nature of my job—and also my personality—I tended to choose relationships with women who wanted the same thing that I did: a hard and fast fling with no strings attached.

For my job, I'd traveled a good amount, and I couldn't take a significant other with me. I also didn't like having to explain myself to women, especially seeing as that explanation often had to be tempered with half-truths and white lies thanks to my little NDA. It had just been easier to keep things surface level and uncomplicated.

But there was something about seeing a dish in my drying rack—two plates together instead of one. Something shifted in my gut as I realized I didn't hate it. Knowing there was another person cohabitating with me. Then again, maybe it wasn't the fact that it was just anyone hanging around—maybe it was the fact that it was Tara Kendrick that had me all swirly inside.

A loud crash from the basement drew my attention away from the damn drying rack. Cursing under my breath, I took the rickety old stairs as fast as I dared, whirling around the corner with a flashlight I'd grabbed off the wall on the way down.

"What the hell are you doing down here?" I shined the flashlight toward the far end of the room.

There, crouched in the corner, was Tara. She was hunched awkwardly beneath a bookshelf that had clearly tipped over. Fortunately, it had crashed against the far wall and hadn't smushed her—it was perched over her like a dangerous child's fort. Dust decorated her hair. I could see wisps of a cobweb on her shirt from across the room.

Tara raised the tiny light of her cell phone and swept it around the room. "Get the flashlight out of my eyes. I'm fine."

"Fine my ass," I said, repeating her favored phrase from the night before. I crossed the room and found that indeed she wasn't quite as fine as she'd said.

The reason she was still crouched was because a stack of old gardening pots—the heavy, terracotta kind, had fallen in front of her. The floor was a mine of piercingly sharp shards. When she groaned, the hair on my neck rose.

"You're hurt." I said it as an accusation. I meant it that way. "Where are you hurt?"

"It's nothing, it's just this stupid pot on my ankle. It's stuck, wedged by the bookshelf."

I grunted. "What were you thinking? If the bookshelf hadn't landed against the windowsill, you could've been killed."

"Okay, Mr. Over-Exaggerator."

"This thing is real wood, and there's a stack of encyclopedias on it. It could've seriously hurt you."

"Well, it didn't, so let's forget it."

While making tense chitchat with Tara, I'd already started moving. I swept through the shards and leaned my shoulder against the bookshelf. It took most of the muscles in my body screaming in protest, but eventually the thing groaned and creaked and shuddered back into its rightful place.

Then I bent, gently lifted the pot that had gotten stuck between the shelves, and heaved it off her ankle. My body had gone into fight or flight mode, my adrenaline pumping on high. My stomach churned with the fear of what could've

JINGLE BELL ROCK

happened, how close she'd come to getting seriously hurt. The thought developed like a side ache, a sudden, abrupt pain I couldn't get to quit.

"There," I grunted, taking a step back to stand the pot upright. The thing had to weigh a hundred pounds. "Now just wait a minute, and I'll—"

Before I could turn back to her, Tara had already tried to stand. The look on her face as the pain arced through her, the wince, the limp, sent shocks of electricity crackling through my already-loaded-with-adrenaline system.

"What are you thinking?" I exploded. "You're fucking hurt."

I swooped forward, grabbed her behind the knees with one arm and behind the back with the other, cradling her to my chest like a pile of feathers. A pile of feathers that kicked back.

"What are you doing? You freaking Neanderthal!"

"I'm bringing you upstairs." I spun away from the bookshelf and made my way up the rickety staircase, leaving the flashlight on downstairs. "You can barely put weight on your ankle."

"You're overreacting. I was just testing it out."

"You didn't get a passing grade on that exam."

"Good thing there's a curve." Tara shifted against me.

I couldn't help my eyeroll. Tara gave another moderate struggle, but when I cinched her tighter to my chest, she finally gave up. When I summited the staircase and surveyed the landing, pausing for a moment, she pointed as if directing traffic.

"There. The nearest couch."

I obeyed her command. Tara seemed eager to get set down. I was reluctant to let her go. But I did, releasing her gently onto the overstuffed, weirdly brown cushions. She let out a sigh as I straightened and took a step back.

I made my way to the kitchen. I peeked in the freezer and saw the loaf of frozen bread—minus the four slices I'd removed to make breakfast. The peas from last night had never gotten returned and were probably warm mush by now. The damn bread was the only thing in the whole freezer. I returned to the couch in the living room and found Tara leaning forward to study her ankle.

Even as I extended the loaf of frozen bread, I felt like an idiot. Tara stared at me like I was an idiot. Tara hadn't been wrong when she'd called me a Neanderthal—when I'd seen her trapped, possibly hurt, all extra parts of my brain had ceased to function. I'd reverted back to my most basic instincts. *Save. Her.*

"Here," I said, when she didn't make a move to take the bread.

"Are you asking me to make you a snack or seriously offering me frozen bread as an ice pack?"

"The latter," I said, then, more irritated, "I wasn't expecting company. I certainly wasn't expecting my company to go rooting around in my dangerous old basement, and you used up the only peas I had last night."

"You gave me permission to hunt for skis!"

"I was being flippant."

"Well, I take things literally."

"Uh huh," I grunted. "I can see that now."

"Did it not occur to you that there is literally a world made of cold and ice just outside your door now?"

"Huh?" I was too focused on Tara. My heart was beating too fast. My brain was a little fuzzy. It took me an embarrassingly long time to process the non sequitur.

"Ice." Tara's face was caught between fuming frustration and bewildered amusement. "Take the bread out of the bag, fill the bag with snow. Success, genius—you have an all-natural ice pack."

It didn't take a damn genius to figure that out, and it was pretty terrible I hadn't done it myself.

"I was distracted," I grunted.

"Someone actually hired you?" Tara clucked. "On purpose?"

"Hilarious. I can tell your brush with death didn't take away your sense of humor."

"Oh, you big oaf, you're overexaggerating everything. It was just a little misstep."

I headed back into the kitchen and tossed the stupid bread back in the freezer. I grabbed a couple of sturdy plastic bags, made my way outside, scooped up enough snow to make a couple of ice packs. I tossed two in the freezer to keep for later, then returned to Tara's side.

Kneeling before her, I reached for Tara's injured ankle. She pulled away at my touch, and I backed off.

"Did I hurt you?" I asked.

"It's just a little scratch." Tara's face was contorted in a grimace. "Stupid pot."

"Can I look? I'm no doctor, but I was trained to know some basic first aid."

"I'm not dying."

"Glad to hear it. Now can you stop protesting and let me help you?"

I took Tara's grudging silence as the closest thing I'd get to a green light, so I tried again to reach for her. Gentler, slower, until I saw the issue.

"You're bleeding," I said.

"You're right," she deadpanned. "You really are a doctor, Sherlock."

My stupid heart raced faster. I was going to be the one needing a doctor if I didn't calm myself the fuck down. I took a long breath, let it out slowly, forcing myself to seep into the state of mind I'd adopted with my job.

Careful, calm, disassociated. I needed to separate my logical thinking from anything emotional. It was how I'd survived years at The Company. I'd needed to be able to be present, sharp, intense. There had been no room for mistakes. Mistakes got people hurt. People killed. I knew. I'd witnessed it.

Yet here I was, panicking at something that had almost happened. The bookcase had *almost* hit her. The pot could've snapped her leg in half if it'd fallen at the right angle. The broken shard could've pierced a really important artery.

That was how my mind worked—prepare for the worst, expect the worst. The only difference was that this time, it bothered me on a personal level. I'd offered her a fucking loaf of bread as an ice pack because I hadn't been properly focused on the situation.

I cursed under my breath as I collected myself. The bleeding was coming from Tara's calf. I could see the jagged line where the sharp terracotta had pierced her skin and dragged down in a Harry Potter-style lightning bolt. It wasn't deep, but it wasn't pretty either.

"You'll be okay," I declared, expelling a huge breath.

"No kidding."

I was already pulling my shirt over my head and wrapping it around her calf, securing it with a brief knot to help staunch the bleeding.

"Who do you think you are, Fabio?"

I looked up at Tara. "Huh?"

"There are a zillion towels in the kitchen. Did you really have to take your shirt off?"

"You're welcome for trying to help." I rose, feeling incredibly dumb and trying not to let it show. "I'm just stopping the bleeding. Then I'll need to clean it and bandage it up for you. I don't think it's deep enough to need stitches, but I'm going to call Doctor DiMaggio just in case."

"Wait, Gavin."

I'd already turned away, trying to hide my sheepishness. I stopped, turned my head to look over my shoulder at her mid-stride to the kitchen. "What now?"

To my surprise, it was her turn to look sheepish. "I'm sorry. And thank you. I didn't mean to startle you."

"Startle me? It's not that, it's just..." I shook my head. "Forget it."

I grabbed my phone from the kitchen counter and returned. I dialed back to Matt DiMaggio, Fantasie's only doctor.

"Hey, Matt," I said. "Got a minute?"

Doctor Matt DiMaggio, Fantasie's most eligible bachelor, answered my video call with a grimace.

"Dude, where's your shirt?" Matt asked.

"Forget it," I muttered, ignoring Tara's I-told-you-so eyebrow waggle in the background. "Take a look at this cut for me."

"Hi, Dr. DiMaggio." Tara groaned. "This is so embarrassing."

"Tara?" Matt DiMaggio gave a smile on the screen at Tara. "How's your mother?"

"She's fine, thanks. Her new dosage seems to be working out perfectly. Thanks to you. By the way, I'm fine too. Gavin's just panicking over nothing."

I flashed the screen downward because it annoyed me how friendly the two seemed. If Tara was single, and the doctor was single... I jabbed the phone closer to the wound.

"Do you need to stitch this up, Doc?" I growled. "Or what?"

Matt gave a short laugh. "It's a little hard to see with you moving the phone around like a light saber, Donovan."

"Oh, for Pete's sake." Tara yanked the phone out of my hand, unwound my shirt from her calf, and dropped the phone so the doctor could see. "I got a little cut. It's nothing."

"It's not nothing," Matt said after a long moment, "but I'm happy to say you'll survive."

"We can't get anywhere in this snowstorm," I barked. "Is she gonna be fine for a few days?"

"Sure, if she's okay with the idea of losing her leg," Matt deadpanned.

Tara gave a good laugh.

"Yes, of course she'll be fine," Matt said. "Clean it out, and if you've got some antiseptic and some bandages, do that whole thing. If it's not better in a couple of days, or whenever you get back to town, pop by the office and I'll take a look. Call me anytime if you need anything else, Tara. Definitely call me sooner if it's showing any signs of infection."

"Thanks, Doc," she said, hanging up the phone. She tossed it back to me with a smug smile.

"Told you so," she said.

"Didn't know you were such buds with Doctor Cutie," I grumbled.

Tara stared at me. "Dude. I live in Fantasie. *You're* the one who's been away."

I didn't have a good reply, so I headed upstairs to my bathroom and gathered my first aid supplies, a warm cloth, some bandages. Then I made my way back downstairs.

As I knelt once more before her, Tara had gone suspiciously silent. Since conversation hadn't been on my side today, I didn't bother to resume speaking. I quietly lifted her foot and washed her wound. She hissed when I applied the antiseptic. Her face had gone a shade paler by the time I finally wrapped it with gauze.

"How's that feel?" I stepped back, retrieved the bloodied shirt I'd initially wrapped around her leg, and discarded it in the trash can nearby.

"It's fine." Tara watched my movements. "I'm sorry I made a mess of things."

"It's no problem," I said gruffly. "What can I bring you? Or where should I bring you?"

"Snowshoes."

"Huh?"

"I saw some snowshoes downstairs. They'll be easier than skis when I break out of here."

"Are you out of your fucking mind?" I stared at her. "Your ankle is hurt."

"So get me an ace bandage or some athletic tape," Tara shot back. "And some snowshoes while you're at it."

I just shook my head at her. "I'm not being an accomplice in you setting sail from here in a blizzard and freezing to death. No way in hell."

"Fine. Then I'll go back downstairs myself."

"No, you won't."

Tara glared at me. "Snow. Shoes."

I cursed a blue streak as I stomped down the stairs. This was my way of calling her bluff. I understood that she was an independent woman and all that jazz, but she was downright nuts if she was planning to head out in a snowstorm. I figured maybe if I brought her the damn shoes, she'd lay off the debate and turn on a movie already.

I retrieved the dusty old snowshoes I hadn't known existed and grabbed the flashlight I'd left on downstairs while I was down there. I stomped back upstairs until I realized any more stomping, and the stairs might just give way beneath my weight. When I reached the top of the staircase, I dropped the snowshoes before her.

Then I went to the kitchen and cracked open a can of soup. I plopped it in a bowl and microwaved it until hot. I got a couple of bottles of water, the jar of peanut butter and a spoon—that counted as a snack, right?—and the TV remote. I returned to the living room, flicked the TV on, and set up the food tray next to her.

"Your snowshoes, soup, and some beverages," I growled. "Can I get you anything else, princess?"

"A little less attitude, please and thank you."

I rolled my eyes. "I can see you're fine, so why don't you just sit here and eat something and put your leg up?" To emphasize my point, I fluffed a pillow and stuck it on one end where her leg would presumably go. "We're not going anywhere anyway, so you might as well settle in."

"And what are you going to do?"

"If I'm being honest, I'm still a little worked up, so I'm going to go rip some wallpaper off," I declared. "I'll be right upstairs. Holler or call me if you need anything. I'll be down to check on you in an hour."

Without waiting for her to respond, I made my way upstairs. I laid into the wallpaper. Nothing like a little bit of fury to fuel a reno project. I flicked on some tunes, not too loud in case Tara called for me, and zoned out. I checked on her once at the thirty-minute mark, just a peek down the staircase, satisfied to see she'd made a dent in her soup and had actually changed the channel to an action movie.

By the time my hour of work was up, I was feeling marginally better. I'd worked off some of my testosterone fueled adrenaline rush. I'd played out the situation in my head, reminding myself that the worst hadn't happened. Tara hadn't been clonked on the head by the bookshelf. She was just fine, as evidenced by her sparkling wit and charming banter, sitting on my couch downstairs.

There was still the slight issue of why I'd overreacted to an embarrassing degree, but I'd had enough Freudian dissecting of myself over the last twenty-four hours that I didn't dwell on it.

I'd chalk it up to a moment of insanity primed by the fact that I was sharing my space with a gorgeous woman for the first time in—God, how long had it been? Many months, we would go with that. Tara Kendrick had always gotten my blood boiling, and thirteen years later, an innocent little brush of my hand against her boob still got me worked into a frenzy.

"Tara?" I came to a dead stop at the bottom of the staircase.

That *boom, boom* of my racing heart came right back. The couch was empty. Soup tray gone. A peek in the kitchen told me the dishes had, once again, been neatly cleaned and stacked on the drying rack. Peanut butter spoon and all.

I expelled a breath, running through a list of profanities in my head. I raced upstairs to the bedroom. It looked untouched—bed made, bathroom clean and towels hanging neatly. But there was no sign of Tara.

Then I saw something moving outside. A human sized something. The list of profanities bouncing around my head like a pinball game returned in full force.

I headed over to the balcony and pulled the doors open. The pummeling snowfall had lessened to a smattering of big, fat flakes swirling down in festive ambiance. Though I wasn't feeling very festive right now.

I stared down, unable to believe the sight before me. Working at a high profile, very expensive, boutique security

JINGLE BELL ROCK

firm had led me to a lot of places. I'd seen a lot of things. Weird shit, cool shit, fancy shit, crazy shit. But I'd never seen anything like Tara Kendrick.

Tara must have gone through my drawers and borrowed some sweatpants. They were massively large on her and ballooned around her legs. Over it, she wore a fancy-looking peacoat that most certainly wasn't warm enough in this weather. She'd shoved on a hat and gloves. Snowshoes were on her feet. Tara Kendrick was plowing her way through the snow in the general direction of the highway.

"Are you out of your mind?" I hollered after her. Then, "You're wearing my pants."

"I'll wash them and get them back to you," she hollered back. "I figured you wouldn't mind. You don't seem to like wearing clothes anyway."

I glanced down and realized I still didn't have a shirt on. No retort there.

"I didn't know I had to wear clothes in my own goddamn home," I shouted back. "Where do you think you're going?"

"Out," she shouted like some teenager. "I'm not your ward, you caveman. It's really none of your business. Consider me checked out of the inn. Money's on the bed."

"You're insane," I called back. "Fucking nuts."

She waved, her middle finger extended through her gloves.

I stepped back from the window, crossed my arms against the chill on my—admittedly naked—torso, and studied the situation. Tara certainly wasn't going to get very far very fast. Even if she did, there was nowhere to go. She wasn't really going to hitchhike home, was she?

Grumbling, I yanked open my drawers, found a second pair of sweats that matched the ones that Tara had borrowed, and jogged downstairs. I'd give her a ten-minute head start. Then all bets were off.

Chapter 5

Tara

"Holy Hannah."

I paused, cursing out the ankle that was most certainly sprained. I wiped at my brow with my gloved hands. There was no way I was sweating when it was twenty degrees outside, right? Except my boob sweat said otherwise. I was downright scorching hot after hauling my ass a mile in snowshoes, up and down sloping, snowy hills in the direction of the diner.

I had on a small backpack I'd found in Gavin's closet that contained my shoes—high heels, since that was the only thing I'd worn yesterday—a bottle of water that Gavin had left for me on my half-assed charcuterie board, and my phone.

I was well aware my little adventure was nuts. There was no real need for me to be hiking outside in the lull of a snowstorm. But on the flip side, it wasn't like I had a lot to do in my spare time. I hated being trapped, and I hated being trapped in a house with Gavin Donovan worst of all.

Being close to Gavin was doing funny things to me. It was messing with my head. Messing with my heart. Messing with my lady business.

Then there was my pride. I had always taken care of myself. The two times I hadn't, I'd had my heart broken. The first time had been my relationship with Gavin. The second with Liv's father.

I'd tried counting on other people twice. It hadn't worked. I wasn't interested in counting on anyone but myself at this point. Things had been going fine, just me and my daughter. We didn't need anyone else in our lives to let us down.

When I made a promise, I meant it. And I had told Liv that I would be home to collect her last night. So when I hadn't been able to make it, I'd been more than a little bit disappointed in myself. There was no way in hell I wasn't making it home today, especially seeing as tomorrow was Thanksgiving. Even if that meant I had to drag myself through the wilderness on foot to call myself an Uber from the freeway.

I just about crumpled to the ground in relief as I spotted the lights on in the diner. I made it the last hundred yards through sheer grit and boob sweat. When my finger closed over the door handle to pull it open, I prepared myself to collapse into the first booth I could find.

"There you are, honey." A woman scurried to the front door as I tumbled inside. "You made it in really good time, sweetie."

"Good time?" I stared at the woman—dark skin, hair tied in a top knot, pretty pink apron tied around her waist. She was probably my mother's age. "What do you mean?"

"Oh, Gavin called ahead and said I should open up shop, seeing as I had a customer getting blown on in by a blizzard."

"Gavin called you?" I finger gestured around. "Is he here?"

"No. He seemed to think you wanted some time by yourself."

The woman smiled, a kind smile that reached her eyes as she ushered me to the counter. She helped me remove my peacoat and gave an amused chuckle as I wrestled off my snowshoes along with the pair of tennis shoes I'd borrowed from Gavin.

I slipped into my high heels, not because I was trying to look good for anyone, but because I didn't feel like clomping around in worn tennis shoes that were six times my size. Plus, this way, I could leave Gavin's shoes behind at the diner for him to retrieve when I got in my Uber and scooted away from here. I didn't want to leave owing the man anything.

"Now sit, honey. I'm Ida." The woman bustled around the counter and tapped her fingers, waiting for the pot of coffee to finish brewing. "Are you hungry?"

"Starved." The soup I'd scarfed down and the two pieces of toast Gavin had left for me this morning had been no match for the calories I'd torched trekking across the world to get here. "If it's not too much trouble. Actually, did you say you had to come here to open up?"

"Well, yes, I did say that. But it's no trouble."

"I'm so sorry! You didn't have to open an entire restaurant for me."

Ida gestured around. "You mean flick on the lights and put on a pot of coffee? Like I said, no trouble. I live right next door. I'll throw on some hashbrowns and an omelet. One for you, one for the hubby. He'll appreciate it. Really, you're doing Charles the favor because otherwise he was looking at leftovers."

I sat back in my seat, finally realizing the extent of my nuttiness. I'd really, truly let my mixed-up emotions for

Gavin tangle with my desire to get home and see my daughter.

"I'm sorry to be any trouble," I apologized again. "I probably shouldn't have left Gavin's place. I just really wanted to get home."

"Honey, there's nothing wrong with a good trek through the snow to get your blood pumping. You know, some people do that for fun."

"Yeah, crazy people," I remarked. "Do you know how hard it is out there?"

Ida burst out in appreciative laughter. "I don't much care to find out. I'm happier tucked under my blanket in a cozy armchair with a good book. Save the snow shooin' and four wheelin' and ice fishin' for someone else."

"Amen."

I gratefully accepted a sturdy white diner mug full to the brim with dark black coffee of the perfect variety. I took a sip and immediately felt it recharging my weary bones. My ankle ached, despite the fact that I'd wrapped a boatload of ace bandages around it.

"So tell me." Ida turned her back to me, exposing the cute bow on her pink apron as she threw a slab of butter on the grill and pulled out some eggs. "You're pretty determined to get somewhere. Care to share?"

"It's my daughter."

There was something about Ida that made conversation feel easy, even in the first five minutes of knowing her. Plus, it felt good to have someone to talk to who I wasn't supposed to hate. I was *supposed* to hate Gavin. Hating him for breaking my heart was easy. Not hating him was complicated.

Ida nodded knowingly. "I've got one of them. A son, too."

"How old?"

Ida waved a hand dismissively. "Grown and gone, but that doesn't mean I don't remember the days when they were younger like it was yesterday."

"I promised my daughter, Liv, that I'd pick her up last night. She's safe, of course, with my mom. I don't even think she noticed I was gone. But I hate—and I mean absolutely hate—breaking my promises to her."

"I understand, sweetie." Ida's spatula scraped in soothing tones against the grill. "We spend all this time worrying about those children, loving them until our insides hurt, and they don't even seem to notice." She turned, rested her hands against the counter as she faced me. "Let me tell you, though, it comes around. Some take longer than others, but my daughter has her own girl now. And let's just put it this way: my daughter appreciates me more now than she ever has before. Makes it all worth it."

"That's good to hear. Because sometimes I do wonder."

Ida sized me up. "Was it a man?"

"Was who a man?"

"The one who broke his promises."

I thought of Franklin, Liv's father. I thought of Gavin and the way he'd left my vulnerable heart in tatters. I thought of my own mother, and the way she'd raised me as a single mom.

"A lot of men," I admitted. "It seems like all my daughter has had in her life are men that don't stick around."

"And your life too," Ida observed. "I'm sorry, sweet cheeks. I had one of them. My first husband. But the second one more than makes up for it."

I was already shaking my head. "I tried twice. I'm done."

"Uh huh," she said with a wink. "That's what I said too. The right one will convince you otherwise."

"I doubt it," I said. "I'm pretty stubborn."

"You don't say." Ida stared pointedly at my snowshoes. "Which reminds me. Gavin told me to ask ya if you were still bleeding. Do I really want to know?"

I shook my head. "I'm fine. But thanks for your very awkward concern."

Ida burst into laughter, then set about mixing something together in a bowl. I recognized it a few minutes later as pancakes. The scent of coffee, the warmth of the diner, the buttery scent of frying comfort food had me forgetting that I was supposed to be hunting for a way out of here, not burrowing in deeper.

"So you know Gavin, then?" I asked, trying to quell the notes of curiosity in my voice.

"Having the job I do, you get to know people." Ida flipped a couple of pancakes. "I like to talk. People like to eat. The two go hand in hand. That's the long way of saying that we've become acquainted since he and Lily bought that place."

"He and Lily? I thought it was Lily's place."

"He put Lily's name on the deed, but Gavin fronted the money for the place." Ida glanced over her shoulder at me, then returned to her cooking. "I've known Lily Donovan for years. We go way back. I grew up in Fantasie, you know.

JINGLE BELL ROCK 69

Moved out this way when I met my second husband. We bought this place together along with the house next door."

"Oh, I didn't realize. I'm from Fantasie too."

"I gathered." Ida smiled. "I could tell. Anyway, Lily and Gavin have a partnership going from what I understand. Not that Gavin would admit it, but Lily likes to rave about her nephew when she comes to visit."

"Huh."

"I'm not surprised Gavin didn't tell you. He keeps things close to his chest."

"It's none of my business," I said quickly, but I was replaying my conversations with Gavin in my head. Everything he'd said had led me to believe that Lily Donovan had bought the place on her own. Knowing that Gavin had swooped in to help out with payment was... surprisingly unshocking. It seemed like the sort of thing he'd do.

"He's a good egg." Ida cleared her throat. "I know you're not asking for my endorsement, but I'm just saying. If you were asking, I'd vote for Gavin."

"Vote for him for city council?"

"More like vote for him as husband material. You know, if you're looking." Ida slid a plate across the counter. It had a pile of pancakes and a serving of scrambled eggs. "Which I know you're most certainly not."

I tucked into the food, losing all fight in me to protest Ida's glowing reviews of Gavin's husband material-ness. I was halfway through my pancake stack before I forgot the real reason I'd come.

"The real reason I came here, aside from these orgasmic pancakes," I said with the wave of my fork, "is because I was hoping to find a way home. My car is stuck at Gavin's place, and I couldn't get it out even if I wanted to. The plows haven't come through."

Ida shook her head, a hint of regret on her face mixed with a hint of amusement. "You can't get out from here either, honey. No taxis, Ubers, none of that can get up this way. Gary, our main plow guy, was out of town this weekend not expecting snow. Morty from down in Fantasie is gonna make his way up here eventually to help out, but it'll take a while. Not to mention the huge tree that got knocked down over the road. That's gonna take a day to clear."

"Maybe if I hike down to the highway?"

"Honey, I think your daughter would rather have her mama make it home alive in one piece *tomorrow,* than get into the car with some random person in the middle of a snowstorm today. Just my two cents."

"I understand, but—"

"I hate to say it, but unless you're prepared to walk miles further, then you're stuck here."

I gave a guttural groan.

"I'm sure things will clear up by tomorrow evening."

"But that means I'd miss Thanksgiving with my daughter."

"Sweet cheeks, you're her mama. That's all you've got to be. You don't have to be perfect. You're human, and it's not your fault things didn't go as planned. It's healthy for her to see her mama having to roll with the punches. Just be honest with her," Ida said. "Call your baby Liv, tell her you wish you were there, but it just isn't happening until tomorrow. Does she like being with your mother?"

"She loves it. Liv couldn't get off the phone with me fast enough yesterday. They had a whole sleepover planned."

"Then you *really* don't worry about it, baby. Let them enjoy their time. If my mama was still here..." Ida paused, cleared her throat. "She's been gone twenty years now, but I'm sure as hell glad she was around to take my babies for sleepovers when they were little. They still talk about their sleepovers with Grandma Pat. The movie nights, the pancakes for dinner, the candy she'd sneak into their tote bags to take home. That's what childhood is about, honey. Let them have some fun. Break some rules. It's good for everyone."

"I suppose things could be worse."

"Of course they could. And if I'm understanding things right and you're a single mama, you could probably use a bath and a book yourself. Or a movie. Or a snuggle date with a handsome man."

"Oh, Ida, don't play me like that."

She grinned. "How's your food, honey?"

"Like I said. Orgasmic. I haven't had a meal like this in a long time. Finances have been a little tight at home, so it's been home-cooked meals, which means I'm cooking. And I sure as hell can't cook like this."

A throat clear sounded behind me. A manly throat clear.

I swiveled in my chair to face my burly prison guard. The man who seemed intent on keeping me locked in his home like Beauty and the Beast. Okay, that was a slight exaggeration, but still. I was used to doing my own thing. I was not used to listening to someone else's opinion on what I should and shouldn't be doing.

"Orgasmic, huh?" Gavin's voice rasped a little. "Shall I give you some time alone with your pancakes?"

"If that involves you leaving, then sure. I was having a nice conversation with Ida here." I gestured toward my new friend behind the counter, but I quickly realized the sneaky minx had ducked into the back room, leaving me alone with Gavin. "Huh," I grunted. "Well, I was until Ida ditched me."

Gavin crossed thick arms over his chest. "She's my friend too. And I'm pretty sure she knows I'd like to have a word with you."

"I don't owe you anything."

"Fine. I'll leave. I'm assuming Ida filled you in about the trees down, the fact that Gary is out of town, and the *other* fact that there's no way you're getting anywhere today?"

"Shut up," I said, but it was a weak, childish attempt at a retort.

My shoulders slumped forward, and I swiveled back to face my food. It was starting to hit me, to finally hit me, that I might not make it back in time for Thanksgiving dinner with my baby girl. It would be the first holiday we hadn't spent together ever. It was making me feel a little weepy, and the absolute last thing I needed right now was a waterworks display to rival Niagara Falls in front of Gavin Donovan.

"What's got you so anxious to get out of my house? Aside from the fact that it's my house."

I shot a bitter look at Gavin. "I don't owe you any explanations."

Gavin heaved a huge sigh and pulled a winter hat off his head. The man was dressed like a lumberjack. He had sweatpants on and a big flannel shirt that looked like it had some very cozy Sherpa lining on the inside. I was instantly jealous. It looked a lot warmer than my missing-a-button peacoat.

Gavin moved a few steps closer then pulled back the chair next to me. He gave an exaggerated hesitation.

"May I?" he finally asked. "Or will you elbow me in the ribs?"

"No promises," I grumped. Then, "Fine."

Gavin plunked himself next to me. It felt like the room increased in temperature by about five hundred degrees instantly. I wasn't sure if he was radiating heat from his hike up here, or if it was just the tension zipping between us. Either way, I removed my peacoat and hung it over the back of the chair, revealing the T-shirt of Gavin's I was still wearing.

"Nice pants," he said finally. "We match."

I shoved a bite of pancake into my mouth. "Sorry for stealing your pants."

"I've never heard that one before."

"I left you money under the pillow for the pants and the room."

"I don't want your damn money."

"This is a business transaction," I reiterated. "We've gone over that."

"I fucking get it, okay?" Gavin's fist rattled my silverware as it came down and landed on the counter. "You don't owe me anything. Understood. I'm just making conversation. Would you rather I leave?"

I glanced sideways at him. I hadn't realized my stubbornness had been eating away at him so much. Needling him until his frustration had bubbled over. Gavin didn't look angry so much as frustrated that I wouldn't let him help. Which was fine and dandy because I didn't want him to solve my problems.

"I prefer to take care of myself," I said, quieter. "I don't want to explain myself to you."

"Fine. Are you done with your pancakes?"

"Huh?"

"You haven't touched them since I've been here. Can I eat them? I'm starving. Two pieces of toast isn't exactly enough to fill my stomach. Especially with the way you're making me chase after you."

"I'm not making you do anything."

"You snowshoed three quarters of a mile on a sprained ankle. You're not dying on my watch."

"How valiant of you."

"Fine. We can sit here in silence. Your pancakes, princess?"

I pushed my plate over in answer. Ida must have sensed the tense silence because she reappeared, grabbed another mug, filled it with steaming coffee. As she passed it to Gavin, she refilled mine. There seemed to be a touch of sparkle in her eye as she surveyed the fact that Gavin was literally finishing my leftovers.

"More food?" she asked.

"Yes," Gavin said shortly. "Thanks, Ida."

Ida gave a nod and disappeared again. Leaving us alone. Again.

A tiny bit of guilt had wormed its way into my insides as I watched Gavin packing away the pancakes like he'd returned from a forty-day famine in the desert.

Yes, he'd hurt me thirteen years ago. But that was a long time ago. He'd apologized and had seemed sincere about it. He had done nothing except help me out—from donating his bed free of charge to bandaging my ankle after I'd gone snooping around his basement. He'd been polite. In fact, he'd been quite the gentleman, considering the circumstances in which he'd found me randomly on his doorstep, bleeding and annoyed at the universe.

"I'm sorry," I said finally.

Gavin's pretty eyes shifted in my direction, filled with confusion. "Sorry?"

"Sorry for being a little bit of a bitch."

"No, Tara, that's not what I meant at all. You're not a bitch in the slightest. You're entitled to your anger. You're entitled to not forgive me. You're entitled to dislike me intensely if that's what you want. I didn't mean to imply any of this was your fault."

"Well, some of it is my fault."

"Yeah, the hiking through the snow on a bum ankle was a little batshit, but you've always been feisty." Gavin let out a little smile. "Still, it was your prerogative. You do have a point: I don't have a right to know anything about your life. I shouldn't have pressed so much."

"I just really wanted to be home for Thanksgiving." I felt a little deflated.

I was finally coming around to the idea that it wasn't looking possible. I'd phoned Liv and my mother this morning, but in true Liv nature, she'd been too busy making bead necklaces to have much of a discussion with me.

When I'd mentioned I might be a little more delayed than I had first thought, Liv had told me to "take my time because she was busy anyway". So, there was that.

"I get it," Gavin said, obviously trying to understand my half-stories.

But I didn't feel like expanding. I didn't feel like letting Gavin in on the nuances of my life just yet. Liv was the most precious thing to me, the pearl in my clamshell. I didn't share her easily, didn't open to reveal my treasure to just anyone. As kind as Gavin had been, it didn't mean I had to invite him back into my life.

"You don't have to get it." I shrugged. "To be honest, I don't feel up to talking about it. I just want to sort of pretend it's not happening."

"Hey, that's fair." Gavin spoke with a tenderness that could become dangerous. "I won't bother you about it again. I appreciate you letting me know."

Ida returned then and slid another platter in front of us. One platter, two forks. More sparkly-heart eyes from her. I groaned.

"I think she's shipping us," I muttered to Gavin when Ida returned to the back of the room. "One plate? Two forks?"

"Ida's a romantic." Gavin dismissed the insinuation quickly, easily, which was much appreciated. "You still dip your sausages in that godawful condiment?"

"You'd best not be insulting my precious ketchup again."

Gavin gave a shy smile, reached all the way over the counter, and plucked a bottle of ketchup from the rail behind it. He cracked open the cap and poured a generous sized Eiffel Tower of ketchup.

"That's good," I said politely once he'd nearly emptied the bottle.

He barked a laugh. "How many sausages do you plan on putting away?"

I stubbornly took one sausage for a little swim through the pool of ketchup. "Wouldn't you like to know."

We ate in amicable silence then, savoring the greasy grub, the buttery toast, the fluffy pancakes. We did a number on the food without speaking. We moved next to one another in a friendly little dance. Passed the coffee pot amicably. Shuffled food from one side of the plate to the other. Exchanged napkins peacefully.

"Kinda like old times, huh?" Gavin finally said. "Or is that off-limits talk, too?"

I considered a long moment. Added some more cream to my coffee. "It does remind me of old times. You know, that diner's not there anymore. The one right outside of Fantasie where we always went."

"I know." Gavin wrinkled his nose. "I subscribed to their e-mail newsletter."

"You did not!" I blinked at him. "I did too. It was the only way to keep track of their weekly rotation of cookie flavors."

"Exactly. Not to mention—" Gavin's phone rang before he could finish his sentence. He glanced down, did a double take. "Sorry. I need to take this."

It wasn't lost on me that Gavin didn't simply talk quietly or move to a corner of the diner to answer his phone. No, he left the building entirely and closed the door behind him before he even said *hello*.

Sneaky Ida returned then and began clearing dishes.

"What's your plan?" Ida asked innocently. "Will you be sticking around here for another day or two?"

"Doesn't seem like I have much of an option," I said. "If I can't leave, I guess I'm stuck."

Ida's eyes darkened more seriously. "Look, hon, I understand the predicament you're in. I've got a mama's heart too, and I was a single mama for some of those years before I met my second husband."

I swallowed, nodded.

"And I can vouch for Mr. Gavin Donovan until the cows come home, but if you're not comfortable staying with him, I want you to know you have a place with me." Ida raised a finger and pointed upstairs. "Charles and I recently renovated the studio upstairs. We were gonna rent it out, but haven't listed it yet. It's yours until the roads are clear if you'd feel safer there."

"I really appreciate that, but trusting Gavin isn't the issue. I know he's a decent person."

"He sure is." Ida patted the countertop, her wedding ring giving a satisfying clink. "Let me put it this way. I'm gonna keep the key to the studio under the front mat. Ain't nobody gonna find it over the next few days anyway. You need a place, help yourself—no questions asked. No money accepted."

I gave her a grateful smile. "I can't tell you how much it means to me."

"You're not all that much older than my daughter." Her voice became gruff. "Like I said, I've got a mama's heart."

JINGLE BELL ROCK

I licked my lips, feeling more emotional than I should've over a short stack of buttery flapjacks, when a wind whistled into the diner as Gavin opened the door. I swiveled to face him, surprised to find his presence a welcome relief.

I wasn't sure what had changed. Maybe Ida was toying with my emotions. Or maybe it was the fact that brunch with Gavin hadn't been terrible. Or maybe it was the fact that if I was going to be stuck alone in the middle of nowhere, it was kind of nice to have some company.

My strange sense of excitement at seeing Gavin immediately quelled, however, when I caught the look on his face. The teasing was gone. The frustration gone. The playful banter a distant memory.

In its place was a slate of granite. The pretty gray gemstones that were his eyes had turned into slabs of concrete. The muscles under his lumberjack shirt seemed flexed, almost swollen with tension. And when he rested his eyes on me, it was possessive. Dangerous. Like he expected me to do what he wanted.

"We need to go," he said. "Now."

"But—"

"I'm not telling you what to do this time because I enjoy seeing you squirm." Gavin swept into the room, carrying a cloud of seriousness with him. "I know you're all hung up on taking care of yourself, being independent, and all that. Please be fucking independent in fifteen minutes once we get home."

"Okay."

"I'm serious, Tara. I can't explain everything right now, but—" Gavin stopped abruptly, did a double take at me. "Wait—did you just agree with me?"

I flashed him a hopeful little smile. Gave a tiny one shoulder shrug. "I mean, I guess you could've asked a little bit nicer, but it's fine. I'll go with you."

A complex emotion seeped into Gavin's eyes, softening those concrete slabs the tiniest bit. Then he gave a succinct nod, so quick I would've missed it if I hadn't been staring directly at him. There was a wave of appreciation that went along with it.

"Thanks," Gavin mumbled. "Do you mind giving me a minute to talk to Ida? In private."

"Uh, yeah, sure." I reached for my snowshoes and began fumbling with them. "Just give me a—"

"Don't be ridiculous."

Gavin leaned over, grasped my thin wrist with his hand. I was pretty sure his fingers could've encircled my wrist three times if he'd tried. His touch was warm against my skin, his grip commanding but gentle. It sent flames licking down my stomach and straight to the space between my thighs. I bit down on my lip, hard.

Gavin felt it too, I could tell. He froze, glanced up at me. We were inches apart, just a breath away from a kiss. We'd been here before, and the moment felt weighty, familiar, new and thrilling all at once. The way my blood was pulsing through my veins, the way I was being pulled toward him, the way—

The swinging doors to the kitchen slapped shut, announcing Ida's presence. For once, her timing was completely terrible, I thought, as Gavin and I righted ourselves, both of us looking so obviously flustered and hot that it was ridiculous. Then again, maybe her timing was perfect. Another few seconds of being locked into Gavin's orbit could've been disastrous.

"I'm sorry," Ida said. "I thought I heard, well, never mind. I'll just—"

"We're leaving," Gavin said. He turned to me. "Leave the snowshoes, Tara. I brought the snowmobile."

I smacked him on the chest. "You had a snowmobile this whole time?"

He licked his lips, still staring at my mouth. "You never asked, babe."

I ignored the pet term, thinking he probably called just about every woman of childbearing age babe. Then I gathered his snowshoes and shuffled into my peacoat and hiked outside to give Gavin some time alone with Ida.

Once outside, I burrowed into my coat. I saw the snowmobile sitting a hundred feet off. I flicked through a list of obscenities in my head about how he'd let me tromp almost a mile through the snow with a sore ankle before coming to my rescue. Then I reminded myself that I hadn't wanted to be rescued, and I got mad at myself all over again.

But that frustration dissipated the second I glimpsed the worn welcome mat between my feet. Ida's comments had helped settle my aching heart a bit. I hated that I couldn't be home with my baby, but the seasoned mother had a point—Liv was in good hands. The best hands. I could hardly find fault with that.

Maybe years from now, this would be a story me and Liv would look back on fondly and chuckle. And in the meantime, wasn't I in good hands too? I was bunking with a man who, at the very least, I knew to be a good person. Gavin wasn't some random weirdo.

Then there'd been Ida who had offered me refuge from the storm with no strings attached. There were good people in this world. Just because I was conditioned to see the worst in others, especially men, didn't mean all people were out to let me down.

I toed the welcome mat, reminding myself not to get teary eyed now. My tears would freeze right on my freaking eyeballs, and I did not need another phone call to the smoking hot Dr. DiMaggio from Gavin's house.

Fortunately, my moment of overly dramatic self-analysis was cut short when Gavin brushed out the front door, carrying a huge bag with him. He cocked his head at me to follow him. Then, on second thought, he reached over and picked me up.

"Excuse me?" I lost my sense of equilibrium as he marched through the snow. "I thought you weren't going to tell me what to do."

"I didn't say a word," he said, a tad smug. "But you're in heels."

I debated fighting him on it, but we were already halfway to the snowmobile, and the thought of having to tromp through a foot and a half of fresh powder made my ankle ache. So I took a page from Gavin's book and kept my mouth shut as he carried me like a banged-up Disney princess through the snow.

"How'd you get your scar?" I blurted. "I mean, the one on your, uh, abs."

Gavin's eyes shifted to my face. "How's that relevant right now?"

"Just making conversation," I said, well aware my face was within kissing distance to Gavin Donovan's lips once more.

"Like you, I don't want to discuss everything," he said pointedly.

"Work?" I asked.

"Sure," he said finally. "We'll go with that."

I didn't press him because, after all, I'd been complaining about him getting into my business. So here I was, not getting into his business.

When we reached the snowmobile, he set me down gently, deliberately, onto the back. He fastened his large bag and my backpack on with a strap, then he climbed on. When he grunted, I took that to mean I was supposed to wrap my arms around him.

I did, letting my hands snake around that sherpa-soft lumberjack shirt. The softness of the material mixed with the hardness of him underneath was, to put it lightly, a bit titillating. Which was hard for me to admit, even in my own currently overly-emotional brain.

As he fired up the engine, giving no sign that he was as affected by any of this as I was, I leaned my head against his back. I just needed to rest. I was exhausted at this point, wiped out and drained from everything that had happened over the last twenty-four hours.

I'd spent a fourteen-hour day decorating yesterday. Driven partway home in a snowstorm. Confronted my first love and life-long nemesis in a shocking twist of fate. And I was stuck away from my daughter for the first time ever on an important holiday. I was ready for a nap.

Gavin stilled when my forehead hit his back. He waited, then leaned backward just enough to whisper in my ear. "Just hold on, babe. A few minutes, and I'll get you home."

Home, I thought to myself sleepily.

Home sounded nice.

Chapter 6

Gavin

I'd never seen anyone fall asleep on a snowmobile before.

To be fair, Tara hadn't exactly conked out, but the way her eyes were practically rolling in circles when I pulled up the driveway at the house, parking it in front of her busted up vehicle, told me she wasn't all that far off. The real tell, however, was when I offered to carry her inside and she didn't bat an eye.

Miss Independent flew off the handle every time I so much as looked in her direction the wrong way. The fact that she let me scoop her off the snowmobile and carry her up the front porch, kicking the door open and hauling her into the warmth, both set my heart on fire and nearly brought me to my knees.

Glancing down at Tara's face, those eyelashes fighting a losing battle to stay open, the soft pout of her incredible lips—it just about turned me into a religious man. I'd never seen a woman so perfect in my entire life.

Except I had. I'd seen her before, and I'd thought she was perfection then. I'd spent the last thirteen years talking myself out of the fact that she was still taking up precious space in my heart. I'd tried to tell myself that my infatuation with Tara had been because we'd been so young, swept up in some love-riddled romance that happened in hopeful summers, a time capsule of hormones and unbridled joy and finding someone I had loved, deep and hard.

Yet here she was, limp in my arms, and she was even more beautiful. Wiser, more cynical, feistier. She packed an even bigger punch than before. Carried an even bigger attitude with her. And she had exactly the same overwhelming, tilt-the-earth-upside-down effect on me as she always had.

I hadn't been wrong. I'd spent thirteen years telling myself lies. I'd told myself that I hadn't loved her as much as I remembered. That she wasn't as perfect as my memories had told me. That I didn't regret walking away from the best thing in my life.

All fucking lies.

I walked upstairs to my bedroom, which I'd happily turn over to her every damn day of the week, and I set her on the bed. I took off her high heels and set them on the floor. I studied her for a moment, then did my best to gently remove her hat and gloves.

It took me a solid seven minutes to peel some of her outer layers off without waking her. Then, I tossed up a prayer to the gods as I decided to try and help her out of those sweats. My sweats. I fucking loved seeing her in my clothes. I knew that I hadn't earned the right to even daydream about making her mine again, but damn if my mind wasn't trespassing there anyway.

I knew I was playing with dynamite taking her pants off, but those pants were covered in a layer of snow that was already starting to melt and would chill her to the bone, so I figured I would take my chances. Keeping a respectful distance, I tugged the pants off and pulled the T-shirt down so it covered her completely.

I hissed in a sharp breath when I saw she'd bled through the bandage I'd wrapped around the cut on her calf. Her foot was still wrapped up in ace bandages. I knew she'd be fine, but it still pierced me like an arrow to know she'd hurt herself on my watch.

Layering a towel over a pillow, I propped her leg up and pulled a blanket over her before backing out of the room. I paused for a moment in the door to watch her sleep. It was the first time she'd seemed truly peaceful, truly content since she'd re-entered my life. She deserved a life of peace and joy. Even if I wasn't the one who could give it to her. She deserved the world.

Shutting the door behind me, I made my way back downstairs. I unpacked the array of groceries I'd mooched off Ida. I'd taken care of the breakfast bill and added a hefty tip, along with enough extra to cover the food supplies. I refused to feed the woman in my house from a half-eaten jar of peanut butter and a frozen loaf of bread any longer than necessary.

Fortunately, Ida had been in the possession of plenty of fresh produce that she'd hoisted on me for fear "it'd go bad before customers could get to her", and I'd happily taken them off her hands. Salad greens, eggs, sausages. Cheese, soda, and—fortunately—a couple of bottles of wine.

The cabernets had come from Ida's personal stash. She'd offered them up as a gift with a wink-wink. I'd rolled my eyes at her not-so-subtle insinuations. But I also hadn't refused. I wasn't sure what that said about me or my character, but if Tara wanted to relax with a glass of wine tonight, who was I to stop her?

Since I had absolutely no clue how long Tara was going to be sleeping, and I also had no clue if she'd want to spend time with me even when she was awake, I decided to return to the old nursery and carry on with my wallpaper removal.

I set to it, letting the soft music work its way through my body as I fought hard not to think about the phone call I'd gotten at the diner. The call had come from Carter Donovan, my cousin and owner of The Company.

The information Carter relayed had spooked me. Enough to haul Tara's ass out of the diner and get home. Or at least, to the place I was calling home for now. I was prepared here at the inn. I had my gear stashed within reach. I could protect Tara here if it came to that. I didn't think it would, but in my line of work, one never could be too safe.

The wallpaper came down easily. I had no clue how long I'd been toiling away as the hours ticked on. I'd checked on Tara once, ensured she was still breathing, and then had left her alone.

When I finally heard a sound in the hallway, a gentle knock on the door, it was as if I was getting pulled out of a trance. I hit the pause button on my music and quickly registered that it was already dark outside. My stomach grumbled. I took all these clues to mean that it must be evening already, or pretty damn close.

"How long was I out?" Tara rubbed at her eyes, the gesture so sweet and innocent it tore me to pieces faster than the wallpaper I'd been scraping off.

I wanted to pull her to me, suffocate her with a hug, warm her with a kiss. Then relax her in a much more intimate way.

I cleared my throat feeling hot and twitchy. In all the wrong places.

"A while?" I scratched my head. "Um, I lost track of time."

Tara looked rested. Peaceful. Her eyes glimmered. "I see your hatred of shirts is still intact."

I glanced down at my bare chest. "I was getting hot."

I was also fumbling my words. Tara was standing in my doorway in nothing but my shirt. Her hair mussed with sleep. The faint smell of fresh winter air lingered on her, along with something more floral, soft and feminine. It gave me a fucking appetite, and not for food.

"Sure." Tara seemed unusually playful.

Her eyes raked down my body, her lips twitching into an amused pout. Then her eyes locked on something, and with a glimpse down, I saw she was looking at my scar. She moved forward, into the room, as if drawn by a force of nature.

My breath hitched in my throat as Tara drew closer. She paused, almost in a dream-like state, as she raised her hand and rested it on my scar. She trailed her finger down it gently.

"Are you..." My throat was dry and scratchy. "Are you awake?"

"Huh?" Tara looked up, confused, but her hand remained on my chest.

"Are you sleepwalking?"

Tara pulled her hand back. "No. Why?"

"You don't seem to hate me, and I'm wondering why."

Tara gave an embarrassed shift of her weight from one foot to the next. "Sorry. I can get back to that pretty easily if you'd prefer."

"No, no." I reached out for Tara, let my hands rest gently on her arms. "I was just caught off guard."

"I'm sorry, really. I don't know what I was thinking touching you." Tara stayed close to me, twining her hands together before her body. "You didn't have that scar last time. It just... I don't know what I was thinking. It looks like you were hurt badly, and I guess..."

"It's fine." My voice was a dirt road. Dry, scratchy. "You're right. I got it at work. Knife wound."

"Yikes." Tara's eyes drew back to the jagged scar. "I'm sorry. What happened?"

"A job gone bad. Someone I thought I could trust..." I thought back to the night it had happened. To the night I'd faced the truth about the only other woman I'd loved in my life. Or thought I'd loved. Turned out it'd been one big joke on me. A joke that had almost gotten me killed. "I made a mistake," I said simply. "That's all. It was on me."

"I see. I was just being nosy. And Gavin, I don't hate you. I guess not anymore."

I leaned in, brushed some hair back from her face. We stood close to one another, wrapped in a halo of nostalgia fueled desire. I knew some of these feelings must be lingering from before, from a love so intense it'd ruined me for every woman I'd met over the last ten years.

I had half a mind to tell her that. I debated, the words heavy on my tongue, afraid I'd startle her.

"You never settled down." Tara said it as an explanation.

It burst something inside of me, and I returned my hand to her cheek. This time, I didn't pretend to whisk her hair away. I simply let my thumb brush against her skin. I watched with deep pleasure as her eyes fluttered shut against my touch.

"Nobody has ever been able to hold a candle to you," I rasped.

Tara's eyes reopened, and if I was reading her right, she was feeling the same thing I was. I leaned in, my hand sliding down to grip her chin. I tilted her face up toward me, though she was so damn tiny I'd have to dip my head half a foot to close the gap between us. It gave her a long time to push me away. She didn't.

I leaned in, my lips centimeters away from making contact, when her phone fired off in a stupid jingle. Tara stepped back, jolted as if she were on fire. She glanced down at the name on the screen and, her chest heaving with rapid breaths, she flicked it open.

"Hello?" Tara's eyes were wild as she looked at me, distracted, as she turned away.

But not before I heard the small voice echo through from the other end of the phone with one little word that just about sent me into shock. "Mom?"

It felt like my knife wound was as fresh as the day I'd gotten it. A sharp pain hit me in the gut at the sound of the little voice on the other end of the line. A girl, a child, calling Tara the title: *Mom*.

Tara looked up at me, obviously watching my face change expressions. "Honey, can I call you right back?"

Tara was still hanging up when I blurted, "You're fucking married?"

She blinked at me. Then she stepped close, gave me a slap across the cheek.

"No, I'm not fucking married. You think I'd sit here letting you feel me up if I was married?"

My hand went to my cheek. Not because her slap had hurt. It hadn't.

"I wasn't feeling you up," I said sourly. "I just figured—"

"You figured you knew me," Tara hissed. "You. Don't. Know. Me. Gavin, dating for a summer over a decade ago doesn't give you any insight to the woman I am today."

Then she turned and stormed out of the room. Rightfully so. I immediately felt like an ass. I debated chasing after her, but I figured she probably needed a moment to cool down. Frankly, it wouldn't hurt for me to cool down a touch as well.

Granted, my burst of indignation had apparently been wrongly directed, and what an awful assumption to make. Of course people could have children without being married. I shook my head, cursing at myself. All it would've taken was one breath. A moment to think things through. Just the two seconds it would have taken to formulate a more intelligent and somewhat sensitive reply to my shock.

But that's what it had been—a shock. And Tara had been right. A part of me did feel like I still knew her, and I had no right to feel that way. She had had thirteen years to grow, mature, change. *Have a child*.

That was the kicker. She had a child. I wasn't sure why I felt so upended by the news. I really didn't have any information about Tara. Once I'd moved away, I'd stopped keeping tabs on her too closely. I'd tried for a while, but it had hurt too much.

I rarely visited home, and when I did, my family members avoided mentioning her. So she'd existed in this sort of void, a time capsule I'd held of her memory while I'd been away. I'd imagined her to stay frozen like the eighteen-year-old she'd been when I'd left. And that was all sorts of fucked up. I owed her an apology. A big one.

I poked my head out of the door and heard conversation coming from the other end of the floor. My bedroom. I headed downstairs, ignored my grumbling stomach, and poured two glasses of wine.

When the conversation came to a lull upstairs, I gave her another twenty minutes. I did wander into the hallway to take a peep into the coat closet to make sure the pepper spray was still there. When I saw it was, I relaxed some.

I made my way upstairs, a glass of wine in each hand, and rapped on the bedroom door gently with my knuckles.

"What do you want?" she huffed.

"To apologize," I said. "And to offer an olive branch."

"Keep your damn olives."

"Okay, what about grapes?"

"Now's not the time to be cute, Donovan."

"I've got wine," I said. "Wine always helps, doesn't it?"

There was no quick retort from her, which I took as a fantastic sign. A moment later, the door opened. Quick as lightning, Tara's hand darted out and nabbed a glass of wine from my hand. Then she slammed the door in my face.

"Great." I spoke mostly to myself. I took a deep drag from my glass. "Well, I'll be downstairs with real food if you get hungry for something other than squished and heavily fermented grapes."

No response.

As I headed downstairs, I mentally gave her an hour before she broke and joined me for sustenance.

It took three.

I was sitting in the living room, feet up, reading over some paperwork that Carter had sent me later that afternoon. Information on my looming assignment. My last assignment.

I glanced up as Tara reached the bottom of the stairs. She'd showered and changed into a fresh set of my clothes. Shorts and a T-shirt. She'd opted for a bra this time.

"Dinner's in the kitchen," I said. "I reheated some leftovers."

"Do you have more squished grapes?" Tara held up her empty glass.

"Sure do. Can I join you?"

"I'm undecided."

"Great. That's better than expected." I led the way to the kitchen and poured us both a big glass of wine. I handed one to her. "I'm sorry."

"Do you have a game? Checkers or something?"

"What?"

"I don't want to talk to you, but I don't want to be alone."

I made my way down to the basement. Flicking the flashlight around, I unearthed a couple of dusty board games that had been left behind by the previous owners. Checkers was one of them. I made my way back upstairs and laid out the playing board without a word. Tara sat down across from me and made the first move.

We were halfway through the first game when I dared utter a sound. Tara's glass of wine was half empty and her cheeks were getting rosy. I figured she'd either be getting angrier with the wine or more receptive to conversation.

"I leapt to a stupid conclusion. It was unfair. Bullheaded. Stupid," I reiterated. "And I'm sorry."

"I wouldn't have led you on." Tara looked at me, hard. "You should know better than that."

Her flushed cheeks brought out a new element to her beauty. She looked raw. Pissed. Vulnerable. Heated. I liked seeing her react to me. I felt like an idiot to bring out a reaction in such a poor way, but it was something. I could work with something.

I made a move on the checkerboard. Sipped my wine. It was going to my head, too. And I knew if I were to ever establish any semblance of trust with Tara again, it had to start with me.

"I thought I fell in love one other time. Five years ago," I said, offering a piece of myself I didn't share with anyone. "The woman worked for the same company as me. I thought things might be different with her. That we might be able to make something work because she understood me, the lifestyle, the danger."

"Plus, you could talk to her about things, confidential things."

"To some degree, that was a big part of it. It felt like we were on an even playing field in a way, like she could just as easily leave me behind as I could her."

Tara watched me without a reaction. Her hand was poised over her black chip, but she seemed too frozen to set it down.

"We dated for eight months. We'd sleep over at one another's place, but when I asked her to move in, she said she'd have to think about it."

"You loved her?"

I licked my lips. "I thought so. It wasn't the same sort of love that—" I hesitated. "It wasn't the same sort of love I'd had before in my life. It was more of a convenient love. Business partners who sometimes slept together. I thought if nothing else it would grant us both an amiable companionship."

Tara clicked her chip down. My move.

I ran a hand over my chest, over the old wound that still burned with memories. "She gave me this scar. She was working for someone I was in the process of investigating. She'd gone undercover at our company to try and get close to me."

"Oh my God."

"I was about to move in on the big baddies," I said in a gross oversimplification, "but instead of letting me take those guys in, she turned on me. They got away. She got away. She left me to bleed out."

"Shit." Tara blinked. "I thought my break-up was bad. But it doesn't hold a candle to that."

"Like I said, it was my own fault. I shouldn't have trusted her. There were signs. Red flags, but I either didn't want to see them or was so desperate to believe it could work that I ignored them."

"Hey." Tara's voice was soft, tender. "It's not your fault for fighting for love. I mean that, Gavin."

The way she said my name made everything worth it. Everything that had led me to her, to now, *with* her. I swallowed hard.

"I am a little jumpy when it comes to trusting people," I admitted. "So when I heard that voice..."

"My daughter," Tara offered.

"When I heard your daughter on the phone, I went into fight or flight mode. I panicked. I don't know, I guess over the last day we've spent together, I just got it in my head that I was starting to re-learn things about you, and I had this picture of you painted in my head. A daughter wasn't in that portrait, so the news threw me for a loop."

"I get it. I can see how it might be a shock. I'm just a little surprised you didn't know. I guess. I mean, it's not a secret in Fantasie that I'm a single mom."

"My family avoids giving me updates on you. I purposefully didn't ask, and I haven't been home in years. I basically isolated myself. It was the easiest way." I left it at that. The pain of not knowing was easier than the pain of watching her go on to live a happy life. To date again. To have a child with someone who wasn't me.

"I get that."

"I've spent the last thirteen years trying to convince myself that I didn't make a mistake letting you go."

"And?" Tara's lips pursed.

I gave her a wry smile. "And I'm still working on the argument. In the meantime, I had to shut my emotions off, or else I'd have gotten hurt. My line of work didn't leave a lot of room to work out emotions. I had to be focused and logical."

"But you did get hurt," she whispered.

"Right," I rasped. "Because I let myself feel something. It wasn't even fucking real, and I still paid for it in blood."

Tara's eyes widened into saucers. "Gavin, I—"

I cut her off, shaking my head. "I didn't mean to make this conversation about me. I just thought it might help you to understand where I'm coming from and why my hair-trigger reaction came out that way. No excuses, just some background."

"It does help me understand. I couldn't... I would never have imagined."

"Not many people would. It's also the reason I've been acting a little discombobulated since you've been here," I admitted. "I'm not always this much of a disaster, I swear, but it's all new to me. I've been a machine for the last decade and I'm having some trouble switching that off."

"I don't think you're a disaster, Gavin. I've thought a lot of things about you over the years, but never that."

"That's too kind of you, but you'd be dead wrong." I looked her in the eye. "I've been trained to expect anything. To prepare for the worst. To act cool, calm, collected in the highest of stakes. But nobody prepared me to see your face again."

Her lips trembled, and she glanced down at the checkerboard. She thwacked a black chip down on the board with shaky fingers, even though she'd gone three times in a row, and I had yet to make a move.

"Anyway, there was no way you could've known," I said. "I kept my life a secret for a reason."

"A good reason, I guess."

"Debatable." I finally laid my red chip down with a snap. "Tell me about your daughter."

"Her name is Liv. Olive." Tara's face broke into a ray of sunlight. Happiness radiated from her as she spoke about the young girl, and it was a pleasure to watch. "She's six years old."

I nodded, feeling the slightest of notches of disappointment. It was stupid, ridiculous. A part of me had wanted to hear that this surprise daughter was thirteen. That there was a chance, that maybe... I shook the thought away as quickly as it'd happened. Tara would've told me if I was the father. She would've found a way.

"Do you have a photo?" I asked instead.

"Do I have a photo," she scoffed. "Do pigs fly?"

I blinked at her. She blinked back at me.

Tara covered a hand over her mouth and giggled, her cheeks turning a shade of peony pink.

"I'm a little drunk," she admitted, flipping her phone around so I could see a photo of her daughter. "Sorry. The wine went right to my head."

"She's phenomenal. A beautiful young woman." I looked up at Tara, feeling a heaviness in my chest. "Liv looks like you. The eyes, the mouth, the hair..."

"She's got her dad's nose." Tara wrinkled her own nose. Then she looked up at me. "He's not in the picture. Us Kendrick women don't have much luck with men."

A somberness descended, resetting my happiness level to an appropriately contrite amount. "I'm sorry to have contributed to that."

"Hey, we were kids. I think we've hashed things out enough. Maybe we can just... move on?"

I narrowed my eyes at her. "How drunk are you right now?"

"I wouldn't pass a breathalyzer."

"Uh huh."

"But I could probably walk a reasonably straight line."

"Bullshit."

"Are you doubting me, Donovan?" Tara's eyebrows shot up.

There was mischief in her eyes, that same mischief that had been responsible for my getting her naked every chance I got for that one perfect summer. I could feel the reminder in my cock. I slammed my hands against the table playfully and leaned over.

"I'd like to see that," I murmured.

"What're we betting?" Tara stood, slammed her hands against the table in a reply, and met me nose to nose over our forgotten checker game.

"If I win," I said, "you aren't allowed to run away again. You wait out the snowstorm until we can get you reliable transportation home and stop making me chase you across the damn tundra."

Tara's eyes went wide as hula hoops. "Fine. But if you win, you take your damn bedroom back and let me sleep on the couch."

JINGLE BELL ROCK

Tara extended her hand to shake on it. I would've much rather kissed her hard on the lips to seal the deal, but I wasn't risking another slap to the face. Two in one afternoon was not a good tally to have.

Our hands locked together, and I felt as if a spell had been cast over our embraced fingers, holding them tight, making it difficult to part ways. I could tell Tara was staring transfixed at whatever current was passing between us too.

Tara snapped back to attention first and made her way to one end of the living room. The fire roared warmly in the hearth. Blankets were piled on the couch. Tara stuck her tongue out between her lips in the most adorable form of concentration I'd ever seen. Things, in this moment, were just about perfect.

Tara spread her arms wide like she was on a balance beam and started marching in a wobbly arc across the room. When she reached the other side, she glanced back, flashed me a wink, and said, "Take that, Donovan."

My eyebrows shot up. "You're kidding, right?"

"Bet you can't do any better," she challenged. "You're as drunk as I am."

"Not a chance."

"Come and get me, then."

That was one dare I'd never turn down. I made my way right across the room, closing the distance between us in an almost hungry march.

"I win." I stood by her side, glanced down at her.

She wobbled, put her hand out to steady herself on me. I wasn't prepared, and the shock of her fingers brushing against my skin sent bolts of electricity through me. I pulled her close against me, closer than necessary.

"Can I kiss you?" I murmured.

She inhaled a breath, and I expected her to say no. Then she nodded.

I didn't let her finish the nod. I wrapped my hand in her hair, dragged her the rest of the way against me, and kissed the ever-living daylights out of Tara Kendrick.

My lips touched hers, a soft, pillowy sensation that warmed me to the fucking core. I was hard as ice within an instant. With one touch, Tara had released my desire. She was playing with fire, with lava. She could set off my dormant craving with one whisper against my cheek, and I'd turn into a damn animal from all those years of pent-up need for her.

"Jesus, baby," I rasped against her lips. "You don't know how long I've dreamed of this moment."

"I thought you'd forgotten about me. I did nothing but think of you, Gavin. For years. Fucking years, Gavin."

"I'm so sorry. So sorry. If you let me try again, I swear to God I'll never let you go."

Tara's lips parted, trembled, and she shook her head. A tear slipped down her cheek. "I can't."

"Because you actually can't, or because you don't want to try?"

"My life is not just about me anymore. I have a daughter. She *is* my life." Tara gulped, emotions obviously bubbling over. "I am not interested in trying again. In getting back together. I have sworn off men. I have sworn off relationships."

"Then what about tonight?" I asked, wishing I felt embarrassed about how desperate I felt. Now that she was here, in my literal fucking arms, I felt like I was spiraling out of control with the idea that she could slip through my fingers like sand. "Give me tonight. We'll go from there."

"I'm not interested in one night."

"You're still a woman. You still have wants and needs," I said. "Why should you deny yourself those?"

Tara sat. "I understand that. But I am denying them with you."

"Why me?" My voice broke.

"You know why." Tara's gaze leveled on me. "If we go here again, and you decide to leave, it will break me. If I involve my daughter, and she came to love you, and you let her down—" Tara shook her head firmly. "No. Her own father already let her down. Her grandfather is not in the picture. I'm not doing that to her again."

"I could promise—"

"I don't want to hear any promises, Gavin. End of story."

I gave a nod. "You've made up your mind, and I respect that. Regretfully, I will back off. Please note that it is with a massive fucking pile of regret."

Tara's expression when she looked at me was a bit taken aback, almost as if she'd wanted me to fight harder for her. The thing was, I did want her. I wanted to be with her. But I respected her more than all of that, and if she wasn't ready, then I wasn't going to be the one to push her to a place of discomfort.

I released my arms from her. "Another round of checkers?"

She licked her lips. "I think I need more wine. And maybe a sandwich."

Chapter 7

Tara

After popping into the restroom for some privacy, and to take a few much-needed deep breaths to calm myself down, I met Gavin in the kitchen. He made good on his word. He poured us some wine, fetched us some dinner from Ida's leftovers, and played me in a game of checkers.

There was no flirting. No lingering eye contact. The one time we accidentally brushed hands passing the salad, he'd looked away and apologized.

I hated every minute of it.

I thought about apologizing to Gavin for turning him down flat, but I couldn't do it. For selfish reasons, I couldn't have Gavin turning back into the man he'd been over these last few hours. A man who was funny, hot as all get out, and kind.

A man who had clearly tried his best to expose his weaknesses to make me feel more comfortable with mine. A man who was trying to be honest. A good man. I knew in my core that when Gavin Donovan promised he wouldn't leave me this time, he thought he meant it.

But minds could change. Jobs could change. Things could happen. Emergencies, illnesses, deaths. He was still employed by some secret security company with only God knew what sort of assignment coming up. His life didn't spell stability, and unfortunately, that meant he wasn't getting a passing grade when it came to what I needed to complement my life.

JINGLE BELL ROCK

Me—and more importantly Liv—needed stability. We needed people who loved us and were here to stay. People who wouldn't go anywhere no matter what. Illnesses, jobs, whatever. I wasn't ready to entertain the possibility of letting someone back in just yet, especially since Gavin and I had only been reintroduced twenty-four-ish hours before.

But this new coldness in him, the distant respectfulness he'd adopted after I'd asked for space, somehow hurt worse. I hadn't realized how much I'd wanted him to want me. How much I'd ached to recreate a glimmer of the magic we'd experienced during that one enchanting summer together. And the magic had shown up in spades. Fireworks. Bells and whistles.

When Gavin had kissed me, I'd thought my lady parts were going to rebel and orgasm on the spot. I'd felt him, thick and hard, even through our clothes.

So what was a girl to do? Let Gavin keep thinking she wasn't interested, so he kept himself as isolated as an island? Or give in to the urges for an enchanting night or two that would surely end with another round of heartbreak?

My phone ringing interrupted the most electrified game of checkers I'd ever played in my life. Every move felt weighted, as if one of us was testing the other in our resolve. Short bursts of eye contact. Little stabs of food with forks. Bites of conversation that tackled exactly zero difficult subjects.

"I've got to take this," I said, wiggling my phone with relief. Then, as an afterthought, I added, "It's Liv."

Gavin nodded. "Of course. I'll clean up dinner."

I excused myself and scurried upstairs, thrilled with the opportunity for a reprieve from Gavin. Sitting next to him, in the same room as him, felt exhausting. Like we were two magnets destined to be drawn together, having to fight the forcefield with every breath. I was wiped.

"Hi, honey." I answered the video call. "How's Grandma's house?"

"It's good." Liv paused, her sweet face centering in the video. "When are you coming home?"

I licked my lips, both torn into pieces that I didn't have a good answer for her, and also grateful beyond relief that she still cared. It was embarrassing how much it had hurt me that she'd practically not noticed my absence. Not that I'd ever say that to her. I was equally proud of her. Motherhood sure was one clusterfuck of emotions that all hit at once.

"I hope I'll be able to get back tomorrow, but I'm not sure exactly what time," I said. "I'm really sorry I'm not there. Do you think you can be a big helper for Grandma to get Thanksgiving dinner ready tomorrow?"

"I guess." Liv heaved a sigh as if she held the weight of the world on her shoulders at having been asked to stir the gravy.

"Good girl. What've you two been up to?"

Liv regaled me with the adventures she'd been up to with my mother. Forts, books, arts and crafts. Movies, snuggle time, cookies. I was envious of their time together.

"I miss you. I wish I was there," I confessed. "You know if I could be there I would, right? I'd do anything to get to you."

"I know, Mom. But you don't have to worry. I'm taking good care of Grandma."

The seriousness once again in Liv's eyes shattered me. My sweet girl, thinking I was more worried about my mother than I was her.

"I know you are, honey." I felt my eyes tearing. I couldn't cry in front of her. I never cried in front of her. "Call me anytime, okay? I'll let you know the second the roads are cleared, and I can make it back to you."

"Okay, Mom. I miss you. Love you." Liv looked over her shoulder. "Grandma wants to talk to you."

"Tell her I'll call her back in a bit." I spoke over the lump in my throat. "Good night, sweetie."

The second Liv hung up, I lost it. The tears came in droves. Little sobs wracked my chest. I tried to be quiet, and it mostly worked, but a little bit didn't.

It wasn't just the fact that I was missing Liv. I knew many parents went on vacation without their kids, or work trips, or just sent their kids to their grandparents' houses for sleepovers all the time. It was everything else that was too much.

It was the dam Gavin Donovan had burst inside of me. Trinkets of an old relationship I'd tucked away in a time capsule that had unexpectedly resurfaced. My own desires as a woman, which I'd all but buried in a glorious Viking funeral that had suddenly returned. The financial difficulties my business faced at having only one woman to do a three-person job. The stress of simply not getting home.

And yes, the damn wine didn't help. I wasn't a big drinker, and I was feeling about as squashed as the those freaking fermented grapes. I was done. Drained. Exhausted.

A knock sounded on the door. "You okay in there, Tara?"

"Fine." A big, ugly sniffle probably didn't help accentuate my point.

"Can I come in?"

"I'd rather you didn't."

"I have hot chocolate and wine. Your choice."

"Can I choose both?"

"The world is your oyster, Kendrick."

"Give me a minute."

I slipped on a clean shirt and a pair of fuzzy socks. Then I padded to the door and opened it, making no effort to hide my red rimmed eyes. The dampness still lingering on my eyelashes. The sniffles that slipped out like annoying little traitors.

"I'm so fucking sorry." Gavin took one look at me. "If any of this is my fault—"

"It's not," I said quickly. Then I cocked my head. "You can come in if you want." I grabbed the hot chocolate. "You've paid your toll."

As Gavin entered the room behind me, I caught the irony of the moment. I turned, gave him a little smile.

"Thank you for not commenting on how I just invited you into your own room. And also, thank you for loading this up with a mountain of whipped cream."

"Whipped cream and ketchup. Your two favorite condiments."

"Whipped cream's not a condiment," I retorted. "Who the hell offends whipped cream by calling it a condiment?"

"Please accept my deepest sympathies for the error."

I glanced at him, gave an involuntary snort of laughter at the dead seriousness on his face. I inclined my head toward him. "I accept."

He sat at the foot of the bed. I sat at the head.

"Let me see your foot," he instructed.

I'd had all the fight knocked out of me with my little cryfest, so I kicked up my feet and sipped my hot chocolate and let him have his way with my foot. He gently peeled my sock back, checked the new bandage he'd fixed earlier in the evening, and then examined the ace bandages.

Then he pulled up the other foot, slipped the sock off, and began massaging the sole. I groaned like a woman who hadn't been touched in a decade. Then again, it might as well have been a decade. It'd been a long, long time since I'd had any sort of intimacy with a man. And yes, I counted a foot rub as intimacy.

"Everything okay with Liv?" Gavin's eyes were serious.

"Yes, she's fine. Completely fine. Too fine." At his questioning eyes, I continued. "I was getting a little worried she didn't even notice I was gone. Or that she wouldn't miss me. Yes, I am desperate to be wanted by my daughter. I realize how pathetic that sounds."

"I don't think that's pathetic at all. I think it makes you the best mother on the planet. I don't know much about Liv, but I do know she's lucky to have you. Damned lucky."

I licked my lips, comforted by the easy conversation. The sweet hot chocolate. The calming foot rub.

"She's the reason I wanted to be home so badly," I confessed. "I had made a promise to her. And after the way her dad left, I just—I can't stand making promises I don't keep.

I'd never in a million years assumed I wouldn't be able to get home when I said I'd be there."

"You're human. It doesn't make you a bad person nor a bad mother."

"That's what Ida said."

"You discussed this with Ida?"

I gave him a look. "She's a woman. A mom. She understands."

"Fair."

"I'm all Liv has," I said. "I've never missed a holiday with her before. Tomorrow will be Thanksgiving. I need to get back there with her."

"Ah."

"You don't sound like you believe me."

"I do. I'm not a mother, but I can understand where you're coming from, why it's important."

"But?" My curiosity got the better of me.

"But obviously Liv *does* have other people. I'm sure Cathy is the best grandma. I'd hardly call Liv being stuck with your mother a hardship." He raised a hand before I could interrupt. "Not that that makes it any easier for you to be away. But I do think Liv will survive, and I hardly think she'll hold it against you."

"Maybe," I sulked. "But that frustrates me a little bit."

"Why?"

"Because I want her to need me. Her growing up scares me to death. She is my life, my world. I literally panic thinking she's going to go off and do her own thing someday." I swallowed hard. "But on the flip side, I'm practically ramming lessons of independence down her throat. I want her to be able to take care of herself. I don't want her to count on anyone else."

"On a man," Gavin corrected gently. "You want her to count on you, just not on a man."

"Is it so wrong that I want my daughter to develop her own mind, wants, needs desires, et cetera before meeting a man?" I shot back. "I think not. I think it's the best thing she can do for herself."

"Maybe it is." Gavin was obviously treading carefully. His hands worked out a tender spot on my foot I hadn't known was there. "But you can't live her life for her. Maybe she falls for her high school sweetheart and chooses not to go to college."

"Nope," I said. "Not an option."

He bobbed his shoulders. "I'm not getting in between the two of you. I'm just giving you another perspective. Liv will have to decide who to let into her life and who not to let into her life on her own at some point."

"I know. Doesn't mean I'm not gonna sulk about it prematurely."

"She's six."

"Moms are supposed to worry."

He acknowledged my point with a bow of his head. "I'm sorry you're missing the holiday with your daughter. I can't imagine how that feels for you."

Gavin surprised me yet again with the tenderness in his reaction.

"Thanks," I murmured. "But I'm still hoping to be home by tomorrow."

"I don't want to give you false hope. It's not looking good."

I felt my eyes watering. Those pesky tears took a trip down my cheek. "I know."

"Baby." Gavin leaned in, wiped my tears.

The motion wasn't romantic at all. His endearment wasn't anything but heartfelt. I raised a hand, let it rest on his as he touched my face. We held there, close to one another, joined by circumstances and nothing more. Or was there more?

"Is there anything I can do to help?" Gavin asked.

"Get me a helicopter home?"

"No place to land one around here," he said, "or I'd try to call in some favors."

I did a double take. "Do you really have incoming favors of that scale?"

Gavin gave a little shrug. Then I remembered who he worked for and decided not to ask.

"No." I gave a monstrous sigh. "I'm tired. I'm going to go to bed. Just ignore me tomorrow when I'm a moping zombie."

"Aye, aye, Cap." Gavin stood and took a step back from the bed with a little salute.

On second thought, he stepped forward and collected the wine and hot chocolate glasses and moved them to the nightstand. He pulled the covers back, helped me shift my legs underneath, then tucked me in. When he brushed a hand over my hair, I thought that was the end of his bedtime routine, but there was more.

As his lips brushed over my forehead, I finally felt a sense of peace, a little bit of drunkenness, and complete and utter exhaustion as it dragged me under.

Chapter 8

Tara

The next morning, I was true to my word. I was the perfect picture of a mopey zombie.

I made it down to the kitchen and uttered a couple of nonsensical words to Gavin who watched me with an attentive gaze. I continued mumbling something about a long bath and a nap, and he let me go, only trying to push waffles on me once when I declared I didn't have an appetite.

I did take a long bath in the soaking tub, feeling bad about myself as I stared out the window at the frustratingly beautiful scenery. I checked my phone incessantly, but it seemed the snow and trees wouldn't be cleared until late afternoon at the earliest. That didn't help much with my busted-up car situation, which would need to be taken care of before I could drive my mopey ass home.

My mood was made worse by the fact that both my mother and Liv kept dodging my calls as if they were *so* busy. I muttered under my breath a lot of frustrated rantings about how busy they could be making Thanksgiving dinner for two. I texted Liv again to call me when she could. No reply.

I sighed, then remembered I had my computer with me. I set up at the little desk in Gavin's room and turned on my headphones. I zoned out, looking at tax forms that made me even more miserable. Finally, I shut my computer in a heap of despair at the giant tax bills heading my way next year.

I'd dismissed several of Gavin's knocks on the door. But when three o'clock finally rolled around, I gave up pushing him away and answered him when he rapped his knuckles more demandingly on the door.

"I'm coming," I said, hauling my depressed backside off the bed. "Keep your shorts on."

I opened the door and was taken completely by surprise. Gavin stood there dressed in jeans and a button-up shirt. He'd showered and shaved, and his hair was still wet. The man looked like a dream. I wondered if I'd slipped into some sort of comatose state of misery and was conjuring him up with my imagination.

"Why are you wearing a shirt?" I blurted. "You never wear shirts. Especially not nice shirts."

His lips turned up in a smile, but he simply held out a hand in reply. "Can I show you something?"

"Let me check my calendar," I said dryly. "I have so much going on right now."

Another laugh from Gavin, but curiously enough, he wasn't taking the bait on my snarky banter.

Mysteriously, Gavin led the way downstairs. A tingling sensation made its way down my spine. Something was up. I just had no idea what.

Then he gestured toward the kitchen, led me inside, and paused. It took me a long minute to understand what was happening.

"Happy Thanksgiving, Tara," he whispered in my ear.

Then I burst into tears. Big, sappy crocodile tears.

Gavin Donovan, pain in my ass, love of my young life, and all-around conundrum, had set up a Thanksgiving dinner for the two of us. On the table were place settings laid out with painstaking attention to detail. He'd scrounged up some real cloth napkins from somewhere in this godforsaken old house. He'd combined the ingredients he'd pilfered from Ida's diner into a spread that looked festive and hearty.

There was a fresh salad, eggs—because apparently Gavin Donovan couldn't eat a meal without eggs—and sausages. Fresh rolls, real butter, a pie on one end for dessert. A bottle of deep red wine already uncorked. It was a real, bona fide Thanksgiving dinner.

But the part that'd caused the cascade of tears was not the food, or the adorably detailed setup, or the fact that Gavin had taken the time to prepare all of this just for me. It was the two little faces staring back at me from the computer screen propped on the table.

"Liv?" I took a step closer. "Mom? Where have you been all day? You've been ditching my calls."

I slid into a chair across from the computer and noted that Liv and my mother were sitting in my mother's kitchen. Snippets of the feast they'd prepared on their end were visible through the video feed. Rolls, turkey, cranberries. Mashed potatoes and green beans. Their feast was admittedly a bit more traditional, but it didn't make mine any less special.

"We were busy," my mother said, not making eye contact with me. It was suspicious at best. "Anyway, Happy Thanksgiving, honey. We thought it might be nice to share a meal together since you weren't able to be here in person."

I looked up at Gavin, and my words vanished. Just evaporated like little drips of water on hot asphalt, leaving me speechless. Gavin flicked a quick smile in my direction, then sat down as if there was nothing more to say.

JINGLE BELL ROCK

"Bon appétit, huh?" he said. "Dig in, princess. Apologies for the half-assed—" Gavin looked up at the computer screen. Guilt crept into his face when Liv giggled at the word ass. "Sorry." He looked to me, his eyes wide, as if he'd already royally screwed up.

"This is an incredible meal." I looked down. "Thank you, Gavin."

Gavin glanced away. "It's not much. I just used what we had."

"Liv, have you met my..." I hesitated, felt my mother's piercing gaze on me. "Have you met my old friend Gavin?"

"Hi, Gavin." Liv flashed her cute smile at him, then turned to me. "Isn't this so fun, Mom? I thought we wouldn't be able to have Thanksgiving together, but this is basically together."

"Except you can't steal my bread roll." I winked at the screen. "So technically, my food is a little safer from a distance, yeah?"

Liv got a kick out of that. "But I could steal Grandma's roll."

My mother pushed her plate toward Liv. "Be my guest. This grandma has eaten more sweets in the last two days than in the last two years of my life. You'd better come back soon, Tara, or you won't recognize me when we come out of hibernation because of all the weight I've packed on."

"Dig in," I encouraged Gavin, as conversation broke into an almost-normal mishmash of Liv interjecting her thoughts on everything between mouthfuls of food. I mouthed to Gavin over the sound of my daughter's chatter, "Thank you."

Gavin barely acknowledged it, but the flicker of satisfaction in his eyes was enough to tell me he knew. He understood. And that was enough for both of us.

"What have you guys been up to?" My mother asked innocently enough, but I could read hidden meaning behind her snoopy question. "Anything fun?"

"Your daughter has taken up snowshoeing," Gavin said, buttering his roll and not looking at my mother. "Tara made quite a dent in the snowstorm yesterday."

I elbowed Gavin. My mother cracked up, using a dainty finger to try and stifle her laugh.

"Mom! You went without me?" Liv demanded. "I told you I wanted you to take me sledding this year, and we haven't been yet."

"I didn't go sledding. Snowshoeing," I said. "And I haven't taken you yet because there hasn't been any snow."

"Do you like sledding?" Liv asked Gavin.

"I do," Gavin said around a mouthful of bread. "I've got a good hill up here at the house. Found a couple of old toboggans in the basement."

"Maybe we can come sledding on your hill sometime," Liv said easily. "We don't have any hills at our house. It's flat as a pancake. We usually go up to my school, but it's always packed, and the big kids build jumps that are too big for me to go off. Charlie Knutson broke his tailbone on one that iced over last year."

"That sucks," Gavin said.

Liv looked up like she'd been shot.

I tried to suppress a grin. "We don't say that word around here."

JINGLE BELL ROCK

"I'm sorry," Gavin said, chagrined. "That *stinks*."

"Sure does," Liv continued. "So maybe you can invite us up to your hill."

"You guys are welcome anytime," Gavin said. "Plus, there's a little pond right down by the river that freezes over, and the last owners told me they used to turn it into a hockey rink. Do you like ice skating, Liv?"

"I've never been!" Her eyes widened like donuts. "But I think I would really love it. Do you have ice skates?"

"Sure do."

"For me, too?"

"Of course," Gavin said. "Just let me know your shoe size, and I'll have them ready. Give the water another couple of weeks to freeze, and the invite's open."

"And Grandma would come too," Liv said.

"Of course Grandma is welcome too. Maybe by that time I'll have the rooms ready for guests," Gavin said with a sideways glance at me. "Y'all can give this place a dry run before Aunt Lily lists it for real."

"Well, what a lovely invitation," my mother said. "That sounds like a fabulous New Year's getaway. Consider us booked. It's the least we can do after all you've done to host Tara so far. In case I haven't thanked you for letting her stay, let me say this: Thank you from the bottom of my heart for keeping my little girl safe."

"Okay, Mom," I groaned. "A little overdramatic much?"

"I'm just saying," she said, "you would've tried to make it home if I hadn't booked you a place with Gavin. Whose inn technically wasn't even open. I think it's perfectly reasonable to thank him for ensuring you didn't end up in a ditch somewhere."

I groaned again. Gavin smiled.

"It's been no trouble, ma'am," he said.

I wrinkled my nose, made a face at him. "Ma'am?" I mouthed. When my mother got up to refill Liv's sparkling grape juice, I whispered to him, "Suck up."

Gavin grinned around a bite of sausage. Then the conversation devolved into a production of Liv reciting her lines for her Christmas school play. It was three weeks away, and she had the role of Singing Angel 3 with exactly *one* line. She rehearsed like she was a Broadway star.

It was over an hour later when we finally bid goodbye to our virtual party. Each side had made dents in their respective pies. Second helpings had been had. Coffees and teas had been steeped and sipped. We were all full, warm, happy... lucky. I wasn't sure how I'd managed to go from a mopey zombie to a happy sunflower, but I suspected it had to do with the man who was currently doing the dishes at the sink while I packaged up the leftovers.

"This was a really, really good day, Gavin. And it could've been a really, really crappy one. Thank you."

A muscle in Gavin's jaw ticked, but he didn't look back. "I'm glad."

"I'm sorry if I said something to make you think I'm upset with you." I took a step closer to him. "I promise I'm not. I know after last night things between us got complicated."

"You don't have to explain." Gavin turned, flashed me a cardboard smile. "It's forgotten. I won't make any more moves; you have my word. As an added bonus, I just finally got a text from Gary—he's back in cell range after being up north with his family. The fallen trees are being cleared now. He'll run the plows through after. You'll be good to go tomorrow morning if your car starts. Even if it doesn't, I can give you a ride."

As Gavin moved around his kitchen with remarkable ease, I felt a sudden emptiness inside me, as if someone had pulled the drain on the tub and the water was swirling away, and I was scrambling to stop it.

As soon as the roads were clear, I was free to get a ride home and get my car fixed. I was free to leave Gavin. I was free to never speak to him again. Hadn't I spent most of my time here trying to escape his presence? So why did I feel practically bereft at the thought of walking out that front door tomorrow morning?

"Before you go, I have one more surprise for you." Gavin interrupted the moping thoughts with another promise. "Are you ready for it?"

"I have no clue."

He raised his hands. "It's innocent, I promise. Now that you know you'll get to return to Liv tomorrow, I thought you might want to half-pretend you're on vacation and relax."

"That sounds intriguing," I had to admit. "Seeing Liv so happy helped a lot. It was so kind, so thoughtful of you to set that up."

"It was nothing. A team effort."

"My mom said you called her last night," I confessed. "Yes, I forced her to tell me what happened, even though you swore her to secrecy."

"Oh, Cathy." Gavin sighed. "She's never been able to keep a secret."

I laughed, a memory from years back tumbling into the forefront. Gavin had tried to plan a surprise date for me the summer we'd been together. He'd gotten flowers, made a reservation, bought me a special necklace. It had been for our one-month anniversary.

My mother had spilled the beans to me an hour before the date, completely spoiling the surprise, and yet Gavin had taken it in stride. I knew my mom had liked Gavin, and better yet, she'd liked him for me. I knew she'd mourned with me when I'd lost him.

"C'mon." Gavin waved for me to follow him, gently tugging me back to the present.

"Let me help with cleanup," I insisted.

He raised a finger and playfully shushed me with a wink, his finger coming to rest against my lips. "I have a feeling you cook and clean plenty at home. Let me handle it tonight. It's almost done."

I wanted to argue, but the touch of his finger to my lips was intoxicating. I felt like my eyes crossed as I tried to look at my own lips. Gavin noticed, pulled his finger away.

"Sorry," he said quickly.

"No, it's fine. Look, Gavin..." I wanted to tell him that it was *all* fine. That he should stop walking on eggshells around me. That he could just be himself, and wherever things led, we'd figure it out later.

He watched me, waiting. Still, the words didn't come. I didn't know how to tell him, how to give him the green light that I was okay with his touch.

Gavin spared me any more embarrassment and snapped out of it first. He cocked his head toward the porch and told me to follow him. I obeyed like a robot.

"Here we are." Gavin pushed open the back door and led me out into an offset screened in gazebo. The air was chilly, and I shivered as I poked my head out from behind him to discover the surprise.

"Gavin," I said. "What is this?"

"Its maiden voyage." Gavin gestured to a hot tub that looked brand spanking new. A couple of fluffy towels were hung up on one side. A huge bucket filled with snow held a bottle of chilled prosecco.

It looked like something out of a fancy, expensive spa. I practically salivated at the thought of slipping into the steaming water, letting my shoulders relax, closing my eyes as the wind brushed around us.

"I thought you might fancy a dip," Gavin suggested. "I had it installed a week ago but haven't had the chance to test it out yet. Thought it might be nice for you to sit out here and, I dunno, relax. Read a book. Watch something. Listen to music. Do nothing. Your choice. I wanted to get you a bowl of strawberries, but Ida didn't have any, so you've got pre-packaged powdered doughnuts as an appetizer."

My lips felt cracked and dry as they parted. Nobody had ever thought ahead to do something like this for me before. To prepare something that was exclusively for my enjoyment without expecting something in return.

On top of what he'd done for me and my daughter with the Thanksgiving meal, I felt almost burdened by his generosity. It felt like a weight, crushing me in the best possible way. Suffocating me with so much goodness that I couldn't even remember why I'd hated him just two days ago.

"It's nothing," Gavin said, peering at my face, obviously trying to dissect what was happening there. "If you're not a hot tub person, that's fine. I just thought... I mean, it's clean. The chemical levels are good. If you wanted to—"

"It's incredible," I whispered. "Thank you."

"Good. Well." Gavin waited a long beat. "I'm glad to hear it. So I guess I'm going to head in then. I know you didn't think ahead to bring your suit, so I'll give you your privacy."

"Aren't you coming in?"

His eyes flashed dark, going from gray to almost midnight. "No."

"But—"

"It's for you. I'll leave you to it."

I reached out a hand to stop him, forcing him to still and hear me out. "I'd feel bad if you're in there cleaning up while I'm out here soaking and looking up at the stars."

"I don't think it's a good idea."

"Look, if you're worried about seeing me naked, don't be. I can wear my bra and underwear. It's no different than a swimsuit. You have a laundry machine."

"Right. It's, uh, not that."

"Are you that opposed to being in the same room as me?"

"That's what you think this is?" Gavin looked down at me, the height difference between us seeming exaggerated by the intensity of his stare. "That I don't want to be near you?"

JINGLE BELL ROCK   125

"I don't know exactly what this is," I admitted, "but ever since the kiss yesterday, you've been completely distant."

"I have to be distant." Gavin's voice was a thundercloud rippling across a summer sky. "Or else..." He stopped, shook his head.

I reached my hand from his wrist, brought it to his chest, rested it there gently. "Or else what?"

"I can't trust myself to let my guard down for one damn second around you," he rumbled. "If I let myself feel for even a moment, everything comes crashing back, and I don't think logically. The only thing I want to do is touch you. Hold you. Kiss you. Make you mine."

"Gavin."

"I know," he murmured. "You're not interested. So I'm sorry, Tara, but you can't have it both ways. I've got no interest in being 'just friends' with you because it's too goddamn hard."

"Gavin, listen—"

"I never stopped loving you, babe. I thought I'd convinced myself that this would never work. That you would've moved on. That you *should* have moved on. But then I saw you, and I haven't been able to sleep a damn wink with you under the same roof as me. So, no. I will not be coming in that hot tub with you because I won't be able to keep my hands off you if I do."

"Maybe there's a different way," I mumbled. "Maybe there's a happy medium."

"There's not."

"What if—"

Gavin leaned in, brushed a kiss against my forehead. "I'm going to respectfully step away from this situation, Tara. If you care about me at all, just let me go. I'm going to go inside, clean up. Please, take this time for yourself. I'll check in with you in a little bit in case you need anything."

Leaving zero time for debate, Gavin turned and walked across the back porch and into the house. The door closed behind him, leaving me outside in the darkness, the warm water bubbling behind me, steam rising where hot air met frigid winter.

I wasn't sure how long I stood there, but it was long enough that my limbs were starting to get chilled from standing outside and my feet were startling to tingle. I had to either get my cold behind in the hot tub or march back into the house.

Gavin had gone through a lot of effort to set this up for me. The least I could do was make sure it didn't go to waste. That would be ungrateful. So I peeled off my shirt. I peeled off my bra. I peeled off my pants and everything else and dipped a toe in the water.

I exhaled a hiss as I slid in. The water felt hot, too hot at first, but it was a delicious mix with the cool air from my shoulders on up. I was still feeling the tiniest bit fuzzy-headed from the wine after Thanksgiving dinner, and the hot tub only exacerbated it.

As I warmed in the tub, watching the dusty snow tumble around the gazebo, I reached for the prosecco, my throat feeling dry. When the cool bubbles met my tongue, I moaned with satisfaction. Then, because I was a child at heart and couldn't resist, I popped a powdered doughnut in-

JINGLE BELL ROCK

to my mouth and savored the mostly-dry, fake sugary taste. I was pretty sure the sweets came from a gas station, and for some odd reason, it hit the spot.

I couldn't have been in the hot tub for more than a couple of minutes when the door opened again. I'd downed one glass of prosecco and the bubbles had fortified my confidence. As Gavin strode across the porch to me, a bottle of water in hand, I knew what I had to do.

Chapter 9

Gavin

I muttered a string of words under my breath as I crossed the porch back to the gazebo. I'd spent the last ten minutes preparing myself for this moment. I was repeating the laundry list of items I needed to do to get the inn ready to go before launch day in my head to keep myself distracted from the sight of Tara in a hot tub.

"Sand the nursery walls. Buy the paint. Another round of stain on the stairs," I mumbled incoherently. "Review the budget with Aunt Lily, ask about upgrading the kitchen cabinets."

I deliberately didn't look up as I reached the gazebo. Like an idiot, I'd forgotten to leave water in the ice bucket with the prosecco. In also relevant news, I knew if I looked up or hesitated for even one second, I'd be in trouble. So I focused on repeating inane chores to myself and keeping my eyes focused on the newly sanded floorboards of the gazebo.

"Gavin."

Her voice woke me from what probably sounded like the ramblings of a nutjob. My head jerked up involuntarily, and I caught sight of Tara. I inhaled a breath like a drowning man, sucking in air in order to survive the moment.

Tara Kendrick looked all sorts of incredible. Her hair was wet, a smooth frame around her face. The face I'd dreamed of for years. A cute little nose, those freckles I never paid enough attention to, the smooth milky skin of her shoulders. Paler now, probably since it was winter.

Before, her body had been tanned with summer sun, a result of the hours we'd spent outdoors together, lounging on the beach, me running my hand over her back, up her legs, around the perfect curve of her ass. Trying to be a gentleman, failing as she'd roll over to face me, giggling as my hands got overeager, wrapping me up in a welcoming embrace. I was a damn fool for leaving, but I'd made my choice. And here we were.

"Tara." I responded like a doorknob because I couldn't think of anything else to say. All I could repeat was the name I'd longed to forget.

Her hair was darker thanks to the water and the dim lighting. Her eyes were black diamonds, glittering in the dark. Magnetic, pulling me to her.

"Come in." Tara breathed the words as much as she said them. "Please."

"But—"

"We don't have to be 'just friends'. We also don't have to be in a relationship." Tara raised one shoulder out of the water in a shrug, and the effect was mesmerizing. Water droplets slipped down her shoulder like a work of art. "Maybe all we need is one night. A memory of the past."

My voice felt gruff. "I don't think I'm going to be able to just move on if we do this."

"And I can't promise you a future. So where does that leave us?"

I shook my head. "I'm just going to..."

My words fucking vanished as Tara Kendrick rose from the water like some sort of ethereal mermaid. She stood, her hands wrapped around her stomach in a show of vulnerability. But slowly, she let them fall to her sides, letting the rest of her naked body come into soft fairy lighting.

My eyes stayed on her face for a long moment. I was going to need fucking dental work for all the grinding my teeth were doing trying not to let my gaze slip, but eventually, I gave up.

My gaze ran the length of her body, slowly, deliberately, with a delicious relish as I studied her like I might a painting. A painting that might go up in flames tomorrow with no replicas. A painting I needed to inhale, memorize, consume like my last meal because once it was gone, it was gone for good.

"Jesus, Tara." The breath whooshed out of me. "You sure as hell know how to test a man."

"So give in."

My eyes moved lower, down the curve of her shoulders, following the map of freckles sprinkled there. Lower, to the mesmerizing curve of her breasts. Small, lovely, a perfect handful. Lower, over her stomach to the sweet belly button. To the little scar that told me she'd had a c-section.

Lower, lower, to the place where her legs came together, to the center I longed to touch.

My cock was straining at my jeans. I made no effort to hide my desire. It would've been a worthless cause, anyway, seeing as Tara's eyes had already landed there. She licked her lips. My dick twitched.

"You are playing with fire," I warned her.

"I can see that." A shy smile slid across her face, then a hint of that shyness crept into her expression. "I know I don't look like I did the last time you saw me naked. I've had a baby, and I'm older. I don't have time to work out as much, so maybe—"

"Stop right there." I cursed again, struggling to come up with the words. "You're more gorgeous than the last time I saw you. More perfect. I want to touch you, Tara, on every goddamn inch of your body. Do you see what you're doing to me?"

I swallowed hard as she looked down at my zipper. She gave a tentative nod, her teeth biting into her lip.

"I want to be inside you." My voice slithered across the distance between us. "But I don't understand what's changed, and I need to know—"

"Why don't you get in here with me, and we'll see where things go."

"I don't know."

"What are you afraid of?" Her eyes sparkled with a pinch of challenge, and a whopping dollop of dismay. "Gavin, I'm standing here naked in front of you. I don't know how much clearer my intentions can get."

I was already ripping my shirt off, sending a few of the buttons flying. My zipper was down, my pants at my ankles by the time I reached the hot tub. As I slid off my boxers, there was an audible hiccup from Tara as my erection sprang to attention.

"Wow," she murmured when I looked up. "I always thought my memory was playing tricks on me. I mean, it's a very nice penis you have, and I guess—"

I stopped her with a kiss that had my cock jumping like it was possessed. Reluctant to take my lips from hers, I climbed over the hot tub and finally, blissfully, wrapped my arms around her body. I'd longed to hold this woman for years.

I'd longed to slide every inch of my cock inside her and fill her with my hot seed. I'd longed to make her mine. To get her pregnant with my baby. To live a quiet life together in a little house with a big dog. But white picket fences had never been my thing, and that image had gone up in smoke.

"You feel as good as I remember in my arms," I breathed into her ear. "But Tara, I don't understand. What changed?"

"You? Me?" Tara floated down so she was sitting on my lap.

Water cascaded down her face. She looked like a vision from a movie with the steam surrounding her like we were in a damn dream.

"What you did for me, for my daughter and my mom. The way you went out of your way to make me comfortable, to ensure I was happy on a hard day. Well, nobody's ever done that for me before." Tara swallowed hard. Her lips were swollen, pink. "Last night you were talking about how we're both adults and have needs. You're right. I want to have sex with you. You want to have sex with me. There's really nothing stopping us. We don't have to get married."

"No, we don't," I said tentatively. "But what about a relationship?"

Tara shook her head viciously. "No. I'm not ready for that either. This is just sex."

"This isn't just fucking sex," I growled. I pressed her down against my lap so she could feel my length against her slit. "I want you to be mine."

"I can't, Gavin. Take my offer or leave it."

JINGLE BELL ROCK 133

I considered. Then Tara didn't just make up my mind for me—she exploded the whole damn thing. She slung her arms around my neck, leaned in close, whispered in my ear a few of the things she wanted me to do to her.

I groaned, feeling like I wasn't going to last past the foreplay at this rate. The way that sweet pussy was teasing my cock made me feel like I was a volcano teetering on the edge of an eruption.

Tara ground her hips against me. Teasing, testing. Her mouth found my ear, bit gently. Then she trailed a string of kisses down my neck. I threw my head back, savoring the moment like it was my last on earth.

"I want to feel like a woman," Tara pleaded.

I opened my eyes, looked into her gaze, startled to find there were tears there.

"Tonight, I don't want to be a mom. I don't want to be a struggling business owner. I don't want to think about the fact that my mom goes back to the doctor next week to make sure her cancer is still in remission." Tara gulped, sounding almost frenzied, on the verge of need. "I just want to be wanted tonight, Gavin. Free. I want to feel good, I want to—"

I put my mouth to her cheek. "I need to be inside you. Let me get—"

"I'm on the pill. I'm clean. I haven't had sex in six years."

She said about the only thing that could've taken me out of the moment while my cock was literally poised at her vagina. "Six years?"

"Since Liv's dad," she confessed. Then, annoyed, "I've been a little busy. You've got a naked woman on your lap, and that's what you fixate on?"

"I'm clean too. It's been a while. Not six years, but..."

Tara hiccupped and gave a little chuckle. Tears mixed in her eyes as steam wrapped a halo around her head. "Please, Gavin."

I really, desperately wanted to take my time with Tara. I wasn't sure that was physically possible. I could see in her eyes how much she wanted to be Tara Kendrick tonight. Not mom, not daughter, not CEO.

As it just so happened, Tara Kendrick was just about the only thing I'd wanted in my entire life.

I lowered my mouth to her breast, taking the pert nipple into my mouth, suckling. As Tara arched against me, pressing her stomach against my torso, I took advantage of her raised hips to bring my fingers to her core. I started slowly, slipping one finger inside. Damn she was tight, needy.

"More," she whimpered against me. "More."

I inserted another finger and pulsed my hand against her slick folds. When I added a swirl of my tongue on her breast, tugging at the tender bud, she let out a soft cry. I pulsed my hand a few more times, then retreated.

"I'm sorry, I'm sorry," Tara murmured against me, her eyes woozy with lust, the expressions flickering through her eyes chaotic and needy. "I'm not going to be able to last long. I need you inside me."

"I want to come inside you," I told her. "I want to drive you mad, then fill you with my come."

JINGLE BELL ROCK

"Yes, God." She rose her hips, perched over me, begging, demanding. "Please, Gavin."

I slid into her, taking my time, feeling her slit part for me. Her inner walls quivered as I slid in another few inches, filling her with my swollen, thick shaft. Her fingernails dug into my skin, and with each inch I eased into her, she quieted her whimpers with little nips against my shoulder.

"You're so big, Gavin, I'm not sure this is gonna work." Tara's eyes widened. "But you feel so good, I don't know—"

She cut herself off with a wild cry as I slid the rest of the way home. I'd meant to go slowly, to gently guide myself home, but she'd arched against me, twitched her hips, and I'd lost control and pressed her onto me.

"Fuck. Tara, are you hurt?"

She could only shake her head at me. Then she moved her ass over my lap. She ground against me, testing, obviously reveling at the feeling of fullness. She gave the slightest of winces, and I gripped her shoulders.

"Am I hurting you, baby?"

She gripped my shoulders back, looked into my eyes. "Make me feel good, Gavin."

Her wish was my command. And her demand unlocked every last string that had been holding me back. I thrust into her, hard, watching her eyes widen in revelation. I gripped her hips hard, raised over my lap, slammed her down.

Tara inhaled sharply. "Don't you dare stop."

I raised her again, then speared her with my throbbing cock. At this rate, I was going to last about three strokes. I stilled, wrapping my hand around her hair. I gripped tight, yanked her head back while I left a treasure trail of kisses down her exposed neck. When I reached her breasts, I sucked hard.

I kept my hand gripped in her hair, keeping her head back, letting those gorgeous tits bounce as I thrust into her.

Finally, she fought off my hands in her hair and threw herself against me, taking over the momentum. She bucked her hips of her own accord, riding me until my mind ceased to function. I let her have her way until I felt the starting quivers of her orgasm, and then I took the reins again.

I rose, relishing the sudden intake of breath as the cold air wrapped around us. I let her legs curl around my back while she clung to me, desperate, needy, and I pulsed into her. Once, twice, another time until I could feel her sobbing onto my damn shoulder.

The second she ascended into her climax, I pressed myself into her, deeper, impossibly deeper, as my balls tightened and I released everything into her. I held her there, my hands wrapped in her hair, my cock firmly inside her, as she milked me dry.

When she finally came down from her high, I eased us both back into the hot tub. I felt drained. My legs were admittedly a little shaky. And when I looked over at Tara's rosy cheeks, her sex-mussed hair, her passion-drunk eyes, I knew this couldn't end with one night.

Chapter 10

Tara

I laid in bed, staring at the door to the bathroom like it was about to burst into flames. My body felt limp, happy, mushy. I remembered that sex with Gavin back in the day had been good. I hadn't remembered it being *that* good. Then again, he'd been my first. I hadn't known what sex was all about then, just that I'd wanted to find out with him.

The man had obviously matured. He'd filled out, gotten bigger, stronger, wiser. And then there was the whole penis situation. Which was a great situation indeed. He used that thing like a magic wand, as far as I was concerned.

Those were the completely random thoughts running through my brain as I lounged in my post-sex haze on Gavin's bed. He'd let me in to shower first after we'd exited the hot tub.

Now it was his turn while I lounged in yet another one of his T-shirts on the bed. I was teetering on the precipice of stealing one of these shirts in a permanent way because I'd gotten so used to sleeping in them over the last couple nights.

When Gavin came out of the bathroom, I told him my thoughts on holding some of his clothing hostage. Gavin grinned, wearing nothing but black briefs that showed off his muscles. A lot of muscles. Muscles of his calves, his thighs, his abs. His arms. When he stretched a hand and slid it through his messy wet hair, his body seemed to ripple with the effect of it. Apparently a career in security work did a body good.

"You can have all my shirts."

"So are you this fit because your job requires it?" I asked looking pointedly at his body. "It's somewhat intimidating."

"I think it's more because I've spent the last thirteen years working out in the gym to release a lot of sexual frustration." Gavin had the gall to wink. "Tonight, I can finally say it's all been worth it. How are you feeling?"

"Fantastic."

"Good."

We stayed there in a standstill. I wasn't ready to do a sleepover. He didn't seem ready to leave.

He compromised by perching on the edge of the bed and pulling my foot into his lap. Then he stilled. "Your cut. You shouldn't have gone in the hot tub."

"The wound's pretty much closed up." I shrugged. "It wasn't deep at all."

He wasn't convinced.

"Seriously," I promised. "Even if it gets infected and I die tomorrow, I'll die a happy woman."

That brought a smile out. "I'm glad to hear it. So..."

"So you never told me why we had to rush out of the diner the other day," I said, quickly latching onto a subject that'd keep us far away from discussing our personal lives and where they were headed now that things had gotten exponentially more complicated.

"Right." Gavin expelled a breath. "I do owe you an explanation."

"Okay?"

"Carter Donovan called me to touch base on my upcoming assignment."

"Your last one?"

He nodded. "Turns out, it might be more urgent than people expected."

"There's more." I watched Gavin carefully. "What are you not telling me?"

He met my gaze, as if to prove that he was telling the truth. "Carter thinks it might be partly personal."

"Are you suggesting this might have something to do with your ex?"

"I don't know," Gavin said on a sigh. "But it's nothing for you to worry about."

"I see."

"There's only one issue," Gavin said. "I'm going to be wrapping up my portion of the renovations on the inn in a couple weeks before we bring in the rest of the contractors to finish the job. When that happens, I've got to figure out a good reason to *stay* in town. Assuming the case goes on that long, I'm going to need a cover."

"In town. Fantasie?"

He inclined his head. I took that to be a yes.

"What do you mean?"

"I mean, I haven't been home in thirteen years. Why now?" Gavin shrugged. "Not exactly flying under the radar. I need a good cover. And unless you want to pretend to be my girlfriend to give me a reason to stay..."

"Gavin."

"I know." He rubbed a hand over his face. "Stupid idea."

"I'm sorry," I said. "But I don't think I can commit to that. Don't get me wrong, I had a great time last night. I've even enjoyed being around you. But when I leave here, I think it's best if we go our separate ways."

Gavin's eyes darkened. "I understand, Tara, I really do. But I'm hoping that means I can at least do this."

"Do what?" I squeaked.

In reply, Gavin sank one hand into the back of my hair, his fingernails cinching tight, as he gently yanked my head toward him. His other hand came up to my chin, and he held me tight as he planted a sucker punch of a kiss on my lips.

It hit me right in the gut in the best way. All the feels wrapped up in one. I understood it to be some sort of goodbye, a thank you, a wish upon a star for more.

The tightness of his hand in my hair gave my scalp a delicious prickle. As he climbed on the bed, settling himself over my lap, navigating my face so it tilted upward to face him, he paused for a breath.

"If the memory of tonight has to last me for twenty more years, I'm going to make it worth it." Gavin lowered his face to mine, nipped my lower lip, then slid his tongue into my mouth and made my brain go all sorts of numb.

"Maybe just once more," I gasped. "Like, really, really quick."

Gavin paused, stared blankly at me. "*Quick* is what you think of me?"

My heart was pounding, and my pupils felt like they were running circles around my eyes. "Um, no. I just meant, you're sitting on my lap already, and I can already feel that

JINGLE BELL ROCK 141

you're ready, so, we might as well. Been there done that, you know. No harm in once more."

"Fuck."

I raised my hand, fisted that glorious shaft through his briefs. If he'd existed in ancient times, the Romans would've made a statue of him. A big, big statue.

"Are you sure—"

"Yes." I cut him off by yanking off his underwear. I stared shyly at him, then muttered, "I mean, I suppose it doesn't have to be that quick. We're already doing it, so..."

Gavin pushed me back against the bed. "Are you asking me to take my time with you?"

"I—"

I wasn't sure what I was asking because at that moment, my mind glitched as Gavin yanked my shirt up and dipped his mouth to my nipple. One swirl of his tongue around the tender bud, and I could feel the heaviness between my thighs, the pressure building. I felt like a bottle rocket whose fuse had been lit, and I wasn't sure my fuse was all that long.

Wriggling down, I tried to slip out of my shirt, but Gavin stilled me by pinning my arms to the bed. I was captive as he perched against me, teasing my entrance with his Romanesque dick. I'd always meant to visit Italy, see the sights. I wasn't sure I had to at this rate.

"Leave it on," he growled. "I've been wanting to fuck you in my shirt since the day you slipped it over your head."

"No kiddin'," I said breathlessly as he slipped a finger into me. "God, Gavin."

"You're fucking wet already, baby."

I nodded, even though there was no question.

"I'm not sure I can ever wash this shirt again," he murmured into my neck. "It's going to smell like you, and I'm gonna need it when you're gone."

"One problem." I hiccupped as he slid in a second finger. My back arched. My bottle rocket fuse was blowing its load really, really quickly. "I'm stealing this shirt, remember?"

Gavin barked a short laugh, but the look in his eye was devilish. "Not this one, baby. Pick any other one. The smell of your sweetness on my shirt..." He inhaled a sharp breath. "Might be dangerous. I'd be walking around with a hard-on all day."

"Okay, maybe less talk, more sex." My hips wanted to buck at the way his fingers were stroking my inner walls, and I couldn't come without him.

Another laugh from him as he curled against me. His arm slid behind my back, and he lifted me, tilting my hips up so he had better access. He teased me with his glistening dome, pulsing in, briefly, then back out. "This what you want, baby?"

"God, yes."

"Say my name."

"I need you, Gavin. Now."

"Open your eyes." He gritted his teeth and commanded, "Look at me, say it again."

"Gavin, please."

Bolts of lightning arced through his eyes as he slammed into me. There was no finesse, no teasing, no gentle easing himself home. He speared me straight to my core as if trying to split me in two, and then pounded, once, twice, until my arms flew from his back and gripped onto the headboard, hanging on for dear life as he bore down on me like the world was going to end.

I wasn't aware of the sound coming out of my mouth, just that my thoughts were wiped clean, my mind a black cloud of glitter as I fell off the ledge and into an abyss of pleasure. I kept my eyes fixed open, locked on Gavin's face as he released a stream of hot seed into me.

He collapsed on top of me, and I realized how long it had been since I'd felt the weight of a man on me. It was nice, comforting really, and just a little bit sweaty. But sweaty in a really, really nice way, if that was possible.

I let my fingers find his back, trail down his skin in tender strokes as if giving their own little apology for the way they'd scratched at his back like a feral cat a few moments before. I hit a tender spot, and he shivered against me, coming back to life, rolling off to one side.

Gavin faced me. I faced him. I could feel my heart racing. I put my hand to his chest, and his heartbeat was equally as erratic. We looked into each other's eyes as if it was the most natural thing, laying here in a post-coital haze prepared to pillow talk about whatever the hell people pillow talked about. It'd been so long since I'd done it, I had no clue what came next.

"You're sure?" he whispered.

I knew what he was asking. Was I sure that I wanted to push him away? Was I sure that this was it, the last time? Was I sure that I was ready to give all of this up?

No, I wasn't sure. I was far from sure. My delicate little teenager heart was still madly in love with Gavin Donovan. I'd been in love with him for the last thirteen years, and even an engagement to a different man, along with a child, hadn't changed that. Which was why I couldn't let him into my life, not now, not yet.

With Gavin, my heart was raw, bruised. His leaving wasn't something I could forget so easily. Maybe if it was just me. Maybe then I could convince myself to put up some walls, have some sex, and see where things went. But with Liv to think about, things weren't so simple. She was my world now.

My lips were dry. "I'm sure."

He nodded. Kissed me on the head. I was pretty sure he murmured something that sounded like "I love you" as he slid from bed, tucked me in, and dragged his thumb down my cheek. But I wasn't sure, just like I wasn't sure exactly when he left the room, because I'd turned my face into my pillow so he couldn't see my tears.

Chapter 11

Gavin

"Good morning."

The two simple words from the love of my life just about sent me into cardiac arrest. I turned from where I was cooking—what else?—more damn eggs. There she was, Tara Kendrick, standing in my kitchen and looking like a summer dream.

She'd changed back into her original clothes, minus the high heels, but her attire had a different feel to it today. She looked more relaxed in her jeans and fancy blouse. She looked like the picture of home.

My heart felt like it'd taken a hard upper-cut of a punch when I realized that I wanted her to belong here. I didn't want her to be appearing in my kitchen, wondering if she was free to leave yet. I wanted her to be standing there because she damn well wanted to be near me.

Instead, I licked my lips and pointed with the spatula at the stove. "Breakfast will be ready in a few minutes."

"Gavin."

Her breathlessness caused me to turn again. I wanted to look at her, but the more I stared, the more those fissures in my heart cracked, and I wasn't sure how much I could take of her being here, but not being mine.

"Thank you," she murmured, her hands clasped in front of her body. "For everything."

I wanted to say more, but I didn't trust my voice not to squawk like a teenage boy's. I flicked the eggs around the pan some more. "Gary and Morty were able to get the tree out of the road last night. Roads are freshly plowed. I texted Morty to come pick up your car."

"But I need to drive my car home."

"Not like that you don't," I said. "You're trying to kill yourself? That car is not safe."

"Technically, I've driven worse."

"I don't even want to know."

"Do you know how expensive a cab would be back to Fantasie?"

"I'll drive you. I don't have anything else to do today."

"I'll hitch a ride with Morty in his truck," Tara said. "He's going back to Fantasie anyway, so it's not out of his way."

My mood was a little sour at the thought of Tara leaving this little cocoon we'd created for ourselves in my half-finished project, but it improved a few notches as I watched Tara eat the eggs I'd prepared. I couldn't cook for shit, but thankfully, she didn't seem to mind the somewhat charred omelet I'd ended up with this morning. Tara Kendrick wouldn't let me help her with much, so I considered it a small win.

"Please let me pay you for—"

"I'm going to stop you right there," I said. "I'm not accepting payment for anything."

A honk from outside let us know that Morty was here. He was the tow truck driver from Fantasie. He rarely wore shirts. He liked to grill. That was about all there was to Morty.

"I guess this is it." Tara stood. "It's been really good seeing you again."

"Right. You too." I wanted to pull her to me for a kiss, but I'd tried that last night, and it had ended in us fucking so violently the headboard had left a scratch mark in the wall paint. So I shoved my thumbs in my pockets.

Tara moved to grab her purse. Grateful for something to do, I lunged for it and got there first. I allowed myself the tiniest of smiles when I noted a bulginess to the little purse that hadn't been there when she'd arrived. A tiny bit of fabric poked out from where the zipper couldn't quite squeeze shut. I'd bet my entire savings account that she'd pilfered one of my T-shirts as a souvenir, and I'd never been so damn proud in my life.

"Thank you," Tara said, tugging it away from me. "By the way, can you please give me back my pepper spray?"

I headed to the coat closet and retrieved the little cannister. I handed it over.

As I did, the front door banged open without so much as a knock or a doorbell ring. There, standing in the entryway, was a beast of a man. Morty the tow guy stood there in, as usual, no shirt. He had thrown on a leather vest over his bare chest, probably due to the chilly twenty-degree temperature.

"Morty," I groaned. "I can see your nipples."

"Good to see ya, kid." Morty gave a half-toothless grin. "It's been a long time, Little Donovan. Looking good."

"Right, Little Donovan." Tara grinned at me. "I like it."

"Ready to go, pretty lady?" Morty turned to Tara. "Your chariot awaits."

Tara looked at me like a deer in headlights as if reconsidering her decision to ride home with Morty. It was my turn to grin back at her. For good measure, I gave her a little ass smack as she walked out the door.

"See you, sweet cheeks." I winked as she yelped on her way out.

Morty's grin brightened a few watts as he looked a little bit closer at Tara. "Glad to see you had a real nice time out here, Miss Kendrick."

I was pretty sure the words Tara mouthed in my direction included a few not fit for children's ears, but if nothing else, it had me grinning. At least, until I shut the door, and then I realized she was gone.

For good.

Chapter 12

Tara

It had been harder to adjust back to normal life than I'd expected.

A week had passed since I'd returned from my three nights stay at the inn, and it felt like I'd returned from a semester abroad. My daily routine was all off-kilter. My mind was scattered. I'd been an hour late to a client meeting, and that had never happened before in my entire life.

Before I'd seen Gavin, I hadn't allowed myself to be a hot mess. I was organized because I had to be. I couldn't afford not to have my life in order. I had a daughter to care for, and that daughter was currently asking me a question that I hadn't heard the first or the second time.

"Mom. Can you just sign it?"

"What is it for?" I asked. "Sorry, I was thinking about work."

"A permission slip for the Christmas field trip our class is taking." Liv groaned at my lack of focus. "We're going to see real reindeer."

"Oh, right. Sure," I said, scribbling my signature on the paper. "Okay, let's go, babe, or you'll be late to school."

Liv's ponytail swished behind her as she headed to the front door. At the last second, she squealed about forgetting her show and tell in her room. I grabbed my mug of coffee and hustled to the front door, unlocking it and pulling it open while hollering behind me for Liv to hurry up.

I moved to step outside, but I was in for a shock. A big shock. A big, manly, grumpy-looking shock. I let out a yelp and jolted back in surprise, sending my coffee sloshing forward onto the figure standing on my doorstep.

"Ow. Fuck," Gavin said, curling his shoulders in as coffee spattered down the front of his shirt.

"Hush now," I said on a reflex. "There are children present."

"Sorry. Shit. Sorry." Gavin brushed off his shirt, still wincing.

I didn't blame him. I liked my coffee boiling hot.

"Why are you here?" I finally found my words.

Still wincing, Gavin also found his words. "Haven't you heard of travel mugs?"

"Haven't you heard of calling before you show up outside someone's house?"

"I was going to knock when you gave me third degree burns." Gavin gave me a small smile. "Oh, and by the way, we're getting married."

"Excuse me?"

Gavin put his hand on the door, picked up the duffle bag that he'd set on the front steps. "I'll explain later. Here's your ring. It's real, so don't lose it."

"Wow," I said. "That's a pretty big rock."

"You're getting *married*?" Liv stood in the entrance to the mudroom from the hallway. "Can I be the flower girl?"

Gavin's face went slack. "I, uh—"

I spun to glower at Gavin, then addressed Liv. "He's just kidding, sweetie. This is an old friend—"

"I know who Gavin is." Liv marched up to him like they were best friends. "This is my pet fish, Fin. I'm bringing him for show and tell. He's named Fin because he only has one fin. Not two fins."

"You're not," I said. "You are not bringing Fin for show and tell."

"But it's the only thing I want to bring," Liv said evenly, as if that ended the argument.

"Cool fish," Gavin offered. "I think it's a great idea for show and tell."

Liv beamed. I scowled.

"Come on," I said to Liv. Then to Gavin, "You can't stay here."

"It's just a work assignment." Gavin's smile seemed frozen on his face. "I'd love to explain later. When we're alone."

"I can't talk now," I said, my heart rate accelerating. Gavin showing up at my door was *not* a good sign. Especially not if it was related to his job. "I have to work."

"How about I ride along with you, then?" Gavin said. "We can talk in the car."

"Oh, yes. I'd really love that," Liv said with emphasis on the *really*. "Are you going to be my dad?"

I let out a giant whoof of breath. "Everybody get in the car. If I hear another word out of anyone before I get coffee in my system, it's not going to be pretty."

"Um..." Liv raised a finger. "So is that a yes to Fin?"

"I'll hold him." Gavin leaned forward, relieved my daughter of her ridiculous fish. "He'll be safe with me."

"Okay. You can be Fin's dad, too." Liv took Gavin's hand, guiding him out of the house toward our car. "So are you going to get me a Christmas present then, if you're my dad?"

As I watched my daughter walk hand in hand with the man that was a very threat to my existence, my heart was doing funny things. For the past week, Liv had talked nonstop about Gavin. She'd asked when we'd be doing another video chat with him. I'd mostly blown off her questions with non-answers, and she'd seemed mildly appeased.

It had irked me how much she'd taken to him. And over the week, I'd let those nights with Gavin build up in my head. To the point I'd become almost angry about it. At myself, for not taking a risk to be with him. At him, for not chasing me harder. At Liv, for liking him so damn much.

Then when Gavin had shown up this morning, it had boiled over all those confusing emotions. Especially since he seemed to be just as pissed about the whole situation as I was.

I groaned as I studied my sexy nemesis, my daughter, and a one-finned fish as they waited by the car like a big, happy family. I blew out a long, slow breath, and prayed that Gavin Donovan had some good answers to my questions. Or else that pepper spray could be making its long-awaited comeback.

***

"Tara, I—"

"*Zzz. Zzz.*" I buzzed with my lips, holding up a finger to shush Gavin in the passenger's seat while the barista prepared my extra-large latte at the drive-thru window. We'd already dropped Liv off at school, but I wasn't yet ready to launch into a full-on discussion with Gavin just yet.

Only once the coffee goddess handed my drink to me, and I'd had the opportunity to fortify myself with a couple of sips, did I glance over toward Gavin. I made sure he could read the dissatisfaction I was feeling with a particularly nasty scowl.

"You can talk now," I offered as I took another drag of coffee. "Please make it good."

"Look, I'm not particularly happy with this development," Gavin admitted. "But apparently word got out that you and I are dating."

"I didn't say anything."

"I didn't say anything either."

We looked at one another. At the same time, we said, "Morty."

I followed up first. "If you hadn't slapped my ass on the way out the door, maybe Morty wouldn't have gone flapping his trap all over town that we were a couple."

"I was only doing that to help you!"

"How was slapping my butt helping me out?"

"I figured Morty wouldn't hit on you if I, you know..." Gavin shrugged his shoulders. "If he got the idea that you belonged to me. I didn't think he'd make a big deal out of it."

"Do you know Morty *at all*? Or Fantasie?"

Fantasie was the town I'd lived in my whole life. It was a little pinprick on a map located in a scenic part of Maine. We were flanked by beautiful rivers with spectacular views when the leaves burst into color in the fall. It was home to the Knitting Committee, or whatever they called themselves, as well as gossip central.

As if to emphasize my point about the size of our little town, I sailed past the Fantasie sign on the highway as I headed one town over to my first client meeting of the day. The sign was worn and weathered, and a little rainbow frowned on top of the letters. Beneath the printed **FANTASIE** text was a handwritten scrawl that declared, *Where dreams come true.*

Which was wholly untrue. Dreams weren't guaranteed to come true in Fantasie. If they were, I wouldn't be a single mother struggling to pay all the bills. With a hot man in the car next to me who I'd spilled precious coffee on earlier this morning.

"I do happen to have a little experience in Fantasie," he said, watching me with a sideways glance. "Though it's been a while."

"You don't say."

"I'm sorry for showing up like I did this morning." Gavin looked straight ahead out the windshield. "I realize I should've called first. Well, technically, I did call first, but you didn't answer."

"You called me at seven o'clock in the morning on a school day. Of course I didn't answer," I said. "I wasn't ignoring you; I was going to call you back when I had a minute."

"No you weren't."

"No, I wasn't," I agreed. "I would have definitely chickened out. Plus, I thought we agreed to go our separate ways?"

"We did, but things changed." Gavin sucked in a sharp breath. "Now your safety is at stake."

"My safety?"

Gavin looked like this was the last conversation he wanted to be having on earth right now. "I'm sorry, but Carter called me early this morning. They've confirmed that my ex is involved in something big, something bad."

I felt the muscles in my neck tightening. "Is that part of the reason why your next assignment is located near Fantasie? Because she's coming for you?"

"It's not that she's coming for me, but..." Gavin heaved a slow sigh. "But I don't think it's a coincidence she's hanging around the area either."

"What does this mean for you, for me?"

"We have to assume that my ex knows where I've been staying. Who I've been seeing." Gavin gave me a knowing look. "If that's true, she'd see you as my weakness. You could become a target."

"Well, then, why don't you leave the area for a while?"

"And go where?"

"Anywhere else," I said. "If you are so worried, let's just stage a breakup and you can take off."

"Doesn't work like that. If she knows you're important to me, or have been important to me, it won't stop her from targeting you."

"But I'm *not* your weak link."

Gavin's gaze slid over the console toward me, and I didn't like the vibes he was giving off. Like I was all sorts of wrong.

"I'll need some details then," I said. "If I'm involved, I deserve to know some of the specifics."

Gavin glanced out the window at the sprawling, snow-covered cornfields as we flew by farm country.

"I'm thinking we pretend to be engaged for a little while," Gavin said finally. "It's too late to hide our relationship from my ex, so we might as well go all in to help quell the Fantasie gossip. If we're together, it will give me a reason to be in town, an excuse to be moving in with you so suddenly."

"How convenient."

"I'll need to be in town anyway. There's a new company that moved in outside of Fantasie town limits a few months ago. A laundromat. The company I work for thinks that it's a money laundering operation, and we're trying to gather intel to prove the theory's correct."

"What if I say no?"

"I thought you might ask, so I'm going to sweeten the pot. How's ten thousand dollars?"

I just about veered right off the road. I righted the wheel then glanced at him once I was sure I'd heard him right. "Just to be clear, this isn't some weird prostitution thing, right?"

"Don't be ridiculous. It's a fake relationship. I won't touch you if that's what you prefer."

"Say I agree—then what?"

"If you pretend to be my fiancée until Christmas, you have my word I'll break up with you in a splashy way by the New Year. And on January 1st, you'll get a cashier's check for ten grand. The threat should be taken care of by then."

"I can't take that much money," I said. "It's probably half your earnings for the job."

"Babe, that's not even close to half." Gavin glanced over, saw my smirk. "How much do you want? Give me a number."

"Twelve grand."

"Twelve." He repeated the number like it was outrageous.

"I mean, you asked."

"Fifteen it is," he confirmed. "I'm glad we have a deal."

"How much do you make, Gavin Donovan?"

"Marry me for real, and I'll show you my bank statements."

I barked a laugh. "Good try. But your proposals need work."

Gavin grinned. "The next one will be better, I promise."

"This is not a done deal yet," I warned. "I need to know more about the logistics. The safety of things."

"That's the other part of this," Gavin said. "I need to be physically close to you and Liv. If anything happened to the two of you, I'd never forgive myself. Living in your house is about the best I can do when it comes to offering you my protection. Protecting people is my job, and I'm damn good at it. You'll be safe as long as I'm around. I'll make sure of it."

"I trust you."

I flicked on a blinker and turned down the main street in one of Fantasie's neighboring towns. I had been booked to prepare for a corporate party at the biggest hotel in a fifty-mile radius. It was imperative that I be at my best.

"Can we finish this conversation later?" I parked in the lot outside of the hotel. "I have a lot of work to do today, and I can't be distracted."

"Let me help you."

"Huh?"

"Look, if we're pretending to be headed toward marriage, you're going to get some perks with it."

"I know. Twenty thousand dollars' worth."

"That's fine."

"Are you serious?" I stared at him. "Do you have twenty thousand dollars to pay me with? Are you going to keep adding to the pot every time I ask for it?"

Gavin gave a short little laugh. "I'm good for the money, Tara."

"I know. It's just..." I shrugged. "It's a lot of money. At least, to someone like me."

"It's fine."

The way he spoke about money, it was like it barely mattered at all. What a privilege, being able to toss out the idea of shelling out twenty grand for a little assist on one of his work assignments.

For me, it was a life-changing amount of money. My mother's prior cancer treatments had wiped out the savings I'd put aside for my business. My mother had no idea how close I'd come to going bankrupt. I was pretty sure she thought I was rolling in dough, probably because that's what

I'd led her to believe. It was the only way she would let me help pay for her treatments.

Otherwise, she'd have had to sell the house. I knew, not because she'd told me, but because I'd bumped into Mickey Michaels, one of the town's real estate agents, Mickey had expressed her surprise at my mom's phone call asking about putting her house on the market.

"I hate to make this about money." When Gavin spoke it was hushed. Tentative. "It's not. I'd give you the entire fee if that's what you wanted. I'm fortunate, Tara. Money's not an issue for me anymore. Your safety is."

"Still."

"I overheard you a couple of times, mentioning things about finances being tight."

"I mean, it's not a secret. I'm a single mom with a fledgling business. It's hardly a leap to make. I follow a budget. We've survived this far and we'll keep doing it."

"Hopefully twenty grand will help make a dent in things. Float you for a few months, maybe allow you to take a little break. I don't know."

"I don't need twenty grand," I said. "I would've done it for ten."

Gavin reached for my hand, gave a squeeze. "You would've done it for free, Tara. That's the sort of woman you are."

I swallowed at his hand tucked in mine. Sitting here, simply coexisting. Finding solutions to problems. Weird problems, sure, but problems all the same. It felt like something a real couple would do, not a fake one.

"What am I supposed to say to Liv? And to my mother?"

Gavin tensed, looked down. "I'm truly sorry about involving your family in this. We'll make it very clear during our breakup that I'm the screwup, and I'm the one walking away. I'll defer to you on the rest."

I sighed. "Liv is already too attached to you for her own good."

"I like her too."

My chest felt heavy as I considered how this might affect my family. My mother would be fine, she could get over it. But Liv?

As I climbed out of the car and headed to work, to the job I needed to do to support my little girl, I knew it wouldn't be easy. But what was the alternative? If Gavin said we were in danger, I would be stupid not to believe him. I couldn't see Liv get hurt, not physically at least, if I could help it. The rest would have to sort itself out in time.

Chapter 13

Tara

It wasn't a terrible way to spend the day, watching Gavin's arms bulge as he hauled stuff up and down, left and right. The man didn't need so much as a water break after I'd given him marching instructions and set him to work earlier this morning.

The local bank was having their holiday party at a big hotel, and I'd been hired on to get the ballroom in shape for two hundred guests in just eight hours. I hadn't been able to get in the doors until ten a.m. due to a breakfast they'd hosted, and I expected to be working right up until five thirty when I'd have to buzz home to pick up Liv from after school theater rehearsal.

Then I'd bring her back with me and let her do her homework while I supervised the final touches of the event. Once the bank's party started at seven, I'd stick around for another hour or two until I ditched out and left cleanup to my very part-time assistant.

"Hey, hon," Gavin called over to me. "You want the star or the angel on top of this Christmas tree?"

"We're working," I said to Gavin. "Be professional."

He winked at me. "I'm marrying you."

"Oh, shut up," I mumbled to him as Dolores—the almost-retired front desk receptionist at the hotel—gave me a huge double thumbs-up.

"Gotta sell it, yeah?" Gavin leaned over, gave me a chaste peck on the cheek.

It alighted something between my thighs. I turned away to grab some tinsel that I could use to hide my rosy cheeks. All day, my nerves had been a bit frayed.

The whole situation had me on edge. Spending this much time close to Gavin couldn't be a good thing. Getting wrapped up in some money laundering investigation. And yet backing out could be even worse if the danger factor was to be believed, so here I was, pretending to be engaged to a man who may or may not be an assassin.

"Who's the hunk?" My very part-time assistant chose that moment to walk into the room. "And why'd he kiss you on the cheek? Yes, I saw that. I asked Dolores about it, but she didn't know squat."

I glanced over at Millie. Her real name was Millicent, but she went by Millie, and she made candles and soaps and all sorts of stuff she sold back in Fantasie. I'd hired her on to help me manage some of the events during the holiday season, especially since I'd need some nights off to take care of Liv. I couldn't afford to turn down clients, so hiring an assistant had been the best I could do to make ends meet.

"He's, uh, some guy," I said. "A friend. Just, can you check on the caterer? I only have a couple hours before I have to get Liv, and then you're going to be in charge, so stay focused."

Millie raised her eyebrows and gave me a surprised look. Her curly red hair spiraled around her face, and her freckles popped on pale skin. She wore round glasses and was as quirky in real life as she looked in photographs.

"Hit a hot button there, I can see." Millie leaned forward and bopped me on the nose with the tip of her finger. "Good thing I know how to get you to talk."

"Huh?" My mind was still on assassins, especially since I was looking at my favorite pretend-assassin's butt as he arranged empty Amazon boxes wrapped to look like gifts under another tree.

"Bubbly prosecco after a late night on the job when Liv is at your mom's." Millie squinted adorably at me. "You always spill all your deepest secrets on the bubbly."

I considered this little nugget of information as Millie swept away in a long, patchwork skirt she'd probably made from her grandmother's old T-shirts to check on the caterer. I thought back to the bubbles I'd consumed in Gavin's hot tub. Things suddenly made a lot more sense.

"Hey, I'm sorry, but I've got to ditch out for a little bit." Gavin glanced down at his phone, read a message, frowned. "I need to check on something."

"Aw, shucks. Is it work again, sweetie?" I tried to sound cute, but it came out a little sour.

"Sure is, babe." Gavin met me with sarcasm, beat for beat.

But to anyone watching from the outside, we probably looked like a real couple discussing real work situations. He was standing too close to me, looking down at me like he might devour me on the spot. I should know. I was feeling pretty hungry myself having worked next to him all day, and my appetite had nothing to do with food.

I lowered my voice. "I thought you were supposed to be protecting me. How's that work if you're not here?"

"I've got a buddy watching the hotel."

"What?"

"Relax. I trust him completely. He's—"

At that moment, a tall, dark, roguishly handsome man strolled into the hotel lobby. His hands were shoved into his pockets, and he looked like he was here for the bank party—a few hours too early.

"Lucas?" I barked. "You sicced your cousin on me?"

"Hey, Tara. How's it going?" Lucas Donovan, Gavin's oldest cousin, strolled over in our direction.

He had a Prince Charming grin that would've melted a woman's panties. Fortunately, Lucas was already taken. He'd married Chloe Brown in a whirlwind romance almost a year ago. Not to mention, I had my sights set on a different Donovan.

"Uh, yeah. Fine." I shook my head. "You don't have to babysit me."

"I'm not here to babysit." Lucas looked confused. "Gavin said you needed a hand, and long story short, I owe him a favor. He's cashing in for manual labor. So, give me marching orders." Lucas raised his thick arms in surrender. "Put me to work, because I hate owing this little shit anything."

Only another six foot plus Donovan could call Gavin names like that. Then again, Gavin actually had Lucas by an inch or so. It got a rise out of Gavin and a smirk out of me.

"Right, asshole. See you later." Gavin smacked Lucas so hard on the shoulder, the lawyer pitched forward into a box of ornaments on the table.

"Great!" I gave Lucas an overly sweet smile. "I guess you can bring those on up to the main ballroom. We're making centerpieces with those."

As "Deck the Halls" thrummed in the background, I huffed after Gavin.

JINGLE BELL ROCK

"What are you thinking, bringing your family into this?"

"You're my family." Gavin winked at me. "Remember?"

"Be serious. It's just you and me standing here right now."

"I am being serious." Gavin stilled, looked me in the eyes. "Your safety, and Liv's safety, is my priority. I didn't come down here to fuck around with you, believe it or not. I came down here to take care of you. To finish my job. To keep you safe until I'm positive you're not in harm's way. Then, if you want, I will get the hell out of here and leave you alone. Until then, you're under my protection."

"But—" I got blustery, but I didn't quite have a retort. I stuttered for a bit until I circled back to, "But I don't want a babysitter."

"I'm sorry," Gavin said. "I have to leave. I've called in a buddy from the company I work for, so if I have to dip out in the future, he can keep an eye on you from a distance."

"Absolutely not."

"You won't even know he's there."

"I said—"

"Until then, you're stuck with Lucas. Give him hell for me, will you? I cashed in a damn big favor for this." Gavin had the gall to wink at me. "Make it worth it, princess."

I huffed back into the hotel lobby, my mind whirring. I couldn't quite process everything that'd just happened. This talk of bodyguards, Gavin calling in familial favors, the frown that had appeared on his face as he'd read his messages. Suddenly, the whole thing was feeling overwhelming.

My anxiety ratcheted up to a whole new level. On top of that, I was still in the middle of working with some of my biggest clients, and I needed to be on the top of my game during my busiest season of the year.

I ducked into the bathroom, took a moment to wash my face and stare into the mirror. I could do this. I just needed to focus and get through the night.

Then, once this job was wrapped and Liv was tucked into her bed, I could sit down with a glass of wine and really think about the day's events and begin to properly process everything. With Gavin sitting across from me at the kitchen table, because apparently we were engaged.

What. The. Hell. Was. Happening.

"Are you kidding me?" The door to the ladies' room burst open and Millie propped her fists on her hips, elbows splayed wide. "Dolores just told me that you're engaged to that hunk, and I've never even heard his name? What gives?"

I stared at her, searching for an appropriate response.

Then I burst into tears.

***

After losing thirty precious minutes to a half-assed explanation to Millie about how things with Gavin, a former flame, had happened very quickly, I promised her I'd fill her in on the rest later. Then I re-applied my mascara, swiped on some lip gloss, and returned to work.

As annoying as my arrangement with Gavin was, I had to admit that having two large Donovan men around for the majority of the day had been a huge help. I would've really had to hustle if I'd wanted to get things ready without them. Even now, things were pushing up to the deadline.

I glanced at the clock, saw it was already five. I had barely enough time to check in with the caterers, set out the centerpieces, and make sure Millie was prepared to take over before I had to get Liv.

"I can get Liv if you want," Millie said, watching me as I flipped through papers and mumbled under my breath like a crazy person. "You seem really stressed."

"No. I promised her I'd pick her up, and I'm going to be there."

"Okay. Just offering."

"Thanks," I said, trying to sound apologetic. "I appreciate it. It's just, I always swore to myself that I would be there for her. No matter what."

"It's just one time."

"Starts that way," I said, "and then all of a sudden, I've hired a full-time nanny and never see my kid."

"That escalated quickly." Millie reached into her flowing skirt, shuffled around some pockets, and pulled out a teeny tiny candle that fit in her palm. From another pocket, she pulled out a matchbook. "I'm going to light this lavender lemon candle for you, and you just take a few whiffs because you need to chill."

"I'm not into all of that incense stuff."

"It's not incense, and you're going to need to get into scents because it's sort of what I do."

"That does smell really good," I admitted, leaning forward. "I think it's helping my headache already."

Millie beamed like the sun had risen inside of her. She looked like a little patchwork rainbow trembling with excitement.

"Really? I am so glad. I'm just testing it out before I add it to my roster of products."

The candle really wasn't doing shit for my headache, but the joy on Millie's face did give me a boost. I remembered those days, the early days of starting a business. The sky was the limit. The options were endless. There was only one way to go—up. There was no talk of balance sheets or brick and mortar storefronts or client rosters. Just dreams.

I took another obligatory sniff of the candle. Really, it did smell quite lovely, it just hadn't miracle cured my headache. But if Millie was coming to me for positive reinforcement, it was the least I could do.

"I'm going to get the silverware set out and check the candy buffet," Millie said, "and then—"

I waved her off as my phone began to ring. Glancing down, I recognized the number, and it sent a pinch of panic down my spine.

"Hello?"

"Hi, Tara. This is Sandy from Fantasie Primary School, and—"

"Yes, I've got your number, Sandy," I said, trying not to sound cross. "Is Liv okay? Did something happen?"

"Um, I was just wondering if you were on your way to pick her up, or...?"

I glanced again at the clock. "I'm just about to leave. She's supposed to have practice for the school play today."

"Play practice was cancelled for today. An email was sent out last week—Mr. Moriarty had a conflict today, so he moved rehearsal to tomorrow. I guess you must have missed the email?"

"What?" I gaped at my phone and looked at the clock for the zillionth time in as many minutes. "Why are you just calling me now?"

"I was on after-care duty today, so I just let her stay with me. I know this time is busy with you for work and everything, so I figured you were just running late. But, well, you know, we're going to be closing up here soon...I'd offer to take her home with me, but I can't do that. School rules and all."

Sandy wasn't only the music teacher at the Fantasie grade school, she was a good friend of mine. We'd grown up neighbors and had remained friendly through high school. We'd been on the same beach volleyball team before we'd both had kids. So I understood that Sandy had been trying to help me out on a personal note today.

"Plus, I mean, Liv kept telling me that you were on your way, so..." Sandy cleared her throat. "I didn't want to make you feel guilty. I know life as a single mom is hard enough."

I cursed. "I'm so sorry. It'll take me twenty minutes to get there. Can you, is there any way you can wait until then?"

I heard the hitched breath on the other end. "I can wait," she said finally, but it wasn't a super thrilled agreement. "It's fine. Just get here when you can. Don't rush."

I understood Sandy's tone of voice. That was the *I'm trying to be nice, but I really have to be somewhere else and wish your ass wouldn't have been late* voice. I knew it well because I'd used it before on playdates with other parents who'd dropped their kid off for one hour and showed up two hours late.

I was in the middle of a stream of curses that would've made most sailors proud when Millie found me as I hunted for keys that I suddenly couldn't find.

"I'm late to pick up Liv," I said. "All this planning, and I missed the fucking email about the school play. I'm dropping balls everywhere."

"Go," she said. "Or maybe there's someone you can call to grab her so you can stay here and stress, like, thirty-four percent less? Maybe your mom?"

"My mom's at book club, and plus, she hates driving in the dark. There's nobody—"

"Your fiancé?" she suggested. At my blank expression, she continued, "Don't look at me like I'm an idiot. If you're marrying the guy, he's going to have to parent with you. Right? Or am I right?"

I licked my lips, glanced at my phone. I couldn't do it. I couldn't interrupt Gavin. But even as my mind protested, I spotted the hard-ass manager of the hotel coming to find me, and if everything wasn't perfect—

"What the hell," I muttered, "it's worth a try."

Millie gave me a little spank to get me scooting off in the opposite direction. "You skedaddle and take care of the Liv situation, whether you get her or someone else does. I'll cover for you."

I had approximately thirty seconds to decide which route to take before I would inevitably get wrapped up in a very chatty conversation with a man I had to impress if I ever wanted to work here again. And rushing out on the manager in the middle of a large event was not a good look.

So I did as Millie suggested and slipped away, dodging the conversation before it ever started. I made my way to the lobby by the time Gavin picked up.

"Where are you?" I asked breathlessly. "I need a huge favor."

Chapter 14

Gavin

"What's up, buttercup?" I was currently crouched next to a dumpster with a gun on my hip. I was a little bit busy, but the note of concern in Tara's voice had me rethinking my priorities in a heartbeat. "What's wrong?"

"It's Liv. I missed the email about her school play practice getting rescheduled, and my friend Sandy is covering for me at aftercare. I really need to pick her up. And also, the hotel manager has been hovering around me like I'm incapable of running my own event, and if I ditch out now—"

"Relax. I've got her." I raised from a crouch. Glanced up and down the alleyway. "She's at the elementary school?"

"Yes."

"I can be there in five minutes."

"Oh my gosh, you're a saint. If you don't mind, you can drop her off here. I can keep an eye on her while I finish up, and you'll be free to continue doing whatever it is you're doing. What *are* you doing?"

I glanced up and down at the laundromat I'd been casing for the last hour. There'd been no activity yet, but I'd gotten wind that a meeting might be happening later tonight, and I was supposed to get a glimpse of who was having this meeting.

I'd been in the middle of installing little cameras that would tell me who was coming or leaving. I hadn't finished up with everything I'd wanted to accomplish, but it'd have to be good enough.

JINGLE BELL ROCK

"If it's okay with you, I'll take her home," I said. "You can focus on your work. She'll be with me the entire night. You can call her anytime you want. She can do her, I dunno, homework or feed her fish or whatever the hell she needs to do without sitting around at the hotel and getting in your way."

"Just get her, and we can figure that out later," she said breathlessly. "I have to go. I'll call Sandy and let her know you'll be picking her up—you'll need to show an ID. Then I've got to get back to work. I'm behind."

"Go," I instructed.

Then I hopped in the car, turned on the feed from the camera I had managed to install, so that I could view live images from outside the laundromat, and headed to pick up Liv from school like the fake-stepdad I now had to pretend to be.

I made it to the school in four minutes, thanks to empty roads and a lead foot. I saw Liv waiting for me, or rather her mother, on a bench out front. She was swinging her legs, little braids looking fuzzy after a day of play. One of her knee-high uniform socks drooped down to her little shoes. A pinch of worry held her eyebrows together.

Her gaze bounced right over my car, and I realized she didn't recognize the vehicle as the one coming for her. The little fishbowl sat adorably in her lap.

I parked out front and gave a wave to the teacher. "Hi there, you must be Sandy," I said, flashing my license. "I'm Gavin Donovan. Here to pick up Liv."

"That was fast." Sandy blinked at me.

The teacher was a pretty Black woman with a slim skirt and fitted blouse. She glanced down at her clipboard and checked it against my ID.

"Gavin?" Liv jumped to her feet. "Where's mom?"

"She was caught up at work," I said. "I volunteered to come and get you. I figured Fin needed a big, bad bodyguard for the drive home."

Sandy was still looking at my license, but her lips twitched up in a smile as she handed it back to me. "That'll work, Mr. Donovan. And by the way, welcome back to town. Are you and Tara..."

Sandy glanced down at Liv, as if gauging how much to say in front of the child. Then I remembered where I knew Sandy from. She'd been a few grades younger than me and had run in some similar circles as Tara. Of course she'd know who I was, and she probably would know about the history between us.

"We're just happy seeing how things go," I said carefully as Liv rose to her feet. "Taking things slow."

"Gavin is my mom's friend from Thanksgiving," Liv chirped happily to Sandy. "He carried Fin to school for me today, even when Mom wasn't going to let me bring him."

"Well, it's a good thing Gavin was here then." Sandy patted Liv's head. "The class loved him. Now, you two have a good night, all right?"

"Okay!" Liv bounced to the car. "Can I sit in the front seat?"

"Um, I think that's for Mr. Fin," I said. "I need to talk to your mother about driving arrangements. I'm not sure..." I looked helplessly to Sandy. "I don't think you're allowed?"

JINGLE BELL ROCK 175

"Back seat only, Liv." Sandy gave me a wink. "Careful of this cutie, Mr. Donovan, or she'll take you for a ride."

I gave Sandy a salute. "Thanks for the tip, ma'am."

Once Liv was all buckled in, and we were headed for home, I realized I knew jack shit about kids. It wasn't that I didn't like kids because I did. But the last segment of my life had been focused on *not* kids. Now here I was, all alone with one very special little girl.

"So what's the plan for tonight, kiddo?" I asked. "Do you want to go see your mom, or..."

"Is she working?" Liv wrinkled her nose. "Maybe we can go home. Do you like movies? I like movies."

"I like movies," I confirmed. "Let's call your mother before I promise things that are gonna get me in trouble."

"You're smarter than you look, Gavin," Liv said on a big sigh that made her sound years older than she was. "I guess we can call her, but I'm not gonna like what she has to say."

I grinned, then I hit dial on Tara's number. I could hear the stress in Tara's voice from the moment she answered. It was incredible, after only one weekend together, how it already felt like the decade we'd spent apart almost ceased to exist.

My feelings for Tara had come back in full force, if not stronger. I could pick out the nuances in her voice as if we'd never stopped loving one another. I could picture her like she was next to me, could imagine the feel of her skin against my hand—

"Gavin?" Tara repeated. "Are you there?"

"Yeah," I said. "We're here. Still in the parking lot at school, haven't started driving anywhere yet. I've got Liv."

"I know," Tara said breathlessly. "Sandy texted me."

"Uh huh. What else did Sandy say?"

The brief pause on Tara's end of the line told me she was hiding something, even as she huffed out a nonsensical response. Then she bumbled on, obviously flustered that I'd called her out on the message from her friend.

"Liv, honey, I'm sorry about today," Tara apologized. "I missed the email, and then I've been at work all day, and—"

"It's okay," Liv said from the backseat. "Gavin didn't forget about me. Please don't make me come to your work."

"What?" Tara asked, sounding truly clueless. "I thought you liked coming with me."

"It's boring, and plus, Gavin mentioned a movie," Liv said, giving me a shy little wink. "I don't want him to be sad. Maybe I can stay home and watch a movie with him?"

Tara hesitated again.

"It's fine, really," I said. "I don't have anything I need to do tonight. I can hang with Liv if it's fine with you."

Tara paused to bark orders at someone in the distance. She returned to our conversation sounding desperate. "Sure, if that's what Liv wants, it's fine with me."

"It's what I want," Liv assured her. "Bye, Mom. We gotta go."

"Oh. Okay. Well, bye then—I love you. See you later."

"Are you going to be okay?" I asked Tara. "Is Lucas still with you?"

"Of course he's still here. You superglued him to my side." Tara sounded much more like her business self. "And he's doing a fantastic job," she said, almost angrily. "Much better than you."

"Good," I said, pleased to see I'd shaken her out of disappointment at the Liv situation. "Funnel your frustration at me into focus on your work, and then you can lay into me once you get home."

Once another laundry list of instructions wrapped up, I disconnected the call. Liv sat back in her seat and blew out a breath that sent wisps from her braids blowing away from her face.

"Oh, my mom," Liv said. "She worries too much."

"Sure does," I agreed. "So, what's for dinner?"

Liv leaned forward, a little gleam in her eyes. "What are my options, Gavin?"

***

Apparently saying no to a little girl was more difficult than I'd expected. Liv had sweet talked me into stopping by one drive-thru for a shake, another for fries—because they were curly there—and yet a third drive-thru for an actual burger. I was feeling a little overwhelmed by the time we pulled up outside of Tara's home.

I let us in through the garage with the code Tara had texted me, then I promptly made a note to myself to change the code. If she'd texted it to me, the digits lived in cyberspace, and someone could get to it. I'd do that later tonight, once Tara got home and Liv was sleeping.

We got Fin snuggled back into Liv's bedroom. I made a half-hearted argument about how we should probably eat at the dinner table with utensils and proper stuff, but Liv made the well-vetted argument that if we wasted time eating properly, the movie would run past her bedtime, and we would be left on a cliffhanger. I wasn't sure there was a cliffhanger in Shrek, but she convinced me there sure was.

So that was how we ended up eating dinner in front of the TV with three different fast food bags before us. I'd grabbed a couple of extra burgers and shakes and shoved them in the fridge for when Tara got home. I figured with the way she was zooming around, she'd probably be starved. I'd watched her call a juice box lunch earlier.

At about the halfway point in the movie, I saw Liv's eyelids starting to look a little sticky. She hadn't touched the second half of her burger, and she was sinking so deeply into the couch I was pretty sure it might gobble her right up. I leaned forward and paused the movie.

"Didn't your mom say something about brushing your teeth and doing homework and getting ready for bed?"

Liv blinked at me. "What about it?"

"Why don't we do that now, and then we can finish the movie," I promised, holding the remote like a bargaining chip. It'd been a long time since I'd been around kids, but I wasn't a complete idiot. I knew how negotiations worked.

She eyed my hand on the power button and gave a sullen nod. "Fine."

"So do you..." I raised my shoulders. "Do that stuff by yourself or do you need help?"

Liv shot daggers at me. It was very reminiscent of the annoyed looks her mother had been sending my way all day long. "Of course I do it by myself. I'm not a baby."

"Okay, then. I'll be waiting here for you when you're ready. With the remote."

Liv hauled herself off to her room. I heard the sounds of a kid doing kid things to get ready for bed. About ten minutes later, she came back wearing a long pink nightgown and holding a threadbare little blanket.

"I don't *need* my blanket," Liv said defensively, holding it against her cheek. "It's just comfortable to take with me."

"Of course," I said seriously. "I know you're not a baby."

"That's right." She plopped on the sofa. "I don't have homework. But I need to practice my line for the play."

"Okay. Hit me," I said. "I can do that."

"You just say 'And the star rose into the sky'."

I said, "And the star rose into the sky'.

"You have to mean it," Liv said with an eye roll. "You weren't trying really hard."

"And the *star* rose *into* the sky."

Liv peered up at me, then she stood, and very solemnly, said three words. That was apparently her line. Then she sat down, and I realized that was my cue.

I gave a rigorous round of applause. "Encore," I said. "Encore!"

She gave a self-satisfied shy little nod. "Okay, we can finish the movie now."

Liv sidled onto the couch next to me. She rested her head against my shoulder, and no more than five minutes later, those eyelids were all sorts of sticky again. It was mesmerizing, watching her doze off. I'd never seen someone fall asleep before like that, so graceful, so innocent. Liv was still practically a stranger to me, and yet somehow, I felt like my heart had swollen full with something resembling care for her in the short time I'd known her.

How could it not? The kind way she'd accepted me into her family, the delightful way in which she sparred with me over what to order for dinner, the way she snuggled against me, trusting herself fully to a man she'd barely known, made my heart ache for her vulnerability and revel in the innocence of her childhood.

And I thought that maybe, in this small interval, I could understand one millionth of the way Tara felt as her mother. The love Tara had for Liv, the care, the reason Tara had plowed through a snowstorm on snowshoes with an injured ankle to get home to this one little girl.

I raised a hand, gently brushed it through her hair, then settled in to watch a talking donkey because I wasn't about to reach for the remote and risk waking Liv.

I wasn't sure how long we stayed that way. All I knew was that I found myself pretending to be wide awake when I heard the click of a key in the front door, and the lock turning. I started, but fortunately Liv was in a deep enough sleep it didn't rouse her.

My heart pounded, but I forced myself to stay still until Tara's face appeared from the hallway, peering around the corner. Only then could I relax, and I held up one finger to my lips.

Tara froze, looking like she'd seen a ghost. Her eyes darted between me and Liv, and I just left my finger on my lips for fear Liv would startle awake.

"Can I move her?" I mouthed quietly.

Tara, still frozen, gave a slow nod. I shifted my weight from under Liv's head and scooped her up against my chest. Carrying a bag of sugar felt heavier than lifting Liv's sleeping figure. Her head drooped over my arm as I tried to juggle her into a position that looked more comfortable. Finally, I gave up and forfeited to the fact that she was just going to be a rag doll until morning, and I shuffled down the hall to the room decorated for a child.

Liv's room was pink and frilly, and there was a gauze tapestry thing hanging down over the bed that I somehow got my head tangled in. I had to fight my way out of it as if I'd gotten stuck in a gnarly fishing line. When I had successfully deposited Liv beneath her comforter, I exhaled a huge sigh of relief.

I took one step back, and there was a huge *squeak*. I stilled, and Liv's eyes flashed open. She gave me a sleepy smile, rubbed one hand over her eyelashes, and the murmured sleepily, "Goodnight, Big Gavin."

"Goodnight, Little Liv."

I turned and just about had another heart attack. I'd been on stakeouts that had been less stressful than getting Liv into bed. Tara was standing at the doorway, her eyes tired, her hair falling out of its ponytail. But the smile on her lips told me that she was content now, being here with her daughter.

"She's all yours," I mumbled, sidestepping around Tara and making my way into the kitchen.

I waited, somewhat patiently, while Tara presumably tucked in Liv and said her goodnights. Or whatever it was she was doing. Ten minutes later, Tara appeared in the kitchen, and I realized she'd washed her face and changed into pajamas. A strappy tank top and lacy little shorts. She'd halfheartedly thrown a robe over her pjs, but it didn't cover up much. Again, no bra. Again, it was an issue for my concentration.

"I got you dinner." My voice came out hoarse. "I mean, if you consider burgers and fries dinner. Sorry, but it was what the boss ordered."

"The boss?" Tara eased into a chair at the little table off to one side of the kitchen. She yawned, looking like she was about to fall asleep with her eyes open. "Oh, you mean Liv?"

"The one and only." I pulled out the three different food bags from the fridge and tossed them onto the table. "Help yourself. It's a smorgasbord."

JINGLE BELL ROCK

Tara looked at the three different bags, the puzzled look on her face as if she was trying to compute some AP Calculus problem. "Why did you go to three fast food places?"

"It's what the boss ordered," I repeated.

Tara stared at the bags then burst into laughter. "Are you serious? You can say no to her, you know."

"Have you tried?" I crooked an eyebrow. "Liv didn't seem to like that word very much."

Tara was still laughing. "You're kidding me. You—big, tough-guy, assassin Gavin Donovan—were outsmarted by a six-year-old?"

"Have you looked into that little face?" I shot back. "She worked some voodoo magic on me."

"Well, I'll give you that. She knows what she wants. And she goes after it."

"Like her mama," I said, firing up the electric kettle so I could make a cup of decaf. My stomach felt a little greasy after the dinner I'd plowed through with Liv.

Tara seemed to be too tired to take the food out of the bag herself, so I grabbed a plate, slapped a sandwich and fries on it, and nuked it in the microwave. Then with a flourish, I slid the plate, along with a sort-of-greasy napkin from the bag and a packet of ketchup down next to her.

"Dinner is served, princess," I announced.

Tara burst into tears. "I hate you."

I slunk backward, mostly wishing I could disappear into the wall. "Sorry?"

"I hate you," she repeated as if the problem was my not hearing her.

"Did I do something?" I asked. At her blank stare, I continued. "Okay, aside from the whole fake engagement thing."

Tara licked her lips, shook her head, and pushed back her chair. Apparently she wasn't too tired to go fish the damn ketchup bottle out of the fridge. I thought our conversation was a little more urgent than her condiment infatuation, but obviously she thought otherwise.

"You don't have to do all this. It just makes it worse." Tara took a huge swipe of ketchup with a single fry and popped it into her mouth. "Pretending to be a part of our family. I get you want to make things realistic while we're fake-engaged, but behind closed doors you don't have to pretend."

"Which part was me overstepping my boundaries?" I asked, genuinely confused. "Letting Liv eat garbage for dinner, or putting said garbage on a plate for you and heating it up?"

A little smile turned up Tara's lips, but she seemed to resist the urge to let me cheer her up. Good thing I was too stubborn for that, and I wasn't going to give up so easily.

"Come on, babe. Talk to me." I sat across from Tara in her kitchen.

Now that I'd spent more than five minutes in her place, I was beginning to see evidence of Tara all over her home. The house itself couldn't have been more than twelve hundred square feet. It was small, compact, old. But filled with Tara's warmth and charm.

Photographs of Tara, her mother, and Liv were propped on various surfaces. The fridge was covered with child-drawn art. The countertop in the kitchen was chipped but perfectly clean. The floor was scratched up but spotless. Liv's pink backpack hung from a single peg near the door. A small poinsettia sat near the sink, it's leaves dripping with glitter. It was neat and homey and perfectly lived in, and I found myself thinking I had no real desire to leave its walls.

Tara must have been watching me study the place. "Where did you live? What was it like?"

I thought of the penthouse I'd occupied in downtown LA. It was clean, too, but at the hands of a team of maids. The building was modern. There'd been wall to wall windows with a view to the ocean. I hadn't bought the place for the views—I'd bought it for the security team that went with it.

It'd served me well while I'd been in California, but when I'd sold it, I'd packed one suitcase with my possessions and that had been the end of it. The rest of my belongings I sold with the place. It hadn't been a home for me. It'd been a home base. Technically, I was mostly homeless right now, but with my job wrapping up and this gig in Fantasie, I'd wanted the freedom to go anywhere.

"I like your place better," I said in a brief summary. "So, want to talk about the waterworks?"

"Not really," she said.

"Try again," I pressed. "Because I'm not going to leave you alone until you start talking. And if you tell me you're not the boss of me again, I'm going to..." I stopped. I didn't have much of a threat. I didn't want to make it a threat. But I had gotten Tara to smile again, so my tactic had worked.

"It was just a long day," she said with a sigh. "Starting with you showing up at my front door. Then there was the stress in the back of my mind about what this means for us for the next couple of weeks. Not to mention the stress of trying to guess at what your secret life is."

"I'm sorry for my part in your stress."

"It's not just you," she confessed. "I had a long day at work. The party went off okay, but it wasn't great. I was completely distracted. Millie helped me carry the load for sure. Having you and Lucas as manpower was a lifesaver."

"Good."

"But it just wasn't... It wasn't *perfect*."

"Well, the manager you were trying to impress is a dick, so I wouldn't care too much what he thinks." I swiped a fry off Tara's plate. "He made an appearance while I was decorating the tree and told me my color themes were abysmal. I mean, it was green and red. Who the fuck hates Christmas colors?"

Tara's mouth twitched upwards again. "Fair, but that's the guy I need to impress to keep working there. If I could get some sort of exclusive contract to work with the hotel, it could really help my business."

"What about—"

"Yeah, the ten thousand dollar check you keep promising me—"

"Twenty."

"I feel like that's robbing you blind."

"It's not. Trust me."

Tara licked her lips. "As generous as that amount is, it will help now, but it's not a long-term solution for my business. I'd like to have a little more flexibility in my schedule to be there for Liv, but I just don't see how I can drop any of my clients."

"You could always hire help to expand without putting all the burden on yourself."

"I really do hate you." She sighed again. "Stop making all sorts of sense."

"It's cruel."

"You're just so damn thoughtful." Tara gave a little sniff like it was a real travesty. "I can't handle this, Gavin. You playing husband, father-figure, whatever. Bringing me dinner. And if it's confusing to me, then it's probably confusing to Liv."

"Tara, if someone bringing you five bucks worth of dinner makes you burst into tears, then, honey, you haven't been spoiled enough in your life."

Tara didn't seem to have a retort to that. It made me feel all sorts of awful seeing her glance away. There was probably more truth to the statement than even I was willing to admit, and it aggravated old wounds. I'd felt guilty for leaving Tara for years, and I thought that'd been bad. I now felt worse.

"I don't want you to think this little arrangement means anything," Tara said. "I need money, you need a cover story, and that's it. So just keep your distance where you can, okay?"

"Sorry. So, no more burgers?"

"I love the burgers," Tara said angrily. Then, a bit haughtier she added, "Thank you."

"You're welcome," I fired back. I couldn't resist ribbing her a little. "Even if I'm unhappy about it."

Tara grinned, shook her head, polished off the first burger. She reached for the second and paused. "Did you get anything to eat?"

"I'm good," I said. "I ate too much already."

"How much did the two of you order?"

"Whatever fifty dollars split across three fast food joints buys you?"

Tara's eyes widened. "I'm amazed you got Liv to sleep after that. Did she sweet talk you into a shake?"

"Sure did."

Tara rolled her eyes. "She's only allowed one shake a week on the weekend."

"I wasn't aware."

"It's fine. I repeat: I can't believe you got her to sleep."

"She was an angel. I mean, except for all those devilish deals she made with me, but I consider that good negotiation skills. Has she considered a career in law?"

"I've considered it for her. It's alarming how that kid can get what she wants. And if you say that means she's like her mama, I'm going to slap you."

"I appreciate the warning," I said, then shut my mouth.

We sat in what I'd consider amicable silence while I waited for Tara to finish her dinner. When she was done, she asked me if I wanted tea, and I agreed. We took our mugs to the couch and sat. Far apart from one another. Shrek was still rolling. We both stared at the TV like it was a crucial 4th down in the Superbowl.

"You really did save me today," Tara murmured, her hands wrapped around her cup as if it was a lifesaver. "Both helping me at the hotel, getting Lucas over there, and especially picking up Liv from school."

"It was nothing. Literally it was the least I could do after getting you wrapped up in all of this."

"I mean, I guess I showed up at your doorstep first, which started everything."

"True, but I slapped your ass and started the rumors of us being together."

"You're right. This is all your fault."

We shared a little smile, then finished the movie in silence.

"Well, good night then." Tara stood. "I guess you're... staying?"

"Couch okay? I don't need anything. Except maybe a shower if you're offering."

"We've only got one bathroom, and I'm showering first. It's in the hall, and I'll set out an extra towel when I'm done. Don't sleep naked."

"Wouldn't dream of it," I said. "Thank you, Tara. For everything."

"Thank you." She spun around in the entrance to the hallway at the last minute. "I mean, really thank you. Liv, well, I don't know why, but she adores you."

"Just like her mother—"

"If you finish that sentence, you're dead to me," Tara said, but she was smiling. "Thanks for taking such good care of her tonight."

"I had fun."

"I actually believe you," Tara said, her eyes flicking toward the TV, then toward the couch where I'd been cuddled up next to Liv an hour earlier. "Just try to keep some distance between the two of you. You're leaving, remember? And she shouldn't be the one to pay for it."

On that somewhat somber note, Tara turned on a heel and marched out of the room. I settled onto the couch, listening to the sounds of the shower flicking on, running, shutting off. Of Tara brushing her teeth, padding down the hall, presumably climbing into bed.

I realized that it was nice, being here. Listening to the sounds of a busy house. Knowing I wasn't alone. Knowing I was staying in a real, loving home for quite possibly the first time in my life.

Chapter 15

Tara

"Mooooooom."

The word was dragged out like a cow's lowing. My eyelids were literally peeled back by tiny fingers. I found myself staring upward into the eyes of my mini me.

"What did I tell you about waking me before my alarm?" I flew up in bed, easing Liv off my body and to the side. It took me a minute to come to my senses. "What's going on, baby?"

"Did you know Gavin stayed overnight?" Liv bounced on the bed, rousing me from sleep a full hour before my alarm clock. "He's on the couch. I went to get some cereal, and there he was. Sleeping on the couch. Isn't that funny?"

"Funny." I groaned.

I'd known this conversation was coming, but I hadn't wanted it to be at five thirty in the morning. I blew out a breath. Glancing in the mirror, I was very relieved that I hadn't wandered out of my room looking like a rooster in front of Gavin.

Although, maybe it would've done some good in keeping him away from me. It was difficult, occupying the same space as someone I'd once loved. And someone I'd seen naked just a few days before. Those magnetic forces had descended upon my house, a push and pull that existed between Gavin and me. The constant reminders of the best times of my life along with the worst. It was exhausting.

"I wanted to talk to you about that, honey," I said. "Gavin's going to be staying with us for a little bit."

"Because he's going to be my dad?"

"No, Liv, it's not like that." I brushed her sweet little flyaways back from her face. "Not exactly. We are just going to take things one day at a time and see where things go."

"This is very exciting," Liv said in an even tone of voice. "How come you're not marrying him if you like him so much?"

"These things take time," I told her. "The situation is complicated. Is that okay with you?"

"I like Gavin." She shrugged. "It's fine by me. Fine if you want to get married, too."

"If you have any questions, you can always ask me. Okay?" I ruffled her hair. "Now go get your cereal. Try to be reasonably quiet and let Gavin sleep. I'm pretty sure he's not used to little girls waking him up before dawn."

"I can be quiet," she promised.

As Liv slipped out of the room, I threw a robe around my pajamas. I slicked my hair back into a halfway presentable messy bun. Shoved my feet into old fuzzy slippers. Then I shuffled my way toward the living room to survey the situation.

"Gaaaavviinnnn." Liv was leaned forward, blowing her morning breath right into Gavin's face as she whispered his name at the highest decibel a whisper could possibly go. "Gaaviinnn, are you sleeping?"

"Liv," I hissed. "Didn't I tell you to be quiet?"

"I am being quiet!" She had the attitude of a teenager as she gave me angry eyebrows back. "I'm whispering."

I fought back a severe eye roll and pointed to the kitchen. "March."

"I'm awake," Gavin groaned. "I'm awake."

"See?" Liv turned a radiant smile on me. "See, Mom? I knew he was awake this entire time."

My eyeballs were still sore from their last failed attempt at an eyeroll, and I pressed my fingers to my forehead to release the tension mounting there. It wasn't even six a.m. Lord help me get through this day.

Gavin was already swinging his legs to the floor. He wore sweatpants and a sweatshirt. I was pretty sure he'd overcompensated with the whole not sleeping naked thing and had dressed like he was going on a hiking expedition in the mountains. I'd meant shorts and a T-shirt. But I appreciated the effort.

"What cereal would you like?" Liv asked Gavin. "Trix?" She paused to give the thumbs-up. "Or Raisin Bran?" She gave the thumbs-down.

Gavin rubbed at his eye. He looked surprisingly childish, adorably so. I looked away.

"Do you have coffee cereal?" he grunted.

Liv looked to me. "Mom?"

"Go get your breakfast," I instructed Liv. "And leave our houseguest alone."

As Liv scurried into the kitchen with a few little skips, I turned to Gavin.

"I'm sorry," I said. "I told her to be quiet."

"She was being quiet." Gavin's sleepy expression flashed amusement. "That kid, I tell you."

"Don't I know." I hesitated. "So. Trix or Raisin Bran?"

He burst into laughter. "Just coffee. Don't worry about me. I think you made it pretty clear you didn't want me to impose on anything last night. So just ignore me, go on with your day, and pretend I'm not here."

A little worm of guilt worked its way around my stomach. I felt a little bad after all he'd done for me last night, from picking up Liv and getting her to bed, to thinking ahead to bring me dinner.

"I mean, I guess we can be amicable," I said grudgingly. "I had a talk with Liv this morning. She knows you're not sticking around and she seems fine with it. So I feel a little better about that."

A look of disappointment washed away the amusement that had sparkled in Gavin's eyes, but it disappeared in a flash. I chose to pretend I hadn't noticed.

"Well, I'm glad we got that straight." Gavin rose. "Mind if I shower? I fell asleep before I could rinse off last night."

"Go ahead. You've got a twenty-minute window before Liv breaks down the door to brush her teeth."

"I'll be out in five."

"Gavin!" The shout came from the kitchen.

Gavin looked to me, then over his shoulder. He turned from his march to the shower and headed toward Liv's voice. I followed him closely, unable to exactly identify what Liv was playing at.

I found out a second later when I entered the tiny kitchen. It looked shabbier now that I was studying, picturing how Gavin might see it. The checkerboard floor had chipped tile. The countertops were not my favorite shade of beige. There were still crayon markings on one wall where Liv had colored.

But Gavin didn't seem to care about any of that. He was staring at the kitchen table where Liv had poured two bowls of cereal. One regular sized bowl for herself. One gigantic sized bowl for Gavin. She'd literally poured Trix into a small saucepan. She'd set the lid on top, but it sat askew since the cereal was piled too high. A puddle of milk ran off the table and onto the floor.

"A big bowl of cereal for a Big Gavin." Liv flashed her arms out wide as if finishing her debut on Broadway and seeking a standing ovation. "You're welcome."

"Wow." Gavin blinked. "Thanks, Liv."

"Make yourself at home," Liv said. "Here, I got you a big spoon for your big mouth."

Gavin dutifully accepted a ladle. Then, with a sideways glance at me, he sat before his bowl of cereal. He dwarfed the table, the chair, the entire kitchen. Liv and I weren't used to having guests, and we especially weren't used to having guests the size of Big Gavin, as Liv had fondly nicknamed him.

"Delicious," Gavin said, scooping a ladleful of Trix and taking a crunchy bite. "Tara, why don't you get ready while Liv and I have our breakfast?"

"You can shower," I said. "You really don't have to do this."

"Do what?" He chewed another crunchy mouthful. "I couldn't possibly turn down the delicious feast Liv prepared for me."

I hid a smile at Liv's beaming face. Then I grabbed a towel, quickly mopped up the worst of the milk, and then took

Gavin up on his offer to get ready for the day. For once, I wouldn't have a little girl firing off a bullet pointed list of random but somehow urgent questions while I tried to apply eyeliner.

I got dressed for the day, fixed my hair, took an extra three minutes to really fortify my makeup, and then made my way back to the kitchen. I found Gavin washing his cereal pot while Liv stood on a chair next to him and dried the dishes. They were currently mid-recitation of Liv's one line from the school play. I wondered how long this had been going on for.

I stood in the doorway for a long moment, watching the two of them with a little ball of warmth fluttering in my chest. That ball of warmth was not welcome, but I also couldn't push it away. I'd lived my whole life, at least these last six years, for Liv. Seeing her like this, really happy, made me feel some sort of way.

"Mom. Gavin said he's coming to my school play," Liv said. "He's been practicing with me, but I told him he needs to see it in action."

Gavin looked panicked as my eyes landed on him. "I didn't say that. *She* said that."

"But you didn't say no," Liv said, a look of hurt developing on her face. "You are gonna come, aren't you? It's really important."

"Ask your mother," Gavin muttered, before fumbling the pot against the lid. A loud clatter broke the tension.

"Clumsy Big Gavin," Liv said, laughing. "Wash one at a time."

Gavin had somehow managed to throw on a pot of coffee while also running lines with Liv, and I gratefully helped myself to a large mug. Gavin came over, helped himself to a smaller mug. He was standing too close to me for comfort.

"You're not gonna throw that on me today, are you?" Gavin asked, eyeing my cup of hot caffeine. "I swear I wasn't volunteering to tag along to school plays. Though I'm happy to if you'll allow it."

"We'll discuss this later," I said under my breath. "For now, you're safe from the coffee burns. I know my daughter well enough to know when she's guilty."

I swore Gavin let out a breath of relief.

"About that shower," he said. "Now's a good time?"

"Fine."

"What's the rest of your day like?" he asked. "You've got to bring Liv to school, then what?"

"What's it matter to you?"

"Just wondering if I could tag along."

"And if I say no?"

"I'd tag along, you just wouldn't know it."

"We'll discuss this later."

"Uh huh," Gavin said, and his breath brushed against my ear.

He wasn't trying to be overbearing. He wasn't trying to be close to me. He wasn't trying to be sexy. It just so happened he was sexy, and my kitchen was small, and it was setting my body on the fritz.

It didn't help that he was gentle and playful and kind to Liv, and seeing the joy in her eyes at having a new friend made it damn hard to remember that this situation was doomed to end.

Chapter 16

Gavin

Each day with Tara grew more and more pleasant.

Before either of us knew it, an entire week had flown by, and we'd been settling into some semblance of normal life. The initial shock of the situation had worn off. The urgency seemed to have faded. The danger seemed somehow less.

Really, it had been a boring week. If life could ever be boring with Tara Kendrick. Our lives had settled into a new little routine, but try as I might, I could not get life in the Kendrick house to feel boring.

I slept harder than I'd ever slept in my life nightly on the stuffed old couch. I woke up to a little voice whispering *Gavin* into my face at the crack of dawn, then forced myself to down a pound of sugar that she called breakfast, just because I couldn't find it in me to disappoint Liv. Though I had coaxed her to put away the saucepot and settle for a regular sized bowl, which had certainly helped.

Then Tara and I would take turns getting ready for the day. We'd take turns putting on the coffee pot, taking out the garbage, changing the toilet paper rolls.

At the start of the week, Tara had insisted on driving herself and Liv to school without me. After two days in, she'd grumpily left the passenger door open for me in the morning, and when I'd climbed in, she'd mumbled something about my wasting gas and causing global warming. So that had been the end of us driving separate.

As fast as the last week had gone, however, that meant the time we had left together was shrinking faster than I was prepared for. I knew it was coming to an end. Tara never missed an opportunity to remind me that I was just a "friend" needing a place to stay and would be leaving very soon. She explained this especially loud when Liv was in the room.

But as time went on, I found myself wondering more and more why our time together had to end. I was on my last job. Once we figured out this laundromat shit and the security breach, I was a free man. I had enough money to live on for a long, long time. Eventually, I could figure out what I wanted to do with my life. In the meantime, what the hell was stopping me from staying in town with Tara and Liv? Why did it have to end?

I hadn't had the guts to bring up this new revelation to Tara just yet. Because it wasn't really a revelation. It was just the same thought I'd always had, but now it felt more real, more possible. All I needed was to prove to Tara that I meant it this time. That I wanted to stick around, not only for her, but also for Liv.

"Come on, Gavin. Hurry." Liv peered over my shoulder.

It was six forty-eight in the morning, and we needed to leave for school in four minutes. I was currently wearing my shorts and a T-shirt and hadn't yet showered. I was also holding a pink glue gun while I stuck a popsicle stick to a posterboard.

"No, a little this way." Liv jabbed her thumb to the left. "This guy is supposed to be a walrus."

JINGLE BELL ROCK

I grunted, sticking myself with a piece of scathing hot glue as I adjusted the stupid walrus's tusk. Apparently Liv and Tara had both forgotten there was a school project due today.

The morning had been a frenzy as Tara had snapped at Liv to pay more attention in school, and Liv had snapped back that she was just a child. I'd stepped between them and taken charge of the project so that both women—the little and the big one—would survive the morning rush hour.

"We've got to go," Tara hollered. "I've got a new client to meet this morning. I cannot be late."

"But Wally needs another tusk!" Liv shrieked. "Do another tusk, Gavin."

I felt like I'd just qualified for the Boston Marathon as I held up the posterboard and declared Wally to be a perfectly two-tusked walrus ready for the car ride.

"He's not perfect," Liv said. "His tusks are crooked."

Tara paused, fastening a necklace, to look at the posterboard. "Did you make him cross-eyed on purpose?"

"If you two ladies are so hellbent on having a perfect Wally, do it yourself," I huffed. "I was on a time crunch. Sorry he's got crooked tusks and eyeballs."

Tara's face crumpled into a smile. "Sorry. Thanks. He's the spiffiest walrus I've ever seen."

"You said hell," Liv said. "You owe me a quarter."

I made sure my next curse was under my breath. I was racking up quite the swear jar tab. Fortunately, Liv informed me that she accepted Venmo or Paypal. Which was good because I was going to need a 30-year loan to cover my debt at the rate I was going.

As the two girls rushed toward the car, I followed, still unshowered and dressed like a homeless man. Then again, I was sort of homeless. And I'd showered the night before. But showering twice a day was sort of a need for me. Seeing Tara walking around half naked in her pajamas was doing a number on me. Mentally, physically, sexually. Did I mention sexually? And mentally? And physically?

I'd taken to wearing jeans around the house more than I'd ever worn jeans before. Mostly because one wrong look at Tara, and my cock started to raise like a damn flag.

I tried to stop it. I couldn't help it. I had tried everything. Counting tiles on the kitchen floor. Looking for patterns in the popcorn ceiling. Reciting Liv's line from the play over and over again in my head, just to keep my blood in my head and not my dick. Nothing worked, though a couple of long showers per day seemed to help. Slightly.

I'd always thought Tara was beautiful. I'd fallen in love with her years ago, but somehow, I loved her even more now. She'd grown more and more beautiful with age. Then there was the whole playing house situation that was going on.

It was my biggest fucking fantasy of all, seeing her in the kitchen, barefoot, hair tousled from sleep (or preferably sex), kids running underfoot. It was everything I'd ever wanted. And almost had. But the picture of it played with my heart, played with my desires.

I wanted her so badly I craved the taste of her. The only reason I forced myself not to make a move on her was because I couldn't tempt her into kicking me out of the house. If I couldn't have Tara as mine, at least I could help keep her safe. Then, maybe, I could finally leave here with a clear conscious when Tara declared our playtime over.

The only light at the end of the tunnel was that I knew Tara wasn't unaffected by my presence. We'd bump into each other once in a while; the house was small, after all. She'd jolt back like she'd walked into an electric fence.

I caught her watching me occasionally, often when I was with Liv, with a sort of faraway look in her eye, and it made me wonder if she was visualizing what this might look like for real. It wasn't all that much of a stretch to imagine. Because we were here, living this reality, day in and day out.

Tara finished ushering us into the car and cruised to Liv's school like she was being chased by a bat out of hell. She all but skidded into the drop off line and planted a kiss on Liv's head with practiced ease, then all but shoved her daughter out of the car.

"Wait, Mom. Gavin too." Liv turned, holding her janky Wally poster in her hand, and came around the car to the passenger door.

When I opened it, she leaned in and gave me a little kiss on the cheek.

"Thanks for your help," Liv said. "Don't forget, Gavin, you have to practice lines with me tomorrow. The school play's in less than two weeks."

"Aye, aye, Captain."

I gave Liv a salute. It was all I could manage. It was the first time Liv had planted a kiss on my cheek like I was someone she really cared about. It made my withered heart swell with something that felt a lot like love for that pistol of a little girl. I purposefully didn't make eye contact with Tara as she pulled away.

Finally, as Tara crept to the other end of the parking lot, I felt her gaze burning holes in my head.

"What?" I said, a little bit snarly, as I whirled to face her. "I didn't ask for that. And you can't possibly expect me to treat that adorable little girl like a piece of shit so she doesn't like me. I'm sorry that you're not happy right now, but if it helps, I care about Liv too."

Tara blinked, looking completely surprised. "I was just going to ask you to buckle up. The bell keeps dinging."

"Oh." My feathers properly ruffled, I jabbed the buckle into the fastener. "Right."

Tara drove quietly through Fantasie past The Bean Counter, the best local café, and toward the tiny office space she owned on a side street off the main drag.

"I appreciate you treating Liv like she really matters," Tara finally said, speaking so quietly I had to strain to listen to her. "I've given up hoping that it won't hurt her when you leave. Of course she'll miss you. She missed you after we Skyped for Thanksgiving, so I guess we'd already dug that hole a long time ago."

"Really?"

"You're all she asked about for a week. When you showed up, I'm pretty sure she expected it. Not, like, she was psychic. Just that she liked you so much she assumed you'd be coming around again."

"About that. Tara, I was thinking—"

"I hate when you start out conversations like that. They never end well."

"What if things don't have to end?"

"Are you crazy?"

"I feel very un-crazy. In fact, it feels sort of wild to me that we ever figured this had to end. I mean, what's stopping us from being together? *Really* being together?"

"Lots of things." Tara's knuckles grew whiter as she gripped the wheel. "For starters, I told you not to get any hairbrained schemes in your head. I am not looking for a relationship. You living in my house does not constitute a relationship. You befriending my daughter does not mean I have to fall in love with you."

"Maybe not," I said. "But what if you could fall in love with me just because?"

The look in her eyes was almost murderous. "I did fall in love with you, Gavin Donovan. I promised myself I'd never do it again."

"Yeah, well, it's too late for me," I muttered.

"What'd you say?" she demanded, veering the car into a parking lot so violently the front wheel bumped up on the curb, and there it stayed.

"You just gonna park halfway up the sidewalk?" I asked her. "You're blocking pedestrian traffic."

"What'd you say?" Tara's voice was level, her gaze loaded as she stared at me.

Just then, my phone rang. I wiggled it. "I've got to take this. Sorry."

I slid out of the car, well aware I looked like I belonged at the gym and not standing outside of Tara's place of business. I would've been a little more embarrassed if I wasn't so busy fuming at the way our conversation had gone.

I was mad at myself for caving and broaching the subject without thinking it through first. I knew it was a question that should've been handled delicately, especially since the very topic could put us at such odds that she'd kick me out of her house, risking her and Liv's safety.

I was equally mad that Tara wouldn't even entertain the conversation. From everything I could see, we liked being a part of one another's lives. I knew in my heart that I'd never let her down again. I was struggling to find ways that I could prove to her I wasn't the same man who'd left town all those years ago.

"Hello?" I answered. "Any news?"

"We've got an updated location on Andrea. She's on the east coast. Jersey." Carter sighed. "I just wanted to let you know. We're trying to keep our eye on her, but you know Andrea..."

I grunted. "Unfortunately. You think she's involved in the laundromat scheme?"

"That's what you're supposed to be figuring out," Carter said. "Watch your back. Andrea won't take kindly to this little engagement thing you've got going on. You know she never got over the fact that you wouldn't flip for her."

I pinched my forehead with my thumb and forefinger. "How'd you find Andrea?"

"Facial recognition from one of the video feeds we had set up on another laundering site. A little deli in Jersey. Andrea was seen going inside last night. This morning, the news hit that the owner of the deli turned up floating face down in a nearby lake."

"Ouch."

JINGLE BELL ROCK

"You heard from Mikey yet?"

"He just got in earlier this week," I confirmed. "He's around, doing his thing."

Mikey was a one-named wonder who had worked for The Company in the past but now freelanced. He had the sort of face that women would describe as average. Handsome, but not standout. His build was medium. Not too tall, not at all short. Not a dad bod, but not huge muscles. The guy could blend in anywhere. He could be a soccer dad one morning and a Wall Street financier by evening.

I'd hired him on my own dime to help me keep eyes on Tara for the last week, and as far as I know, she was completely clueless about the fact that there was a new set of eyes on her. Mikey was damn good at his job, which was exactly why I'd hired him.

"I'm glad to hear it. And Gavin—don't underestimate Andrea this time, or you might not get lucky a third chance." Carter paused for a beat. "Oh, and tell my mother hello."

Chapter 17

Tara

Ever since Gavin had brought up the unspeakable question in the car on the way to my office a couple of days ago, I'd danced around him like he was a firecracker ready to go off at any moment.

We'd been doing so well cohabitating, living in a cozy little bubble. We'd both known that bubble would eventually burst, like all bubbles do, but we'd found a way to enjoy the situation while it lasted.

Until Gavin had gone and blown it out of the water. Blasted it away like Squirtle while still halfway in the drop off line at school. Gavin had gotten Liv into Pokémon, and now freaking Squirtle had worked his way into my vernacular. Not to mention the new poster of Wally that Liv had insisted we hang in our living room since it'd earned her a gold star.

So for the last three days, ever since Gavin had abruptly dropped me off at my office then began looking glowering and snapping into his phone, he hadn't brought it up again, and neither had I. We'd both retreated into our separate bubbles, but it somehow felt a little less shiny, the walls a little thinner, the whole biodome ready to collapse with one gust of wind.

I'd been even more surprised this morning when Gavin had encouraged me to drop Liv off at school by myself. I'd done a double take, then did as he'd said because, after all, that was what I'd been asking for this whole time—for him to leave us alone.

Liv had pouted the whole way to school. She'd barely scrounged up a kiss for me at drop off because she'd been convinced it was my fault that Gavin had stayed home. And really, it *was* my fault. It killed me to see my daughter feeling so down about it. But what was the alternative? Letting her get attached to a man who, historically, disappeared without warning?

I was now at my office, a tiny little studio that was the cheapest office space I'd been able to find in walking distance to The Bean Counter. I had one desk and a coffee maker I rarely used.

I didn't need much; I used this space to do my paperwork, meet with potential clients, and store some of the supplies. It did the job, and I loved my little nook. I remembered the day I'd gotten the keys to it, the day it felt real, like I'd *actually* started a business. Even now, walking through the door of my own office never ceased to give me a little hit of dopamine.

"Oh. Hello." I stopped as the little bell I'd installed jingled as I entered my office. "Um, how'd you get in here?"

A woman stood. She'd been sitting behind the desk, her blond hair cut in a neat little bob. She turned, smiled.

"Oh, hi. You must be Tara." The mystery guest stood and extended her hand. "The door was unlocked. I emailed you about a meeting?"

"You did?"

"I'm Finlay Cometeer. I'm new to town," she said, then gave a little shrug. "I know I'm a little early, so I figured I'd just wait inside for you."

I glanced at my watch. "You're an hour early."

Then I looked sideways at the door as if the handle had unlocked by magic. As far as I knew, I'd never left the door unlocked. I made a note to check if Millie might've stopped by with the spare key. I doubted it because she usually would tell me, but I supposed it was possible.

"I thought you might be in early." Finlay thumbed at the door. "When I tried the handle and it was unlocked, I figured I'd just wait for you. I've only been here a minute or two."

"Okay. Well, I guess we'll get started then. Can I grab you a coffee?" I gestured to the machine and made my way around to the other side of my desk. "What brings you in today, Ms. Cometeer?"

"Finlay." The woman gave me a little smile as if I was an insider on some big secret that was her name. "Please, it's Finlay. As I mentioned in my email, I'm in the process of moving to town. I'm thinking of hosting a New Year's Eve party as sort of a housewarming thing for some friends. I hear you're the best event planner in town."

"Can I ask who referred you?" I asked.

"I forget his name," she said. "I was in the coffee shop, and your name was tossed out when I asked around. I looked you up, emailed you, and the rest is history."

"Do you have a budget in mind? A theme?"

JINGLE BELL ROCK 211

"Budget's not really an issue." Finlay wrinkled her nose. "As for theme, I'm thinking extravagant. Maybe Great Gatsby?"

"We can definitely do that." I pulled out a notebook and started jotting down some notes. "And you want the actual date to be New Year's Eve?"

"Yes, please. Are you free?"

"I have a small event earlier that day. But let's discuss a little more—I might be able to have my assistant take the lead on that one to free up my time for your party."

"That would be lovely. I really would just like to work with you." Finlay smiled. "I'd pay a premium."

"Not necessary," I said. "Where'd you say you're moving to? I assume you're buying a property?"

"Oh, yeah, on the outskirts of town." Finlay waved a hand. "I'll send you the address."

"I was born here, so I know pretty much every property. Is it the old Hanson place?"

"I can't remember. My real estate agent handles the transactions for me." Finlay's smile turned a little crooked.

"Can you excuse me for a minute?" I asked. "My daughter just texted, and I need to give her school a call really quick."

"Of course." Finlay sat back in her seat. "Kids come first."

As I made my way out of my office and toed the curb, I dialed Gavin's number. Something wasn't sitting right in my stomach with this woman.

"Gavin," I said when he answered. "What does your ex-girlfriend look like?"

He gave a sharp inhalation of breath. "Petite, dark hair. Blue eyes. Thin nose. Why? What's wrong?"

"There's a woman at my office who had set up a meeting with me, but I don't know. Something seems off. I just thought..."

"Fuck. Stay right where you are." The line disconnected.

I stared at my phone, a little shocked that he'd hung up on me. I was in the middle of feeling a little bit miffed about his quick dismissal of my phone call when a tourist climbed out of his car in the parking lot.

"Excuse me," I said, as the man walked by me, a little too closely.

The man had a ball cap on his head, a camera strapped around his neck. His white socks were pulled up too high. His cargo shorts were almost comically full of stuff in his pockets.

The man stopped next to me. "You know where a guy can get a bite to eat around here?"

"Yeah," I said. "The Bean Counter is that way. Best coffee you'll get for sixty miles."

"Great." He grinned, then gave a nod. "I'm Mikey, and I'm a friend of Gavin's. Okay if I poke my head into your office?"

My head spun. First, at the rapid whiplash I'd gotten from assuming the guy was some random tourist. Second with the realization that the fact he'd gotten here so quickly was probably a testament to the fact that Gavin had been having me followed. Watched.

"No, it's not okay," I said. "Did Gavin hire you to stalk me?"

"I'm not at liberty to say. I'd just like to—"

"Fine. Whatever," I snapped. "But just FYI, you're fired."

Mikey gave me a good-natured salute, then strolled toward my office. He pulled the door open, poked his head inside, then pulled his head back out.

"She's gone," he said. "You called Gavin about a woman in your office, right?"

Obviously the reason Gavin had dropped my call like a hot potato was so that he could get on the phone with his tourist-buddy named Mikey.

On one hand, it seemed so completely unreasonable that the man in front of me could work for the likes of Gavin. Gavin was all tall muscle and brooding eyes. He *looked* like he could be an assassin. Mikey looked like he was ready to cheer on his toddler at dance camp, then take his family out for burgers and fries afterward while wearing his high school ball cap.

"Yes," I said. "Finlay can't be gone. There's only one door. I mean, there's a back door that leads to the storage room, but that was locked."

Mikey inclined his head toward the door as if asking permission to enter. "I doubt it's locked anymore."

I threw my hands up. "Do what you need to do, I guess."

Mikey did another of his salutes. Then he took off his sunglasses, his fanny pack, his camera. The ball cap got spun to the side so it was more naturally cockeyed. And like that, I realized that Gavin's hiring of Mikey was not silly, it was ingenious.

The guy could fit in anywhere. He'd fooled me, and of all people, I should've been able to recognize someone who didn't belong in Fantasie. I'd believed him to be a tourist without a second thought.

The squeal of wheels sounded as a car flew into the parking lot. I knew who it belonged to before I turned around. Mikey slipped through the door to my office like he had no interest in being around when I got a chance to lay into Gavin. I didn't blame him. Even I didn't want to see what I had to say to Gavin. I was feeling pretty annoyed about this mystery man stakeout business.

Gavin got out of his car. Made his way to the sidewalk. The first word I'd use to describe his expression would be livid. The second would be terrified. I figured that my face probably told a similar story.

"What the hell, Gavin?" I threw my hands up for the second time. "You were having me followed?"

"I had to take care of something this morning." Gavin practically spat out the phrase as he stepped onto the sidewalk. He put his hands on my shoulders, studied me, as if looking for dents or scratches. "Where is she?"

"I don't know. Your buddy Mikey is in my office now. He said she's gone."

Gavin bit his lip, and I couldn't figure out if he considered that to be good news or bad news.

"Fuck, Tara. I'm sorry. I should've never left you alone."

"That's exactly the problem. You *should* have left me alone. What were you thinking siccing some private investigator on me?"

"Mikey's not a private investigator. He worked with me at The Company for a while. He's the best at what he does."

"Then what would you call it?"

"Protection," Gavin said. "Because obviously, we have an issue here. And you're blind if you can't see that."

I felt my eyes well with tears. "You're an asshole, Gavin. I didn't ask for any of this, okay? Have fun with Mikey. Maybe you can bunk with him from now on. Obviously, he's in town. Obviously, he's watching me anyway. I don't think you should stay with us anymore."

"Tara, you're overreacting."

"I'm overreacting?" I shook my head. "I don't think so. I just want my life back. My normal, boring life. Yes, I realize I stayed at your inn, but that doesn't make any of this my fault. The engagement is off."

"There you two are."

Gavin looked as shocked as I was that someone had encroached on our territory without either of us noticing. Then again, we'd both been pretty heated, our eyes locked on one another.

I spun around, pulse racing, to find Lily Donovan, Gavin's aunt and the owner of the Fantasie Inn, standing behind me. She was a tiny woman in a pretty white dress that just about dwarfed her with the amount of fabric fluttering around her feet. When Lily smiled, it was impossible not to return the gesture.

The little laugh lines around Lily's eyes creased, her teeth showed, a sparkle crackled in her eyes. She seemed positively thrilled at the mere thought of being alive. At once, I felt almost guilty at the streak of rage burning inside me. Another of her smiles, and I felt the flames of my annoyance extinguishing further.

"Hi, Lily," I said, swallowing the biting remarks I'd been saving for Gavin. "It's good to see you."

"It's Aunt Lily now." Lily laughed, then handed over a bouquet of tulips. "I can't believe the two of you haven't made it to one of my Friday dinners yet since you've been engaged. Gavin, I'm disappointed!"

"It's busy season," I said weakly. "I've been working a lot."

"That's not an excuse." Lily waved a hand. "I always knew the two of you would find a way to cycle back to each other. Like I told Lucas when I heard the news, it's always been fate."

Gavin and I stood next to each other. I couldn't look at him. Our little ruse was seeping into more corners of our lives than I'd ever anticipated. When Gavin had handed over the engagement ring at me, I hadn't had time to think about how our little ruse might affect others. Other people who might be hurt when they found out they'd been deceived. I'd been so tunnel vision focused on my life and Gavin's, and the intersection, that everything else had fallen by the wayside.

"Uh huh," I grunted.

"We're thrilled," Gavin managed with a throat clear.

"So, a Christmas Eve engagement party then?" Lily asked. "Surely the two of you will be celebrating the holidays together. Why not use the opportunity to get together with family who"—she paused, poked Gavin in his massive chest—"haven't seen the likes of you *once* since you've been in town."

"I've been working on the inn," Gavin said weakly.

"And spending your evenings here holed up with Tara." Lily winked. "Not that I can blame you two for wanting some alone time. Tara, your daughter must be thrilled at the idea of a wedding for her mama?"

"She's feeling some type of way," I hedged.

"I hate to cut this short, but Tara here was just on her way to a client meeting." Gavin leaned in, kissed his aunt on the cheek. "It's been great seeing you, Aunt Lily."

"Of course. Honey, I'm going to get on the phone with your mother." Lily pointed at me. "I don't want to usurp mother of the bride duties, but I think a Christmas Eve engagement party at the Fantasie Inn would just be..." She did a chef's kiss with an extra loud smack.

"Right," I said. "I'm sure my mother would be thrilled to hear from you."

"Yes, let your mother and I fuss over the details for once. You just show up looking like your ravishing self," Lily said. "And you two, get yourselves to a Friday night dinner before I have to send Lucas and Noah to kidnap you."

We waited, both with awkward smiles on our faces, while Lily whisked herself and her flowy dress off in the direction of Main Street. Once she was out of sight, and the parking lot was abandoned, I took the liberty of whacking Gavin in the chest with my bouquet of tulips. A few petals hit the ground, which was a real shame.

"You jerk!"

I raised the tulips again, fully intending to give him another thwack with the flowers, but Gavin's hand came up and encircled my wrist, stopping me in my tracks. His entire hand fit around my arm like it was a pencil. His touch stilled me. I hated that he still had this effect on me, even when I was fuming mad.

"You did this to me." My eyes filled with tears that cascaded down my cheeks. "I never wanted to hurt anyone, and now this whole thing is turning into one giant mess. Fix it, Gavin. And then get out of my life. For good."

Gavin took my other wrist in his hand, he pulled me to him. Close, too close. I was inches from him. His eyes softened, a true cocktail of sadness and fear and frustration.

"I'm sorry," he whispered.

Then he let my wrists go. I let my arms drop, the tulips dangling from one hand. I gave a nod. Then I got into my car, took a few deep breaths, and drove away, his eyes following me all the way out of the lot.

Chapter 18

Gavin

"What'd you find?" I stalked into Tara's office, letting the door swing shut behind me. "Was it her?"

Mikey turned from where he'd been kneeling before the back door studying something. "I didn't get a glimpse of her. Andrea was waiting for Tara, so I didn't see her go in the building, and she snuck out the back while I was busy out front."

"Right, but it had to be her, right?"

"I'd say so." Mikey took a few steps toward the desk.

He reached over, picked up a short, handwritten note. He slid it across the white surface toward me. I took one look at it and cursed.

Gavin,
She's pretty.
—*A*

"Fuck," I said again, holding my head in my hands. "How did Andrea get this close to her?"

"I'm sorry," Mikey said, "but you'd just asked me to tail your girl. I didn't know you wanted me to clear places before Tara went inside."

"Nah, it's not your fault. I didn't think Andrea would be this daring. Things are escalating faster than I expected."

I could see the camera and fanny pack he'd been wearing sitting on the desk. He still looked like a tourist. Nobody in their right mind would guess the man was an incredible shot and one of the sharpest minds The Company had ever seen.

"What's going through your head?" Mikey asked.

I licked my lips, sat in the chair opposite Mikey. He sat, too.

"I'm pissed. Terrified," I admitted. "Tara could've been killed today because I let my guard down."

"You can't protect everyone all the time," Mikey pointed out. "Look, I talked to Carter before I took this job, and he warned me this job would be dangerous in a personal way. Andrea is pissed at you and obsessed with you, and that's a dangerous combination."

"That night, Andrea really thought I'd switch sides." I shook my head. "I don't know why she ever thought I'd flip and work with her, betray The Company. I'd never insinuated anything of the sort. And when I held my ground, threatened to turn her in..."

"I know, trust me," Mikey said. "But it's obviously left Andrea with a bad taste in her mouth. I imagine that's only gotten worse, now that you're happily engaged to another woman."

I raised my eyebrows. Mikey raised his eyebrows back.

"I'm not here because of the money, Gavin," Mikey said. "I'm here because I owe you one. This is my one."

"Just keep Tara safe," I said. "She peeled out of here. Can you do me a favor and go after her? I have a feeling she'll be annoyed if it's me watching her today."

Mikey's hand drifted near his waist, and I was sure there was at least one weapon hidden in those bulky pockets of his dad-pants. "Sure can. But I need you to keep me in the loop, or someone is going to die. What else do you know about Andrea?"

"I've heard she's cleaning cash for the guys in the Jersey mob. That's what the laundromat is supposedly all about just outside of town. My guess is she lays low for a few days after a stunt like this."

"Where'd your girlfriend go?"

"I'll text you the address," I said. "Tara's on a job this morning."

I pulled out my phone and sent Mikey the details. He slapped me on the shoulder as he left the room. I took that to mean we were all good. Even though things weren't good.

Then I sat in the chair for a long, long time. I watched my phone until Mikey texted me that he'd caught up with Tara. True to form, she hadn't skipped out on work, even though she would've had every right to head home and hole up in bed for the rest of the day.

But the Tara Kendrick I knew and loved would put on a brave face and show up at her job no matter what. As I sat in her office, I glanced around at the sparse furnishings. I pictured Andrea sitting here, encroaching on my space—*her* space. I knew Andrea had selected Tara as her target because Tara was the closest thing to a weakness for me.

I wondered what Andrea looked like now. I'd need to confront Tara sooner rather than later to interrogate her about the details. She was the only person who'd seen Andrea recently enough that we might be able to get a sketch artist on it.

But I figured Tara needed some time to cool down from the incident. I also figured that Andrea would already be changing her appearance again, chameleon that she was. After all, that's what The Company had taught her to do, and she was highly trained and intelligent, if nothing else.

I figured I'd give Tara the day, seeing as Mikey would be watching her like a hawk, and I'd talk to her tonight after Liv was in bed. When I could have her full attention and really plead my case. That is, if she let me in the door.

I stood, headed out of the room, locking the door behind me. When I turned, I started as if I'd seen a ghost. In a way, it felt like I was dredging up a ghost of relationships past, seeing as the last time I'd seen Cathy Kendrick in person had been thirteen years prior.

"Gavin." Tara's mother smiled at me. "Fancy seeing you here."

"Mrs. Kendrick. Hi."

Tara's mother studied me closer. "I just got the funniest call from Lily Donovan."

"Oh?" A pit developed in my stomach. "I was just coming to chat with my daughter about it, but I suppose you might have some answers for me."

Cathy Kendrick was even more petite than her daughter. But somehow, even though I was looking down at a tiny, five-foot-tall woman, I felt like I was a shrimp. I wouldn't have minded sinking right into the pavement.

"Is that right?"

"Your aunt seems to think that you and my daughter are engaged. I hadn't heard the news." Cathy's voice was piqued with curiosity. "I know a good man like yourself wouldn't have asked for my daughter's hand in marriage without asking for permission first."

"Right." I coughed. "I'm sorry about that. It's just—"

"Don't tell me it's an outdated practice." Cathy's smile turned even sweeter. "Don't tell me my daughter is an independent woman and can decide who she wants to marry all by her lonesome. I know all that."

"Well—"

"I know you, Gavin, and I think you're honorable enough that you might've thought to mention it to me beforehand. Heck, even after-hand. Why am I finding out about an engagement party for my daughter from someone else?"

My mind raced through any sort of reasonable explanation. For starters, I couldn't believe that Tara hadn't gone ahead and shared the news with her mom, false or otherwise. I knew how close the two were. I knew how much it must have pained her mother to find out from a third party. I was completely baffled as to how I'd ended up feeling gunned down in broad daylight by Cathy's questions.

"I think you should talk to your daughter about that," I said. "I'm sure she wants to share the news with you."

"You know..." Cathy pressed a finger to her lips. "When I heard Lily Donovan sharing the news, at first, I was hurt. I was about to burst into tears. My only daughter, who I love more than anything in the world, keeping secrets from me of this proportion?"

I wasn't sure where this was headed, though I was pretty sure it wasn't the time for me to start fucking my way through a lie of an explanation.

"Then, I realized that something felt off. And I've learned to trust my instincts over the years, and I just couldn't shake the feeling that something wasn't right. So,

I went ahead and gushed with Lily about how exciting it is that the two of y'all are getting married." Cathy shifted high onto her toes then settled back onto her feet in anticipation. "But I know something isn't right here, Gavin."

"I'm sorry?"

"Don't apologize to me, young man. Look, I gave you the benefit of the doubt. My granddaughter seems to love you. My daughter seems inexplicably drawn to you. That was a real sweet thing you did for our family on Thanksgiving."

I cleared my throat.

"I got to thinking that maybe you've really changed over these last thirteen years. Maybe Gavin Donovan is worth all that trouble he put my Tara through." Cathy licked her lower lip. "But now I'm starting to think that trouble just follows you all around."

I stared into Cathy's eyes. Her gaze was searing, as if she was x-raying me on the spot. It took a minute before I could speak around the knot in my throat.

"You're right," I said softly. "Mrs. Kendrick, I'm sorry."

"Sorry for?"

"For coming back into your daughter's life at all. I understand I'm causing her nothing but trouble," I said, meaning every word of it. "I also knew that I couldn't possibly stay away. I've never stopped loving her."

"There's got to be a huge *but* somewhere in this story."

"The situation is complicated," I admitted. "Just give your daughter the benefit of the doubt. Don't hold anything against her—she'll tell you the truth of it all when she's ready. Just keep in mind, none of this is her fault."

JINGLE BELL ROCK

"I don't like you talking in circles around me, Gavin Donovan." Cathy blinked. "I can remember the way my daughter looked at you, even as a teen. I saw the way her world was wrecked when she lost you. Don't you dare hurt her again. Or else."

Cathy Kendrick tapped her purse, her head of gray curls flopping back and forth with the threat. I wasn't sure if she had knitting needles in that floral bag or a loaded pistol, but I was pretty certain it was a threat. And I was pretty sure she was good for it.

I reached forward, grabbed Cathy's hand. "I need you to understand one thing, Mrs. Kendrick. I have always loved your daughter. I would never, and will never, voluntarily hurt her."

Cathy stared at me for a long, long time, those calculating eyes watching mine. She gave a nod, as if whatever she'd seen was to her satisfaction.

"Very good then, Donovan." Cathy gave me a cheeky little smile then, and another nod. "I don't know what's going on here, but when you decide to marry my daughter for real, you come to me first. Understand?"

"Of course, Mrs. Kendrick."

"Good. Now buy me a coffee like a good son-in-law. A decaf. My nerves are already in tatters today." Cathy Kendrick hooked her arm through mine, and before I knew it, we were promenading down Main Street toward The Bean Counter for the entire world to see.

I wasn't sure exactly what had happened. I wasn't sure if I was supposed to be happy about it or terrified. But I was pretty certain I knew one person who would be livid.

Chapter 19

Tara

"You did *what* with my mother?" I lowered my voice, then repeated. "Gavin Donovan, get your ass in here. My phone has been blowing up all day long."

Gavin looked properly sheepish as he stepped into my house. When I'd received the first text earlier in the day about Gavin and my mom seen together at The Bean Counter, I was mostly confused. Then I'd gotten three more texts of a similar nature with all sorts of winks. Then had come the demands from my friends for more information. Ironic since I was the one who wanted more information, first and foremost.

"This is a good start," Gavin said dryly. "I was pretty sure you'd pepper spray me upon sight. I'm happy to see it's only words you're shooting my way."

"Don't tempt me." I turned and stalked into the kitchen, keeping my voice in a pissy whisper. "The only reason you're here is because we need to talk. Then you're kicked out."

"Understood."

Gavin flicked on the kettle with the comfort of a person who lived in my house. Still annoyed, I went over and yanked the kettle off its base.

"Don't make yourself at home," I instructed. "Sit down and start explaining."

"Your mother confronted me," he said. "Me buying her a coffee was basically a hostage situation."

I was pretty sure my jaw was hanging open. "You're going to need to rewind the tape a little further. You're talking about my gray-haired, book club obsessed mother?"

Gavin looked longingly at the kettle. I lifted it and dumped the water into the sink. He sighed.

"I'm sorry about earlier. I owe you a big apology about how I reacted to the situation," Gavin said. "You have to understand, Andrea is—she gets under my skin. It's been a long haul."

"I *don't* understand. You've been telling me about twenty percent of the story. So how could I possibly understand?"

"Sit," Gavin said. Then, seeing my face, he tried again. "Please sit and hear me out. Then I will leave."

I grabbed a beer. I didn't offer him one. Then I sat.

"I told you about my history with Andrea. We dated, but that's not where things ended." Gavin gave another heavy sigh. "Our breakup was messy, as you know. Afterward, she developed an odd sort of obsession about it. She couldn't understand why I wouldn't turn against The Company to be with her."

"Okay."

"Meanwhile, I'd been realizing that I'd never actually loved Andrea. I'd loved the idea of her, the face she presented to me. But none of that was real."

"I get that," I said softly. "I felt the same way with Liv's dad."

"You haven't told me much about him."

"Because I don't owe you any information. It doesn't involve you," I said. "Unlike your dating history, Liv's dad might've pissed me off, but he's not stalking me."

"Fair."

"Have you had contact with her after she tried to gut you?"

"Not explicitly," he said. "Though there've been times I wondered. Times when I'd be in a grocery store and think I saw her, moments I'd notice a car tailing me. Stuff like that. Nothing concrete."

"You think she's been watching you?"

"More like keeping tabs on me. Understanding what I'm up to." Gavin cleared his throat. "Making sure I'm not getting too happy and content without her in my life."

"How sure are you that it was her in my office?"

Gavin pinned me with a look. "She left a note. About you."

"What'd it say?"

Gavin fished it out of his pocket and passed it to me. I read it, feeling a shiver rock my spine.

"It worked then," I said. "Our fake relationship. It was the bait you needed to draw Andrea out of hiding."

"It fucking backfired," he grumbled. "She got closer than she was ever supposed to get."

"What now?"

"I'd offer to break up with you and leave town, but I just don't think anything good will come of that. Andrea's too close. She has you in her sights, and she doesn't let things go easily. She's competitive to the nth degree. I don't think she'll just forget about you because I leave town."

"Not to mention," I chimed in, "you'll be looking over your shoulder until you catch her."

"While that's true, if I thought leaving was the way to protect you, I'd leave in a heartbeat and gladly look over my own shoulder the rest of my life. I just don't think that's the answer."

"I think you're probably right. So what's next?"

"Well, you've made it clear that I'm kicked out of the house, so I'm going to do my best to keep you and Liv safe from a distance."

I bit my lip. A part of me wanted to let him stay. I could see how much it pained him that he was causing such complications in my life. But I wasn't ready yet to welcome him back into my safe little bubble with Liv.

"Gavin!" A tiny little screech interrupted our conversation. A moment later, a flurry of princess dress and ruffled hair bolted across the room and shot into Gavin's arms like a cannonball. "Where were you after school?"

"Gavin's actually not staying with us for a while," I told Liv. "He's found alternate accommodations."

Liv frowned. "That's not fair. You promised he'd be here through Christmas."

"I didn't promise anything," I said. "I just said he'd be staying with us for a little while."

"You *said*!" Liv emphasized with a pouted lip. "You specifically said. You can't break your promise. He was gonna get me a Christmas present, I just knew it."

"She can't remember to wash her hands after playing outside," I muttered to Gavin, "but she remembers every word that comes out of my mouth."

"Gavin." Liv turned very seriously to him. "We have to get a Christmas tree tomorrow. It's the weekend. Mom said we could get a tree. We were going to cut one down ourselves."

"No, we weren't," I said. "We were going to buy one from the store."

"Well, you always said we needed someone big and strong to help us carry a tree," Liv said, once again showing off her penchant for selective hearing. "Gavin is big and strong. Big Gavin, you can carry a tree, can't you?"

"I, uh..." Gavin specifically didn't look at me. "I've been known to carry a tree or two in my day."

"I told you so." Liv informed me with a haughty head tilt. "So I guess that settles that."

"Gavin's not staying here," I said. "He's busy tomorrow."

"My school play is next week. I am going to be very, very disappointed if you don't show up." Liv talked to Gavin sternly. "You'll be there, won't you?"

"Get back in bed, Liv," I said gently. "It's very late."

Satisfied, Liv gave Gavin a pat on the head. Then she leaned down and gave his knee a little peck, probably because she couldn't reach his cheek.

I extended my arms for a hug, but Liv was already rushing out of the room, calling behind her, "Goodnight, Mom."

I shot Gavin a look filled with poison darts.

"Don't look at me like that," Gavin said. "I didn't ask for any of this."

"Do you see the mess you've caused?"

"I can apologize until the cows come home," Gavin said. "Unfortunately, the only way out of things is through it at this point. Sorry, sweetheart."

I bit down on my lip, feeling tears prick my eyes.

JINGLE BELL ROCK 231

"I respect you to the ends of the earth, Tara." Gavin stood. "I care about you. I care immensely about Liv. And from the bottom of my heart, I'm sorry."

I gave a reluctant nod as he made his way toward the door.

At the last second, Gavin paused, turned around to face me in the kitchen. "And I'll apologize in advance, but there's no way in hell you're keeping me away from that damn school play."

"But—"

"It's open to the public."

Then Gavin turned on a heel and let himself out the front door. I wasn't sure which part changed my mind. The way he was leaving peacefully, without pestering me to stay? The part where he seemed hellbent on not letting Liv down in any way possible?

I stood, hurried to the front door. I yanked it open, a cold wind blowing at me. I saw Gavin hunched over as he made his way to the car.

"Hey, asshole," I called after him. I raised a blanket I'd grabbed off the back of the chair. "Make your shower fast. I'm going to bed."

Gavin did his best to hide the little grin that appeared on his face.

"I'm not happy about this," I informed him, as he returned inside the house. "I'm not doing it for me, I'm doing it for Liv's safety."

"Trust me," Gavin said. "I can tell how much you hate it."

Chapter 20

Tara

I'd had plans for how this day was going to go in my head. I'd already prepped myself for another year of a small Christmas celebration with just our little family. Me, Liv, my mom. It was the way things were around here. I'd never in a million years imagined someone else coming into our house and encroaching on our Kendrick traditions.

And yet here Gavin was, boomeranging back into my house. My life. My family. And if he had it his way, my heart.

I had no intention of letting Gavin get his way. The only thing he'd consistently brought into my life was trouble, and I wasn't looking for trouble. I was looking for stable. A stable husband. A stable father figure. A stable man to be by my side day in, day out—or no man at all.

Yet here he was, asleep on my couch. It looked like someone had appeared and dropped a lumberjack on my sofa. One of Gavin's arms was stretched up and over the back of the couch. His legs were all askew in a position that couldn't be comfortable.

I wasn't sure how the physics worked with Gavin's huge form actually fitting on the couch, and a part of me felt a little pinch of guilt at shoving him there. But I didn't have a guest room, and he wasn't sharing my bed, so those were the breaks.

The part I didn't expect to see, the part that made annoying body parts of mine tingle, was the part where Liv was perched atop Gavin like a little parrot. She'd folded her legs under her body, pulled a blanket around her shoulders, and balanced a cereal bowl in her lap. Her eyes were glued to the television where some obnoxious cartoon was blaring. Gavin seemed to be completely oblivious to the fact that a little girl had parked herself on his chest.

"Liv!" I hissed. "Get off Gavin. Let him have his space."

"I woke him up." Liv turned to me with those wide brown eyes. "I asked if he wanted to watch cartoons with me. He said yes, but…" She gestured down at the lightly snoring Gavin as if that explained everything.

"Get down," I said, reaching for her. I lifted her right off Gavin's torso and set her on the floor. "Don't sit on people."

As I headed to the kitchen, I filed that in the list of weird things you say when you have kids list. Right next to "Why are you naked?" And "What's in your mouth?"

I made coffee. Grudgingly, I set out an extra mug. Gavin had earned his morning caffeine when he'd effectively turned into a table for Liv's breakfast bowl.

The coffee pot was just finishing when the floor creaked behind me. "Liv, you have to eat something else besides Trix—"

I sucked in a breath when I found Gavin standing in the doorway. He looked like the last piece of dessert I really, really wanted to eat but knew I probably shouldn't. He wore a thin T-shirt and gym shorts. His hair was mussed, his eyes sleepy, his five o'clock shadow making him even more lumberjack-ish than usual.

"Oh, it's you," I said. "Good morning."

"I could probably stand to eat less Trix too," Gavin said evenly. "I've had more Trix in the last couple of weeks than in the whole rest of my life."

I barked a short laugh. Then I fixed on a much more annoyed face.

"That for me?" Gavin watched my face and delicately changed the subject.

He'd spotted the extra cup of coffee. When I nodded, he helped himself, brushing past me. The heat that burned off him was like one of those old radiators that'd scorch you if you touched it. He was my walking, talking radiator.

"I've got good news for you." Once Gavin had taken a sip of coffee, he turned to face me. "I was up late. Hence the reason I couldn't keep my eyes open for Paw Patrol this morning."

"Oh?"

"I spoke to Carter this morning. Claudia, one of the computer geniuses at The Company, was able to break into Andrea's computer. She got some good intel on the aliases Andrea has been using, including credit card numbers, burner phones, that sort of thing. Claudia thinks she might've found a couple of addresses that could lead us to find where Andrea's holing up."

"Wow. That's great news. And fast."

"I work with a good team. Claudia's the best." Gavin gave a nod. "Anyway, I thought you'd be happy about it. As soon as Andrea's taken care of, I'll be out of your hair."

"You keep saying that." I reached into the fridge, pulled out some creamer. I added a hefty amount to my coffee, watching it bloom into a milky shade of latte. "*Take care of*

JINGLE BELL ROCK

Andrea. What does that mean? You're not the police. You can't just arrest her. Right?"

Gavin shifted uncomfortably. "Sometimes we work with the police."

"That doesn't answer anything."

"Do you need an answer? I think the less we discuss the details, the better."

"You told me you don't freaking kill people."

"It's not like that," Gavin said. "Nobody's killing anyone. Hopefully."

"You say that like it's supposed to make me feel better."

"We're teaming up with the feds," Gavin said. "Hopefully we'll be able to pass them the information they need to make the arrest in time. If Andrea's as associated with the Jersey mob as we think she is, then it'd be under their jurisdiction."

"So many alarming things in that sentence. Also a helluva lot of 'hopefully.'"

"Andrea moves fast. She can be hard to keep up with."

I gave a shake of my head. "I don't like any of it. So, I guess, I hope this Claudia's as good as you say she is, and the FBI can arrest her before…"

"I have another proposal," Gavin said.

"You've proposed to me one too many times, Donovan."

That got a laugh out of him. It made me feel good. Then annoyed at how much pleasure I got from making Gavin Donovan smile. We'd been under a lot of tension lately, and I hadn't realized how much I'd missed seeing his smile.

"Can we start over?"

I stared at him. "How many times do you think we can just start over?"

"I don't mean totally. I just mean, can we wipe the slates a little bit so we're not making each other's lives miserable for the next few days?"

"You're not making my life miserable," I lied. "That would mean I cared about you one way or another."

Gavin eyed me like he knew I was a complete liar. But he was kind enough not to call me out on it. "You let me stay here last night. I appreciate that."

I grumbled something. Even I wasn't sure what I'd intended to say.

"Look, I really enjoy Liv's company. Maybe we can lay down our pepper spray canisters and just enjoy the next few days. Even if you can't do it for me, can you do it for Liv? Give Liv a fun holiday season."

"She'd have a fun holiday season even if you weren't here. We've done it the last six years."

"Sure. But you can understand what I'm asking. If we're stuck together for the holidays, at least maybe we can make it a memorable one for Liv. I'd hate her festive spirit to suffer because I had to stick around."

I considered. I did know what he was asking. It was exhausting living with a person when we were both always on edge. I hated it. And frankly, I couldn't keep up with the list of reasons I wanted to stay mad at Gavin.

Sure, he'd gotten us into this mess, but I knew deep down he hadn't meant to. He was a good person who'd been dealt a difficult deck of cards. At the core of things, he was doing what he could do to protect me and Liv. Maybe that counted for something.

"It will make things easier on both of us," Gavin said, still rolling with his argument. "I'll be able to concentrate better on work if I'm not concerned with breathing wrong around here."

I crossed my arms. Gave him a good, solid glower. He got points for not flinching.

"Then in a week or two, I'll kindly say goodbye to Liv. I'll give her a nice Christmas present to make the parting easier. I'll keep in touch with her, if you'll let me. A few phone calls a month until she's forgotten all about me."

I swirled my coffee. Took a sip. I'd added too much cream, and now it was cold. I drank it anyway.

"Fine," I said.

"Fine?" Gavin's eyebrows shot up.

"I don't have much to lose, I guess," I said. "Either way, you're gone soon enough. I guess we can call a truce on everything that's been said so far. But our truce goes out the window if you piss me off again."

"Fair. I'll do my best not to do any such thing." Gavin extended a hand. "Shake on it?"

I steeled myself for his touch. When our hands clasped, Gavin took a step closer, and I smelled him—fresh, woodsy, a hint of cinnamon. I wanted to keep moving forward until I could lean my head on his chest. The memory of his hands on my body, of his ragged words whispered in my ear, burned bright. I forced myself to step back.

"Thank you," Gavin murmured.

The ending music to the cartoon rang, and sure enough, Liv sauntered into the kitchen a few minutes later. "Great, you're both up. Time to go get our Christmas tree?"

Liv looked between us expectantly. Gavin raised his brows and looked in my direction for guidance. I shoved the remainder of my cold cup of coffee in the microwave and hit the power button.

"Who knows where one can cut down a Christmas tree?" I looked at Gavin over Liv's head. "If you're staying here, you can earn your keep and chop us down a tree."

Gavin's eyes sparkled. "I know just the place."

Chapter 21

Tara

Gavin's special place was behind the only mechanic's shop in Fantasie.

"This is my cousin Noah's place," Gavin said as he parked the car in a long, snowy driveway. A neon sign that said **NOAH'S** pretty much gave that away. "He's got a couple of acres. Told us to pick any tree we wanted so long as we don't chop it down on one of the cars in the lot. He's not working today, or else he'd say hi."

"I know Noah," I pointed out. "I do live in Fantasie, and I own a car. He's my mechanic."

"Right." A flush appeared on Gavin's face. "I forget you know more about my family than I do at this point."

We climbed from the car. Liv hauled her sled out from the back.

"Pull me, please, Horsey!" Liv plopped into her sled and waited expectantly.

"She's talking to you," I said to Gavin.

"Horse-y?" Gavin echoed faintly.

"This is my horse drawn carriage, and I'm the snow princess." Liv sounded as if that were the most obvious announcement in the world. "I need a horse, and you're the biggest person here."

"Right," Gavin mumbled. "Horse it is."

Gavin reached for the string attached to the sled and pulled it along behind him, watching cautiously to ensure Liv stayed firmly on the sled. He made it look like she weighed nothing more than a pillow. I knew, from many years of being the horse, that wasn't the case.

"Don't you need to neigh?" Liv asked. "You *are* a horse."

"Yeah, Gavin," I said, unable to stay mad at the man who was pretending to be a horse for my daughter's sake. "Let's hear a whinny."

"I'm not fu—" Gavin stopped himself before he could add to his swear jar debt. "I don't know how to *neigh*. I'm like... a strong and silent sort of horse."

"That's interesting," Liv said. "But I've never heard of a silent horse before."

"Now you have," Gavin said.

I couldn't help but crack up into my mittens as I strode onward. Gavin's face, when Liv had asked him to neigh, had been priceless. A little slack-jawed, a little incredulous, a little terrified.

I had to give the man credit. Gavin had been a good sport all day. Before we'd even left the house, Gavin had helped to fasten Liv into her pink snowsuit—she'd insisted it be him and not me to zip her up into her marshmallow attire. He'd then loaded up the car with sleds, a thermos of hot cocoa, and the menagerie of stuffed animals that Liv had wanted to bring along for the ride.

Gavin had proceeded good-naturedly to pretend that he knew the words to most of the Christmas songs. The only reason Liv hadn't noticed that Gavin knew jack about Christmas lyrics was because she'd been belting them loud enough for all of us.

"Okay, what are you ladies thinking?" Gavin asked. "See any good trees around here?"

"You're not very good at being a silent horse," Liv noted.

Gavin chomped on some gum. "Uh huh."

"That's still not silent."

Gavin gave me a pleading look over her head.

"I mean, she's got a point." I couldn't help my grin. "Then again, you could always just neigh and get it over with."

Gavin stared toward the high heavens, and I sort of wondered if he was hoping the clouds would part and dump a snowstorm on us so we'd be forced to turn tail for home. When no such thing happened, he continued marching forward while Liv gave a dominatrix-style yank on her pretend reins.

As Gavin and Liv traipsed through the snow, I followed at a much more relaxed pace behind them, enjoying the rarity of not being the one needing to provide entertainment to my daughter for once. Liv was, for lack of a better word, completely smitten with Gavin. No amount of my interference or reminders that he wasn't here to stay seemed to make a difference.

And yet, I could hardly blame Liv for how she was feeling. Didn't Gavin have the same effect on me? For all the trouble he'd brought into my life, I still found myself thinking about him when I shouldn't be. My mind wandering while I strung up mistletoe for my clients, wondering what my life might look like if all of this were real. If Gavin's reentry into my life, my home, and even that stubborn little piece of my heart that wouldn't let him go...wasn't just a ruse to keep my family safe.

What if we *could* become a family? Of course I had reasons that things shouldn't work out with Gavin—our past, my commitment issues to men, the fact that he was staying with us because of his crazy ex-girlfriend—but all of those reasons seemed to crumble away during moments like this. Moments when Gavin played the part of doting husband and father a little too well. Moments when Liv looked up at him like she wanted him to stay. Moments when I remembered the feel of Gavin's skin on my body, the way he moved against me, the way we meshed so perfectly together in so many ways... Until we didn't.

Maybe the problem was that a part of me wanted this. The same part of me that would never—*could never*—completely fall out of love with Gavin. The piece of me that had pictured this moment since I was a little girl. Gavin doting on what could have been our daughter, winking over his shoulder at me, sending the blood rushing through my veins in a way that nobody had done before him or after.

I sipped my toasty hot chocolate, reveling in the quiet of the moment, trying not to feel the racing heartbeat, the instincts screaming at me to beg Gavin to stay. To make this moment real. To be the man that I'd always wanted him to be for me, and now for my daughter.

I smiled at Gavin as he made good on his word of being a silent horse. Liv hummed "Jingle Bells' under her breath. Flakes of snow drifted tenderly down from the sky, gifting us the perfect day for a Christmas tree hunt.

My mittens wrapped around my mug, and I felt snug and warm in the almost-thirty-degree day. Our feet crunched through the perfect couple of inches of crisp snow that'd fallen the night before. We'd already made it well out of range of Noah's garage, and the only thing in sight was miles and miles of glittering white on the ground and trees stretching bare limbs into the skies above us. Plump green evergreens. The occasional command from Liv.

"Whoa, Nelly!" Liv shouted. "Whoa means stop."

Gavin looked at me.

"She's talking to you," I clarified again.

"Right," he said, looking at Liv as if she was far more intimidating than a tiny girl armed only with faulty logic and enthusiasm. "Can I speak now?"

"Sure," Liv agreed. "I guess you don't have to be a horse anymore. Now you can be a lumberjack."

"Wonderful." Gavin swiped his hat from his head. "Have you decided on your tree, Little Princess?"

Liv laughed at the nickname, and it struck a funny chord in me. He'd called me princess on occasion back at the inn, and I'd known he was doing it with sarcasm. But when he sweetly teased my daughter, it hit differently. It hit deeper than I felt comfortable admitting.

"This tree." Liv plopped out of her sled, took a moment to right herself. Once she was on both legs looking like a pink marshmallow, she wobbled ahead and pointed to a tree that was technically more of a stick in the ground with a few little branches tottering out of it. "This is the one. Our Christmas tree."

"It's a little small?" Gavin ventured.

"It's really cute," Liv squeaked. "It's just the right size for my stuffed animals and Fin and me."

"You make a solid argument." Gavin knelt next to her.

I gave them their space, feeling like this was something for them to do together. Liv had always, always wanted to cut down her own tree. I didn't own an ax. A saw. Whatever the hell a person used to cut down a tree. I didn't love the snow. I didn't trust myself to do it alone. This was the first year we hadn't been alone.

"Will you help me?" Gavin asked. "I need someone with big muscles."

"Yeah, I can do that," Liv said. "I ate my peas last night."

"Then you should be good to go with those guns." Gavin retrieved the saw he'd hauled with us. "Come here, careful now."

My heart raced a little faster, the way it did anytime little kids and big tools were in the same space bubble. But I forced myself to stay back. I trusted Gavin. I knew Liv was as responsible as I could hope for a little girl. I liked the image of them together.

My fluffy pink marshmallow sat on Gavin's lap, crunching her face up in serious concentration as she focused on helping Gavin drag the saw across a tree trunk that couldn't have been thicker than a number two pencil. I was almost certain Gavin could've snapped it right off with a nail clipper, but he let Liv take a few good slices before he made the cut himself and let the tiny tree flop onto the snow.

"Timber!" Liv announced gleefully.

"I mean, I could've done that myself if I'd known that was the sort of tree she wanted," I offered, but Gavin only gave me a cheeky little wink. He returned Liv's little embrace.

"And how about for you?" Gavin's drawl as he spoke to me was low, warm, soothing.

"I guess we should probably find one that can actually hold an ornament since we're out here."

"Your choice," Gavin said. "Your wish is my command."

Every one of his words seemed to be layered with a little something more, but I couldn't tell if I was reading into things, or if it was actually happening. I took another sip of hot chocolate, letting it warm my belly, before I set my sights on a perfectly slim but very full five-footer. I pointed it out. Gavin winked at me, proclaimed it a done deal, and my warm belly did a little flip flop. Were we moving back to flirting territory?

"All right, Liv," Gavin said. "I'm going to need you to whip out those muscles again."

As Gavin carefully guided Liv to help him with a few novelty strokes of the saw against the larger tree's base, my eyes smarted with tears. I hadn't thought of Liv's father much since he'd left.

He'd left abruptly, firmly, with no remorse. Not so much as a glance over his shoulder. We'd been engaged, both in agreement on the fact that kids were an option in the future, but not a necessity. We'd been in happy agreement that we would make the decision day by day, year by year, as our lives progressed. If we decided to try for children, so be it. If we never got around to it, we'd both been fine with that too.

So when I'd gotten pregnant while on birth control, he'd given me two options. Terminate the pregnancy or he was leaving. It hadn't taken me more than an hour to pack his bags and set them on the porch for him to collect after work.

He'd never called. Never asked to meet Liv. I hadn't kept up with him. He'd never lived in Fantasie on his own. We'd met while he was on a temporary job in the area, and he'd decided to stay. But when our relationship had gone up in flames, so had his ties to our little town.

It was pretty incredible how closely two lives could be intertwined in one moment, and then in the next, the bond completely severed. I'd pleaded my case for him to stick around and meet his daughter exactly once. He's said it wasn't the right time. But as soon as I'd seen the positive marking on the pregnancy test, I'd known in my mama heart, that wasn't true. It was exactly the right time.

Now, years later, I'd finally come to terms with the fact that the timing had been even better than I'd thought. In retrospect, I was grateful Liv had happened before I'd married that asshole. While our parting had hurt, it'd been simple on a logistics level. No messy divorce. No shared house.

But my history didn't help the fact that I was feeling a little skittish with the way Gavin was wiggling his way back into my heart now. Both men I'd loved had left abruptly, without leaving room for me to have a say in things. Was it any wonder I didn't trust the men that I loved?

"Okay, go stand back by your mom," Gavin was saying. "I'm going to use some real lumberjack muscles to get this tree down before we lose feeling in our toes."

Liv skipped back toward me, resting one hand on my hip while she watched as Gavin bent forward and worked the saw against the trunk. I loved it, those little touches she gave me without realizing it. I remembered the days when it was just me and a little baby, and the way I would feel so touched-out by the end of some days. A little girl, desperate for me and only me, without much of a support system. It had been exhausting.

My mother had been around to help, but she'd been going through chemo around the time Liv had been born. She'd had enough of her own issues to deal with, so I'd done my best to put on a brave face and do it all myself. Because that had been my only option.

Now, those touched-out days were long past, and I mourned Liv's quickly escaping childhood. Feeling a surge of love in my chest, I knelt down, clasped her to my chest, and hugged her to me. She let me hold her as we watched Gavin chop down the tree, and it was my own little Christmas wish come true.

"Timber," Liv announced again, this time with more reverence, her eyes gleaming. "Do you see that, Mom? It's the perfect tree."

I swiped at my eyes. Swallowed around the dryness in my throat. "That's gonna look good at home."

"Can we decorate it tonight?" Liv asked. "Please?"

"Of course," I said. "I don't see why not."

Liv rushed to help Gavin load the tree onto the sled. He let her think she was helping a heck of a lot more than she actually was, but if I'd had to judge by the grown-man level of groans Liv was giving out, she was lifting the whole dang tree by herself.

Once the big tree and the baby tree were flopped onto the sled, Gavin sidled over to me. Without seeming to notice he was doing it, he swept the portion of my hair visible beneath my hat away from my face.

"You good, Tara?" he asked roughly.

I blinked up at him. "Yeah, fine."

"You sure?" The way Gavin studied me, serious, concerned, had my heart racing.

"Yeah," I said, gave a shrug. "Just having a nice time."

"Yeah," he murmured. Then he looked over to where Liv had just fallen on her behind while trying to pull the sled forward. "Me too."

"Come on, Horsey," Liv instructed. "Time to pull the sled before we freeze our toes off. And can I get a ride on your back like a real horse?"

"Guess I'm up to bat." Gavin gave me a cute little wink as he headed for Liv.

In one motion, he scooped her up with one of his big lumberjack arms and settled her easily onto his shoulders. Liv shrieked with glee, then gripped onto him like her world depended on it. She gave a little buck of her legs and shouted for him to, "*Giddyup.*"

Another wink from Gavin to me as he picked up the rope to the sled and started off. And, as they marched on ahead of me toward home, I might have even heard the faintest sounds of a neigh making their way out of Gavin freaking Donovan's lips.

Chapter 21

Gavin

I hadn't had a day like this in years. Hell, maybe ever.

Growing up, my mom had been lackluster at best at remembering there was a holiday at all, let alone taking the time and effort to celebrate it. And even if she'd remembered, and even if it'd tickled her fancy to celebrate that year, we hadn't had the funds to do much of anything anyway.

I did remember chopping down my own Christmas tree one year. I'd sniped it from behind Jerry's Grocery, a little pine that'd been barely as tall as I'd been at the time. I couldn't have been much older than Liv.

I'd dragged the damned thing home myself, propped it up in a five-gallon bucket full of water, and had proudly waited for my mom to notice. When Christmas Eve came and went, and Christmas Day came and went, and there were no presents under the tree—and I was well and truly pissed that Santa had forgotten my house again, I'd dragged the tree back outside and left it on the sidewalk. That was the last time I'd tried to celebrate Christmas with any real oomph.

Then I'd gotten older, and I hadn't cared as much. Or I'd pretended not to, even as other kids showed up at school with new clothes and gadgets, while I had my same scuffed shoes and holes-in-the-knees jeans. I'd done a good job of learning to blend into the background.

Of course, Aunt Lily had shuffled a few new items to me here and there, which I greatly appreciated in retrospect, but at the time it'd felt like charity. I could see now, through my adult goggles, that Aunt Lily hadn't meant it that way at all.

But it was hard not to get a little bitter about it when the emotions of a teenager were messing up all trails of logical thought. I'd been torn between accepting Lily's kindness and feeling damn embarrassed at the fact that I needed to.

Then there'd been the last ten years in the California penthouse. My maid had once put a fake little Christmas tree on my counter. I hadn't mentioned it, and it'd eventually disappeared as quietly as it had arrived. That had been her first and last attempt to coerce me into the holiday spirit.

"Did you ever have a tree as big as this one?" Liv asked as we fastened the tree to the car. "This is the biggest tree I've ever seen in my whole entire life."

"Nope," I said, meaning it. "This is the biggest I've ever seen too."

I caught Tara looking at me, and there was a part of her gaze that I could tell meant she thought I was just saying things to make Liv happy. But the longer she stared at me, the more I could tell she wasn't taking me at face value. That she was really, truly trying to read if I were telling the truth or not.

But today wasn't a day for sob stories, mine or anyone else's. Today was a day for celebrating, if for no other reason than because a little girl deserved it, and damned if I was going to ruin this holiday for her.

"Climb in, girls," I said, as I finished fastening the tree onto the roof of the car. "Time to head home."

Tara's cheeks bloomed a bright pink at my words, and it took me a second of rewinding to understand exactly what

JINGLE BELL ROCK

I'd said. I hadn't meant anything by calling Tara's place *home*, but I could see how she might feel some type of way about it.

Once my girls were situated in the car, and I had double checked the tree was on the roof good and tight, I slid in the passenger's seat next to Tara.

"Sorry," I said, soft enough so that Liv couldn't hear. "I didn't mean anything by it."

"I know," she said. "It's fine. I didn't think twice about it."

That was a blatant lie, but before I could wonder what that meant, Liv poked her head in between the front seats. "Can we stop for a cappuccino from The Bean Counter?"

Liv was looking at me, so I glanced to Tara. "Are we sure she needs coffee? Seems to me she's got enough energy without the caffeine."

Tara burst into laughter. "She *thinks* she's ordering a cappuccino. Chuck gives her warm milk with whipped cream."

"In that case, drinks are on me," I said. "If it's okay with your mother."

Tara's breath caught in her throat, and I had a hard time figuring out why until I realized that ordering at The Bean Counter would mean we were going out in public, the three of us, for no real reason at all. The sort of thing real engaged couples did.

Of course, I'd been trailing around town behind Tara like a puppy dog since I'd moved in a few weeks back, but that's all it had been—me trailing behind her. Riding along to school drop offs and pickups. Tagging along to job sites, sometimes lending a hand when she needed help hauling stuff. That sort of thing. We hadn't ever actually been out in public together, on purpose, for fun.

"Please," Liv wheedled. "It's a special occasion."

"Fine," Tara said. "But just a short stop. We'll take our drinks to go."

We made it to The Bean Counter, a little café built into one of the many brick buildings on Main. The owner, Chuck, was short, round, dark-haired. He had two sleeves of tattoos from his days as a motorcycle guy and a handlebar mustache.

He'd taken over the place before I'd ever left town, and he'd gutted the building and made it new and shiny on the inside, while the outside blended into the quaint face of the town's main tourist drag.

Driving down Main Street with a tree strapped to the car had me feeling like we were in some damn Hallmark flick. I'd never once compared my life to a Hallmark movie, but this evening felt like we were in some sort of snow globe, trapped here until the glass shattered and the prettiness inside spilled into the reality beyond its walls.

Christmas lights flickered from every storefront. It was late afternoon, and already the sun had mostly set, leaving the city in a sparkling blackness that glittered like gemstones. Santa figures perched on roofs, waving mechanical arms. Rainbow colored lightbulbs dangled in storefront windows. Little tendrils of smoke curled up from chimneys.

I hadn't been back in town for Christmas since I'd moved away. I'd been invited every year by my Aunt Lily, but I hadn't been able to shake the feeling that it was charity. The same feeling that had dug its claws into me when she'd slip new socks and underwear into my closet, and I'd shamefacedly mutter a thank you when we passed in the hallway at one of her Friday night dinners.

It'd been easier to just stay at home in my penthouse over the holiday season with the ready-made excuse that I had to work. Which was usually true, technically. The security business tended to ramp up during the holiday season—high profile people gave concerts, traveled to events, visited family. It'd never been hard to pick up hours and keep plowing right on through the holidays like they didn't exist except in some parallel universe.

It was a little shocking to me to see not only the lavish Christmas displays all down Fantasie's Main Street, but it went beyond that. The sheer camaraderie that Fantasie managed to pull together during the holiday season was outrageous.

People who normally wouldn't be seen together banded together to raise food for those who couldn't afford it. The Fantasie Quilter's club gave away blankets they'd made in droves. There were little holiday parties every day of the week, and it seemed everyone and their mother was invited.

I'd barely made it known that I was back in town, and already I had an invitation to Holiday Happy Hour at The Cow Tipper, my cousin's local bar. I had an invitation to the community theater production of The Sugarplum Fairy. And of course, there was the Christmas Eve engagement party that was being thrown for me and my fake fiancée by my very own family.

Tara parked the car, and the second I stepped outside, we were greeted by a group of carolers barreling their way down the street. They were more intimidating than a pack of bulls, and I stepped out of their way before anyone tried to rope me into singing another damn Christmas carol. Liv had already exhausted my repertoire of known songs, though that wasn't saying a lot.

"There you two are." Clarice, the Fantasie town psychic (self-declared), popped out of the caroling group. She wore a plush burgundy cape that looked like it was real damn heavy, and she grinned at me first, then at Tara. "I'm so thrilled to see you two stepping out in town together. Long overdue."

"Clarice," Tara said evenly. "Good to see you too."

Clarice was a tall, lean woman who had delicate facial features and golden blond hair. She was almost elvish in nature, or at least, maybe that was just because she was wearing a pointy, burgundy velvet hat with piles of fur lining her face. It matched her cape and made her seem very fantastical indeed. Very Narnia.

"I'm looking forward to your engagement party," Clarice said. "Have you set a date for the wedding yet?"

"No," Tara said. "If you don't mind, Clarice, maybe you could just let us have our privacy with the engagement. It's very new."

"Of course," she said with a wide smile. "I predict a spring wedding. That should give him time enough to heal."

"Heal?" I asked, my tone feeling gravelly as it came out of my mouth. "What are you talking about?"

"From—" Clarice started, but Tara stopped her mid-sentence.

"I appreciate it, Clarice," Tara said. "But we're running late for something, and your caroling troupe seems to be missing you."

Clarice winked. "Of course. Good evening. Enjoy yourselves."

That little wink seemed like Clarice was letting me in on some secret. Unfortunately, I'd missed whatever the actual secret was and shrugged it off as another of Fantasie's quirks.

"What do you think she means by heal?" I walked ahead of Tara, pulling open the door to The Bean Counter. "That's a bit cryptic."

Tara sighed. "Clarice loves to be cryptic. I wouldn't read into it. For all we know, she's talking about healing your chi-energy or something. Forget she said anything. She still thinks we're getting married. A real psychic would be able to tell this was fake, don't you think?"

Tara flashed her hand at me, and I realized she'd put the diamond onto her finger. I hadn't pinpointed the time she'd actually started wearing it, but it gave me a shiver down my spine. I told myself that the only reason I felt anything about her wearing a ring on *that* finger was because it meant she was committed to finishing out this little ruse together. Definitely not because I liked pretending it was real.

The warm air whooshed over us, and I let our little interlude with Fantasie's token psychic fade into the cool air behind us. A bell chimed merrily as the three of us entered. A fire roaring in the hearth welcomed us with feisty crackles, and the Christmas tunes filtering through the speakers got Liv all sorts of revved up as she recognized another one of her many spirited jams.

"What can I get the three of you?" A young barista I didn't recognize smiled at us from behind the counter. She wore elf ears and an elf dress and a little elf hat. If I didn't know how much this town truly loved Christmas, I'd think the locals were downright mocking it. But no, this was real, and the young woman behind the counter seemed genuinely cheerful to be serving coffee dressed like one of Santa's helpers.

"One cappuccino and a cookie, please." Liv was on tiptoes peering over the counter at Chuck. "The biggest cookie you have, if possible."

The elf gave a little tinkling laugh. "Of course. And for you, Tara?"

"Decaf café au lait? No, wait." Tara furrowed her brow. "I'll take your light roast café au lait. We've got a tree to decorate tonight, and I'm thinking it'll be a late one. I'll need the energy."

"The same," I barked, well aware I sounded like an idiot, speaking too quickly, too loudly. I'd never heard of a café au lait before. A damn ice cream cone could turn up for all I knew.

Tara stared at me. The elf nodded happily and punched something into the register. Liv surveyed everything like she was the project manager.

But this situation was sort of making me see black around the corners of my vision. It was too real. Too perfect. Too ideal. A beautiful woman wearing the ring I'd put there. Her adorable daughter looking at me like I was some sort of hero lumberjack who'd saved Christmas. Me, feeling like the Grinch, knowing that things would have to come to an end.

Once Liv was satisfied with our order, I extended my credit card to her and she took it, handed it over to the high-

JINGLE BELL ROCK

ly caffeinated elf. She had to be highly caffeinated for her face to be so smiley and cheerful all the time, right?

Then Liv retrieved my credit card and led the way to a little table near the hearth. I caught Tara's longing glance toward the door, but I wasn't going to be the one to throttle Liv's enthusiasm. Apparently Tara wasn't either, so dining in it was.

A few minutes of Liv kicking her legs merrily from her chair, and a large platter arrived in front of us carried by none other than Chuck himself.

"We didn't order that," Tara said, frowning as she saw the large cast-iron pan filled with an ooey, gooey chocolate chip cookie. "Liv just wanted one of those little regular cookies."

"The warm cookie's on the house," Chuck said, clapping a hand to Tara's shoulder. "Congratulations to the three of you. I hear some bells are jingling in the future, and they've got nothing to do with Clarice's caroling squad out there."

"Ah, yes. This." Tara stared at the ring on her finger like it was an errant piece of lint. "Thanks. So happy."

I caught Tara glancing over at Liv, as if hoping that Liv wouldn't notice this chitchat about bells. Fortunately, Liv was so engrossed in the steaming cookie before her that she was oblivious to anything happening around her.

"It's hot," Tara said, grabbing Liv's hand and pulling it back. "Wait a minute, honey."

A woman from the quilter's club or whatever the group of women sitting in the corner of the café stabbing needles together like they were going to murder someone was called, shuffled on over and elbowed Chuck out of the way.

"Congratulations, you two lovebirds. Nice to see you out and about." The woman, barely five feet tall, draped a blanket full of holes around Tara's shoulder. It was then that I recognized her as Ruby, one of the old principals at the elementary school. "I crocheted you a special bridal shawl. I'm working on a blanket. I'm using this yarn that supposedly promotes fertility or something like that, so I'm hoping Liv won't be an only child soon."

Tara's face looked like it was melting. She cast a worried glance at Liv.

"Is it still hot?" Liv asked, still blissfully oblivious to her mother's discomfort.

"Yes," Tara said. "Can you go grab us some waters, Liv?"

Liv leapt out of her chair with the same enthusiasm as if she'd been tasked to find gold in the wild west, and Tara expelled a breath as soon as her daughter was out of earshot.

"Thanks so much, Ruby," Tara said with a smile that looked painful with every second it lasted. "I really don't need a bridal shawl, but—"

"Nonsense." Ruby patted Tara on the shoulder. "I knit one for every bride in Fantasie. Well, every bride that I like. Granted, that list isn't all that long." Ruby paused with a frown. "I do like you, so a shawl it is."

"Wow. High praise," I said with a smile at Tara while she glared back at me.

"I'm about halfway through the fertility blanket. It'll be done in time for the big day. Which is when?" Ruby raised painted on eyebrows that nearly reached her frizzy perm. "So far as I know, nobody's seen a date go on the calendar yet."

"No date," Tara muttered. "We're counting on a long engagement."

"Uh huh," Ruby said with a wink. "That might change once I get my fertility blanket your way. Then again, I'm not sure if the two of y'all are gonna need help in the baby making department."

Tara choked on air. "What's that?"

"It seems like the two of you have been holed up in a little love nest since you got back to town." Ruby's eyelashes fluttered. "I assume there's a good, reasonable explanation for that."

"Right," Tara said, after a coughing fit so strenuous I was seriously worried her eyes might pop out of her head. "A good excuse. I've been *working*."

"*Hard* work." Ruby winked again. "I'll leave y'all to your cute little family date. Looking forward to the engagement party."

"So you did hear about that," Tara groaned. "That's really happening?"

"Everyone's coming," Ruby said. "It was supposed to be small, but I guess word got out, and so..." She shrugged as if to say there was nothing to do about it now.

Liv came back at that very moment. "Is it still hot?"

"Dig in," Tara said without even looking at the dish.

Ruby skittered away. Tara fended off a few more congratulatory advances from good-intentioned locals. Mostly good intentioned locals. There were a couple I was convinced were just jonesing for intel as to the wedding date, but the rest seemed to be genuinely happy for Tara.

And, I supposed, for me. Though I could count on a couple of fingers the number of people who'd said a word to me, while it seemed just about the entire town had something to say to Tara and Liv.

As a young man locked eyes with Tara and seemed to beeline for the table, I saw the look on her face go from tolerable to plum exhausted.

"Hi, Trevor," Tara said. "Nice seeing you here."

"Congratulations," he said. "I heard the Donovan family was expanding, and as Lucas's assistant at the law firm, I just wanted to extend—"

"Thanks, Trevor." I added an uber cheerful smile. "Appreciate it, but we're actually on our way out. Talk more soon."

I stood, giving Trevor who was, I was sure, a perfectly nice young gentleman, a love tap on the shoulder. He lurched forward like he'd been burned. Tara gave me frowny eyebrows, but the relief on her face told me a different story.

The three of us filed back out of the café, carrying with us the tiny bit of cookie that was left and Tara's café au lait that she'd barely had time to sip because of all the interruptions.

"That was fun," Liv said. "We can still decorate the tree tonight, right?"

"Sure." Tara closed her eyes briefly as we reached the car.

"Let me drive," I volunteered softly, resting a hand on her shoulder.

"It's not far," Tara said. "I can drive."

"I know you can. But let me. Please."

I spun Tara toward me so she could see that I didn't mean anything by it. A little assist to a woman who looked like she was going to fall asleep sitting up. Tara thought on it for a minute, and I could see the independence in her warring with the tiredness. Finally, she gave a single nod.

When Tara fumbled over the keys, my hand closed around hers, and she left hers there for much longer than I expected. I stilled, not sure where to go from here. I wanted to respect her boundaries but I also didn't want to push her away.

"Thank you, Gavin." Tara leaned up, gave me a little peck on the cheek.

I felt like a fucking teenager who'd gotten a body part signed by an idol, like I never wanted to wash that cheek again. The kiss had been tender, genuine, and though it was probably just for looks since the entire town was watching from the café windows, I'd take it.

"Thank you?" I echoed.

"Don't you see the look on her face?" Tara nodded toward the car without turning her head, as if she didn't want to tip off her daughter that we were talking about her. "Look at Liv's eyes."

I looked, right over Tara's shoulder, to the little cherubic face staring out of the window. Liv looked like an angel seated in the backseat. She'd rubbed a small circle to clear the fog from the windowpane, and her face was perfectly framed by little ice crystals. Liv's cheeks were pink. Her eyes glittering. She was waving with vigor at the café windows, probably to the quilter's club, of which Liv seemed to be an honorary member.

"She's not always like this," Tara whispered, "and Lord knows I don't want to admit it, but the only difference I can figure is you."

"I'm just new and shiny. It'll fade."

"Yeah. I guess." Tara's face fell a little.

"But it doesn't have to fade." I reached a hand out, touched her chin.

The two of us were impossibly close, a little halo of streetlight circling us. The carolers down the road were at a pleasant distance, and only the gentle hum of music reached our ears. Light glowed from windows all around us, the charm of this town un-fucking-mistakeable. A group of people that loved their own. A group of people who watched over Tara and Liv. A group of people who were cautiously happy for Tara while rightfully wary of me, the outsider.

"You can't possibly mean that." Tara's eyes watered. "We're playing house, Gavin. It sucks. Liv loves you, no matter how much I've tried to keep her from getting attached. I feel so awful for letting things happen this way."

"Hey, baby." I tilted her chin upward, unwilling to tear my eyes off this selfless woman's gorgeous face. I memorized every line, though it was familiar now—already memorized thrice over. "I love her too. In my own way, I mean." I cleared my throat. "I hope that's not weird."

"Of course it's not weird. Who doesn't love Liv? She's..." Tara shrugged. "She's lovable."

"And so are you, Tara. I've never stopped loving you."

"You don't mean that."

"I mean that with every fucking fiber of my being, and all you have to do is say the word and let me prove it to you."

"There is nothing about our situation that says stable. I need stable in my life. I need it for Liv."

"I can give you stable." My words felt like tires on gravel as I spoke, low, husky, feeling like I'd won the lottery with this tiny, tender spark that I had to keep alive at all costs. "I can give you whatever you need."

"We can't have a one-way relationship," Tara said. "What if we can't give you what *you* need?"

"I only need one thing."

"What's that?" Tara blinked, a tear fell down her cheek.

The poor woman was exhausted. Probably stressed. I hated that I had been a huge cause of her anxiety. Yet I loved standing here, my thumb on her cheek, her chin firmly grasped in my hand, both of us frozen like ice sculptures not caring who in the world saw.

"You." Then I dipped my head, crushed my lips to hers, fully prepared for Tara to sucker punch me straight to the gut.

But she'd had ample time to say no. She could've moved from my touch anytime in the last several minutes. She could've swatted me away. As I'd dipped my lips to hers, she could've dodged me.

Tara did none of that. She met my lips with hers, ready and willing, her arms folding together in front of her body as she curled against my chest to ward off the chill winter breeze.

Both her hands came up, clutched at the front of my coat and yanked me toward her, hard. She tugged me closer, desperate and needy, and I knew she wanted me to take the lead. Hell, I would've taken her right then and there if her daughter wasn't in the car a foot away from us. I wanted to feel her legs wrap around my waist as I pressed her back against the car. I wanted to let everyone in this town know that Tara belonged to me. For real.

Tara nipped at my lower lip, and I parted her mouth to ease my tongue in, to taste her. The hot coffee, the sugary cookie. She tasted like warmth and happiness and home, and I wanted to stay wrapped up in her forever.

In the distance, the sound of a cheer rose. The fucking carolers. But it was the little knock on the window that startled me and Tara from our spontaneous mini make out session.

"Ew," Liv offered from inside the car. "Change the channel."

"Change the channel?" I stepped back from Tara, not letting go of her hand, feeling ten shades of flustered. "What is Liv talking about?"

Tara's cheeks were pinker than her daughter's. She looked like a little Russian nesting doll in her fuzzy hat, overly flushed cheeks, a fantastic little smile lingering around her lips. I was certain she'd enjoyed our interlude as much as me. And the best part of all was the fact that our kiss had chased her tears away. She was dry-cheeked, perky as an elf on a shelf.

"Change the channel," Tara repeated, her voice husky and bothered. "It's what she says if we're watching a show and there's, you know, kissing on the screen. Cooties. Gross affection."

"So gross," I agreed. I held up a hand to Liv in apology. "Sorry."

Liv shrugged. "We should probably get our tree in water before it dies."

"Right." I opened the driver's car door.

When Tara started to step foot inside the driver's side, I caught her around the waist and hauled her back out.

"Other side." My lips brushed against her ear, her cheek. My hands grazed at her slender waist. I wanted to plunk her right down on my lap for the drive home, but that definitely wouldn't be setting any sort of example for the rule-enforcer in the backseat. There'd definitely be some commentary about seatbelts and channels that needed changing.

The entire car ride home, aside from soothing Liv's fears that the tree would not spontaneously drop dead, we were silent. But the air in my ears felt loud. Throbbing, even, because Tara's hand was latched in mine.

We didn't make eye contact. I barely fucking breathed, not wanting to break this, whatever was happening between us. So I drove home well below the speed limit, definitely in violation of some sort of speed laws, thankful I could use the excuse of slippery roads if need be, even though Morty had plowed the roads and spread salt an hour before.

And then we reached home, and my gut pinged in resistance as Liv squealed in happiness, and my precious time of being in physical contact with Tara came to an end.

"What's taking so long?" Liv groaned. "Let's go inside and get this tree some water already. It's parched."

The only part that made the looming separation a little more bearable was the fact that Tara seemed just as reluctant to let my hand go as me. As if once we left this car, something would sever, and the moment would be as gone as sand passed through an hourglass. Slipping away, never quite able to reclaim it in the same way.

"Come on," Liv interrupted. "We've got plans. Hot chocolate. Tree. Hello, people."

Tara gave a barely imperceptible little sigh, and she released my hand first. Probably a good thing, or we'd have sat there all night long until Liv took the damn keys out of the ignition and threatened to let herself in the house.

"All right, sweetie." Tara climbed out of the car. "What do you say to Gavin for the treat at the café?"

"Thanks, Gavin," Liv said. "Now can we please go inside? I have to go to the bathroom."

That got us moving. The three of us leapt out of the car, and I passed the keys off to Tara, relishing in that little moment of physical touch. It was addicting. She'd given me an inch, and I was ready to take a lot more than a mile. I'd circumnavigate the world three times over, and it still wouldn't be enough.

While Liv and Tara headed into the house, I unloaded the tree which was, according to Liv, fucking parched—minus the f-bomb. I carried it inside and waited patiently for the girls to return to the living room.

I could hear Tara rattling around the kitchen and had half a mind to join her, but for some reason, I kept my distance. As if we were allowed a second alone together, I wouldn't be able to keep my hands off her. Liv was our buffer for now, and I needed to keep it that way.

It didn't take Liv long to scurry back, and Tara followed shortly after—almost as if she'd had the same thought as me, that waiting in the wings was the only way to keep things uncomplicated. Or as uncomplicated as we could hope for, all things considered.

"Hit it." Liv pointed at her mother. "Hit it, Mom."

I wasn't sure what Liv was talking about, but Tara didn't miss a beat. She gave me a teasing little smile.

"Gavin Donovan," she said as she pulled out her phone. "You don't know what you've gotten yourself into."

It didn't take me long to figure it out.

Apparently I'd gotten myself into a helluva lot of Mariah Carey.

As Christmas songs erupted through the speakers mounted on the walls, Liv broke out in very enthusiastic dance moves. Limbs were kicking and flailing. A head was bobbing. Her entire body was bouncing around like a pogo stick, once landing on my feet with surprising force.

Tara was more subdued, humming along with the tune, bobbing her head a bit. Until Liv pogo-d over to her mother and grabbed her hands.

"C'mon, Mom," Liv said. "What's wrong?"

"Nothing's wrong." Tara's gaze shot to me. "We have company."

"Gavin? It's just Big Gavin." Liv shrugged, her ponytail still flopping around as she yoyo'd between her mother and me. "He doesn't care. Do you Gavin?"

I rubbed my hands together and shot Tara a perfectly polite smile. "Of course I don't mind. Cut loose, princess."

Tara rolled her eyes. She seemed very reluctant to do whatever it was Liv was encouraging her to do. I had a good feeling I knew what it was.

"Mo-*om*." Liv intoned. "Your favorite part's coming up."

Liv disappeared for a moment, then returned a beat later with one of those plastic play microphones that warped voices. Liv shouted into it. I was pretty sure she was speaking in English but I wouldn't swear to it on the stand. Then she handed the microphone to her mother as the song rose to a height only Mariah Carey could physically hit.

"It's tradition," Liv insisted. "Don't ruin Christmas."

Something in Tara's eyes flashed, and I knew Liv had hit a pain point, whether on purpose or accident. But Tara finally accepted the microphone. Bobbed her head with a little more intention. Had some toe taps that started out simple but quickly turned into a little more, then a little more, until finally—Tara Kendrick was singing—hollering?—into the microphone, dancing around in fuzzy socks that went up to her knees, her messy bun bobbing dangerously on top of her head.

I felt the grin splitting my face in two, and there wasn't a goddamn thing I could do about it. I stood there, balanced against a thirsty Christmas tree, watching the two girls I cared about more than anything in the world as they ping-ponged around the room with more vigor than I'd ever seen in my life.

Tara looked like a sugar plum fairy—whatever the hell that was supposed to look like. It seemed festive and magical and a little bit unbelievable, which was how I felt right now.

When Tara reached out and tugged the binder out of her hair, releasing her long locks to flutter around her shoulders, I was pretty sure I'd made Santa's good list this year. I could die a happy man now, seeing this, experiencing it. Being a part of it. A welcome part of this happy, happy household.

When the song wound down, Liv and Tara collapsed against one another, tumbling onto the couch in a fit of giggles. Tara took heavy breaths, looking happier than I'd ever seen her, as she rested a cheek against her daughter's forehead. Their sweet snuggles lasted for only a second until another Christmas jam popped over the Bluetooth, and Liv and Tara resumed their roles as tone-deaf pogo sticks.

This display of festive exuberance lasted for some time, until Tara begged for a break, and Liv—energy fueled by copious amounts of cookie dough and Christmas spirit—bounded my way, bouncing on my toes like a trampoline and thrusting the microphone in my face.

"Your turn, Gavin."

"Yeah," Tara called from the couch. "Your turn, Gavin."

I shook my head. "I already fu—" I coughed. "I fudging *neighed*. That's enough festivity for me."

"Fudging neighed?" Liv repeated.

Tara rolled her eyes. "Ignore him, sweetie. Anyway, I think it's getting late, don't you?"

"No," Liv said, sounding so reasonable indeed that I was sure she could convince me the earth was flat. "We didn't decorate the tree yet."

"I don't suppose that I can convince you it'd be a good idea to save tree decorating for the morning?" Tara didn't even try hard to sound like she believed her plea would work.

Liv was already on her way to one of the huge Tupperware boxes that Tara had stacked neatly against one wall earlier in the day.

"I think my favorite little ornament is in here," Liv said. "Gavin, do you want to do the first ornament this year?"

Tara stilled. I suspected Liv's question wasn't as innocuous as it sounded on the outside.

"I don't know," I said cautiously. "Should I?"

"Of course," Liv said. "The first ornament is the special one. It's the only ornament my dad gave me. I figure since you're basically my dad now, you can do it."

The room seemed to slow in an almost comical way. As if the air had been sucked straight out of my lungs. The walls felt like they were pressing in on me, and I didn't dare look at Tara.

"I don't know, Liv." I shifted my weight from one foot to the next. "I think you should do it."

Liv walked over to me. She handed me a little ornament of a snowman—or snow-woman, rather, cradling a baby snowman. There was a tenderness to the ornament that, despite the fact the figures were snow people, scratched at old emotional wounds that had no business being opened by a darling little girl.

"Mom says my dad gave it to me when he found out that I was going to be born." Liv dangled it in front of me. "Then he had to go away. But isn't that little snowman just so cute? It's me, you know. I'm the snow-baby."

"It's adorable," I said, though it sounded like I was chewing on a rock. My throat felt scratchy, and I felt miserable knowing Tara was having to witness all of this. "But I think you should do the ornament since you're that cute little snow-baby."

I gave her a little poke in the belly to emphasize my point. She giggled, collapsing in on herself, wrapping herself around my outstretched arm. I gave her another tickle that

JINGLE BELL ROCK 271

was received by shrieks of laughter, and I couldn't help but grin despite the chains tightening around my heart, constricting my blood flow.

"I've got an idea," I said in the sturdiest growl I could muster. "Why don't we do it together?"

Liv was already in a sloth-like position dangling from my arm, so it didn't take much effort to lift her off the ground and support her with my other hand. I raised her toward the tree, which I'd gotten fastened into the supports during one of the interludes of the dance party, and let her wiggle herself into position as she extended her arms toward the tree.

With a tiny tongue sticking out in concentration, Liv furrowed her eyebrows as she tried and failed a couple of times to loop the ribbon over a branch. When she finally succeeded, she burst into such rapt applause for herself I nearly dropped her. I curled her against my chest, caught my balance, and went to set her down. But Liv's arms were locked around my neck.

"Maybe you can help me decorate the top of the tree," Liv said. "You can be my own personal ladder. Mom always says the tree is naked above where I can reach. But now that we've got you, that won't be a problem. Hey, can I do the star this year? Mom never lets me because I can't reach but..." She gave a huge shrug and poked a finger against the ceiling to demonstrate her height. "Now I can."

"Yes, sure, you can do the star," Tara interrupted. "But give Gavin a minute to gather himself. Liv, will you do the honors of sorting the ornaments and pulling them out of the boxes while I speak to Gavin for a minute in the kitchen?"

"Sure!" Liv didn't look back as she flew from my arms toward the storage boxes. "Gavin, I'll make you a pile too. We'll have less ornaments in each pile, but it's okay because I can probably help you do yours."

I gave her hair a little ruffle as I passed by her en route to the kitchen. Tara's voice had sounded like she was doing everything she could not to show emotion. My problem was that I wasn't sure which emotions she was hiding. Sadness? Disappointment? Anger? All the above?

When we made it to the kitchen, Tara beelined for the wine rack and pulled down a bottle of red. She began uncorking it without saying a word. I gave her a few moments of silence, unable to tear my eyes away as she worked, her shoulders tenser than I'd ever seen.

When she finally relieved the bottle of the cork, she let the bottle opener fall into the sink. Her hands gripped the counter top and she leaned forward, and it wasn't until I saw those steadfast shoulders trembling that I realized she was crying. Not a little cry. Big, silent sobs that she'd tried and failed to hide.

"Hey, honey." The second the situation clicked in my brain as to what was happening, I strode across the distance between us in two steps.

Without thinking, I caged her against the counter, letting her feel the warmth of me near her. I didn't want to embrace her for fear she'd push me away, that I'd overstep my boundaries. I simply wanted her to know that I was here for her. I could be her support. I wouldn't leave.

"I'm so sorry," I whispered in her ear. My hand came up, unable to resist the puppet-like tug that I was feeling to touch her. I rested my hand on her neck, gave little, gentle, soothing rubs to the muscles there that felt like taut rope knotted beneath her skin. "I am so sorry for everything. For tonight, for Liv..."

"No." Tara wriggled, turning to face me, her cheeks red and salt stained. "You don't have to be sorry for anything."

"I got you into this mess."

"We discussed that. It's forgiven. We agreed to move on from that." Tara blinked. "I'm not dwelling on it."

"But your tears." My hand slid around to her face, my thumb brushing at that damp cheek.

I couldn't help feeling my body heat at how close we were. She hadn't seemed to want me to move away, so we were close now, my body pressing hers into the counter. Tara looked lost, forlorn. She brought up her arms and shivered, curling herself into a little self-embrace.

"Can I hug you?" I asked gruffly.

Tara gave a nod. I wrapped my arms around her, and when her chin hit my chest and my cheek hit the top of her hair, I knew I was home. This was it. This was happiness. This was where I should have been all along.

"I wasn't sure what to say out there," I murmured. "Tara, honey, I love you. I will do anything for you."

"You love me." Tara echoed my words back. Words that weren't new to her, but it seemed like they hadn't sunk in. She looked into my eyes as if hoping that would make everything click.

Her gaze held universes in them. Layers of desperation and hope, stars of disappointment and grit. Constellations of bravery and love.

"I've always loved you." My voice was hoarse. "I will do anything for you. It's why I'm here. Andrea must know that too. It's why you're in danger."

Tara looked at me, a long, exhausted, completely drained look. As if all the fight had left her body. It gutted me.

Then, without warning, she threw herself closer to me. Her hands came up, gripping at my face, dragging me to her. Her lips hit mine, hot, ready, swollen from the way she'd been nervously biting them the entire time I'd been talking.

Tara's tongue darted into my mouth, and she tasted just as she had outside of the car. Sweet. Caffeinated. Floral and sugary and delicate and like a Christmas cookie. I could spend lifetimes devouring her. I slid my hands around her head, gripping her hair, pulling her to me until we were both starved for oxygen.

Then she took a breath, and I took a breath, and we stared at one another. Fire recognized fire, and I knew there was no extinguishing the flame this time. I lifted her onto the counter, relished the moment her legs locked around my waist.

I was so fucking hard it was a miracle the zipper on my jeans hadn't pinged right off and shattered a window with the force. It felt wrong to be this aroused when Tara's face was still wet with tears, but it was a different sort of desire.

There was no logical thought associated with it. This was primal. Basic human need. I felt like an animal, everything but my feral instincts fading into the background. The room around me went dark. The music was nothing but white noise. The only thing I could smell, taste, touch was Tara.

JINGLE BELL ROCK

Tara ground her hips against my length, and I barely stifled the bottled-up growl into a low murmur. Her hands were on my back. I could feel her nails digging through the flannel shirt I hadn't had time to take off yet.

"God," I hissed. "I can't. I can't give you up, baby. Please tell me—"

"Gross. Change the channel."

Tara and I sprang apart so quickly it was almost like we were in a comedy sketch, and this was the record scratch moment. I spun around, a guilty look on my face, swinging my lumberjack shirt off to hold it in front of the bulge in my jeans.

Unfortunately, that meant I'd let go of Tara, and she'd pushed off me with such force she'd propelled herself directly backward and into the sink. In doing so, one of her arms knocked over the wine bottle. The other arm knocked the faucet and the water began spraying directly into her lap.

Liv stood in the doorway, blinking. "What are you guys doing?"

I glanced at Tara. Her face was red, embarrassment scrawled over every inch of her. Then she burst into laughter, shut the water off, and hauled herself out of the sink sopping wet.

"That's one way to take a cold shower," she mumbled under her breath. To Liv, she said, "Gavin was helping me open a bottle of wine."

"Yeah, he's strong," Liv said. "Well, I've got your piles of ornaments all separated out. Are you ready to do trade-sies? And can I have some sparkling apple juice?"

Chapter 22

Tara

I wasn't sure what I was thinking anymore.

As Gavin, Liv, and I wrapped up a surprisingly aggressive round of Ornament Trade-sies — a new game in which Liv made up the rules as we went—I looked across our little circle on the floor and saw Gavin arguing intensely over why he should get the Grinch ornament and Liv should have the weird beekeeper ornament we'd inherited from some garage sale.

"Them's the rules," Liv quipped, probably parroting something I'd said to her at some point. "Sorry, Charlie."

Gavin broke into a smile. "Fine. I'll take weird beekeeper. You get the Grinch. Are we ready to start?"

Fortunately, I was pretty sure Liv hadn't seen much between me and Gavin in the kitchen. She'd taken one look at us kissing and we'd broken apart like a Jenga game with all the pieces collapsing in a heap. And a load of water splashing right onto my crotch. A sign from God? I hoped not, because I was pretty sure I wasn't in any sort of mood to listen if that were the case.

Something had broken in me today. I had broken, but I'd surprised myself. In breaking, I was finding the potential to build something new in the future. Where a crumbling wall had stood before, Gavin had blasted through it, leaving rubble behind to make way for a new structure.

Instead of walls built by years of disappointment, I had finally decided that I wanted to try building something on my own. Something newer, sturdier, shinier. Something that brought joy and hope and, yes, fear—but good fear. The fear of losing something, instead of the fear of loving in the first place.

Because I'd lived with the fear of loving someone for a long, long time, and I was sick of it. What sort of example was I setting for Liv, teaching her that all Kendrick women were unlucky in love? Didn't I want to see my little girl happy down the line, whatever that looked like for her?

Whether confident and alone, or happily married with a family, I wanted Liv to have the tools to make that choice for herself. I'd grown up with the knowledge that us Kendrick women were cursed when it came to men. That narrative hadn't gotten me anywhere, and maybe it was time to close that chapter of our book and start a new one.

We launched into the next phase of decorating the tree. Mostly with Liv pinning ornaments at six-year-old height. But this time, I had help decorating the top, and so did Liv. She spent a good portion of the first half an hour of tree decorating on Gavin's shoulders, looping her pile of ornaments to the top.

"Okay, okay," I said, reaching up to peel Liv from Gavin's shoulders. "We've got the opposite effect. The tree's so top heavy it's starting to droop. Scram, kiddo. Have some apple juice and decorate at your own height."

Liv giggled, looking at the Grinch-like droop at the top of the tree.

"Okay," Liv said, "but I get to do the star."

"Sure thing, captain," Gavin said with a little salute.

"Thank you," I said, wrapping my arms around Gavin's neck the second Liv had disappeared into the kitchen to pour herself more sparkling juice. I didn't care if she spilled the entire freaking bottle on the floor. If it stole me a minute alone with Gavin here and now, it was worth a little cleanup. "I've never seen her this happy decorating the tree."

"I've never decorated a tree before."

Gavin's admission came out of left field. I was in the middle of going in for a kiss when I processed what he'd said. "You've never decorated a tree? Are you serious right now?"

He looked embarrassed, as if he hadn't meant to share that little nugget with me. "It's not a big deal. We didn't do Christmas like this at my house."

I thought back to Gavin's past, remembered what he'd said about his mother not having the tools she needed to care for him properly. I'd just never realized *how* awful things had been.

"A Christmas tree?" I repeated. "I'm sorry, Gavin. That's terrible."

"It's not so bad." Gavin brushed it off, nodded at the tree. "That ornament really from Liv's dad?"

I nodded, glanced behind me. I saw Liv nuking something all secret agent like in the microwave and figured she'd probably gotten into the s'mores supplies. Good for her, since I wasn't ready to let this moment with Gavin lapse. I'd deal with the sugar detox tomorrow.

"Yeah," I said with a sigh. "I'm sorry I haven't said much about him."

"You didn't owe me any explanations."

"There's not much to say. We met while he was here on a job, dated a few months, got engaged. Neither of us was sure we wanted kids. We were going to get married, wait a few years, discuss the possibility of growing our family later on."

Gavin's hands were working small circles on my lower back.

"Then I got pregnant. It wasn't in the plans. I was on birth control, and we were both shocked. He asked me to get an abortion. I kicked him out the same day."

Gavin muttered some words under his breath that had me double checking to see that Liv was still up to her elbows in sticky marshmallows and chocolate. One look in the kitchen told me she was going for round two. That was my girl, all right.

"I'm so sorry." Gavin held my face between his hands, strong as a vice holding my gaze so I couldn't look away. "You didn't deserve that. You did the right thing, in my opinion. Anyone who wouldn't stick around to support you and a child—"

"I could support both of us," I interrupted him. "It wasn't about that. I'm independent."

"I know, baby," Gavin said. "I meant that he should *want* to support the two of you—not only financially, but to be there for you, with you for everything. How could he have not wanted to look into his daughter's face and know that precious girl?"

The way Gavin glanced over my shoulder and caught Liv in his gaze told me the only thing I needed to know. He loved Liv. That was the long and short of it. I'd seen the two of them getting there over the last few weeks, and even though it had happened quicker than I'd ever thought possible, there was no denying it.

I knew Gavin would do anything for her, for me. He'd been trying to prove that since I'd walked back into that inn after all these years. And really, he'd never given me a reason to doubt it yet.

I knew, then and there, that I was doing the right thing by letting myself fall. Opening my heart to Gavin was the only way forward at this point because, dammit, I'd never truly fallen out of love with the man. Somehow, that love had only grown stronger, multiplied exponentially as I watched him fall in love with my daughter, the person who mattered most in my life.

I raised onto my toes, gave him a tender, slow kiss. A ribbon of heat wrapped its way around us, the sensuality of the moment enhanced by the low music thrumming in the background, the warmth from the electric fireplace, the glow of the Christmas tree lights. Our home felt complete for maybe the first time in my life.

"I want you, Gavin," I murmured to him. "Tonight, please."

He groaned against me, his fingers digging into the flesh at my hips. I'd changed clothes from my wet jeans into gnome Christmas pajamas that matched Liv. His thumbs dug their way underneath the waistband, tempting me.

"Is it bedtime yet?" Gavin winked, stepping back from me. "I'm kidding. That girl isn't going to sleep for about twelve years with the amount of s'mores she thinks she secretly shoved into her mouth."

"I know, right?"

Gavin's eyes darkened just the slightest amount. "I'm sorry to bring the conversation around again to this, but did Liv's dad ever reach back out? Is he in your life at all?"

I ran my tongue over my teeth. I felt a tornado of fire whirl around my gut every time I took long enough to actually consider the fact that Liv's father had no interest in knowing her.

"No," I said. "I sent him pictures of her when she was born. I sent him more when she turned one year old. When she turned two, I swore it was the last time I'd reach out. Not because I wanted him back in my life, but just because..."

I felt those freaking tears coming back. Now that the emotional well had been cranked open, it was flowing like beer on tap. I swiped them away.

"I mean, look at her. What sort of person wouldn't want to know Liv?" I said. "Especially her own flesh and blood?"

"I can think of a few choice words, but I'm not going to start now," Gavin said, a plume of heat swirling in his eyes. "I know you know this, but it's his damn loss. Do you believe in fate?"

"What?"

"Fate," Gavin said. "You know. Destiny."

"Sure. I believe things happen for a reason."

"Maybe this was the reason."

"What?"

Gavin lowered his lips, told me his answer with a kiss. It was barely a breath when he spoke.

"Us," he murmured, his lips still pressed against my cheek as he whispered. "It's obvious to me that Liv belongs to you, so maybe your ex came into your life for a reason, to give you her. Maybe he wasn't meant to be her father figure, as much as that sucks. Maybe..." He cleared his throat. "Maybe you could give me a chance."

"I don't know, Gavin, I think—"

"I swear to you, Tara Kendrick. I won't fuck it up."

I felt my eyes crinkling in a smile as I looked at him. "What I was going to say is that I think it's already too late for that. She's already made the decision for herself." I leaned against Gavin's warmth, feeling his heartbeat against my cheek. "I don't have any desire to change her mind."

"Fuck," Gavin breathed against my hair. "I love that little girl, but I really wish it was bedtime. I need to be near you, Tara."

"I know," I whispered, giving him a little nip on the ear. "Soon enough. I give her an hour before the sugar high knocks her out."

I gave him a little wink, and we stepped apart as a little crash sounded from the kitchen. We both turned to find Liv standing on a chair, looking guiltily toward us as an entire sleeve of graham crackers landed on the floor.

"No problem," I said with a clap of my hands. "There are more ornaments out here that need hung. Get to work, Liv. I'll clean this up."

Liv scurried out of the room with only one double take at me, as if wondering how she'd gotten out of that mess without so much as a wrist slap. I whistled as I swept up the crumbs. Then I looked out at the living room where Liv was giving instructions to Gavin on where to hang the popcorn balls she'd made at school.

We spent the rest of the night celebrating Christmas much later than Liv's bedtime, stringing tinsel around the tree, bleating out spontaneous Christmas songs into the microphone, pausing for snack breaks on the couch.

Between drill sergeant Liv handing out marching orders—a trait she likely inherited from watching her mother work—Gavin and I managed to sneak in little touches. Glances over Liv's head. A kiss behind the ear as he reached for a candy cane, a touch on the back as he stretched to put an ornament over my head.

When Liv disappeared to use the bathroom, we snuck into the kitchen for a short, hot make out session against the wall. The heat between my legs was on the verge of combusting. Poor Gavin had to stay in the kitchen for fifteen minutes pretending he needed a drink of water before he was presentable enough to return to the living room.

When Liv requested a movie, we all crashed onto the couch, knowing it was the fastest way to get her to fall asleep. We turned on *The Santa Claus*. Liv snuggled between us, delicately spreading a blanket so we all had a piece of it on our laps. Gavin set his arm over the back of my couch and lazily tickled my shoulder with what felt like the heat of one thousand suns.

"Isn't our tree the greatest ever?" Liv murmured sleepily, one hand on my thigh, the other resting on Gavin's. "Look at it, guys."

Gavin and I turned to look at it. The tree was horrendous, really. Many of the branches had gotten bent and dinged up. Piles of pine needles were on the floor. The top was so heavy it was curved to almost a ninety-degree angle.

The top was so full of ornaments and the bottom equally as full, but the middle was downright empty. It was a weird-ass tree.

"Beautiful," Gavin said.

"Perfect," I murmured.

But Liv was already sleeping.

"Can I?" Gavin asked a few minutes later, nodding toward Liv.

I nodded back at him. "Please."

Gavin lifted her, dwarfing her small figure with his huge one. He carried her into her room, and I followed behind, resting a hand on his back as he gently deposited my daughter into her bed. I tugged up the comforter gently, brushed Liv's hair back, pressed a kiss to her forehead.

Then I curled into Gavin, and we watched as Liv's face melted into that sweet angelic expression of a child sleeping. Dark eyelashes fluttered against her cheeks. The smell of sugar clung to her pajamas. Her thin arms looked downright spindly spread across her pink sheets.

"She's beautiful, Tara," Gavin murmured, his face pressed to me. "She looks just like you. She's lucky to have you."

"I'm lucky to have her," I said, feeling an ache in my chest for how much love had flooded there for my girl. Then I turned to Gavin. "And we're both lucky to have you."

Gavin's eyes turned downright black with desire as he took my hand, tugged me out of Liv's room. I closed her door, then followed Gavin to my room. I closed my door, too, and locked it.

I stood before Gavin. Not ready to admit I loved him out loud, but also not ready to let him go. All I knew was that tonight, we needed to be together, and the rest would come with time.

Chapter 23

Gavin

I'd seen something change in her eyes.

I'd seen the start of it after our trip to the café. I'd seen it compound in the kitchen. Then, in the living room when we'd been alone, I'd seen the final phase of her transformation. Tara was giving me a chance. She was really, truly giving me the opportunity to take up a little bit of space in her life, maybe in her heart, and I wasn't going to fucking blow it.

We stood in her bedroom, precious cargo sleeping a few doors down. I wouldn't let Tara down. I wouldn't let Liv down. As far as I was concerned, I'd do anything it took for the chance to one day call those girls my family.

"I mean it, Tara," I murmured, my throat thick. "I have always loved you."

"I know," she whispered. "I don't think I ever stopped loving you either. Not really. Or, maybe not successfully, even though I wanted to."

I nodded. I understood. At one point, I'd felt the same way. Until I'd forfeited my heart to Tara whether she wanted it or not. I'd come to terms with the fact that I'd love her in some way, somehow, until the day I died. There was no way around it.

"I think it's why my marriage didn't work. Or my engagement, I should say," Tara murmured. "In retrospect, I realized I barely knew my ex. On paper, he was what I thought a husband and a father looked like. Stable job. Generally the same wants and desires out of life. And it still didn't work. It wasn't enough."

"His wants and desires weren't fucking correct," I said. "The only man who deserves you is the one whose only want and desire is to be with you. Everything else is a moot point."

"That's not true," Tara said, her eyes pleading as she looked back at me. "You can't *only* want me. It doesn't work like that."

"Baby, I've had everything else." I peeled her shirt off her body. Tara raised her arms to make it easier. "I've stashed away more money than I'd ever dreamed of in my bank account. I've had the nice condo. The exciting career. None of it was enough."

"It doesn't work like that, Gavin."

"The only thing I want is you." I pressed a kiss to her forehead. One to her collar bone. Another to her neck. I felt immense pleasure to see her skin flush where I touched her, like there was some spell interlocking the two of us together. "With one amendment. I want a family. You. Liv. Hell, I'd have ten kids with you if you wanted."

"I don't..." Tara's eyes flashed. "You'd have kids with me?"

"A whole soccer team," I promised her. I slid her bra strap down her shoulder. "I want nothing more than to get you pregnant with my child. To make that ring on your finger something real."

"Gavin, you can't..." Tara's breath was coming out in little bursts.

"I love Liv, honestly," I said, my mouth still on her flesh. "And if you were to ever allow me into your life, I'd love her like my own child. No doubt about it. But just think:

we could give her a sibling. Siblings. Fuck. Enough talking. I want you."

Her breath was coming in little bursts, and I was so goddamn hard I couldn't bear to be outside of her any longer. I yanked her shorts down. Her hands tore at my lumberjack shirt. A button flew, then bounced off the wooden door behind me.

"I want you too," she murmured. "Now. Here. Fast."

"Not fast," I said. "Slow. I've been waiting for weeks. Hell, years. I want to take my time with you."

Whatever she'd been tempted to say, Tara lost her train of thought as her head flew back when I raked a trail of kisses down the side of her throat. I released her bra with a touch of my fingers, and the fabric fell to the floor.

"Jesus, you're incredible." I studied her for a moment, dragged a hand down her neck, let it drop to her breast.

Tara was busy fumbling with my jeans, and though I was loath to remove my hands from her, I put her out of her misery as I released my button, lowered the zipper, and then dropped my pants. My erection jerked free like an animal that'd been kenneled for far too long.

"I know it's only been a couple of weeks," she said, her eyes fixed on my boxers, "but I thought for sure my memory was playing tricks on me. That you weren't really so, you know—*nice*."

"Are you talking to my dick or to me?"

Tara's gaze jerked up. She looked sheepish. I barked out a laugh, dragged her face to me, tasted her.

"Feel free to continue the conversation," I said, feeling as lighthearted as a kid on Christmas morning. "With me or my cock."

She studied me for just a second more, as if trying to discern if I was making fun, then she threw her head back and burst out in laughter. Somehow, seeing her laugh, half-naked in my arms, brought me to a new level of fallen. Fallen for her heart, mind, body, soul.

It wasn't one thing about Tara that made me weak. It wasn't those perfect breasts, the nipples tempting little buds pointing at me like spotlights. It wasn't the soft curves of her hips, her pale stomach, the wetness that waited between her thighs.

It wasn't the fact that she was a good mother, the very best. Or that she was a thoughtful daughter, a hard worker, an independent woman through and through. It wasn't that everyone in this damn town seemed to love her like a sister.

It wasn't even the fact that I'd missed her like she was a part of me. Both for these last few weeks, but also for the years and years that had gone by before.

It was everything. The way she laughed, the happiness that rocked through her when she was happy. The tenderness that was her whole heart, the way she cared for everyone from her daughter to her clients to me—the man who had complicated her life beyond measure. It was Tara as a whole, my person—the only woman for me without a shadow of a doubt. And I wanted to make sure she fucking knew it.

Before I could get to having my way with Tara, her hands clasped around my cock through the material of my boxers, and I cursed like I'd been shot. Tara, still wearing her panties, dropped before me and tugged at my boxers with a bit of a malicious gleam in her eye.

"No, baby," I gasped. "I want tonight to be about you. This isn't—"

"This *is* about me," she said, and then she closed her lips around my dick.

I was pretty sure my pulse jerked to a dead stop. I was frozen in place, feeling like I was floating out of my body while being insanely in tune to every sensation, every touch. The way her breath warmed my cock, made it twitch and jump. She was playing me like a goddamn fiddle, and I was powerless to do anything but stand as still as an ice sculpture.

When she began to move, her tongue working circles over my skin, I finally snapped back to reality. I sank my hands into her hair, held her, gritting my teeth to avoid coming in her mouth then and there. This was the stuff fantasies were made of.

I glanced behind her at the mirror on the dresser, her perfect figure, those gorgeous curves. That fucking incredible ass I couldn't wait to get my hands on. The way she was working my dick wasn't going to leave much time for fun extracurricular activities with the two of us, so I let myself enjoy one more minute of my hands tugging on her hair, watching her move up and down my shaft, before I growled something that definitely wasn't English and pulled her off me. Much to my chagrin.

"Fuck," I said. "Where'd you learn how to do that?"

Tara gave me a little bit of a sheepish look as I laid her on the bed.

"Actually," I growled, dipping my head to take one of those rosy nipples in my mouth. "Don't tell me, or I'll have to fucking kill him."

Tara barked a laugh, a laugh that was quickly stifled when I bit down gently, tugging at the bud on her breast. Her back arched, her ass thrusting upward toward my body as I balanced myself on one hand, planking over her.

"I told you," she managed to spit out, "I haven't had sex in six years. I mean, before you. And with Liv's dad, well, he wasn't into that."

"Into what?"

"You know." Tara's cheeks turned into red apples as I stood before her. "Oral sex."

"Come again?" I blinked.

I'd thought there wasn't anything that could take me out of the moment. Then I'd heard that.

"Fucking what?" I spit out.

"Don't stop," Tara insisted, her chest rising and falling. "I don't want to talk about other people. I want you inside me."

"Are you telling me he never..." I dropped to my knees before her, sank my fingers into her skin, and dragged her hard across the bed until her thighs were parting before my face. "Tasted you?"

"No. He thought it was weird."

I was well and truly fine to never speak of the man who'd fathered Liv ever again. As far as I was concerned, he didn't exist any longer. I'd learned everything I'd needed to know about the idiot.

"His fucking loss." I dragged my thumb down her panties. "You're already wet for me, baby. You're soaked through."

"You made it hard to focus tonight."

"You want to talk to me about fucking hard?" I popped to my feet, letting Tara have a good, long look at my cock. At what she did to me. I'd never been so hard in my life, and the way she looked at me, bit that little lower lip as she reached one of her sweet little hands in my direction, made me want to fill her with my seed.

I gently swatted her hand away before she could touch my dick again and turn me on like a volcano on the verge of eruption. I returned to my perch, rubbed my fingers along the outside of her lacy panties for a moment longer, inhaling the scent of her. The pheromones. The wine that'd spilled on her when she'd fallen into the sink. The smell of baked cookie lingering in her hair. It was fucking glorious.

"You're not touching me," I said. "Not yet."

"But—"

"Don't you want me inside you?" When Tara didn't immediately answer, I poked my head up and looked up and over her stomach, past the swell of her breasts, to those eyes hooded by her lashes. "I asked you a question. Do you want me inside you?"

"Yes, Gavin. Yes," she whimpered. "Please, just get on with it. You've been teasing me all night."

I shifted her panties to the side, slipped one finger inside. The hitch of her breath hit me like jet fuel. It invigorated me. Gave me sustenance as if I'd been a starving man.

I added a second finger. She bucked for me, and I'd never felt such power before. The gentlest power, the most precious, the sort of power that I knew she didn't give to just anyone. It humbled me. Destroyed me.

I dipped my mouth, pressed my tongue to her slit, tasted the nectar that was more intoxicating than any cocktail. I let my fingers work inside her while I massaged with my tongue, letting my hands and my mouth play together in a little orchestra that seemed to be working, judging by the way Tara seemed to be breathing like she was on fucking fire.

"Gavin." The word was hurled my way. A beg. A threat. A plead.

"I know," I murmured over the core of her while my fingers pulsed once, twice. "But I can't get enough of you."

"Please," she said. "I'll do whatever you want. Just come up here. I need you."

It was hard to argue when she made deals like that, so I gave her another thrust or two with my hand, a swirl with my tongue, and then let my fingers drag slowly, slowly out of her so she felt every second of the looming emptiness.

"What is it you want?" I perched over her, caging her against the bed.

Tara seemed so small, so vulnerable. Naked, chest heaving, eyes hazy with desire. Her lips were swollen. Those sweet hands of hers came up, felt around on my torso. Slid around to my back, and her nails dug in as she urged me closer to her.

"You know what I want," she whispered against my cheek.

"I want to hear you say it. Again." I cleared my throat. "I'm never going to get sick of hearing you say that you want me. So get used to saying my name."

She blinked, nodded. I reached for her chin, tipped it upward.

"Got it?" I repeated.

Tara's eyes flashed open. "I want you so badly, Gavin. I want to be with you. I want to love you. I want to have your babies. I want us to be a family, but I'm not sure if—"

I cut her off before she could continue. Before she could ruin the most perfect words I'd ever heard in my life. I pulled off those lacy panties, lowered myself down to her, pressed my cock against her entrance as I continued to kiss the fucking daylights out of her.

Her tongue slipped between my lips. Tara dug her fingers into my back so hard there'd be scratch marks tomorrow. I didn't care if she gave me a damn scar, so long as it made what we had permanent.

Tara moaned as I teased her entrance with my swollen shaft. I'd never been so swollen with desire, so hard in my life. I wasn't sure she'd be able to take all of me, but I was willing to try if she was. As she moaned again, a sound I took as an invitation, I eased into her. Just an inch. Slow, but perfect. Sweet as a fucking rose.

"God, I'm so full." Tara's voice was faint, soft. "More, Gavin."

Another inch. She stretched for me, those lips parting to let my erection through. Where it longed to be. Home was here. Wrapped around Tara, my cock inside her, already glistening with precum. Threatening to fill her with my seed.

"I want you to be my wife," I rasped to her. "I want to give you more kids. As many as you'll have. I want a family with you, and I'm not fucking going anywhere."

Tara looked up at me, blinked, a single tear pooling in her eye, filling slowly with every ounce of emotion the poor woman had inside of her. Then the tear fell, cascading from the crease of her eye down the side of her face, leaving a salty trail to her ear.

"I'm scared," she whispered to me. "I'm scared to love again."

"It's too late, baby," I whispered back to her ear. "If you feel even a fraction of the way I feel, then we're both too far fucking gone."

"I do love you, Gavin."

At the words, I couldn't help it. I pressed myself the rest of the way inside her, sliding home, hard, making Tara jerk against me, curling off the bed as she clung to me like a goddamn koala. I wrapped her around me, balancing her as I pulled myself to a standing position. Her arms slid around my neck, her legs cinched tight around my waist, my cock splitting her down the middle.

"I love you, too, baby," I said. "And I promise you this is forever."

Tara lowered her mouth to me, pressed those soft lips to mine, and then she ground her hips against me, taking me deeper into her sweet pussy than I'd ever thought possible. She flinched, almost as if it were too far, and I felt like someone had punched the wind right out of me.

I let my hands dig into her ass, unable to regulate the force with which I grabbed her. I managed to mutter something about if I was hurting her, and fortunately, Tara understood my garbled, sex-infused nonsense.

"You're so deep inside me," she said spoke against my neck, her breath leaving a hot trail of goosebumps. "And somehow, I want more. Don't hold back, Gavin. I fucking mean it."

That was all I needed to hear as I lifted her by her ass, then plunged her back down onto my cock. We rocked together, the moans escaping her like little nuggets of adrenaline that forced me onward, upward—more, harder, faster.

But I didn't trust myself to come inside her while I was standing. I was pretty sure my legs would give out. Hell, I might go into a coma at the rate my brain seemed to be glitching at the feel of Tara, the words she'd added to the swirl of lust and love and hope.

I laid my gorgeous girl on the bed, perching her head on the pillows so her hair formed an auburn halo around her head. It was difficult to pull my cock out of her, to leave her empty when I hadn't yet finished, but I needed to do this right.

Reaching a hand up, I tucked her hair away from her face. I looked into her eyes. A question was poised on her lips, but she paused, watching me, sensing there was more to this moment than sex. More than a climax. More than the fucking five minutes I was about to last before spilling myself inside her.

I leaned down, kissed one cheek. "Do you trust me, baby?"

"I've always trusted you." Tara's hands came up, toyed with my hair. Gentle, rhythmic motions.

JINGLE BELL ROCK

I sent a hand down to her clit. Relished the look that swarmed into her eyes at my touch. I let myself explore her for a few minutes.

"Do you believe that I love you?" I whispered. "Do you believe I'm not going to leave you?"

"Yes to the first," she hummed softly. "The second is complicated."

"Why?"

"I believe you don't *want* to leave me," she said.

There it was. The crux of the issue.

I pressed my lips to her forehead. Gifted a tiny kiss to her nose. Reached a hand upward, tipped her chin until her eyes flashed and her gaze locked on mine. Our breath mixed like an enchantment, a potent spell that would bind the two of us forever.

"You are the only thing that matters to me now," I said. "It will take the devil himself to drag me away from you."

"But—"

I crashed my mouth to Tara's sweet pout.

"All I'm asking for is the chance to prove that to you."

Tara took a deep breath. "You know it's not just me this time, Gavin. Liv is more a part of me than anyone, or anything else. We're a package deal."

"Marry me," I instructed Tara. Hell, it was a beg. I'd grovel. "I'll adopt Liv tomorrow and love her like she's my own daughter. Do you believe that?"

Tara's hands stilled in my hair for a second. Then, in a moment that I'd remember on my deathbed, she pulled my face toward her, gentle, the tenderness seeping from every inch of her perfect body.

"I believe that more than anything else." Tara's eyelashes fluttered, wet, as another tear joined the first. "I see the way you treat her, the way you look at her. To be honest, it's what convinced me that you were worth the risk."

"Fuck, Tara." I pressed kisses down the trail the tears had left.

My lips were salty with the essence of Tara's love for her daughter. I touched a finger to my lip, feeling like she'd given me a piece of herself. A little bit of magic. The ultimate vulnerability that I needed to protect more than anything else in this lifetime.

"I love you," I murmured. "I need to come inside you."

She nodded. It seemed all she was capable of doing.

"Do you want me to use a condom?" I managed to gasp. I realized it was a little fucking late, seeing as I'd already been sheathed to the hilt inside her sweet sex, but I owed her the option at the very least.

Her eyes flashed, she shook her head. "I'm still on the pill. I mean, as long as you're okay with the risk. I did get pregnant on it before, so there's no guarantee."

The insinuation hung there. I closed my eyes, urging my goddamn cock not to explode on her stomach before I could even put myself inside her.

"The thought of having babies with you..." I shuddered, then before I embarrassed the shit out of myself, I thrust myself fully into her waiting sex.

Tara shivered, her nails digging into me with the force of it. I couldn't wait this time. I couldn't ease every inch into her one bit at a time, I needed her to feel the full force of my desire. The drive she put into me to have her, claim her, mate her, make her mine. Like years of dreams had built up into this one release.

Because this was more than sex. This was it.

I pounded into her, once, twice, and then she was reaching up, digging into my skin with her fingers, her tits bouncing in my face. I used one hand to cup her breast, pinch at the bud. When I did, she jerked, and I could feel her walls starting to quiver. But I wanted to hear it one more time. My name.

It was like she could read my damn mind.

"Gavin," she cried, our sweat mixing, her juices slick on my body, the taste of her on my lips.

And with that single word, I let the waves roll over me as I emptied every last ounce of myself into her. We tumbled together, headfirst over the abyss as our lips locked for one last, aggressive kiss while I poured myself into her gorgeous body.

We rode out a climax that seemed to last through the ages, through one kaleidoscope of colors, emotions, desire, until finally, we were both drained. Exhausted. High as a kite.

I rolled off her to one side, tucking her into my arm as we let our heartbeats return to normal. She threw a naked leg over me as she snuggled in, and my hand came to land on her ass. My cock twitched against her as my palm made contact with her skin.

"Are you serious?" Tara lifted her head, stared down my dick like it'd just performed a miracle. "That thing still has life left in it after that? I don't know what the hell we just did, it was something."

"Babe." I gave her another smack on the ass.

That said enough. Tara gave a happy laugh, and finally, she looked carefree. The shyness she'd had at being naked in front of me seemed to have faded. Her hair was mussed, her eyes bright and shiny. However, the longer she stared, the more hints of vulnerability that appeared.

Tara traced little circles on my bare chest. "That was nice."

"Babe." Another little slap to the ass.

That was all the conversation I could muster. Sure, I was halfway to a hard-on, but apparently every single ounce of energy in my body was being funneled there. I still couldn't get my hands off her, but she didn't seem to mind.

"Nice is the understatement of the year," I finally managed. I did have to lift my hand off her adorable ass cheek in order to groan out a sentence. Couldn't take my eyes off her, though. "Mind blowing is a little closer."

"But during it, I mean, if you didn't mean what you said..." Tara looked down. "I would understand. We were both in the heat of the moment."

The circles on my chest intensified. She seemed to be writing in cursive across my skin as if it might help me to understand what she was trying to say.

And just like that, my energy levels filled. At least enough to send some conscious thought back to my brain so I could compute what she was saying.

I rolled her onto her back. I took her hands in mine, pressed them against the comforter so she was restrained. Her breasts spilled below my chest. I was poised over her, and though I didn't want this to be about sex, I couldn't help the thing my cock was doing. I could hardly blame it, wanting to be back where it belonged, but I ignored it and focused on her eyes.

"The sex was great. Mind blowing. Best I've ever had," I blew through the list quickly. "But what made it fucking heaven on earth, Tara, was you. You offering me a little piece of your heart. Opening a door to let me in. We could've not had sex at all tonight, and this would've been the best night of my life. Do you understand me?"

Tara looked into my eyes. Trying to read between the lines.

"There are no lines to read between," I said, trying to guess what she was thinking. "I love you. Period. End of story. The only thing I want is to make you and Liv my family. Full stop."

Those beautiful eyes welled with tears. "I believe you. It's what I want too."

And then because the moment felt right, and Tara was squirming beneath me despite the fact that my hands were pinning hers to the fucking bed, I pressed my cock against her entrance. She was slick for me.

"Do you want me again?" I whispered.

"Please," she said, and it sounded like a prayer.

I didn't let up on her wrists as I slid myself home. This time I did move slow. My cock was just as hard as it had been, and where it'd gotten its stamina from, I had no clue. But I was damn grateful.

Because this time wasn't about the sex either. It was about the promise.

We'd banged hard the first time, fucking like our lives depended on it. Rocking against each other, pounding so hard the bedframe had knocked against the wall.

This time, she let me have the control. She let me slide myself in and out of her. She gasped, and I watched her eyes darken with every inch I pushed into her.

A few slick thrusts, slowly. A nip of her tender breast. A kiss to the throat. Our tongues tangling as we met, her hips curving off the bed to strain against me in the only way she could while I kept her restrained.

Slow, beautiful, perfect. The extra credit to what had already been a dream night. Then I lost all my breath as she started to tremble beneath me, and the room turned into a vacuum chamber and the only thing I could do was slide in, painstakingly slowly, slide out, painstakingly slowly, in a rhythm that damn near made both of us lose our minds.

This time I dragged the climax out of us with intention, and when I could feel the end closing in on us, I nudged her chin up with my nose, keeping her pinned beneath me. She was letting me have control of her pace this time. I felt like I was holding her in the palm of my hand, and my one focus was to protect her at all costs.

"Look at me," I said. "Now."

Her eyes flitted open, and the second her gaze caught mine is when it happened. It was the thing that tipped us over the edge. The piece that had been missing, our ultimate connection, and she let out a guttural cry that I stifled with my mouth.

She bit down on my lip, and I felt her orgasm hit her, and mine followed mere seconds later, until I couldn't swallow any more of her climax as she forced mine out of me, and I grunted and wrapped her against me, finishing with one long, slow thrust that left both of us trembling against one another.

"Holy cow," Tara murmured when we finally rolled next to each other. "That was..."

"Yeah."

"If you get another hard-on in the next five minutes, I'm calling the Guinness Book of World Records."

"Please don't," I begged. "My mind's willing, but my body's not."

She laughed, laid her head against me. "I love you, Gavin."

"I love you, too, baby."

We laid there for a long, long time. So long I had no clue if it was night or day, this year or the next, this lifetime or a new one. There was just me and Tara, and it was the only thing that mattered.

"You know what it was?" Tara whispered.

"What was?"

"The neigh."

"Huh?"

Tara popped her head up, grinned at me. "When you agreed to be the horse for Liv. I just thought, any man who would *neigh* for my daughter is okay in my book."

I leaned my head back on the pillow, grinning like a madman. "The fucking neigh."

Chapter 24

Tara

In the five days since I told Gavin Donovan that I loved him, he'd made good on his word. He didn't leave my side for a second, except to take a phone call, and even then, it was like his eyes were following me through the window of the car as he stood ten feet away, boring a hole in my skull.

He came with me to all my job sites and hauled more Christmas trees and untangled more strings of bulbs than any man should ever have to in his lifetime. The real highlight was when my Santa canceled at the last minute for a children's event I was hosting, and with a little cajoling and the promise that I owed him a big fat IOU, Gavin stepped into the jolly red suit—white beard and all—and pulled off a very studly Santa look.

Then there had been the nights. The nights that seemed warmer now that I had a literal heater sleeping beside me. In all actuality it seemed like Gavin Donovan's resting body temperature was boiling point. When we weren't tangled together between the sheets, he had one arm over me, or a foot touching mine, or a finger wrapped in my hair, as if he couldn't bear to let go of me even in sleep. If I wasn't so freaking hot all the time, I'd have thought it was adorable.

But I wasn't going to complain. Gavin had made the promise to me that he wouldn't leave. That he would make this family situation work, and every minute since he'd made that promise he seemed to be working to prove to me that he'd meant it. Each day I believed him a little more. Each day, my love for him grew. Each day, we became more and more of the type of family unit I'd always dreamed of having.

Then there was the sex. We had a lot of sex to make up for after being separated for thirteen years while secretly pining for one another, and Gavin Donovan didn't waste an opportunity.

There'd been the surprise visit to my office between client meetings that had required me to pull the drapes to the parking lot. The quickie while my mom had taken Liv out for some hot chocolate. The luxurious lather, rinse, sex, repeat in the shower when Liv had gone sledding with a girlfriend from school.

In between the sex, there were the kisses. Some hot and fiery. Some slow and languid. Some perfectly innocent pecks on the cheek that still managed to get my lady parts tingling with anticipation.

There was the handholding. The movie nights on the couch. The game nights with Liv—a big deal because now we could expand on our two-player games that we'd grown bored of into the wild west of three-player games. Every single moment was tinged with more meaning than the next. If this was my life now, then I was one lucky woman.

"What's changed?"

I blinked in the mirror, surprised by the figure standing in the doorway. I turned and found my mother standing outside my bedroom. She was looking at me while I perched over the vanity, adjusting my earrings.

"Sorry to startle you." My mom's eyes crinkled into a smile. "We *were* planning to drive to the event together tonight?"

"Of course," I said. "You usually knock at the front door. Caught me off guard is all."

"I did knock." My mother entered my bedroom carefully. "When you didn't answer, I used the key. I even called your name when I came in the door. So, sorry to barge in like this, but I was a little concerned."

"Sorry. I guess I was distracted."

Distracted was an understatement. Tonight was finally the night of Liv's school play. In other news, it was an odd night for Gavin to have disappeared on us. He'd been away for hours without a word, without a text. I assumed he had Mikey watching the house, but I hadn't asked. I'd been too busy curling Liv's hair for the play and focusing on tempering my daughter's excitement for the three big words she had to deliver so she didn't puke from the adrenaline.

Now that I stopped to really think about it, the last time I'd seen Gavin was early this afternoon. It wasn't entirely unusual for Gavin to have to duck out here and there for a couple of hours—I knew he was still dealing with his work assignment, whatever that looked like, though he did a good job of keeping that separate from his home life with us. I'd almost forgotten there was any danger at all, now that we'd settled into the warmth of our cocoon.

This afternoon, he'd gotten a text on his phone that had changed his expression. It'd been fleeting. A single look in his eye. The whisper of something that didn't belong. A darkness that felt out of place in our sunny home.

Then Gavin had pressed a kiss to my cheek, said he had some business to take care of, and that he'd check in later. It was later, and I hadn't heard from him, but only now was I starting to get worried.

It was six o'clock. Liv's play was scheduled to start at seven, and Gavin hadn't returned the text I'd sent him fifteen minutes ago asking if he was going to be driving with us or meeting at the auditorium separately.

"Is everything okay?" my mother asked. "I feel like you're not really *here* tonight."

"I'm fine," I said. "It's just—"

"Did Gavin call yet?" Liv bounded down the hall as she shouted, screeching to a stop in the doorway my mother had evacuated moments before. "Oh, hi Grandma."

"Hi, honey." My mother bent, gave Liv a kiss on the head and a squeeze on the shoulder. "I can't wait to see you perform tonight."

"Uh huh." Liv turned to me. "Where is he?"

I swallowed hard. "Gavin's still working. I'm really sorry, sweetie. I'll let you know when I hear from him. Why don't you get your costume on because if we don't leave soon, we'll be late."

"I don't want to leave without Gavin." Liv added a pout. "He said he was going to be there."

Frankly, I wanted to pout too. I didn't want to leave without Gavin either, yet the man wasn't here.

"Believe it or not, he can drive himself," I said with a gentle ruffle of Liv's hair sprayed curls. "Maybe his plan is to meet us there. Or maybe he's just really busy at work. Either way, it's gonna be fine. Me and grandma are going to cheer so loud you won't notice anyway."

Liv gave me a look that told me she thought I was nuts, and I didn't totally blame her. It took a lot of effort to drag my gaze back to meet my mother's because I knew the sort of look she'd have plastered there.

"Gavin's gone?" The way my mother asked the question brought back an avalanche of unwanted memories.

It'd been a loss for her, too, when Gavin had left the first time. And unlike me, my mother hadn't spent nearly as much time with Gavin as me and Liv this holiday season, so it was taking her longer to fall back in *like* with him. It wasn't that she hated him; she'd kept her walls up.

I cleared my throat. "It's not like that, Mom."

"I know, sweetie." My mother stepped toward me, tucked some hair behind my ear like I was still a little girl. "I can't bear to see you like this again. Not now, not after all this time."

I gave a long sniff. I plopped on the bed. My mother plopped next to me. That was the thing about being an only child to a single mother. We'd been thick as thieves most of my life, best friends in a special sort of way.

I'd respected her as a parent, but she'd also been my confidant. The person I went to when I needed help, advice, a shoulder to cry on. I had told my mother everything. Or just about everything. I hoped the same would be true for me and Liv as my daughter grew older. I felt an overwhelming rush of gratitude that she was here for me now.

I leaned a head on my mother's shoulder, and she stroked my hair. Not pushing me to talk, not chastising me for the fact that I should have known better. Just waiting.

"Gavin didn't leave," I said finally. "I think something's wrong."

"Wrong?" Her figure stiffened. "Like, call the police wrong?"

"It's complicated. His work is..." I swallowed again. "The situation is complicated, as I'm sure you've guessed, based on the way our engagement news came out."

"Yes, that was a hard pill to swallow until I figured..." My mother's lips turned up in a thin smile. "I know there's more to the story, sweetie. I'm not asking because I trust you to come to me when you're ready. The only thing I want to protect is you and your heart. What can I do?"

"Nothing." I felt the tears dampen my cheeks. "He should be here, and he's not. That's it."

"You really don't think he left?" My mother cradled my face in her hands, forced me to look at her.

"I know you probably think I'm stupid," I said. "But I do love him, Mom. And his leaving wasn't on purpose, I'm sure. Even the first time he left, it wasn't right the way he did it, but the situation was complicated."

My mother let out a ragged breath. "I know."

"You know?" I sat upright. "You *knew*?"

"No, I didn't *know*," she said quickly. "I mean, I didn't know any details. But I saw the way that man looked at you, honey. Even when he was still nothing more than a child, he had the sort of love for you that never goes away."

"But you were upset when he left too."

"Because he did it in a crappy way." My mother gave me a tender smile. "You have always been my little girl. Of course

I never wanted to see you brokenhearted—I'm on your side, no matter what he was thinking."

I licked my lips, nodded.

"I also talked to Lily Donovan back then," my mother said softly. "I understand he had a rough home life growing up. It sounded to me like Lily had done all she could to help, but..."

"Yeah." I played with my comforter. "I don't know all the details, but it didn't sound easy."

My mother smiled at me, this time warmer. "The only thing I can tell you now is that I am *certain* Gavin Donovan didn't leave you this time. His heart belongs to you. I could see it from the moment I saw him outside your office. I don't know if that makes you feel better or worse, but I'm confident he loves you."

My heart lurched. That was what my gut told me too, but I had been starting to doubt my own judgment. To hear my thoughts reciprocated from my mother's lips did wonders for my confidence.

"I know," I murmured back. "That's why I think something's wrong."

My mother's gaze flicked to the clock. "He promised you and Liv he'd be at the play, right? It's all my granddaughter has been talking about for weeks, Gavin coming to watch her."

"Exactly."

"Well, the play's going to start in less than an hour. Realistically, your safest bet is to go to the play, put on a brave face for Liv—she's a nervous wreck *without* worrying about

JINGLE BELL ROCK 311

Gavin—and we'll deal with it after. What's one more hour at this point?"

"You're right. I know. It's just hard."

"Of course it's hard, honey. I know it's hard." She sighed. "And if he still hasn't shown up after the play, then I'm afraid it might be time to call Sheriff DiMaggio. Just give Finn a heads-up that Gavin hasn't been in touch and see if he's heard anything."

"That's a good idea," I said. "Maybe I'll call Finn first. Just to let him know."

My mother kissed me on the forehead. "Good idea, my sweet girl. Go make your phone call, and I'll get Liv ready, and then let's watch our little star shine. It's the only thing you can do."

It didn't feel right, knowing the only thing I could do was wait, but my mother was right. So I picked up the phone and called Finn DiMaggio, Fantasie's town sheriff and Gavin's cousin.

When Finn answered, I dove right in and explained the situation. "I just can't help the feeling that something's wrong," I confessed, finishing up my rush of words. "It's not like Gavin to be so...away from us."

"Thanks for the heads-up, Tara." Finn's voice was hard and gruff around the edges. "I'll keep my ear to the ground, but I haven't heard anything yet. Unfortunately, Gavin hasn't been gone long enough to really dig into a missing person's report, and if you don't have a license plate for me to put a BOLO out on, I'm afraid my hands are tied. At least locally."

"Yeah, I know. So are mine," I said. "I was hesitant to call you, so I guess just consider this a little off the record chat.

If you see Gavin, maybe you could, I don't know—give me a nod?"

"Absolutely, Tara. I'm glad you called. If you don't hear from him by midnight, shoot me a text. And if he's still not back by morning I think we can start making some serious movements to find him. In the meantime, I'll call my cousin and see if Carter has any thoughts on what might be happening here."

"Thank you."

I could hear Finn pausing on the other end of the line. "You know, Tara, I don't want this to come off the wrong way, but Gavin Donovan's past is complicated. It could be that—"

"Gavin didn't ditch out on purpose," I said flatly. "He's in trouble, Finn."

"Understood." The sheriff sounded like he believed me. "That's all I needed to hear. Talk soon."

I hung up and turned to my bedroom door to find my little star gleaming bright. Literally. Liv looked supremely adorable in her little star costume with a blinking round light taped to her hat. She smiled shyly, did a little curtsey, and I burst into tears.

Chapter 25

Gavin

I glanced down at my watch, cursed when I saw the hour. The countdown to showtime was ticking along much faster than I'd anticipated. I'd thought we'd be done by now.

"How's she?" I barked into my burner phone. I'd left all other means of communication far away from this place.

"Tara's fine. Loading into the car now with her mother and daughter. You?" Mikey asked. "Any sight of Andrea?"

"None."

For the zillionth time, I wondered if Claudia had gotten her information wrong. She'd turned up the location of Andrea's home base, or at least one of them. The closest she could pin down to Fantasie.

The place Andrea was supposedly holed up was two towns away, not more than a half an hour's drive. The house itself was a brick colonial with a three-car garage and a picturesque front yard. No Christmas decorations. The front walk had been shoveled. Judging by the tire tracks, it looked like only one stall of the garage had been used.

The house wasn't as fancy as Andrea normally went for, but she wasn't stupid, and if she'd wanted to fit in, she couldn't shell out the big bucks in these small towns without making waves. So she'd done what she'd learned to do at The Company—blend in with her surroundings. Even if it irked her to not have *the best* of everything.

Not that the woman had skimped. Andrea refused to go without comfort if at all possible, as I'd found out the moment I'd stepped foot inside her rented place. The interior of the home she was staying in had been gutted and redone recently, as evidenced by the huge range over the stove, the updated white cabinets, the massive slab of marble on the island.

I sat at the island, my toe tapping against the ground in anticipation. Not about seeing Andrea. She didn't make me nervous. But I was scared shitless about missing Liv's debut on mini-Broadway. I knew in my heart of hearts Liv would never forgive me if I wasn't there when she looked out as the literal star of the show.

"It's been a long time since I came home to a nice hot meal."

I set my phone down as the words rang out behind me. I turned, found Andrea waiting for me in the doorway that led to a hallway, then a mudroom beyond. I'd memorized the layout of this place five times over. There was no room for mistakes tonight.

"Are we going to do this the easy way or the fun way?" I said. "You've kept me waiting, and I have somewhere I need to be."

"Claudia?" Andrea asked. "She was the only one who could ever keep up with me."

"It was only a matter of time before we found you. You were playing with fire coming to my hometown."

Andrea stepped into the kitchen, closed the distance between us. She extended her red nails, manicured way too long, scraped them gently against my chin. "You know I can't stay away from you, baby."

"Get your hands off me." I gritted my teeth, my skin feeling tinged with poison where her nails had streaked against it. "Let me take you in, Andrea. You can cut a deal. The police don't want you. They want the guys bigger than you. You'll get off with a fine and a wrist slap."

"That's cute you think I want to be caught." Andrea winked her long lashes at me.

It was hard to imagine how I'd once seen beauty in her. Andrea was a mirage and nothing more. Her body was trim and fit, manicured to be that way through hours in the gym and a strict diet. Her nails were talons. Her lips painted a bloody shade of lipstick. The waves in her hair had been created in a salon. Even her eye color changed depending on her mood and the contacts she kept on hand.

I couldn't help but compare everything about her to the true love of my life. Tara contained mountains of beauty inside her, the sort of beauty that radiated to the outside. The sort of beauty that couldn't be bottled in an expensive serum or blown out in a salon or trimmed by hours of exercise. Tara contained that elusive beauty that originated from the sort of person she was, the way she mothered her daughter, the way she looked at me and made my goddamn heart weep with joy.

I took a second to beat myself up for letting Tara creep into my thoughts. It wasn't that I didn't want her there—on the contrary. I couldn't think about Tara because she was my weakness. The only one. If I allowed myself to take her into account, I was as good as dead because Andrea didn't have a weakness, a person she loved—not like me.

Andrea might think she still loved me, but she was wrong. What we'd had was a one-sided obsession. Andrea was the sort of woman who wanted what she couldn't have, and when that had become me, she hadn't taken the rejection easily. As evidenced by the knife in her hand.

"I'm not armed," I said, raising both of my hands. "Put the knife down. I thought we could have a civilized conversation."

Andrea raised the butcher knife she'd taken from the kitchen block and ran her fingers along the flat side of the blade. "Nah. I'm good. You were pretty stupid if you came in here unarmed, trying to take me in. It didn't work the first time you suggested a deal, what makes you think I'd change my mind?"

"I just want to have a conversation. Leave us alone, leave town, and we'll be good."

"Stand up."

I stood, raised my hands. I'd known this was coming. Andrea frisked me, spending a little longer than she needed around my waist, winking at me when she finally straightened and took a step back.

"You were telling the truth," she admitted. "Good boy."

"I was never the liar."

"Ouch." Andrea tapped the knife to her lips. "So what do you want to talk about?"

"Admit you were helping launder money. The laundromat here. The food truck in Chicago. The casino in Minnesota."

Andrea raised a shoulder. "What about it?"

"Did you kill Felix Kismet?"

JINGLE BELL ROCK

"Oh, babe. This is not some tell-all confessional at the end of the movie. I'm not the villain here. I'm just a businesswoman doing what a girl's gotta do to make ends meet."

"So you're admitting to murder? Or just the money laundering?"

"Get out of my house, Gavin."

"You paid Tara a visit, and that's personal."

"I wanted to see your girlfriend for myself. Figure out what was so special about her." Andrea tapped the knife against the open palm of her hand. "I'm still bamboozled, to be honest. She's so...*average*."

"You're wrong," I said. "She's not my girlfriend."

"C'mon, Gavin. You've been living with her for months. You're really going to play that card on me? I'm not stupid."

"She's my fiancée."

"You can drop the charade now," Andrea said. "I figured out you were just pretending to be getting married so nobody in town would be suspicious about you living together. It wasn't a very good charade."

"It worked well enough to help us fall in love all over again," I said. "That's gotta piss you off. You drove us together. And now we're getting married."

Something in Andrea's eyes flashed. Maybe our fake engagement charade hadn't worked as it had been intended to work. But it had worked in an entirely different way, and I could see her wondering, doubting. I realized then that Andrea did, in fact, have a weakness. Her weakness was me.

"I will never love you like I love her," I said. "Even when we were together. There was always something missing, and we both knew it."

I moved a step closer to her. She stilled, coiled like a snake, and I could feel her instinct to pounce growing.

"It was Tara." I pressed Andrea on her hot spots. I needed more than she was giving me. "Tara was always the wedge between us because I couldn't stop fucking loving her."

"You asshole!" Andrea shrieked.

She jabbed at me with the knife, but it was a reflex of anger, not the poised strike that I knew she was capable of. I'd been lucky, but also, I'd been prepared. I had been egging her on. Trying to get her to crack, just enough, just a little more.

"You can't fucking handle that I told you no," I said. "You moved an entire business operation to Fantasie to taunt me. And it will be your downfall."

"I'm not going down for the laundromat," she spat. "Nor am I going down for the casino. I'm un-fucking-touchable, Gavin. Ask Felix Kismet. He never saw me coming."

"Because you were a coward," I retorted, the anger in my voice real. "You shot Felix in the fucking back."

Andrea sucked on her lower lip, gave a little shake of her head. Lipstick streaked her front tooth like a scar. "You heard wrong because I looked him in the eyes when I shot him."

We stilled. She stood close to the stove. I'd danced around to the other side and put the kitchen island between us. I waited a beat longer, got the confirmation I needed, then popped the wireless bud out of my ear.

"Thanks for that," I said casually. "We're done here."

"What the hell?" Andrea's eyes flicked toward the device in my hand.

I could see her brain whirring almost audibly, processing at the speed of light. Then she shook her head, a devilish look clouding her face.

"Oh, you almost had me there." Andrea gave a little chuckle. "You? Gavin Donovan wearing a wire? If it were anyone else, I might be concerned. But you? First rule of The Company: Never involve the police. You wouldn't involve the police if your life depended on it."

"You're right. *I* wouldn't," I said dryly. "But this time it's not my life that depends on it."

"What the hell are you talking about?"

"I'm getting married, remember?" I flicked the earbud to her. "Say hello to my little friends."

Andrea raised the bud to her ear, heard the crackle of activity on the other end. The earbud fell from her fingers to the floor.

"You bastard," she said, and she hurtled toward me just as the feds busted down the door on either side of the house.

Andrea skidded over the island, and though I dodged her, it wasn't perfect. Her knife dragged down the side of me drawing a bloody line down my rib cage.

A surface wound. I fucking hoped.

By the time I'd pulled myself to my feet, she was in custody of the FBI. Her knife had been taken from her, someone was reading her rights, and a set of cuffs was being snapped on her wrists. She looked positively feral as she watched me silently as I backed out of the room.

"Donovan, we need a statement," one of the agents called to me. "Don't leave yet."

"Good work," said another. "That's how it's done, Gavin. A little cooperation goes a long way."

A third agent clapped me on the shoulder, then glanced down at her hand. "You're bleeding, Gavin."

"Just a scratch," I huffed. "Listen, I'll give you guys a statement later. I'll tell you every detail you need, but I've got somewhere to be."

"You can't leave," the female agent said. "You need to—"

"I'm going to go find the medic outside, get this shit taken care of." I raised my shirt, gave the agents a view of the trickle of blood down my stomach. I chanced a glance down. My surface wound analysis wasn't quite right, but I wasn't going to die. Probably. So that was a plus.

"Yeah, sure thing," the agent said agreeably. "We'll catch up with you in a minute after the paramedics bandage you up."

Once outside, I slipped between the feds swarming the charming colonial until I found the vehicle I'd parked at the scene hours and hours before. Unbeknownst to the feds. I'd let them talk me into cooperation with some of their plans to catch Andrea, but that didn't mean they had to be privy to all *my* plans. I hadn't even told Mikey about the car, a rental I'd picked up from a few towns over for this very reason.

I climbed into the rental, pulled a U-turn away from the flashing lights at the house behind me, and headed toward the only thing that mattered to me.

Chapter 26

Tara

"Honey." My mother reached down, clasped my hand in hers. "It's okay. He'll be fine."

I blinked back the stupid tears that had filled my eyeballs again. "Gavin's really not coming. I just thought...he'd *never* miss this."

"Don't talk like that, sweetheart. I'm sure Gavin will turn up with a perfectly good explanation." She leaned up, kissed my cheek. "That man has always had secrets. It doesn't nullify the fact that he loves you."

I gave a shrug. The production had started twenty minutes ago. Gavin was officially late. I knew from watching the rehearsals that our little star would be making her appearance in just under five minutes.

I wasn't sure how I was going to explain to Liv that her self-proclaimed Number One Fan, Big Gavin, wasn't here to cheer her on. And worse, as my heart was breaking for Liv, I wasn't sure I'd be able to forgive Gavin myself.

I wasn't built for this kind of life. I wasn't built to be married to a man who disappeared without warning. Who, even with the best intentions, let my daughter down. Even though I loved Gavin Donovan with every fiber of my being, I was starting to think we were simply not meant to be.

I felt him before I saw him. This giant warmth beside me, too big for the little folding chairs that had been set up in the school's gymnasium. Sliding into the spot I'd saved with my purse in the event that Gavin would be here.

"Gavin," I breathed.

Gavin gripped my face with his hands, pushing my hair out of the way. He leaned forward, pressed a rough, sloppy kiss to my mouth that was bereft of finesse but overflowing with passion.

Gavin let me go when mutters started in the row behind us. If I hadn't been so out of it, maybe I would've cared about the elbow jabs and little finger points happening all around us. The staring eyeballs. The Karens and the Nosy Susans who were probably already writing up complaints in their head about indecency at a school function.

When Gavin took his hands off my face, I felt wobbly. I leaned against him, and he pressed an arm around me so tightly it was like he was telling me he'd never let me go. I leaned my head against him telling him that I believed him.

Gavin had made it. By the skin of his teeth, he'd made it. As I snuggled against my man, I glanced over at my mother, and saw a happy smile tugging at her lips as she stared straight ahead, seemingly indifferent to the sizzle happening right next to her.

I was absolutely sure lightning bolts were zipping between me and Gavin, welding us together on every level. Where his body ended, mine began. All doubt I had vanished. And then, when he pressed his cheek to the top of my head, I knew it was a done deal.

"There's our girl," he whispered into my hair.

I looked up, saw my little star beaming on stage, the janky bike light on her head blinking out at the crowd. My baby rose onto the tips of her toes, glanced out at the crowd. When she saw Gavin, her eyes lit up like a lighthouse. She waved so enthusiastically she knocked her hat right off her head.

Gavin took his arm off me long enough to give her a little salute back. Then his hand was right back where it started on my shoulder, his thumb raking circles on my lower back, shooting a spicy warmth to the ends of my fingers and toes and everywhere in between.

Then Liv said her one line, and me, my mother, and Gavin went wild. One would've thought she'd just bought herself a ticket to Broadway. More finger pointing from the Karens and Nosy Susans, but I couldn't care. We were here, as a family, and that was all that mattered.

"I love you," Gavin whispered into my hair again. "I'm so sorry about today. I'll explain everything."

"I know." I patted him on the chest, the rock-solid chest I'd grown so used to being around. "I love you, too."

Then I leaned over to kiss him, a little peck on the lips. But as my hands slid around his torso, my fingers felt tacky, like I'd touched something sticky. I withdrew my hand from the flannel button up he'd slipped over a black T-shirt, and looked down to my fingers and saw red.

"Gavin?" I looked up at him. "Are you—"

Before I could finish the sentence, I noted his face was too white. His grip on the seat before him too tight, his knuckles too clenched. He'd gritted his teeth together, his words forced and tense.

As I reached for Gavin, he seemed to lose hold on what little control he had left. He started to crumble, sliding down his chair, his consciousness evaporating before my eyes. No matter how much I tried, I couldn't hold him upright. He weighed double what I weighed.

"Help," I called out. "*Help!*"

I yanked up his shirt, saw a bandage along the left side of his torso running from his ribs down to his hip. It almost overlapped the other scar he had, the one from Andrea's knife.

"Gavin," I murmured, my tears wet as I yanked off his shirt and stuffed it against his wound. "What happened?"

He shook his head. "It's over, baby. It's all over."

***

Luckily there were some big, strong men in Fantasie.

Even luckier, several of them were in attendance at the school play.

In fact, Gavin was hoisted to his feet so quickly and hauled away by a few dads in the rows behind us that the play didn't even stop. There'd been a brief commotion, but Gavin had been whisked away so quickly most people hadn't figured out what had happened until it was too late.

"Hey, gang." Doctor Matthew DiMaggio strode into the nurse's office of the elementary school, snapping a pair of gloves onto his hands. "This had better not take long, Gavin. One of my nieces is in that play, and she'll kill me if I'm not there watching her line."

The doc winked at me, showing he was kidding, and I appreciated the levity. I prayed it was warranted.

"Welcome back, big guy." Matt approached Gavin's side. The two men were cousins. "Thanks for letting me know you were in town."

"Oh, hell," Gavin muttered. "I'm never going to live this down."

"What do we have here?" The doc quickly cut away Gavin's T-shirt and took a look at the bandage. "Who bandaged you up, Donovan? Have they ever seen a medical school, let alone attended one?"

"It's that bad?" Gavin asked. "I thought my first aid skills were improving."

"You're lucky. It doesn't look like anything important got hit, or your charming wit wouldn't be working right now, and you'd be dead." Matt DiMaggio stared him in the eye. "Dare I ask what happened?"

"It's confidential," Gavin grunted.

"Uh huh." Matt rolled his eyes. "You're going to need to come down to the hospital."

"The hell I will," Gavin said. "Just put on a new bandage."

"The hell I will," the doc parroted back to him. Matt turned to me. "Can you make him come to the hospital with me, or do I need to sedate him?"

I could feel my eyes go wide. My mother, who had come with us, rested a hand on my shoulder. "Go with Gavin, sweetheart. I'll take Liv and explain—well, something. I'll handle it."

"We're going," I said to Gavin. "Stop arguing, or we're not getting married."

"Well, fuck." Gavin looked to the doctor. "Are you driving or am I?"

Once we got Gavin to the hospital, all checked in and finally hooked up to an IV and whatever Doctor DiMaggio had ordered, I finally expelled a breath. I was still shaky, but I was finally starting to believe that maybe Gavin wouldn't die.

"That was a lot of blood," I whispered. "What were you *thinking*?"

"I'm sorry, Tara," he said. "I didn't think it was so bad."

I swallowed. "You got stabbed with a knife. *Again*. And you didn't think it was bad?"

"Not bad enough to miss Liv's show."

JINGLE BELL ROCK

"That's what this was about?" I gaped at him. "You didn't go to the hospital because you wanted to see Liv's play?"

"You can't tell me she wasn't pissed as all get-out that I wasn't there earlier today to drive with y'all."

I didn't answer because technically he was correct. He'd described Liv's mood very accurately, in fact. I waited to respond while a nurse popped into the room, adjusted a few things, gave a satisfied nod. Once she was gone, I eased into a chair and scooted close to Gavin's side.

"Do you know how ridiculous you are?" I reached for his hand and squeezed it. "You are insane."

"I made a promise." Gavin studied me, looking more at ease since the pain meds had kicked in. "I wasn't about to renege on it. Liv's been looking forward to that show for weeks."

"Maybe you need to back up and tell me why you were bleeding in my daughter's school gymnasium in the first place."

Before Gavin could respond, the door opened and Matt stuck his head in.

"Can we get a Do Not Disturb sign on the goddamn door?" Gavin barked. "I'm trying to have a conversation with my future wife in private."

Matt took Gavin's outburst in stride. "You do realize this is a hospital, not a B&B? Or can I get you a mimosa to go with your brunch?"

"Am I going to die in the next five minutes, Doc?"

"Happy to report that's a negative, Donovan."

"Then give me five minutes. Please."

Matt winked at me. I mouthed, "Sorry" back to him, but he brushed me off with an amicable wave. The perks of everyone knowing everyone in Fantasie was having an easy understanding without needing to say a whole lot.

"I went after Andrea," Gavin said, cutting straight to the chase. "I couldn't stand this back and forth, this waiting game. I want us to get on with our lives. Me, you, Liv. I want to fucking marry you, Tara, and start our family. And I didn't want it dictated by a psychopath."

"You mean your ex-girlfriend."

"I had questionable taste at some points in my life," Gavin said dryly. "And for that I truly apologize. But I got one thing right."

"Oh yeah?"

"Yeah." He leaned forward, kissed my knuckles. Our hands were still interlocked. "I think the day I left you is the day my life went off the rails. You ruined me, Tara. For everyone else."

"Okay, Mr. Overdramatic."

But in his eyes, I could see that he'd meant it. And in a way, didn't I feel the same? Hadn't he broken something in me that'd never quite been repaired until he'd returned to stitch up the wound himself?

"You said this is over," I pressed. "Does that mean—where's Andrea?"

"I didn't kill her," Gavin said simply. "I did something I never thought I'd do."

"I thought you just said you didn't kill her."

Gavin licked his lips, gave a smile. "I cooperated with the feds."

"You did what?"

"Andrea had gotten into money laundering for a branch of the mob based out of Chicago. I went to a few agents I knew with a proposal, and they took me up on the offer. We staged a sting together."

"Seems like you got the raw end of the deal," I said. "I'm betting none of them are bleeding."

"I had to be the one to wear the wire," Gavin said gravely. "It was the only way for things to work. We got enough on record to arrest her. Plus, I'm not dead, so I'm calling that a win."

I leaned forward, rested a hand on his chest away from his bandages. "She admitted to the money laundering?"

A storm cloud shifted across his eyes. "Yes. Among other things."

"Worse things?"

"Yes."

A shiver rocked my body. To think this woman had been watching me, my daughter. She'd sat across from me in my office.

"I see that look in your eye," Gavin said. "And I won't blame you if you get cold feet about marrying me."

"Gavin—"

"But first, I need to tell you this is it. Andrea is arrested. She'll be convicted on some big charges and put away for a long, long time. This is over."

"And what about the rest of your career?"

"What career? I'm done. I am officially out. No more."

"And when you get bored? Then what?"

Gavin's eyes sparkled. "I'm not going to get bored, Tara. I've got nights with you to look forward to."

My cheeks flushed, but I wasn't backing down so easily. "That's not enough."

"Look, babe, I'm not going to get bored. I've got plans."

"Would you like to cue me in on them?"

"I thought maybe I could help you out during your busy seasons. I'll be your strapping lackey hauling oversized Santas and setting up lights on high ladders. I'll put on the red suit and the fluffy beard when your real Santas don't show."

"Keep talking."

"I liked redoing that old inn up for Lily. I've got a few things to finish up for her there, and then I've got enough capital to purchase another property. We could do it together. My handiwork, your eye for design, it could be a whole new business opportunity."

"I'm still listening."

"If all else fails, I've got enough socked away to be a stay-at-home dad for a long-ass time. That'd be nice for the kids, wouldn't it?"

The way he said kids made my stomach bubble and fizz like crisp champagne. It seemed for all the world that he was serious about this. Putting down roots with me, starting our family. Together.

"You're sure about all of this?" I asked. "You're sure you're not giving up so much that you'll regret it in three years, five years, ten years?"

"Baby." Gavin leaned toward me, groaned, shifted so he could reach my lips in a kiss. "I'm coming home. You complete me, and that's all I'll ever need."

I sank into the kiss he initiated, easing him back onto the bed, relishing the feel of his hands on my arms, his tongue parting my mouth, the way he claimed it as his own, even as he was hooked up to monitors and IVs and wearing a hospital gown.

"All right, kids. Whoa." Doctor DiMaggio paused in the doorway, his eyes giving a playful twinkle as he studied us. "I guess you really did need that Do Not Disturb sign. Let me remind you, this isn't *that* sort of room. Y'all need to get a real room without so many sharp objects for the direction y'all are headed."

Tucking my hair nervously behind my ears, I patted myself down and stood just out of reach from Gavin, as if should I take a step closer, we'd both burst into flames like two lovesick phoenixes.

"So when's the big day?" Matt asked as he glanced down at a chart. "When did y'all decide to get hitched?"

"Shit," Gavin said. "We never decided on a date."

"I guess we'll figure that out," I said. "We'll need time to plan, and—"

"Christmas Eve?"

"What?" I stared at Gavin. "You're out of your mind." I looked at the doctor. "How many painkillers did you give him?"

"Tylenol." Matt grinned. "The crazy in him is all natural."

"I'm serious," Gavin said. "The family's already got an engagement party planned for us. I don't want to wait."

"You *do* know what I do for a living, don't you?"

"Sorry," Gavin said quickly, "I realize you plan weddings and parties and decorate stuff, but I don't want you to have to plan your own wedding like it's a job. Let's just go to the courthouse, tie the knot, and show up at Lily's party hitched. My aunt and your mom already have the food and decorations on order. Everyone'll be in the Christmas spirit. It'll be great."

"I guess, but still, I don't want to make Christmas Eve all about us."

"Hell, *I'll* make it all about us. You don't have to do a thing," Gavin said. "Plus, I don't want to wait to start our family. I want kids with you yesterday."

"Can y'all wait until the damn ink's dry on the discharge papers before trying to procreate in my hospital room?" Doctor DiMaggio gave a good-natured groan as he scribbled on his clipboard, but he was hiding a smile. "I guess I'll see y'all back here in about nine months in the maternity ward, huh?"

As the words came out of the doctor's mouth, Gavin's expression looked downright ravenous. I felt the tinglings of embarrassment at having this conversation in front of the doctor, but Gavin didn't seem to give a damn, and that was a little bit sexy. I liked that he didn't care who heard that he wanted me. A family. A life together.

"I love you," I whispered.

"I love you, Tara," Gavin murmured back.

The doctor threw his hands in the air. "I give up."

Epilogue

Tara

Snow flurries fell from the sky as I held hands with Gavin, tripping down the street, giddy on champagne.

I stopped in my heels, the train of my white dress soggy and damp as it trailed against the ground. Gavin wrapped his arms around my waist, spun me close to his chest while I threw my head back and stuck my tongue out to let the frosty flurries land there.

"I don't think so," Gavin said, his voice husky as he backed me against the brick wall of Jerry's Grocery. "The only thing I want you tasting tonight is me, Mrs. Donovan."

I gave an exaggerated shudder. "Oh, I do like the sound of that."

"Do you think we actually have to go to the party?"

It was pretty easy to feel that Gavin had no interest in going to any sort of party judging by the hard length pressing against me while he pinned me against the wall, shielding me from the snowfall. Frankly, I didn't care about a party either at this rate.

"I don't know?" I murmured, not remembering what the question was, or even if there had been a question in the first place.

We were on the precipice of being happy-tipsy, the warm and cozy and laughter-filled sort of drunk that came only with a side of true joy. To be honest, I wasn't sure I'd ever felt this sort of unhinged form of happiness.

The day Liv had been born had absolutely been one of the best days of my life, but it had been wrapped up in a complicated ball of emotions. Fear at being a single mother. Disappointment and mourning that her father had abandoned us. Sheer terror at the fact that the hospital was sending me home alone with a baby and zero instructions.

Today, this evening, I had no reservations about our situation. I felt only the overwhelming love that flowed to me from the direction of Gavin, as if it were a tangible ribbon feeding back and forth between us, keeping us on a high.

Gavin's hand raked down the sides of my wedding dress, a little number I'd picked up from the local seamstress who'd been able to alter it for me on a rush order. It was lacy with a V-neck and a little train, solely because Liv had been wanting to carry my train down the aisle.

We'd been married at the city hall with my mother and Liv in attendance in an intimate and absolutely perfect ceremony. Then my mother had shuffled Liv into the car with the duty to pick up a wedding cake and meet us at the party. Gavin and I had opted to walk the few blocks to the Fantasie Inn, needing the freezing temperatures to cool our jets so we didn't show up at the party needing a wrench to pry us apart.

"Gavin, this is someone's place of business," I muttered as he tugged up my dress so he could get a hand on my bare leg.

"I know," he murmured. "I can read the damn sign, but I don't think Jerry's gonna mind. This is our honeymoon."

"I guess—" My breath hitched and words ceased to exist as he found the little garter I wore around my thigh.

Gavin snapped it, dragged his hand higher. His eyes glassed over as he got the first feel of the panties I'd chosen for the special night. He bit his lip, inhaled a sharp breath.

"Shit," he murmured. "You know I'm not going to last through a party."

Fortunately, most of the town was shut down, seeing as it was Christmas Eve. Windows brimming with golden light spilled their warmth onto the side streets, but Main Street was all but deserted so people could be with their families. There was something supremely romantic about being alone on a quaint, abandoned street.

Despite the lack of people, the main drag wasn't without lack of decorations. Christmas lights twinkled from every shop front. Golden orbs dangled from wires hung across the street. Candles flickered from windows, Santas waved from roofs, window boxes were stuffed with evergreen branches. It felt like we'd walked into a storybook world created just for us.

"Come on," I urged. "We've got to get to the party before Liv realizes we're missing."

"There's cake. She doesn't care about us."

"Touché," I said, then hiccupped as one of Gavin's fingers dipped underneath my panties.

He slid his finger into my slit, blowing out a hiss as he felt my readiness for him.

"You're already wet, baby," Gavin said. "It's a sin to go to this party and not take advantage of this situation."

"Gavin, we can't have sex on the street."

He looked like he was seriously taken aback by this rule, but after a moment of processing, he gave a reluctant nod.

"I suppose you have a point, but just know... I don't plan on staying long."

Gavin stepped back, gave me a little space to breathe. Then he gave me a clap on the ass as he tucked me under his arm, shifting the white faux-fur I'd draped over my shoulders to keep warm. I hadn't needed it, considering the temperatures zipping between us were well above boiling point.

We reached Lily's inn, and I noted that my mother's car was already parked out front, signaling she and Liv were likely inside. Gavin hauled me against him roughly for one more kiss in private before we burst through the door.

"You know once we get in there we'll be mobbed," he said, his voice husky. "But damned if I'm gonna let you out of my sight. Fair warning."

"Noted." I blinked at him, feeling like this were an out of body experience.

We were married. I had a husband. My husband was Gavin Donovan.

Taking a deep, fortifying breath as Gavin pushed the door open, I took his hand and followed him as he led the way inside his aunt's bed and breakfast. She had more than enough room with an oversized dining room and a sizeable lobby and sitting room to host an intimate party.

Of course, intimate was relative. For me, intimate meant my mother, me, Liv, Gavin. My assistant Millie, and one or two girlfriends. For Gavin, the list was even shorter.

But Fantasie had a different idea of intimate. As we sidled shyly into the room, I caught sight of a couple of Lily's grown kids—Lucas and Noah, the latter from whose property we'd nabbed our Christmas tree. Then there was the

JINGLE BELL ROCK 337

DiMaggio clan, including Doctor Matt DiMaggio, Sheriff Finn, and most of their brothers.

Clarice, the town psychic, never failed to invite herself to these events. The Fantasie Quilter's club had set up shop in a little corner. I wasn't sure how Chuck from the café had gotten wind of the party, but he had set up shop near the bar and was looking a little jollier than usual as he eyed the fruitcake with an almost romantic gaze.

As we stepped deeper into the room, it was as if we'd entered the slow-motion portion of our evening promenade. Heads swiveled to face us, one at a time. The double-takes followed. Then came the gasps. A whisper. And yet, nobody spoke.

"Here's the happy couple," Lily said, coming around the corner with a big smile on her face. When she laid eyes on us, she came to a dead stop.

Her eyes took in my gown, Gavin's suit. Our hands clasped together like Gavin was my lifeboat and I his. Then eyes turned to Liv who bounced up to us wearing her fluffy, bursting-with-white-tulle flower girl dress.

"You got married without me?" Millie blurted, then she burst into rapid applause.

"Married," Lily exclaimed. "I don't have a wedding cake!"

"It's chilling outside," my mother said, rushing up to Lily's side. "I wanted to tell you, but these two made me cross my heart and hope to die that I wouldn't spill their secret agenda."

"Surprise," I said weakly. "We're married."

"Ladies and gentlemen." Matt DiMaggio raised a glass. "To the newest Mr. and Mrs. Donovan."

The room erupted in applause, and Gavin crushed me to him, dipping me low in front of the eleven-foot Christmas tree in the lobby. The tree was fat, so dripping with ornaments the branches seemed weary with the effort of standing at attention.

Phones came out, clicked pictures. I knew in my heart of hearts that we didn't need professional photos. This one, the picture of us smooching in front of our family and friends, the Christmas tree blazing behind us, Liv—an out of focus ball of tulle and lace twirling around us—was the only photograph I'd ever need to remind me of the feeling on this Christmas Eve.

"Before we celebrate," Gavin said, clearing his throat, speaking louder as the crowd cheered, "I have one more thing I'd like to do."

I felt my heart starting to palpitate. I wasn't aware of *this* part of the secret agenda.

"Haven't we had enough surprises?" I muttered under my breath. "I'm good. Let's just fade into the background and eat cake."

"Cake," Liv said. "It's time for cake?"

"This won't take long. Liv, do you mind coming over here?" Gavin dropped to one knee. He pulled me to him. Pulled Liv to him. Liv hoisted herself right up onto his knee, threw one arm around Big Gavin's neck, and swung her feet until she was comfortable sitting on Gavin, causing a rift of laughter in the watching crowd.

"Tara Donovan," Gavin said, a crooked smile on his face. "I have loved you since I laid eyes on you. I loved you thir-

JINGLE BELL ROCK

teen years ago when we spent one summer together, and I've missed you every damn day since I left."

"Swear jar," Liv chirped happily.

Gavin licked his lips. "Sorry."

"It's fine," Liv said. "I've almost got enough saved for another fish to be Fin's friend from all your swears."

Another little ripple of laughter. But mostly anxiousness as the crowd waited for Gavin to continue.

"We've done everything backwards," Gavin said. "I regret every second that we spent apart, but I can understand now that it had to happen that way. Or else we wouldn't have gotten our Liv."

Someone in the crowd let out a little sob. Probably Millie. Possibly Lily. Maybe my mother.

"Though we've spent years apart, the day you walked into that inn with a can of pepper spray in your hand and a bloody lip, I knew you were still mine. And I've always been yours."

I felt my lip quiver at the way he was looking at me. The way he had one hand on mine, the other around Liv, holding her steady to him.

"Now Liv." Gavin turned so his gaze was level with hers. "Thank you for letting me marry your mother. I promise you I'll love her until the day I die."

"When are you going to die?" Liv mused. "How old are you?"

"Hopefully I'll be around a long, long time."

"Okay. That'll be a lot more swears for my savings account."

"I can do that," Gavin said with a gruff little laugh.

"I knew you were gonna get me a good Christmas present," Liv continued.

Gavin cleared his throat in confusion. I looked at Liv, also confused.

"You're gonna be my dad, right?" Liv shrugged. "I've always asked Santa for a dad."

Gavin buried my small child in his arms, and it broke my heart, little shards separating into a million pieces. Pieces that rebounded right back together into one whole puzzle, the three of us. Meant to be.

"I love you," Gavin whispered in Liv's ear, for only her to hear. "I'd love to be your dad if you'll let me."

The crowd cheered, hooted and hollered as Gavin lifted Liv and me in a hug. He pressed a kiss to my lips, raised our locked hands together to another round of raucous applause.

My mother disappeared during the applause and came back with a towering three-tiered cake she'd pre-ordered and kept chilled outside in the car. Gavin and I did the whole feeding one another cake while Liv swiped her finger through the frosting.

The next hour was flooded with well-wishes and nosy questions we mostly dodged. It was pretty easy to dodge questions because there were so many people trying to talk to us, so we could dip from one conversation to the next pretty seamlessly.

It was during one of those dips between conversations that Gavin dragged me out of the room and tugged me up the stairs. Lily's bed and breakfast had several rooms upstairs.

"Liv's knocked out on your mom's lap," Gavin mumbled. "I booked us a room."

"Here?"

"Yes, here." Gavin grinned. "I had a feeling I wouldn't be able to resist Tara Donovan in a wedding dress for long."

"Stop."

"Come on, it won't take long."

"That's what I like to hear," I teased.

Gavin winked. "The first time. I'll be back for more later tonight—you can count on it. But I don't want to keep you away from your reception for long. It's the only one you're getting, baby. You're stuck with me."

"Good."

Gavin could barely figure out the key in the lock he was pressed so tightly against me, his hand not even subtly splayed across my ass. Fortunately, the upper landing was empty, and nobody witnessed our sloppy make out session against the door while the poor man fumbled with the lock in a string of curses.

We fell into the bedroom in a heap of lace and train and righted ourselves using one another for balance. Tumbling toward the bed, we were giggling and stripping clothes like it was the first time we'd done this. When Gavin got frustrated with how long things were taking, he got me flat on my back on the bed, pinned my hands above my head with one of his.

"I meant it," he grunted, leaning to press a long kiss to my neck, "I won't keep you long the first time. But no promises for later."

"I'll hold you to that."

Gavin had already finagled the zipper of my dress down, and I was pretty darn grateful I hadn't opted for buttons because the heavy pressure between my thighs was begging for release from my brand-new husband.

Gavin took his time pulling the straps of my dress down over my shoulders. Then the bra popped free. Pretty soon all that was left was the garter around my thigh.

"Good thing I bought a lingerie set," I said, staring forlornly at my pretty undies on the floor. "You didn't even look at it."

"Time for pretty underwear later," he promised.

"Yeah, but, *oh*. Okay. This is much better."

I lost my breath as Gavin sank between my legs, primed me with a few well-placed kisses. He added a stroke of his finger between my thighs before he straightened and shrugged off his shirt, his pants. His erection loosed, and I reached for him, hungry to touch him.

"I'm sorry, babe, but we don't have time for that. I need to be in-fucking-side you." Gavin gently brushed my hands off his length, pressed himself against my entrance. "Are you—"

"Yes, please," I begged. "I need you, Gavin."

And just like that, Gavin thrust himself inside me with enough force to rock the headboard against the wall, and I prayed there was decent soundproofing in this place. If nothing else, I hoped everyone was too drunk and high on Christmas music and figgy pudding to worry about where the lovesick newlyweds had disappeared to.

"Fuck," Gavin hissed. "I can't believe I get to do this for the rest of my life. I hope I live forever, and even that's not enough time to be inside you."

Gavin pressed his heaviness to me, his bare chest on mine. He massaged a breast, teased the nipple with his teeth, all the while moving inside me with a ferocity that even we'd never managed before.

I arched my back into him, and he dipped his fingers to the sensitive area between my legs. I just about imploded when he slowed the pace, pushed so far inside me I was sure he couldn't possibly fit more, and then he did the impossible—he slid his entire shaft the rest of the way.

With a growl, he pulled out, pushed in, and began to thrust, a few slow, then harder, faster, until I had to hold onto his back, digging in with my new manicure to stabilize myself against the full force of Gavin Donovan bearing down on me like a freight train.

"Jesus," he murmured. "You're incredible."

I brought my hands up to his scar, gently pressing my fingers there. "Do you hurt?"

"No," he said. "Can't feel a thing."

I wasn't entirely sure he was telling the truth, but the doctor had bandaged him up good, and he seemed to be healing fine, or at least putting on a good front.

"Don't you ever leave me again," I whispered in his ear.

"Never," he groaned into my ear. "You're mine, beautiful. You're mine, Mrs. Donovan."

And with that, we released together, Gavin spilling himself into me, the force of his orgasm obliterating any of my remaining brain power. Finally, mercifully, I let myself spiral toward him with the velocity of a shooting star, desperate for a safe landing, and here I'd found it—my safe haven in Gavin Donovan.

Gavin collapsed on me, lifting himself just enough to the side so that he wasn't crushing my lungs. We lay there, naked bodies heavy, while he toyed with my fingers in his.

"There's one more thing I wanted to ask you," he said.

"What's that?" I mumbled. "I can't think of anything right now. Except maybe another piece of cake."

"Like mother like daughter," Gavin said with a soft chuckle. "On the subject of Liv..."

"What is it?" I propped myself up slightly, though it was difficult because my muscles felt like jelly. "What about Liv?"

"I'd like to adopt her. Formally. If it's okay with both you and her, of course. But I wanted to ask you first. Now that we're married, I was just thinking..."

"Yes."

"I thought—"

"The answer is yes," I said, ducking my head to his chest, resting it there. "As long as she's fine with it, but I don't foresee any pushback."

"That child is saving for a fucking aquarium with her swear jar fund. I am 93% sure it's the only reason she keeps me around."

"And at the rate you're going, she's going to have it by the end of the year." I kissed his nose.

"I'm getting better."

"You are," I promised him. "And it's only going to get better and better from here on out, I can feel it."

Neither of us were talking about swear tallies anymore. We lay together in bed for another few moments, interlocked in a tender embrace. Snow fell outside, the moonlight streamed into the inn's windows, lighting us in a silvery glow.

A low thrum of chatter filled the home from below, from the heart of it, the kitchen, where everyone we loved was gathered. Christmas music piped through the house. The smell of cinnamon and sugar and hot chocolate permeated the very fibers of the house.

"I'm happy," I whispered.

"Me too," he said back. Then Gavin looked at the clock which had just ticked past midnight. "Merry Christmas, Mrs. Donovan."

THE END

Author's Note

Thank you so much for reading! I hope you enjoyed this installment in The Donovan series!

Finn and Josie's story is already up for pre-order in YOU ARE MY SUNSHINE!

LINK: https://bit.ly/SunshineLK

Sign up for my newsletter at LilyKateAuthor.com or find me on Facebook for more information on releases, cover reveals, ARC opportunities and more!

***

Lastly, if you happened to enjoy the story and can spare five minutes out of your day, honest reviews at the retailer of your choice are always welcome and appreciated.
Thank you so much in advance!

Printed in Great Britain
by Amazon